GENERATION WITCH:

REBIRTH

Nanci M. Pattenden

Generation Witch

Rebirth (Book 1)

Detective Hodgins Victorian Murder Mysteries

Body in the Harbour

Death on Duchess Street

Corpses for Christmas

Books 1 to 3 Collection

Homicide on the Homestead

D.E.M.ON. Tales Series

Assassin Eco-Corpses

Bobcat Got Your Tongue?

A Craptacular Understatement

Double Dog Dare Ya

Even Equines Don't Like Liver

ACKNOWLEDGMENTS

I'd like to say a great big thanks to Omar and Ashley, owners of Cardinal Press Espresso Bar in Newmarket, for providing a wonderful environment in which to work. They have a lovely coffee shop with a super atmosphere, yummy goodies, and friendly regulars, creating the perfect place to call "my office."

As always, thanks to my editor, MJ, of Infinite Pathways, and Chris, my graphics guru.

THANK YOU

ONE

I survived the first week. *Maybe this job will finally be a keeper. It is a bookstore, after all.* I repeated those words in my mind.

The bell dinged when someone pulled the streetcar cord for the corner. My stop, too. Only two other people exited, as it was still too early in the day for the summer tourists to be out.

After my usual detour to We Brew, I slipped over to Page Turners, a gemstone's throw from Lake Ontario, and rapped on the glass door. My co-worker smiled and let me in. Sally? Or was it Sarah? She wasn't wearing her badge yet.

"Morning." I held out a second coffee. "Extra-large. Black, right?"

"You're a lifesaver, Marcy. I needed some liquid energy?"

Good question. We barely knew each other. "Shot in the dark. It's a beautiful summer morning and I have a feeling we'll be busy and need all the energy we can get."

Susan clipped the badge to her lapel. Well, at least I knew her name started with an S.

Turned out I was right about being busy. A steady stream of people kept the little bell over the door singing all morning. By mid-afternoon, the flow thinned and Susan asked me to help shelve the shipment of new books waiting in the storage room.

"I'll be gone in a couple of weeks. Haven't told the boss yet." Susan sliced the packing tape and dug into the box. "School starts in September and I want to use this time to get ready."

"Hope you have better luck than I did." I tied back my strawberry blond hair, picked up the box cutter and sliced open another lid.

"What happened? Sorry. Is that too personal?"

"Nah. Too boring. Barely made it through the first year. Been winging it ever since. Over the past year, I've gone through at least a half dozen jobs." I considered that, then counted on my fingers. "Let's see, worked at two coffee shops, a clothing store at Yorkdale, cashier at Wal*Mart, construction crew holding the stop/slow sign, and a local animal shelter. That one lasted the longest. Six jobs, unless I forgot something. I love books, so maybe this one'll last. Maybe one day I'll oust Hagatha the Hag and take over here."

"I know I'll stick out school. I love animals and want to be a veterinarian."

I smiled. "You'll be a great vet." My phone dinged, ending the conversation.

"Marcy, you're not supposed to have your phone on while working." Susan did a great impression of The Hag.

I swiped the icon, trying not to laugh. "Hello… Yes, this is Marcy Adhamh… Oh, my God! I'll be right there.

Susan stopped unpacking and reached for my arm. "You've gone white. What's wrong?"

"Granny. Gotta go to the hospital."

I grabbed my purse and headed to Hagatha's office to explain.

"I'm sorry, Marcy, but you just started. You haven't accumulated any time off. Your shift ends in a couple of hours. You can go then."

Hell no. Granny was way more important than a stupid job.

"Ya know what? You can take your job and shelve it."

※ ※ ※

I skidded to a stop at the hospital's reception desk. The nurse raised an eyebrow and smiled. "How can I help you, Miss?"

"Someone called." I gulped in air. "Said Granny's here. What room?"

"I'm afraid I'll need a little more information. What's your Granny's name?"

"Adhamh. Francine Adhamh."

"I'm sorry, Miss, but I don't see Francine Adams in the computer."

I shook my head. "No, Adhamh." I spelled it out, tapping my fingers against the counter, anxious to get to Granny.

She clicked away on her keyboard, studying the screen. "Here it is. Room 4107." The nurse pointed down the hall. "Elevators are at the end."

"Thanks," I called over my shoulder. Both elevators sat at the top floor, so I took the stairs. By the time I reached the fourth floor, I felt like passing out. *I really should exercise more.* Bracing myself against the wall, I leaned forward, hands on my knees. A nurse entered the stairwell. I grabbed the door when she opened it, rushing through before she could say anything.

Hand on my side, I tried to push away the throbbing stitch. A quick glance at the room number sign and I sprinted off. Darting around the corner, I clipped the edge of a cart piled with meal trays, earning a scowl and rude comment from the nurse. The aroma of the hospital food, mingled with the over-sanitized stench of the ward, made me gag. Swallowing the rising bile, I mumbled a meaningless sorry and hurried along, turning down another hall.

Each corridor grew progressively colder as I searched for Granny's room. I rubbed my arms to warm up, puzzled by the people I passed fanning themselves. *The A/C in this place is ridiculous. How can they be hot?* I reached up and rubbed the emerald pendant hanging around my neck. Normally, it helped me maintain my psychic wall. Today, I needed it for protection against enchantment. *Why do I sense magickal danger?*

I finally found room 4107. I stepped inside, jolted to a stop, and froze. *That pale, fragile woman can't be Granny.* Nearly seventy-six, she normally looked closer to fifty. This woman had to be close to a hundred. I took a step back, but a weak voice stopped me. "Marcy?"

"Granny?" The spell broken, I rushed to her bedside. "Holy Heliodor." My voice cracked. "What happened? Were you in an accident? The doctor who called wouldn't tell me anything. Why do they do that? Don't they realize it just makes you worry more? Why can't they just—"

Granny shook her head slightly and tried to speak. Only a puff of mist came out.

"What is it? Why's it so cold in here? I can see your breath."

The air in her room had to be ten degrees colder than in the hallway, and the plant on the side table looked frost-bitten. I checked the A/C under the window, but no air blew from the unit.

I dragged over a chair and lowered the side rail on her bed. The room had that horrible, sterile smell, combined with the slight scent of the rosewater Granny always wore. My eyes grew moist as I desperately searched for the strong-willed, independent woman who'd raised me, hidden beneath the pale skin of the old woman in front of me. She had one of those oxygen things up her nose, and an IV stuck in her arm; skin paper-thin. That couldn't have come from any accident. She'd always been very active and had a warm, healthy complexion. *What would've caused her skin to change?* No one in our family had ever required a doctor before, never mind a hospital.

"Should've told you sooner," she whispered.

I leaned forward, touching her arm. Cold and smooth, like an icicle. *Why isn't her arm covered in goosebumps?* Gently, I placed a blanket over her, cursing myself for not coming home more often. Granny was all the family I had, at least in Canada. I couldn't lose her. "Should've told me what?"

Her eyes widened. "He's—no—ed." Her voice rasped, making it hard to understand.

"Who's Ed? You're not making any sense."

"No. Dead. Caught me off guard." She coughed, choking. I reached for the glass of water on the bedside table, but she batted my hand. The coughing stopped, replaced by shallow breathing.

"What are you talking about, Granny? I don't understand."

"Your mother..." Her eyes closed, lips still moving. I leaned in but couldn't make out the rest.

The machines beeped, their sound and pattern steady. I took that as a good sign and relaxed, just a little. Her eyelids fluttered.

"We should do this when you're better. Whatever it is can wait."

"No, can't wait."

Her eyes narrowed. Uh-oh. I knew that look. She raised her hand, and I sandwiched it between mine. Frustration and concern flowed from her.

"Damn, Granny."

She had always been stubborn, even when ill, apparently. "Fine. Tell me what's so important, but keep it brief. You need to rest and get your strength back."

"Promise me you'll come back to the craft."

"The craft?"

"Important." She tried to sit up, but fell back. "Promise me."

I knew that look. Sick as she was, her anger flared. "What could be so important that I need to accept my psychic abilities? I'm not sure—"

"No," Granny said, between coughs. "Must promise. Now." The beeping grew rapid, the lines spiking and dropping.

"Granny!" I reached for the call button, but she flailed, ripping it out of my hand. Somehow, her strength returned. She grasped my arm.

"Promise," she hissed between clenched teeth.

 "OK, I promise."

She relaxed. I tucked the blanket back around her and rested my hand on her cheek. "Now, tell me what's going on."

"He's powerful." The beeping increased. "Tell Priscilla—" Granny's face twisted in pain. "He's back! No, not yet." She gasped. Her eyes rolled up.

The machine flat-lined.

"Granny!" I ran to the door, yelling for the nurses to come. They rushed down the hall with a cart.

When Mother died, I should've gotten closer to Granny. Not pushed her away. Panic rose. The nurses seemed to move in slow motion. Just before they reached the door, I turned back. A tiny orb floated over Granny's head. It pulsed, changing from white to pale blue, then zipped out the window, right through the glass.

TWO

Several of Granny's regular customers graced me with their presence at the funeral home. I tried speaking with them, but my mind wouldn't focus. I sat in the front pew, silently acknowledging anyone who came near.

"Marcy, dear. How are you?"

Mrs. Beech hobbled towards me, arms outstretched. I braced for the impact and hug. I opened my arms and mumbled into her hair, "I'm fine, considering." She smelled of lilacs and had been at Mother's funeral, too. She was older than Granny and had always seemed happy to stay long after picking up her orders. Everyone else paid, then hurried off, as though embarrassed to be seen at Granny's house.

Earlier in the day, I'd provided the funeral home with pictures of Granny, Mother, and myself, and they'd been placed around the room. A few people stopped to look at them, fingering the crystals I'd left with the photos.

A short funeral followed the visitation. The few people in attendance began slipping out as the funeral director closed the coffin, signalling the end of the service. I followed, watching as the pallbearers placed the coffin inside the hearse. I got in my car and waited for them to begin the precession.

Alone, I followed behind the hearse in my lava-orange Smart Car. The gravel laneway curved around the church towards Church Hill Cemetery. It seemed strange that my mother, and now Granny, would both rest there. I could only imagine what everyone would think, especially the minister, if they knew my family wasn't Baptist, but Pagan.

I didn't know anyone able to perform the type of ceremony Granny wanted, and something normal was expected by the community. The cemetery sat behind a Baptist Church, so a Baptist minister seemed appropriate, for now. Just like Mother's funeral, there'd be two; one public, one private.

Granny would rest under the canopy of several large maples, near the back of the grounds. When she'd made the arrangements after Mother passed over, she also purchased the two adjoining plots; one for her and one for me. We'd lie in a row, one generation following the next.

I pulled to the side of the lane and parked behind the hearse. While they removed the coffin, I took a moment to steady my nerves before gathering up the bouquets, both made of flowers and herbs from Granny's garden. I followed the pallbearers towards two matching grave markers. Pinkish granite stones, lettering engraved and filled in with black, sat side by side. Both had an etching of angels, one in each top corner, looking skyward. Mine would be the same when the time came. I knelt and brushed away blades of grass that clung to Mother's stone, carelessly flung by a lawn mower. Placing one bouquet on top of her headstone, along with a piece of polished citrine— her favourite gem—I whispered, "I miss you."

The emptiness in my heart weighed heavy. I'd never felt so alone. I kissed my hand, then touched it to the cold granite before rising.

Brushing away a tear, I squared my shoulders and looked around. The cemetery was as empty as the road. My hopes rose as a car approached. *Someone decided to come to the cemetery after all?* My heart dropped as it drove by. I turned and lay the other bouquet on Granny's headstone.

I half listened as the minister spoke at the graveside. Tears clung to my lashes and left streaks on my glasses with each blink. I ran my fingers across the inside of the lenses in an attempt to see better. *How could Granny be gone?* She'd always been so healthy. A hundred thoughts raced through my head, but one kept repeating; the promise. At the time, I'd felt guilty lying to her, but soon realized I'd been lying to myself.

Something brushed across my bare arm. I jumped. It was only the minister. "The service is over, dear."

I mumbled a *thank you* and moved to the empty space between Granny and Mother, barely registering him leave. I planned on coming back at midnight to perform the same ceremony Granny and I did for my mother. *Our* ceremony.

We'd always tried to fit into the community, something I never understood. Everyone knew my family was psychic, different. The funeral was just for show, an attempt at normalcy. The body was simply an empty shell after death, and we weren't concerned with what happened to it. Some Pagans preferred cremation, but we liked the idea of being returned to the earth. Granny had insisted on one of those new bio-coffins, and I rather liked the idea, too. They weren't available when Mother died, but Granny heard about them and made me promise to bury her in one. Gifting ourselves to Mother Earth. It seemed like the right way to do it. The cemetery was far enough outside town it felt like we were in the country, so it suited our love of nature.

Crouching, I read the verse on Mother's marker, wondering who the unknown author was.

> *Believe in faeries that make dreams come true,*
> *believe in the wonder of the stars and the moon.*
> *Believe in the magick from the faeries above,*

they dance on the flowers and sing the songs of love.
And if you just believe and always stay true,
the faeries will be there to watch over you.

I knew when I stopped believing and recalled the day I told Mother my decision. My grade seven teacher had assigned a team project and paired me with my best friend. We worked on it at her home after school, but it didn't go as planned. I'd raced home, stumbling off my bike in the driveway, twisting my ankle. Mother watched through the kitchen window and rushed out.

"Dry your tears, honey. Tell me what's wrong." Mother knelt in front of me and I fell into her arms, burying my face in her shoulder.

"Patsy's mom won't let me play over there anymore. I can't even talk to her." My tears left a dark spot on her bright yellow blouse when I pulled away.

"But you've been friends since kindergarten." She held me at arm's length. "What happened?"

I sniffled, wiping my bare arm across my face. "We were in the dining room working on our project and I said her dad was calling to say he was going to be late for supper. Then the phone rang. Her mom gave me a weird look as she listened on the line. When she hung up, she told Patsy they'd be eating late, then she was sent to her room. Mrs. Billings turned to me and told me to go home, and said I wasn't to speak to Patsy again."

Mother pulled me close. There was a slight edge to her voice. "I guess I should have seen it coming. How many times have I told you to hide your skill?"

"I'm not going to do it anymore. Not ever. I don't want to be like you and Granny. I want to have friends."

I shook my head to clear my thoughts. I didn't want to remember how our relationship changed that day, and could only imagine how hurt she must have felt. If only I'd known she'd be dead two years later.

The pallbearers followed close on the minister's heels, leaving me on my own. I sat cross-legged on the grass between Granny and Mother.

"I know you were both disappointed and hurt by my choice, but you respected my decision. Several times I'd heard bits of conversation between you two and almost changed my mind, just to make you happy. Then I remembered how you always said to be true to myself and not do anything just to please someone else. I've made another decision."

The promise made in haste weighted heavy on my mind since Granny's passing. It'd been hollow, made in the moment to quiet Granny so she could rest. I'd felt guilty afterwards, then realized what caused the void I'd been feeling all these years.

"I'm ready to embrace it now, and I'll make you proud."

A flash of orange off to the left caught my attention. I turned my head and watched as two Monarch butterflies sailed towards me. They landed briefly on my knees, then one flew to Mother's headstone, the other to Granny's. I sat straight and held out my hands, index fingers pointing. The Monarchs came to me, landing on my fingers. I slowly brought them close to my face.

"I promise," I whispered.

They fluttered their wings three times, then flew off.

As I stood, an intense surge of foreboding hit me. My chest grew heavy, and a chill ran through me. The hairs on my arms rose. My head spun. I reached to the headstone for support as my psychic senses kicked in. Even though I'd blocked them over the years, in extreme conditions, they surfaced.

It had never been this strong. My heart rate accelerated, pounding in my ears. I closed my eyes and breathed deeply. My head cleared, but only a little.

No one remained in the cemetery, but I knew someone watched. I tried to clear my mind, focusing only on the feeling, trying to zero in on its location. The sensation didn't come from any one direction—it enveloped me. The air grew heavy. My throat tightened, causing me to gasp for air. I managed a few shallow breaths. My thought process slowed.

Where did I leave my car? Disoriented, I stumbled around Granny's grave, climbing over the pile of earth beside it. I lost my footing and slid off, stopping beside the open hole.

A sharp pain tore through my head. My eyes watered.

Why isn't my wall working? Concentrate. The pain subsided enough to allow me to crawl to the car. Grasping the handle, I pulled myself upright and opened the door. I fell in and hit the lock button.

A deep, guttural laugh shook the ground. I almost dropped my keys in my desperation to find the ignition. Blinking away the tears, I tried the key again. It found its mark. The gravel flew as I sped out of the cemetery.

THREE

I sat in the driveway, hands clenching the steering wheel. *What the heck is going on? Did I really just experience something evil, or is my imagination running wild?* Normally, being in a cemetery wouldn't phase me. *Is it the stress?* That had to be it. I convinced myself nothing actually happened and went inside. After savouring a cup of camomile tea, I headed upstairs.

I spent the rest of the day arranging some of my meagre possessions throughout Granny's, no, *my* house. I always knew I'd inherit it one day. I had already sold most of the furniture from my apartment in Toronto. It was just cheap second-hand junk. I lit a stick of frangipani incense and placed it on the dresser in my old bedroom before surveying the room. Apart from the furniture, it sat empty. Kinda summed up my life.

Some of my clothes were here, and the items I'd kept after selling most of my belongings sat in several battered cardboard boxes salvaged from behind my old apartment building. I wasn't ready to move in yet, but I wanted to make a start. It would be easier to rent out an empty apartment anyway.

I sat my suitcase on the bed, planning to sort my clothes later, then placed my frequently used crystals on the single shelf on the wall opposite the window—quartz, citrine, amethyst, and black tourmaline. Rare gems sat in a jewellery box on the dresser. The rest were in a carved wooden box consisting of a dozen tiny drawers. They were the only items I'd kept when I put the craft behind me, as they helped suppress my ability.

Next, I loaded the bookcase by the window with all my frequently read books. I'd kept one fairly large portrait of myself with Mother and Granny painted on my tenth birthday, two years before denouncing my skills. The nail in the wall still stuck out. Standing on the bed, I hung the portrait back in its original spot. As I stepped off, a wave of anxiety washed over me. My stomach fluttered, my heart rate increased. Someone watched me. Tires squealed as someone sped away.

I stood at the window, trying to see if anyone lurked around the house. Unfortunately, the trees around the property prevented me from seeing the road. As the sound of the motor faded, so did the fluttery feeling. *Were the two things connected? Had to be teens showing off. Why would anyone be spying on me?*

Despite putting my family's psychic skills behind me, it'd been necessary to maintain a wall around myself to keep out the thoughts of anyone nearby. The crystals aided with that, giving me strength, as well as helping me relax. Besides, they were pretty. I definitely needed to bone up on protection, what will all the weirdness that suddenly seemed to follow me. I remembered some rituals, but I'd need to do a lot of research as I only knew the basics. My gut emphasized this was the number one item on my to-do list.

The sun gave way to the waning moon, forcing me to stop puttering around my bedroom. I needed to prepare for the ceremony over Granny's grave. I searched through my wardrobe and changed into the brightest clothes I could find. A cornflower blue ankle-length skirt, a hot pink tube-top, and a white gauzy blouse. I grabbed one of the now empty moving boxes, filled it with the items I'd need, then loaded it into my car. The drive back to the cemetery was fast, as most people were sleeping, but I watched to see if anyone followed. It approached midnight by the time I arrived, so I had to rush in order to get everything in place to start right at twelve.

I removed the box from my car and ran over to the grave site. Like during the funeral, the cemetery lay deserted. The few farmhouses I'd passed were dark, the occupants long since asleep.

Leaves rustled somewhere among the trees. Not loud enough for a person, probably a racoon. Crickets chirped, stopping when I approached. Setting the box on the ground behind Mother's headstone, I stood silently and listened. The eerie quiet set my nerves on edge. *Was it like this when we came for Mother?* Wishing I had someone with me, I let my psychic wall down just enough to probe the atmosphere, searching for that feeling from earlier.

Nothing. It really had been my imagination. But just in case, I whispered a thank-you to the gods and asked them to keep me safe. I took a moment to ground, first removing my sandals so I could set roots and draw the energy from the earth. It was time.

I pulled a bundle of multi-colored ribbons from the box. The tree branches were too high up, so I had made do with the nearby shrubs. One by one, I tied the ribbons to the branches. I smiled as a gentle breeze swirled around them, reminding me of tiny ballet dancers pirouetting on a stage of green. Next, I placed a lavender candle on top of Granny's headstone. Then I took the remaining candles from the box and stuck them in the ground around the grave, starting on the east side. First a white candle, then pink, then gold. I repeated the pattern until I was back at the headstone, ending with a white one.

Candles in place, I lit them, then stood at the foot of Granny's grave, arms outstretched, palms up. I hesitated, unsure of myself. Too much time had passed since I gave up the Pagen ways. *Should I have spent more time reading over the ceremony? Would the spirits, gods, and goddesses hear me? More importantly, would they help? Would the blessing work?* It had to.

"I'm sorry," I whispered, "but I'm back. Please help me take care of Granny."

I looked to the sky.

> "May there be peace in the East,
>
> May there be peace in the South,
>
> May there be peace in the West,
>
> May there be peace in the North.
>
> May there be peace throughout the Universe."

Arms still raised, I moved to the east side of her grave.

> "Spirits of the East, Powers of the Air, I call on you to bring me bright memories of Francine Adhamh. Blessed be."

I continued around the grave, stopping at each side.

> "Spirits of the South, Powers of Fire, I call on you to keep the fire of my love for Francine alive in my memories. Blessed Be.
>
> "Spirits of the West, Powers of Water, I call on you to let my tears and love flow. Remember Francine, who loved life, her friends, her family. Blessed be.
>
> "Spirits of the North, Powers of the Earth, I call on you to bring me strength. Remember Francine, to whom you gave strength and wisdom and embrace her in her passing. Blessed be."

Blessing done and fingers crossed the words were correct, I dug a hole between the two headstones, then removed the final item from the box beside me. A small Blue Star juniper. Planting trees wasn't allowed, but the administrators of the cemetery had approved the low-growing shrub. Energy whirled around me as I circled the grave, lifting my mood. My heart lightened, my entire body tingled. In my soul, I knew Granny was safe and would be watched over. Knew she was now with my mother.

The finality of the ceremony sunk in. The swirling energy subsided, leaving me drained. I dropped to my knees, truly alone. My heart ached. I missed them so much. How was I ever going to figure out what to do without their guidance, love, and support?

I couldn't afford myself the luxury of self-pity. *Time to grow up, Marcy. Time to take responsibility.* The only person who could help me was me.

I rose, thanked the gods and goddesses for their assistance, then said my final farewells. I blew out the candles and untied the ribbons, the juniper the only evidence remaining of my late-night visit.

FOUR

*A*fter putting on my PJs, I went into Granny's room, sat on her bed, and leaned back. Pressure from info-overload filled my head. My brain couldn't process everything.

A week had passed since the lawyer called me to go over the will. The shock had been so great I didn't even remember the drive back to the house. *Why didn't she leave anything to her sister?* Along with the three-story gothic house, I inherited everything; contents, money, investments, plus there was the insurance settlement. I'd no idea she was so well off. The contents included what could be considered some pretty strange stuff. Strange to most, normal to me.

Moving into the house, rather than selling, required zero thought. Despite my zombie-like state, that one decision needed no thought. A week of driving back and forth from the city before the funeral, with the rest of my belongings, finally began to take its toll. I'd been going non-stop since Granny passed. After barely recognizing my reflection in the mirror, I knew I had to slow down. I'd spent the last few days looking for someone willing to let my tiny apartment. Now it was time to veg.

By the next morning, the oversized luggage under my eyes was more like carry-on and the redness had finally vacated. Still needed to work on those lines across my forehead, but at least I looked like Marcy again. *This is the first full night in my house.* That was going to take some getting used to.

I didn't really need the room the enormous house provided. It's not like I throw parties or anything like that. I'd rather have my nose buried in a book, not an e-reader. The feel of the pages and the special musty smell of antique books can't be duplicated.. But those weren't available from Kindle or Kobo. The best are the really old ones.

My favourite was a hand-written book on healing crystals from 1625, discovered on a trip to Paris many years ago. No clue who wrote it. It was simply titled "Journal" with the initials BNT inside above the year. Early on, both my mother and Granny made certain I knew as much as I could about crystals and herbs. I wasn't interested in the rest.

Mother was always saying, "It's important, Marcy. You need to learn more." *Wish I'd listened.*

Rather than take the largest room, Granny had picked the one at the back. On more than one occasion, I'd tried to convince her to move her antique chest of drawers to the space beside the balcony, but she always smiled and shook her head.

The balcony overlooked the garden, her pride and joy. I crossed the hall from my room in the turret to hers and padded barefoot across the hardwood floor to the wrought iron French doors. The moon gave little illumination, allowing all the solar lights the opportunity to show off. I'd forgotten how pretty the garden looked at night, especially from above. I opened the doors and stepped out onto the narrow balcony, inhaling the scents that wafted up.

The property was far enough from town not to be contaminated with noise, except from crickets and frogs. Something rustled among the plants. *Most likely a racoon or skunk.* I wrapped my arms around me as a slight breeze chilled the air, causing me to retreat.

Glancing around the room, I spotted the doorstop. A cast iron black cat, back hunched, mouth open, a non-existent hiss escaping. I could almost hear the hiss. It triggered a memory.

My last Hallowe'en with Mother, she gave me a book called *The Sixteen Principles of Homeopathic Medicines*. Before she died in that crash six years ago, Mother tried to get me interested in developing the family talents that were handed down from generation to generation, but I threw it all away when I was twelve. Everything except for the power of the crystals and a bit of the homemade potions.

It was late, and I needed sleep, but seeing the set of drawers sitting just inside Granny's bedroom still bugged me. I couldn't sleep until I'd dealt with it. *Never could understand why it was so close to the door.* Anytime I walked into the room, if I wasn't paying attention, I'd clip it with my little toe, or bump it with my arm. Besides, it would look so much nicer against the opposite wall.

I gave it a shove. It wouldn't budge. As far as I knew, it only had clothing it. No reason for it to be so heavy. *Maybe I'm just too tired to summon any strength.* Grabbing the back of the unit, I braced myself against the doorframe and tried to push it away from the wall. I only succeeded in chipping a nail.

Good god Granny. You got rocks in here or something? Maybe if I removed one drawer? I took the top one out and placed it on the bed. Nothing but t-shirts— no rocks. With the drawer gone, it was easier to get a grip on the dresser. I braced myself against the doorframe again, gripping the open edge where the drawer used to be. Just as I was about to give it a shove, I noticed a nail near the top of the dresser going into the wall behind.

I stumbled over to my room and came back with my backpack. Forcing my eyes to stay open, I dumped the contents on Granny's bed. I grabbed my little flashlight and shone it behind the dresser, spotting another nail on the opposite side. *Weird.*

My glasses got in the way when I tried to get my face closer. Since I wasn't totally blind without them, I dropped them on the carpet and smushed my face against the side of the dresser. I spotted two more nails about half way down. Something against the wall near the floor caught my attention. I gasped. My hands shook. *It couldn't be.* But I had to know. I removed the bottom drawer to get a better look.

I rubbed my eyes and cleaned my glasses with my PJ top. *Couldn't be.* After putting them back on, I removed the next drawer. *Holy heliodor.* Startled, my back smacked against the footboard of the bed. *What the…?*

Crawling forward, I reached through the opening. *Maybe it's just a painting.* Frozen with my fingertips an inch short of the wall, I took a deep breath. Reaching farther, my fingers brushed against it. It had texture, depth. *Nope, not a painting.* I scrambled backwards to the bed, hitting it hard enough to knock something onto the floor.

A Fae door sat on top of the foot-high baseboard. At least, it appeared to be a door. The house was filled with some pretty strange stuff. *But why a Fae door? Why in this particular room? Why was it barricaded?* Should I be afraid or curious?

FIVE

Stretched out on my side, I shone the flashlight on it again. The tiniest door I'd ever seen stood about a foot high, with a little bitty ladder leaning against the wall below it. Like most century houses, the floorboards were wide and the baseboards quite high. *What needs that tiny ladder to enter the door?*

Something niggled at the back of my mind. The door. What was it about the door? *I should know.* Curiosity won out. Most Fae folk aren't supposed to be dangerous, so I crawled back over and reached in again, putting my thumb and index finger on the little knob. As usual, *think before acting* didn't enter my brain. I always seemed to get that backwards.

A jolt, then a tiny spark. I tried to turn the knob. Locked. *Or is it? I should know about this, but what? Locked Fae doors. Hmm, is it locked or is it just me? Think. Something about humans accessing them.*

I looked over at the stuff I'd dumped on the bed for anything that might open the door. Nothing in my wallet would work, and my keys were too big. Even the little luggage key was much too large. My foot connected with something beside the bed. My set of eyeglass screwdrivers sailed under the bed. Kneeling, I pawed at the carpet, trying to grab the case. My fingers hit the edge, pushing it farther from reach. After crawling under the bed to retrieve it, I removed the elastic that held the case together and took out the smallest in the set before tackling the Fae door.

For once, I thought before acting. *What if a living creature actually lived on the other side?* I decided to only open it a crack. If something lurked, waiting, one quick shove would close the door. If only one hinge was removed, maybe the door would move enough to dislodge the latch.

It was awkward trying to work the screwdriver through the gap left by the drawer, but I finally got the first hinge off. The door refused to budge, so I removed the second one. A shuffling noise came from the other side. Then muffled voices.

Now, a normal person would hesitate, maybe even be scared. But I've never been considered normal. Besides, if there were Fae folk living here, I wanted to meet them. At least I thought I did.

Granny's home always fascinated me, and this just made it all the more interesting. Not just the appearance, which was pretty cool. The dark bricks gave the house a spooky look. It would have been perfect for a Hallowe'en party. Multiple peaks stuck up all over the roof, a black wrought-iron railing closed in the top-most point, each corner finished off with a skull. A flat section contained a small peak just tall enough for a door. *A widow's walk, Granny called it.* My favourite feature was the two-story turret on the north side of the house. My room was inside it on the second floor. The house practically screamed of weirdness. But voices in the wall? For some reason, they sounded familiar.

I finished removing the screws on the second hinge when I heard it again. This time, they sounded closer, followed by scurrying feet. *What is in there?* I got the last hinge off and popped the door out. I shone my flashlight into the opening. It flickered. *Damn batteries.* The light lasted long enough to see something vanish around a corner about six inches in, most certainly a foot. Not an animal paw, but a foot. With a shoe. *What the heck? Where did it go?*

I got up and went to the bedroom doorway. The hall ended a few feet past the door. *Is there something behind the wall? Could this old house have secret passages? Why are my memories so faint?* Maybe there was a reason the door had been locked and blocked off with the dresser. I yawned, too tired to deal with it, so I put the little door back and replaced the hinges. Put the drawers back too, just in case.

I spent the next couple of days searching the house and exploring. The locked Fae door made regular appearances in my mind. So far, I'd found no other piece of furniture nailed down. Did that mean the door in the bedroom was the only one? It'd been a long time since I'd had a good look around, most visits being brief. Normally, when I put in an appearance, I only stayed from mid-morning to late afternoon. Now I wished I could go back in time and visit properly.

The house was filled mostly with antiques. Granny had an old roll-top desk. I couldn't resist opening every draw, hoping for a hidden treasure. All I found were stamps, paper clips, note paper, and pens. Lots of pens. No hidden compartments, at least none that I found.

Occasionally, I heard scurrying in the walls. Even though I tried to convince myself it was simply mice, I didn't believe it. Mice don't need doors. Periodically, I'd knock on the walls, listening for a change in sound, like in the movies. The only change occurred when I knocked on a wall stud.

As I wandered through the house, I realized none of Granny's books were around. I'd been with her when she bought some of them, so they had to be somewhere. The past few days had raised many questions, but no answers.

Since I didn't have many items to place around the house, I decided it was as good a time as any to go through Granny's clothing. It wasn't something I'd been looking forward to. Granny took care of that when Mother died. Most everything just seemed to vanish, except some personal items. I'd have to go through all of Granny's possessions and decide which things to let go. No matter what, the memories would stay with me.

Since the day promised to be warm, I opened the door to the small balcony, allowing all the fragrances from the garden to make their way into the bedroom. *Stop stalling.* I glanced at the chest of drawers by the door, then turned my attention to the closet. Too soon to go near that tiny door.

A few years ago, Granny had made a passing remark about not wanting her stuff to go to waste after she was gone. We had different tastes, so I wouldn't be making use of anything, except possibly some of her t-shirts. Most of her wardrobe wasn't fancy, just regular everyday wear. Blouses, dress pants, jeans, and tees. The latter two for gardening. She had a few fancy dresses for when we all went out on birthdays and Sabbats. I placed Granny's outfits in a box and started on the dresser. It still sat in the way, blocking the tiny door.

Tucked behind her delicates, as Granny called them, sat a box. A plain, wooden box, with a slight scent of cedar, about eight inches long. Funny, she hadn't normally gone for plain anything. Most of her silver and wooden items were covered in engravings, either symbols or vines. Inside was an envelope addressed to me. Below my name Granny had written: *for your 21st birthday.*

I know Granny and Mother considered this birthday a special one, but it meant nothing to me. Until now. Part of the promise I made to Granny included going through with the ceremony. Alone. I sat on the bed and let it all out. The guilt of not having time to heal the rift with Mother. Not spending enough time with Granny.

My body shook. All my life I'd kept my emotions to myself, but I couldn't contain them any longer. Years of held-back tears spilled out. By the time I stopped, the front of my t-shirt was soaked.

All I had left now was that letter. Desperate to rip into it, I told myself to wait in order to share my birthday with her. I kept looking at it. *What's in there?. Can I wait six weeks?* I picked it up, took it to my room, and stashed it at the back of a drawer. *Out of sight, out of mind, right?*

I picked up a framed photo from the dresser. Me, Mother, and Granny, standing in front of an old building in Edinburgh, hidden away down a small alley. I remember wondering why they called it a *close*. It was the last trip we took together. Mother died several months later. Running my fingers across her face, the memory of the day I was told of her death surfaced.

Grade ten. The principal sent word to my math teacher for me to come to the office. As soon as I saw Granny, I knew something was wrong. *Why hadn't I felt it earlier?* I was dumbstruck when she told me. On the drive to Granny's, I stared out the window, too much in shock to even cry. Mother was an excellent driver. How could she have crashed her car? My former BFF, Patsy, had left a phone message that evening, but I never returned her call. Granny swooped in and cleared out most everything, then Mother's house was sold off and I moved to Granny's.

At the time, I didn't even know what she did with our belongings. Maybe I could find Mother's pendant. It was special, and I wanted to have it. I'd discovered some boxes on the third floor about a year after the accident, but could never bring myself to go through them.

Needing to take a break and clear my mind, I put the photo back and headed down to the kitchen for a coffee. The sunporch had always been the perfect place to relax and think things through. I settled in and looked out at the beautiful garden. A few childhood memories scrolled through my mind like a movie. A six-year-old version of myself running through the flowers, up and down the herb spiral, talking to my imaginary friend. *Wait. What?* I couldn't recall having an imaginary playmate. The vision of the foot in the wall popped forward. *Could there be a connection?*

A missing piece of information niggled at the back of my mind. Something I was certain I already knew. I'd gone through the house from top to bottom, and I still hadn't found the workroom. Mother had one, and I knew Granny did too, but I couldn't remember where it was. I used to help Granny with some of her potions, but that was in grade seven, before I tuned out that part of my life.

My trips back since leaving for university became less and less frequent, and helping Granny was something I hadn't done for a long time. I missed her and Mother now more than ever. Neither would be here to guide me through the ceremony on my birthday. Granny had almost made it, but she died two months too soon.

Since I'd put it all behind me years ago, the birthday ceremony wasn't something I thought I'd ever bother with, but I was determined to keep the promise I made when Granny was in the hospital. Now that I was back in the house, it was more than an empty promise, made simply to satisfy Granny so her heart rate could settle down. I really wanted to learn about my family and our special psychic skills. Something had been lacking in my life, and it was time to change that.

I'd made friends at university, but none as close as Patsy had been. At least, until her mom banished me. Didn't want to risk getting close to someone again. None of them knew about my family and I wasn't going to tell. All anyone at university knew was that my parents were dead. How could I admit I had no idea who my father even was? Initially, I lived in the dorm, but I moved into my tiny apartment mid-way through the first year. My roomie had questioned my home-made remedies for headaches and sleep, and made snide comments about my crystals. I told her the remedies were homeopathic, but I couldn't risk anyone finding out the truth.

Even though I'd shut down my psychic abilities as much as possible, I still relied on the potions. Nothing to do with my family. The potions were simply healthier. It wasn't really a lie when I said they were homeopathic. A few were bought from a naturopathic store. Ever since I put the craft behind me, I felt off. Somehow, I had to fill that void. I *needed* to fill the void. It wasn't just lack of friends and family that left me feeling flat. My visits to Granny had become less frequent for a reason. I felt out of place there, and she knew it.

SIX

The second most interesting discovery came mid-morning in the living room. A tall, solid oak case sat against the wall beside the doorway to the dining room. Granny always kept it locked. Remembering a tiny key on the keyring the lawyer gave me, I retrieved it from the silver bowl by the front door. It fit. My breath caught at the contents. Every shelf was filled with crystal balls. Twenty-seven in varying sizes and colors. They belonged to Mother. Her private collection, not ones she used with clients. Granny must have placed them as a remembrance. I hadn't been back enough to notice.

The absolute most amazing discovery turned up in the drawer at the bottom of the oak case. A collection of crystal wands, each neatly wrapped up in a piece of black velvet. My mind reeled as I tried to recall what each one was. A few were unfamiliar. Since crystals had always fascinated me, as well as aiding me with my psychic wall, I knew what they could do. Each gemstone has a different benefit or use. Many people use them to balance their chakra. So far, my only use was to channel my thoughts to maintain a wall around me to block other's thoughts from intruding. My wand of choice was made from opal. It helps absorb energy and vibrations of people around me. It's not really intended to block, but it works for me. *Do they belonged to Granny, or are some Mother's?*

Exhausted, both physically and mentally, I lit a stick of vanilla incense and stretched out on the sofa to enjoy a moment of quiet. Granny's landline rang constantly, so I had unplugged it. My old friends from high school offering condolences; my old, nosey roomie even called. I'd hoped to hear from Patsy.

When her father died a couple of years ago, I'd sent flowers. Wouldn't surprise me if Mrs. Billings tossed them in the garbage. A few of the calls were from Granny's clients, asking if I'd be continuing her business. I hadn't considered that, but I needed something to occupy my time. Helping her with the elixirs had been fun.

I desperately needed to get my shit together. I'd quit the Earth and Environmental Science program at the University of Toronto shortly after I moved out of the dorm, simply because it bored me. The geology course was somewhat interesting, but the rest? Dull, dull, dull. And I'd quit job after job. But more importantly, I had quit *me*. When I denounced my psychic abilities almost eight years ago, it left a tiny hole that I'd ignored. Nothing had been able to fill it. That empty space grew into a chasm the size of the Grand Canyon.

After lengthy soul searching, my hollow promise to Granny needed to be filled in. I actually meant what I'd said at the cemetery. I intended to follow through, not for Granny or Mother, but for me. If I'd kept up with my family studies, I'd know by now what my thing was. Each of us excelled in something: Mother telling fortunes and connecting with spirts, Granny, herbal medicines. I used to enjoy helping Granny, so maybe I'd take a shot at that. She must have a recipe book somewhere. *I need to find it.*

Somewhat rested, I hauled my butt off the sofa. The kitchen seemed as good a place as any to start. It took up a large section of the east side of the house. Lots of cupboards, counter space, and drawers. Starting at one end seemed the most logical.

The first drawer was stuffed with tea towels and dish cloths. The next contained small items for cooking; tea strainers, garlic press, measuring spoons. So far, I'd found nothing unexpected. Granny kept the kitchen organized. Extremely organized. In frustration, I almost pulled the next drawer right out. I even checked the cutlery drawer, which I'd been in many times before. The cupboards contained exactly what I expected—cups, plates, bowls, containers, mixing bowls. Everything one would expect to find in a kitchen, except a cookbook. Slamming the last door, I swore. *Where in holy heliodor is it?*

As I turned, I noticed the calendar on the wall and flipped the page. A bright red circle enclosed July 2. Mother's birthday. Granny's was the 30th. My birthday on the 31st was circled too. I let the page drop.

Twenty-one: the magick number when so many things would be revealed. I'd been excited before, but now I was scared. The more I thought about it, the faster my heart raced. *How can I go through the ceremony on my own? Why hadn't I listened when they tried to teach me something other than crystals and herbology?*

Maybe Granny kept her book in the little closet in the hall, just outside the kitchen door. It was difficult to see the contents as there wasn't a light inside, and the lighting in the hall was dim, but I spotted a package of bulbs. Reaching up, I grabbed it and read the side. They were sixty-watters. Time to brighten up the hallway. I took the bulbs in one hand, and the step ladder in the other.

It was the only place in the entire house Granny had screwed in the low wattage ones, and it was a shame. The hall and the two front rooms had beautiful oak wainscoting. They'd sparkle with better lighting. She always gave me one of her "I know something you don't" smiles when I suggested increasing the wattage.

I opened the ladder and set it up below the first light fixture. As soon as I replaced the one closest to the kitchen, the hall transformed. I lightly ran my fingertips over the oak before moving down to the light near the bottom of the upstairs staircase. What a difference the two bright bulbs made. Despite the pile of empty boxes I'd tossed carelessly after unpacking them, the front hall became welcoming, warm. The mirror on the antique hall stand reflected the light, making it stand out. Mind you, the stand was far from plain and stood out anyway. Made from the same coloring of oak as the wainscoting, it was elaborately carved from top to bottom.

I remembered playing on it as a child. The top portion had a large rectangular mirror in the centre, with coat hooks fastened on both sides— two at the very top, two mid-way down the sides. The bottom portion had a bench with a hinged lid about two-thirds of the way across, with an umbrella stand at the end. I used to sit on the bench and pretend to be a princess sitting on her throne.

I lost my balance as I climbed off the ladder and reached out for the wall. My hand slid to the top of the wainscoting and brushed a lump. I took a closer look and realized it was a button. Loose, but definitely attached.

A memory broke free. I pressed down and heard a click. A section of the wall popped out, leaving a gap just wide enough for my fingers to slip in and pull it open. It barely made a sound. I ran my hand down the edge and marveled at how smooth it was. Whoever crafted it had done a spectacular job. Even the hinges were practically invisible. The movable section was a little taller than me, just over six feet, and about two feet across. Pretty much the size of a standard door, but not as wide.

Half a memory zipped through my mind as I pulled the section open the rest of the way and stepped into what felt like another realm.

33

SEVEN

The hall light shone in, revealing a bare bulb hanging from the ceiling, just inside the opening. I pulled the thin chain that hung from the fixture and a soft glow filled the space. *Damn Granny. Great hiding spot.* That explained her smile. A landing, about three or four feet square, crowned a staircase leading down. Another light also came on inside the room below when I pulled the chain. This was so much better than Mother's room. Hers was just a room on the second floor that would have been a spare bedroom in most people's homes.

Being in the house dislodged another forgotten memory. I played hide and seek down there as a child, and Granny and Mother had always pretended not to know where I was. Standing on the landing inhaling the cool, musty air before padding down the steps, a little of my brain-fog dissipated. Snips of memory briefly surfaced, then vanished.

The stairs were eerily silent as I descended. Made sense. If she had to retrieve something while one of her clients waited in the front room, she'd need to go down without being heard. Feeling energized as soon as my bare feet hit the earthen floor, I dug my toes in and wiggled them. Dug may be a bit of an exaggeration. The ground was hard from decades of being stomped on. The earth was cool, but didn't make me feel cold. It was as though the earth and air mingled to create just the right temperature and atmosphere.

The walls were concrete, but the floor had been left as nature intended. Made sense as the earth was a conduit for energy. I could picture Granny standing at the heavy wooden table that stood in the centre of the room, energy coursing through her as she mixed herbal remedies. The room was surprisingly warm, not cold or damp.

Bookworm that I was, naturally, the first thing I gravitated towards was the shelving covering an entire wall, each shelf jam-packed with books. *Bingo.* I knew they had to have been stashed somewhere. Funny how after the purchases I couldn't recall ever seeing most of them.

Some books were printed over a hundred years ago, many hand-written. Most of the books were on herbs and healing, with very detailed drawings. I walked along the case, running my hand over the spines. I recognized some books from our annual trips to places like England, Scotland, Ireland, and Germany.

One book about eye level caught my attention. A little larger than the others, the binding had faded from many years of use. It wasn't torn, but it was a little frayed around the spine. Granny must have consulted it numerous times. Gently, I removed the book, surprised at its weight, and placed it on the table. I turned the pages.

Some recipes read more like spells. That could explain the crystal ball and wands, but I'd never heard Mother or Granny do spells. Why would they? Crystals made sense as they were an aid in healing, and Mother used a crystal ball when she gave people readings.

Another memory niggled. I vaguely recalled being with her once when she'd purchased a small but expensive quartz ball. None of the recipes in the book seemed to make use of crystals, but there were symbols on some pages. Granny had added a few of her own notes, occasionally mentioning a specific-colored candle or incense. Lifting the book to my nose, I inhaled.

No musty antique scent lingered. Since the book wasn't able to guide me towards any magnificent epiphany, I turned my attention to the shelving on the wall opposite the books.

The contents complimented the books. Shelf after shelf of bottles filled with dried herbs, spices, and some crystals, candles, and a box of wooden matches. These ingredients would certainly be used to create Granny's recipes and potions. A thin rope ran across the room just above my head, bunches of herbs hung drying. *Probably from Granny's garden.* By the looks of them, she must have picked them shortly before she passed over. Most were dry and dropping leaves on the table and floor.

Against the far wall, almost hidden in the shadows, a small table sat adorned with a piece of black velvet fabric draped over something. I removed the fabric and found a piece of crystal larger than any I'd ever seen. A two-foot-tall, six-inch-thick, clear crystal wand—flawless and exquisite. I reached to touch it. My hand lingered about six inches away. A tingling surged through my fingers and up my arm, like tiny shots of electricity, but without the jolt. Afraid of its power, I put the velvet back over it, then walked around the room.

In the far corner, another tiny door, floor level this time. I tried to open it and discovered it unlocked. I didn't get the same spark that the one in Granny's room gave off. *Odd. The door in the bedroom was hidden and locked, but this one was out in the open.* The knob turned freely, but the door wouldn't budge.

Of course not. I don't have permission.

How did I know that?

I took one candle from the shelf and lit it so I could get a better look at the door. I chose a long, white tapered one. Crystals and candles were among the first things Mother and Granny had educated me on, so I instinctively knew what to use. White stood for truth and protection. I wanted to learn the truth and hoped I didn't need protection.

I knelt in front of the door and listened. Silence, except for my heartbeat. The earth under my knees felt alive. The movement wasn't strong, more like a gentle undulation. Nothing like the power I felt from the crystal wand. This soothed. I drew in a little of its power, then moved the candle closer to the door.

Symbols were etched on the top and down both sides of the little door. I recognized one of them. Mother's missing pendant had the same symbol on it. Four loops and a circle; a witches knot, or magick knot as some people referred to it. It hit hard that the only two people who could finish my special education were gone.

How could I have been so stupid? Born with a special gift and ashamed of it. *Could I have been embarrassed by Mother and Granny?* I was beginning to realize just how selfish I'd been. Less than two years had passed between burying my skill and Mother's death, and most of that time was filled with tension. Thinking back, there *had* been a hurt look in her eyes that I'd ignored. It wasn't quite as bad with Granny after I moved in, but it wasn't all rainbows and fluffy bunnies either.

I clasped my emerald pendant and closed my eyes. "Mother, Granny, I'm so sorry. Please forgive me and guide me through this. I can't do this alone."

Almost immediately, a presence warmed the room. Not like in the cemetery. This was soft and welcoming. "Thank you."

There had been no movement behind the little door, so I pushed it to the back of my mind and returned to browsing. *Surely one of the books can tell me what I needed to know.* Books were always my go-to when I wanted to find out anything. Too much nonsense on the internet.

First, I wanted to rifle through the little drawers in the antique desk that sat beside the shelf of herbs. It reminded me of an old post office table. So many little hiding places. I opened them one at a time and eventually found Mother's missing pendant. I kissed it and tucked it into my jeans pocket. Also found an old black-and-white photo in the same drawer. Even though it had been taken decades ago, I recognized two of the children—Granny and her sister Priscilla. Had no clue who the little boy was. I set that aside.

Another drawer contained five tiny keys. They looked about the right size for the Fae doors. I took them out and went over to the little door. The third key I tried fit. I hesitated for a moment, struggling between common sense and curiosity before turning the key. The lock clicked. *Am I doing the right thing? Are there going to be consequences from tampering with the door in Granny's bedroom?*

Obviously, she hadn't been concerned about them being in her workroom, whatever they were. Yet she barricaded the door upstairs. Didn't make any sense. Since I didn't know what these creatures were, I wasn't taking any chances. I relocked the door, then deposited the keys back in the drawer and turned my attention to the bookshelf.

So many books, most appeared vintage. I missed the annual European treks as a family. My favourite place was Denmark. We only ever went into bookstores; never visited Tivoli Gardens, Madame Tussauds, the Eiffel Tower, or any other standard tourist attractions in any of the cities. That would be just plain normal. None of that in my family. It would be nice to go back and fully explore the cities and villages sometime.

Initially, I was scared on those trips. Every place we visited took us away from the regular tourist spots, and through many back alleys and questionable neighborhoods. Kinda got used to it over the years. As I got older, I became fascinated with the old bookstores they visited and began looking for them here. I found a few, but they weren't the same as the ones in Europe. Not old enough, but interesting nonetheless. There was one in town I visited often. The store itself wasn't old, but it contained mostly first edition or hard-to-find books. So far, I hadn't come across any books published after 1900. I really liked the owner, Mr. Barker, and visited him as often as possible. He felt like a grandfather rather than just a friend or storekeeper.

As I scanned Granny's shelves, a book a bit smaller than the others caught my eye. No title on the spine. I reached out and pulled it off the shelf. No title on the front either. I opened it up to just handwriting. A journal, and the writing looked like Mother's. *Jackpot.* If Mother kept a journal, maybe Granny did too. *Could this be a way to complete my special education?*

I read through the first few entries, but guilt got the better of me. The little I read was private, and I didn't feel right reading it. *But what if it contained information I needed?* My thoughts drifted back to the letter from Granny, safety tucked away in the back of a dresser drawer. Much as I wanted to read it, I knew in my heart I needed to wait until my birthday. They had always made such a big deal out of my twenty-first birthday. *Maybe I should wait.* It was only six and a half weeks away. But could I hold out that long?

Granny's journal sat on a different shelf. Somehow, it didn't seem wrong to go through her journal. I couldn't resist. *Reading a little won't hurt, will it?* It's not like I was going to do anything with it, just read it. Besides, I might need to prepare things in advance. *Yep, that sounds logical.* After all, there must be preparations to make, right? Granny's journal would have more information in it since she would've started it decades before Mother. I began to go through it, then changed my mind, deciding to put it back. I hesitated with the book, just touching the edge of the shelf.

"Granny? Do you mind if I read it, just a little? It's the only way you can help me." The journal moved, nestling back into my hand. "Thank you."

I settled on the bench at the work table and opened the book. The lighting over the table was more than bright enough. It would have to be. Can't make mistakes when mixing the herbs and oils.

The first section was on crystals. Made sense. That's what they'd started me off with, but it contained way more. The start of the journal read like a story. She described lessons much like the ones they had taught me years ago. *Never knew Granny had such a flare for writing.* Mid-way through, I found the account of her ceremony.

EIGHT

July 30, 1960.

I stood in the yard and looked up. The moon was full and surprisingly large. The second full moon this month and clearly visible even though it was afternoon. Mother called it a blue moon. They are special. Six thirty-seven, she had told me. That's when I should start my ceremony. It took me weeks to figure out what I wanted to do. Something short and simple suited me best.

I heard the back door open and Mother came out, carrying the large six-sided crystal. It was a flawless white quartz that she kept covered and tucked away in her special room. I had never been allowed to touch it. I could have carried it myself, but I wanted it to be passed over to me to begin the ceremony. A sudden breeze stirred the white silk scarf I had around my neck. Mother stood in front of me and began to recite.

> *I call upon the Maiden, the Mother and the Crone,*
>
> *I call upon the Spirits of Earth, Air, Fire, and Water,*
>
> *To witness the vows of Francine into the craft,*
>
> *So mote it be.*

She handed the crystal to me and I held it high, pointing it towards the moon. I could feel the energy flowing into my hands, down my arms, through my body. I carried it to the pond at the back of Grand-mama's property, stopping to light each of the candles I had placed along the trail. Oh, how magnificent it would have looked had my time been later in the evening.

I was with her as she moved along the trail to the pond. It was easy to picture Granny performing her tasks, deliberate and with such conviction.

Conviction. Do I possess enough? Granny mentioned spending weeks writing her ceremony. How was I going to do that with no guidance? Could I borrow some of what she did? And what's with the blue moon? I've heard people say 'once in a blue moon' but I didn't think there really was one.

I pulled out my iPhone and googled it. *A blue moon is a second full moon in one month. Nothing about why it's called blue. I really doubt it changes color.* According to the website, the next blue moon would be July 31. My birthday. Ok, that's freaky. My ceremony will be on a blue moon, and so was Granny's. And Mother's? The website listed all the blue moon cycles. I scrolled down to 1985 and checked to see if there had been one on July 2. *Yep. Double freaky.* Didn't want to dwell on that too long. I wanted to read more about Granny's ceremony.

We went inside Mother's special room. I was excited and scared. When she opened the door, I gasped. It was beautiful. Lighted candles sat everywhere. There was a table in the centre of the room with a black velvet cloth draped over it, a large gold pentagram embroidered in the centre. She took the crystal wand from me and placed it in the centre of the pentagram. A stick of incense sat at the edge of the table, filling the room with a strange, earthy smell.

I couldn't understand how I could have such a gap in my memory. Recollections gradually surfaced. I was getting a sense of Déjà vu. *How could I have forgotten the panel in the hallway?* I closed the journal and put it back on the shelf. As I turned away from the books, my gaze drew back to the little door in the far corner. The doors were cute, mysterious, but also a tad scary. I was pretty sure they hadn't bothered me when I lived here in high school, but that memory, unfortunately, lay buried at the back of my mind. *What is it about these Fae doors?* Maybe Mr. Barker at the bookstore would know something. I checked the time. Ten thirty. He opened at nine on Saturdays. There was no one else to talk to, and he always seemed to know exactly where to find whatever I was looking for. I almost took the journals upstairs with me, but I figured Granny kept them in the work room for a reason. The secret room was magickal, and, well, secret. What better place to keep something safe?

After putting them back where Granny had tucked them away, I went upstairs and closed the entrance. The edge of the door was visible. That explained the dim bulbs. Decided I'd better put them back, but first I had to head into town to Mr. Barker's store. It had a very creative name, Antique Books. *Must have taken him days to come up with that one.*

✳ ✳ ✳

Over half an hour later, the little bell tinkled when I opened the front door. The drive wasn't far, but parking had been a bitch. Totally forgot about the Farmers' Market.

"Mr. Barker? It's Marcy. I could use your help."

"Back here, dear."

The shuffle of feet grew louder. A pristinely dressed gentleman appeared from behind a stack of shelves. In some ways, he reminded me of Mr. Rogers. Neatly pressed slacks, and no matter the weather, a buttoned-up cardigan. Much older, though. Never could get used to how strong his voice was when he looked so frail. If I had to guess at his age, just by looking at him, I'd say around three hundred, give or take. OK, maybe not quite that old, but he seemed ancient. Funny, he was only a little older than Granny, but he looked more than twice her age.

He moved with care, his feet barely lifting off the floor. *Wonder how he manages stairs?* He hunched, just a little, and his hands shook all the time. His health seemed to have deteriorated over the past few years, but he managed to keep his moustache trimmed quite nicely. He kind of looked like an older version of Johnny Depp. In his younger days, he must have had a flurry of women around him all the time.

I followed Mr. Barker to the back, glancing at the titles of leather-bound books adorning the shelves, then waited as he fumbled with the keys, looking for the one to unlock the private room. The aroma of freshly brewed tea wafted into the hall when he opened the door.

"I wondered when you'd be dropping by. Thought you might have a parcel of questions. Come in and sit down. My grandson will look after the store."

I sunk into an easy chair that sat around a small antique table. One of those little round ones with drop-leaf sides, complete with little clawed feet. In the centre rested a silver tray containing a teapot and two China cups.

"Grandson?" I looked around and didn't see anyone.

"He flew in a few days ago to help. He's in the storage room, sorting out last night's shipment. Had some books flown in from London. You'll want to read them."

He reached across the table and patted my hand. "I'm terribly sorry to hear about your grandmother. I would have attended the service, but I was under the weather. You know, I'm here to help any way I can. You're not twenty-one yet, are you? Francine was so excited about your special birthday. End of next month, I believe?"

I nodded. "So, you know twenty-one is special?" I got the impression he knew about my ceremony, but I wasn't certain just how to broach the subject.

"Yes, I know. Now tell me how much *you* know."

I shrugged and took a sip of tea. "Not much, really. Granny and Mother taught me some about crystals and gemstones. I really enjoy working with the crystals and learning about their unique properties. I feel a burst of energy from some, while others are calming, like emeralds." I reached up and rubbed the stone that always adorned my neck. I hesitated.

"You know about us?" I whispered. "I was always warned not to discuss it with anyone outside the family." A mixture of shock and puzzlement swirled through my mind. How could he know so much? Surely, Granny wouldn't have discussed our various psychic abilities with anyone, not even an old friend like Mr. Barker. I felt like I'd been kept in the dark about things. Was I being punished for deciding not to develop my skills? Had I become an outsider?

Mr. Barker laughed. He had one of those deep, throaty laughs that fills the entire room. "I'm what used to be called a *cuideachaidh*. It's Gaelic for helper, so we just go with that. I know about your family and I know it's not to be discussed. One of you would have to bring it up first. Basically, it's one of those secrets that everyone knows but no one talks about. Understand?"

"No, not really. I guess it's just one more thing to put on my learning to-do list. Tell me, what's with the Fae doors?"

He looked startled and put his teacup down with a clatter. "Fae doors?" He sat upright and shook his head. Just as he spoke, a head popped around the door.

NINE

A guy about my age held out a book. "Hey Gramps. This the one you wanted?"

Mr. Barker held out his hand, which shook more than usual. The guy walked in and gave the book to him. *This has to be the grandson.* Striking resemblance. He had a little of that Johnny Depp look too, but not quite as much as his grandfather. At first glance, I thought he had the same pale blue eyes as Mr. Barker, but when he looked directly at me, I could see they were grey, no, silver. *Who has silver eyes?* They were mesmerizing.

The little bell at the front door tinkled. The grandson winked at me before heading out to help the customer. My entire body tingled. My skin prickled. *What's happening?* No guy ever had that effect on me before. Everything in the room vanished briefly as my head spun. All I could see was the grandson, like I had tunnel vision. The sound of my heartbeat pounded in my ears. A magnetism surrounded him, following him into the hallway. He was only in the room for a few seconds, but his aura lingered, almost enveloping me. And his scent. Familiar and relaxing, but my brain was too frazzled to identify it. I jumped when Mr. Barker spoke.

"Your grandmother ordered this a few weeks ago. I guess it's yours now. Fully paid, so don't worry about that."

How did he know to have his grandson pull that book for me? I took it from him and looked at the cover. No title. I turned the next few pages, careful not to tear the fragile, yellow paper. Four pages in, I found it. *The English Physician Enlarged with Three Hundred and Sixty-Nine Medicines Made of English Herbs.* It was extremely old looking. I checked for a date—1775.

"Definitely something Granny would have wanted for her collection."

"So, tell me more about this door."

"Not much to tell. I found two. One behind the dresser in Granny's bedroom and another in, um, the cellar. Do you know what they're for?"

He wrinkled his brow. "Not certain. Haven't you seen them before? You lived in that house for several years."

"I feel as though I should know, but it's not coming to me. I don't feel afraid of them, more curious."

"A few thoughts come to mind. As I said, there are things that aren't normally discussed, and this would be one of them. I'm surprised Francine invited them in, but it depends on the species, of course."

"Them? Them who?"

"Well, I'll have to check a few things. Won't take too long, but a bit more information about them would help me narrow it down somewhat. Don't worry, but please, keep the doors shut. Block them if you can."

"OK, you're freaking me out."

Mr. Barker laughed, but it was more nervous. Not his usual laugh. "Nothing bad happened to your grandmother, so there's nothing for you to worry about. And you lived in that house all through high school. Nothing bad ever happened to you. But since you're alone, I'd just feel better if you kept the doors locked or barricaded until I know exactly what they are."

I thanked him and headed out front to the store. His grandson stood behind the counter, waiting for the customer to finish a transaction, but he lifted his head long enough to smile at me and wink again. There was something special about him. I released my block and let my psychic abilities reach out to him. *A helper. Hmm, I'm sure he could help me with a thing or two.* Surprised at where my thoughts were going, I threw up my block and almost walked into one of the easy chairs. I deked around the chair and out the door.

As soon as it shut behind me, the enchantment broke and my thoughts returned to the Fae doors and Mr. Barker's reaction. *Is whatever lives on the other side of the door dangerous?* Granny wouldn't have had any animals in the house that weren't safe. But it wasn't an animal foot I'd seen. Maybe it was just a trick of the light or possibly an illusion caused by my exhaustion. The door in the bedroom was locked and blocked. The room in the basement with the other door was now locked, so if it got out, it was confined to that one room. Nothing to worry about, right?

TEN

When I got home, I placed my ear against the hall panel with the secret door. Nothing to indicate anything moving around inside, so I slowly opened it, reached in, and pulled the chain on the light. No movement below. Creeping down the stairs, I looked over at the tiny Fae door on the far wall. Still closed; hopefully still locked, too. Curiosity about the symbols around the little door niggled at me, so I decided to look through the books for clues. *Surely, one must have symbols in it?*

Book after book about natural medicines, herbs, and crystals lined the shelves. I pulled out one of the more current books: *Cunningham's Encyclopedia of Crystal, Gem & Metal Magick*. Hadn't seen that one before, so I set it on the table to read later. A small book sat at the back of the shelf, hidden behind the others. I moved them out of the way and reached in.

It was bound in the softest leather I'd ever touched and, once again, no title on the front. I ran my hand over it. Something was embossed on it, but the book was so old it was impossible to decipher. I set it on the table and carefully turned the yellowed pages.

The handwriting was beautiful. Other books I'd read contained similar writing, but not like this. They had taken extra care to sculpt each letter, much like a piece of art. It wasn't the easiest script to read, but I'd poured over enough old books that I was used to it.

Chapter after chapter of folklore filled the pages. Stories about elves, faeries, goblins, and several creatures I'd never heard of. *What the devil were Lamia, Girallon, and Lammasu?* I looked over at the little door. *Faeries are small. Don't think they live in walls, though.* Some of the wee creatures were elementals. Granny was really into plants and herbs. *Could there be an Earth Elemental living here? There can't really be a mythical being living in Granny's house, can there?*

I gently smacked the book against my forehead a few times. My thoughts were ridiculous. *We're psychics, not… Nope, not going there.* I couldn't help picturing Granny in the garden. She'd always spent a lot of time out there, frequently talking to herself, or so I thought. *Could there be the slightest possibility an Earth Elemental lives here?*

A sound caught my attention, so soft I almost dismissed it. It came from behind the wall where the Fae door sat. I moved closer. *Mice?* No, it sounded more like shuffling feet. Then the rattle of a tiny door knob jiggled. I looked and I swear it moved. More shuffling feet, then silence. *What the heck?*

Was it still locked? *Must be.* Whatever lived inside the walls hadn't opened the door. I crouched down and reached out, then remembered the look on Mr. Barker's face. His reaction when I mentioned the Fae doors. My hand hovered inches from the tiny knob.

Despite Mr. Barker's warning, I was certain whatever was moving in my walls wouldn't harm me. Like he said, I'd lived here for a few years and nothing hurt me. Granny lived here for decades and remained unscathed. Yet, Granny barricaded one door. *Nope. Leave well enough alone, at least for now.* I stood, but couldn't take my eyes off that door. Granny must have spent most of her life in this room. *If anything harmful inhabited the house, why didn't she block this door?* I sat on the end of the table, legs swinging, staring at it. Whatever lived in there was small. How much harm could it inflict? I chewed the inside of my cheek. *Do I? Don't I?* I slide off the table, never taking my eyes off their target.

Oh, what the heck. I retrieved the ring of tiny keys and knelt in front of the door. When the lock clicked open, I froze, key still in place. Did I really want to do this? I reached for the knob, every muscle in my body tense.

"Whoever's in there, I hope you don't mind the intrusion, but I need to know what you are." No shuffling feet, no muffled voices. "Are you there?"

I turned the knob and pulled. The door opened. *Guess they gave me permission.* Nothing rushed out at me. Relieved, I leaned down, getting as close to the door as I could. It looked like a tunnel ran parallel to the wall, with a faint light coming from somewhere in the distance. No creatures. Strangely disappointed, I closed and locked the door.

Before starting upstairs, I picked the book off the floor and put it back on the table. My stomach told me to fuel up. Maybe some time in the veggie garden would relax me. I kept my eyes fixed on the door as I ascended until it was out of sight. Granny's garden basket sat by the back door and I grabbed it on my way through the kitchen.

I went out through the sunporch and walked around the grounds. Even though we weren't that far from Newmarket, it was almost as quiet as being out in the country. The long driveway set the house well back from the road. The trees formed a wall around the property, muffling the traffic, and the back and south sides of the three acres formed a mini-forest, separating us from the neighboring farms.

The fragrance of the different varieties of flowers helped calmed my nerves on the way to the vegetable section of the garden. Heading towards the cucumbers, I thought I heard someone clearing their throat.

I looked around. No one anywhere in sight. I shrugged and knelt to rifle through the vines for a ripe cucumber. Schist! *Why hadn't I grabbed the garden gloves?* I sucked my finger where one prickle stuck me.

Again, someone cleared their throat, but I couldn't see anyone moving around.

Should I be concerned? My neighbors were too far away for me to hear, but my spidey-senses weren't tingling. There was no heaviness in the air, no suffocating feeling. I felt no threat.

Standing, I stretched and looked around for whoever made the noises and removed the kinks from my back. No one in view. I continued on to the herb spiral—the centrepiece of the garden.

Starting at ground level, the slope gently increased as I walked around. It was larger than normal, at least eight feet across, with just enough room for a narrow footpath. A row of stones wound through it, outlining the spiral with the herbs planted along one side. The centre towered about four feet off the ground.

As I snipped at the herbs, the familiar scents tickled my nose. Lemon thyme. *That's what I smelled when the grandson popped into Mr. Barker's back room.* Odd fragrance for a man, but pleasant none the less. *Why hadn't I asked his name? Wonder how long he's staying?*

Movement through the branches of the weeping willow caught my eye, interrupting my daydream. The tree sat several yards away, just beyond a jungle of hostas. I headed straight for it, tripping over the rocks lining the spiral. The basket of veggies and herbs flew from my grasp and I did a face-plant in the strawberry patch. I groaned. Those stains probably wouldn't come out.

Keeping an eye on the willow branches, I retrieved my harvest and sat the basket at the edge of the garden before continuing to the tree. When I moved the branches aside, another of those Fae doors sat in the tree's trunk. The door stood ajar and a tiny hand held the edge. A whisper came from behind, too faint to tell if male or female.

"Please don't lock all the doors. We need to be able to get out. We won't harm you." Then the door closed.

"Uh, O-OK," I stammered. *What was that?* I sat down and stared at the door, waiting to see if it opened again. It didn't.

.

ELEVEN

My hands shook even though I didn't feel threatened by the voice. I don't know why. I'd witnessed odd things before. Mother speaking in a man's voice during a reading, Granny finding a pretty much dead plant and having it fully restored overnight. So, why not Fae? I'd been brought up to believe in the powers of nature, and I'd heard Mother speak of the Fae often.

That niggling in the back of my mind stirred again. As soon as I started to remember, something slammed the door shut. It was so frustrating. But the pictures of faeries I'd seen in books had wings. *Why would they need doors? They could just fly in a window, or down the chimney.* I'd have to read that book I left on the table in the workroom. Maybe I could figure out which type of Fae shared the house with me.

Several minutes passed before I forced myself to stand. My feet tangled. I stumbled and half-ran back to where I'd left the basket. Determined not to allow myself to be spooked out of my garden, I wandered through the plants, inhaling the calming scents of the herbs until my nerves steadied.

Granny had some lovely lavender plants in the garden, and I wanted to dig up a few small ones to pot and take inside. I loved the scent and it would make the house smell wonderful. *Maybe one in my bedroom to help me sleep.* As I dug up two small lavender plants, invisible hands grabbed my throat. It hit without warning. *What the devil is happening to me?* Clawing at my neck had no effect. It squeezed tighter, like whatever happened the cemetery.

I dropped to my knees and leaned forward, balancing on my hands. My breathing became shallow, my head light. The air filled with laughter and the invisible hands let go.

After crawling out of the garden, I lay on my back in the grass, gulping in air. After a few moments, the dizziness passed, allowing me to sit up without swooning. The presence wasn't coming from the willow, so I was pretty certain it had nothing to do with the tiny hand. I tracked it south. *Whatever it is, it meant to kill me, then changed its mind.*

I ran into the sunporch and dropped the basket on the floor. Without really thinking about it, I threw up a protective mental shield. After taking two deep breaths, I stood straight, picturing a white wall of energy surrounding me, safeguarding me. The laughter finally faded, taking the presence with it.

My fingers trembled as I tried to prepare my salad, my mind bombarded with questions as I put the herbs and veggies in a strainer and ran cold water over them. *What's happening to me? How am I supposed to deal with it?* I splashed the cold water on my face, then ran my wet fingers through my strawberry blond hair. A mixture of sweat and dirt trickled into my eyes. I blinked and dampened a paper towel to clean my face, relishing the coolness of the water. Feeling slightly cleansed, the tension dropped away.

The voice in the willow had sounded pleasant enough, scared even. *No, not scared, worried. Could whatever it was actually be afraid of me? And what was that horrible feeling following me? Did I somehow attract something evil in the cemetery and bring it home?* I shuttered at the possibility.

Mindlessly, I started chopping the veggies, one by one. Glancing down at the sink, red spots dotted the white porcelain. *I sliced my finger!* Now that I saw it, the pain surfaced. *Schist!* The phone rang. It slid from my wet, bloody fingers, hitting the countertop.

"Ya? Sorry. Hello?" I cradled the cell between my ear and shoulder.

"Sorry to bother you, Marcy. It's Mr. Barker. I think I've figured out what the doors are, but I need to ask you a few more questions. Would you mind if I came over after I close up?"

I leaned against the counter, watching the wad of paper towels change from white to pink, then red. *Do I need stitches?* "Not at all. I really need to speak to you, anyway. I've so many questions about Mother and Granny, and I have a feeling you can shed some light. Why don't you stay for dinner if you don't have plans?"

"I don't drive much anymore, so my grandson will be with me. You met him briefly today."

Heat rose up my neck and crept across my face. "That's fine. Can we talk freely in front of him? I mean… oh, I don't know. This is just so weird."

Mr. Barker laughed. "Cooper is helping me with my research. Members of our family have been helping your kind for generations. I'll pick up a pizza from Toppers."

Your kind? What was that supposed to mean?

"Toppers? Great. I just picked some veggies from the garden so we can have a fresh salad with it." I glanced at my finger and made a mental note to rewash everything. At least the bleeding finally stopped.

"We'll be there about six thirty."

I hung up the phone and searched the cupboards for a bandage. *What did he find out that I needed to know tonight?* It must be good news. He didn't sound concerned. And Cooper would come too. My heart fluttered. Why was I so excited about seeing *him*?

Cooper. I liked that name, and it suited him. Not an overly common name, perfect for someone far from ordinary. Cooper. Strong sounding, but not overbearing. I found my tablet and looked it up. A person who makes or repairs barrels or caskets. OK, so that's not something to get the senses reeling. The urban dictionary had a much better definition: *one sexy individual who oozes appeal.* Yep, that one works. *And those eyes. My God! I've never seen anyone with silver eyes. They looked right through me.* I nibbled a few carrots, then went into the basement to get that book with the write-ups on faeries, goblins, and such.

Goblins? Please no. Nasty creatures, what with their slime and snot. I hurried down and plucked the book off the table—*or should I be calling it an altar?* I looked at the tiny door in the corner and recalled the voice in the garden. There'd been nothing threatening about it. It actually sounded sad. *It.* I wasn't sure it if was male or female. Did faeries come in male and female versions? Picture books always showed faeries as girls. 'Course, those were just children's books written by people with no actual knowledge. They probably didn't even believe the wee folk existed. I certainly didn't until a short while ago.

Feeling guilty, I got the keys out of the drawer, found the one that fit the little door, and unlocked it. The one in the bedroom would stay blocked and locked for the time being. I'd have to go looking for the doors the two remaining keys fit, but I was okay now with the thought they might be unlocked. After hearing that tiny, worried voice, most of my apprehension had disappeared. *Maybe the other doors are outside, too. Doesn't matter right now.* I put the keys back in the drawer, grabbed the photo I'd set aside, and took it, the crystal encyclopedia, and the faerie book, into the front room. The easy chair by the bay window had been a favourite of Granny's. I curled up in it and gently turned the time-worn pages of the faerie book.

Whoever had written it had been organized enough to put the Fae in alphabetical order by element. I was certain these were Earth Elementals, so I turned to that section. I'd never heard of Ban-Tighes, who apparently look like elderly peasant women. *I wonder if they even still exist?* The hand I'd seen in the garden didn't belong to anyone old. The next one listed was a Bwbach. That sounded vaguely familiar. *Males who wear loincloths.* I didn't think I liked the idea of half-naked, tiny men living in my walls.

Elves. Maybe there were elves in the house. Might not be so bad. They could sew, but they could also be quite mischievous. *Maybe not. How about a good old-fashioned gnome?* They sounded pleasant enough and, according to the person who wrote the journal, they were also kind to animals. *Maybe I should just wait for Mr. Barker to get here. And Cooper. My God, Cooper. Come on, Marcy, stay focused.*

TWELVE

An hour later, I wedged the book between me and the chair and stared out the window. The graceful branches of the willow swayed off in the distance, only partially visible around the corner of the house. That tiny voice, the dark presence, the promise, all weighed on my mind. *What have I gotten myself into?* My life was a mess—I was a mess.

Maybe I should go back and finish my degree? I needed focus. Time to act like a responsible adult, or at least reasonably responsible. Since Granny left me a boat-load of money, I could easily afford the tuition and living expenses. There wasn't enough to last me the rest of my life, but more than enough to tide me over for a few years, allowing me time to get my shit together, and find a job I enjoyed enough to keep. *But how exactly?* I had no one to guide me, advise me. Sure, there was Mr. Barker and his hunky grandson, but they could only help so much. I squeezed my eyes tight. An avalanche of tears tumbled down my cheeks.

"Damn!" My nails dug into my palms as I balled my fists. I *would* get through this, somehow.

I settled back in the chair, reached for my emerald pendant, closed my eyes, and stroked the smooth stone. Its warmth flowed through my hand, arm, my entire body. My breathing became slow and shallow. Bit by bit, my muscles relaxed; my mind cleared. A light touch brushed my shoulder. The faint aroma of rosewater filled the air. I wiped away the tears. *Granny*. Drawing in one deep breath, I let my mind reach out. She would help me. Smiling, I drifted off to sleep.

✷ ✷ ✷

The doorbell chimed, jolting me awake. I checked my watch. Six thirty-eight. I'd slept the afternoon away. I ran my fingers through my hair and hurried to the door.

"Sorry we're late. Hope you like pepperoni." Mr. Barker smiled. He held a large box that smelled wonderful.

Cooper held his hands up, a paper bag in each. "Got some garlic sticks and grabbed a bottle of wine."

"Come in. May as well take them straight to the kitchen and I'll finish the salad. Sorry it's not ready, but I fell asleep. I didn't realize how tired I was."

"You've been under a lot of stress. I can't imagine you've been sleeping well." Mr. Barker put the pizza box on the table.

I put three plates on the kitchen table, then looked into the empty sink. *Where are the veggies and herbs?* I opened the fridge and found them on the middle shelf, still in the strainer. *When did I do that?*

I transferred the veggies to the cutting board. An awkward silence filled the kitchen, disturbed only by my chopping. Mr. Barker casually walked over to the cupboard and took out three glasses for the wine. *He seems quite comfortable here.* Granny never mentioned him visiting the house.

I had no clue how to begin such a strange conversation, so I focused on finishing a blood-free salad. Occasionally, I glanced over my shoulder and smiled at my visitors. The pizza box sat open. Cooper munched on a garlic stick, watching me, and winked. Flustered, I turned away and flicked water on my face. *Why doesn't the stupid A/C kick in?*

"Ready," I announced, placing the large bowl in the center of the table. "Fresh dressing too. Just whipped it up last night." I retrieved my concoction of oil and herbs from the fridge and sat it beside the salad, along with three small plates.

We ate without speaking. My feet did a little tap-dance on the floor. *When did Mr. Barker plan on telling me what he'd found?* When I looked up at him, he stared at me, one eyebrow raised.

"Sorry," I mumbled, and stopped tapping the floor. Instead, my legs bounced. At least that made no sound. Out of the corner of my eye, I noticed Cooper catch a piece of hot, stringy cheese hanging off the end of his slice. The temperature shot up at least ten degrees. I emptied my wine glass as I watched him wrap the gooey goodness around his tongue. *Oh God.*

Fumbling for the bottle, I almost knocked my glass over. I refilled it and with one continuous gulp, I emptied it, breathless when finished. *What is wrong with me? Come on, girl, stay focused. Breathe.* Gradually my air intake and heart rate returned to normal, almost.

"I guess you're wondering what you are and what you have living in your house?" Mr. Barker put down his slice and leaned forward. "I'm afraid I have found little about the doors. I'm still worried you may not be safe."

My mouth full of pizza, I nodded, not certain I wanted to hear more. My chest tightened, my entire body tensed.

"Normally, you'd learn all this from your family, but since your mother and grandmother are gone, and you have no other family here, I don't suppose it would hurt for me to fill in some gaps."

"Please do. I have a feeling there are things I've forgotten." I half-shrugged, not certain why the memories were buried. "As well as everything I didn't learn for not wanting to know."

His expression was grave, his stare intense, and he no longer smiled. *Did I really want to hear this? Have I bitten off too much? Would he tell me to sell the house and return to the city? Shut up, Marcy, and listen to the man.*

"The members of your family are special, but I guess you already know that. Each member has their own talent, and their mother or grandmother trains the children. Unfortunately, your training was interrupted. Do you have any other family? I recall Francine mentioning a sister."

"Yes, Granny has a sister, Priscilla, who lives near London. Any time we went there, we always stayed with her. I stopped going over several years ago, so I haven't seen her for quite some time–gosh, five, maybe six years."

"I'm certain Francine's sister will help you. Can she come over?"

"No, but I could fly over there. It's not like I have a job to keep me here. I guess I'll have to phone her again. When I called to let her know Granny died, we were both too upset to talk long. She's afraid to fly, so she didn't come over for the funeral."

"That's a shame. If she was here, she could have started the preparations for your birthday. Does she know you haven't turned twenty-one yet?"

"Beats me. I don't think so. She never mentioned it."

I glanced towards the end of the table at Cooper. He was busy with his pizza and didn't seem to be listening. This time, instead of my heart racing, it almost stopped. He seemed totally uninterested in what might happen to me.

"Don't worry about him. Like you, he's in training. As I mentioned earlier, we're what you call *helpers*. When someone like you can't locate a special book, or any significant item, you come to us and we let you know where to find what you're looking for, or we purchase it on your behalf. Your family trains the daughters, and my family trains the sons."

"Helpers. I can't recall either Mother or Granny ever mentioning helpers, or maybe it's yet another thing I've forgotten. How did they find people like you in the first place? It's not like you could hang a sign in your window advertising your special skill. And why can't they find the stuff themselves?"

I stole another glance at Cooper. For someone in training, he didn't appear to be doing much.

Mr. Barker laughed, but it caught in his throat.

"Are you all right?"

"Yes, I'm fine. Must be catching a cold. To answer your questions, finding things is our special skill. Not many of your kind can locate items as easily as we can. You can find misplaced items quick enough, but you can't always locate items you've never owned. As to finding us, we're sent to towns where people like you live. It's all very organized, you know."

I didn't know.

"If one of your kind desires our assistance, they register at a special website. It was much more difficult before the internet. When I was young, we wrote letters. Prior to that, it was challenging, as I'm sure you can imagine. The internet has expedited the process immensely. Might even replace us one day. Anyway, if there isn't one of us in the general area, you reach out to the membership. When my son was old enough and finished training, he moved to Halifax to fill a void. Cooper will be ready to find a location of his own soon."

"An organization? I guess I shouldn't be surprised. It must have been a nightmare before the postal system."

"Yes, it was extremely time consuming and took much longer to pair up people."

"So, if I had a brother, he wouldn't be trained like me?"

"It's rare for families such as yours to have male offspring. I'm not really sure how they're dealt with. I've never heard of one."

No males? How odd. I really need to look into my family's history. "Can Granny's sister complete my training? Is that allowed?"

"I don't believe there are cut and dried rules about that. I'm not really familiar with how things work in your family, but I suppose as long as someone is willing to take the responsibility, they can train you. Does your great aunt have children? It's always nice when there are a few people to help."

I nodded. "Yes, she has one daughter, Susan, and a granddaughter, Drew. Drew is a few years older than me. I guess I should call Priscilla tonight."

Cooper finally spoke. "Tomorrow."

"And what's wrong with tonight?"

"Five-hour time difference. She'll be in bed." He winked.

A flush of heat rose up my neck and into my face again. I really hoped it didn't show.

"Right. I'll call her tomorrow." I turned back to Mr. Barker. He was here to answer questions, no matter how strange. Still, it was awkward. I mulled things over before speaking. "Something happened after the burial and I don't know what to make of it."

I pushed the abandoned pizza crust around my plate. My anxiety rose as I remembered being almost suffocated, shuddering when the sound of that laugh filled my head. The need to get it off my chest won out. *Maybe Mr. Barker can help, or at least push me in the right direction.* He was a helper, after all. It came out in a rush.

"There's no one else I can tell, but I'm sure someone, or some *thing*, was nearby, watching, both at the cemetery and here. Something evil. I felt like I was being smothered by the air. It happened again earlier today, but not as strong."

I bit down on my stubby nails, hoping for an answer, trying to read the expression on his face. Puzzlement?

"I wish I could help, but that's out of my area of expertise. You need to take precautions. If you remember any protection rituals, do one right away, and ask your aunt for help. That type of power can be extremely dangerous."

Schist! Not what I want to hear. "And what about the doors? Found another one in the garden."

"The garden, you say? Definitely Earth Elementals. Unusual to have them both in the house and the garden."

"Earth Elementals is what I thought, too, after doing some research in Granny's books. They seem OK. Couldn't tell from the voice if it was male or female."

"What? You spoke to them?"

"One of them opened the garden door and asked me not to lock them in. Couldn't see what it was, though. The door was only open a crack. I saw a hand, but that's all."

Mr. Barker stroked his chin, bringing his hand down the length of his pointed grey goatee. "I'm certain you have gnomes, but I don't know which type. People like you rarely speak of such things to my kind. The occasional slip may occur, but is never elaborated on. I'm glad you feel you can trust me. You probably have a house gnome, but the door in the garden is puzzling. Wood gnomes, sometimes called garden gnomes, are a different species. Cross breeding has been known to happen, though. You might have a half-breed. Rare and special. The knowledge of both rolled into one. No way to tell. They have similar appearances and neither are at all harmful. Nothing to worry about, my dear. You're actually quite lucky."

"How did you find out you had your special power, or whatever you call it?" Cooper leaned forward, elbows on the table.

"Cooper, we're not allowed to ask such questions," Mr. Barker said.

"That's all right. I don't mind talking about it. It's been difficult not having someone to confide in."

I got up and popped an Earl Grey K-cup into the machine for Mr. Barker. I knew it was his favourite. *How much should I tell them?* Neither said a word as I waited for the tea. I knew I could trust Mr. Barker. He'd obviously visited Granny numerous times. *How else could he be familiar with the kitchen? Were they more than friends?* Never occurred to me before. They were close in age, after all.

Question is, do I really want to reveal something so personal? We'd only ever spoken of books, history, and my trips to Europe. I desperately needed to discuss everything with someone, and my only family was an ocean away. *Time to start opening up.*

Ready as the last drops fell into the mug, I placed it in front of Mr. Barker and started my tale.

THIRTEEN

"It was grade two. We were out playing at recess when a sudden feeling of dread hit. 'Course I didn't know what it was. Don't think I even knew what dread meant. I just stood, terrified, looking around the playground. When I saw Missy skipping rope on the narrow laneway that went around the school, I knew it was her I felt scared for. I ran over and grabbed her arm. Told her I wanted her to play on the teeter-totter with me. She dropped the rope and followed me. About halfway there, we heard a crash. A delivery truck had flipped over."

I turned and fumbled to remove the empty pod from the machine. The words stuck to the back of my throat.

"The end of Missy's rope stuck out from under the truck," I croaked. "If I hadn't had that vision and pulled her over to the playground…"

I stopped and wiped my eyes.

"Sorry," I mumbled, as I turned back and dropped into my chair.

Cooper reached over and put his hand on my arm.

"I'm OK. Really. I haven't thought about that for years. I just got an image of the truck in my mind, like it happened only moments ago. When I told Mother, she was so excited. Said she'd been waiting since my birthday. Turns out seven is a magickal number. It's connected to spiritual awakening and awareness. Anyway, she called Granny and that weekend they started educating me on crystals and gemstones. They fascinated me. Still do. They were beautiful and powerful.

Then Mother and Granny started playing a guessing game with me. They'd point out some random person and ask me about them. It was difficult at first, but eventually I could pick out people who needed help."

I leaned back in my chair, relieved to finally have someone to talk to. My shoulders dropped. The tension oozed out. I closed my eyes as I thought back to another day years later.

"In grade eight, my friends started to distance themselves. I was over at Candice's house after school when her father prepared for a business trip.

"I'd stopped my lessons a few months earlier in order to be *normal*, but the feeling was so strong I couldn't hold back. I told him he should change flights. He didn't. The engine stalled at take-off and the plane crashed at the end of the runway. No one was hurt, but Candice told everyone, and I think her parents told some of their friends, too. I became *the freak*, and that stayed with me all through high school." I almost told them about Patsy, but strangely, that memory still hurt.

"You've led a very solitary life, my dear. Now that you're back home, maybe you should look up some of your old classmates. Many still live in the area."

"Why? So I can become the town freak again?" I winced at how sharp my voice became.

"People change, Marcy. Don't be afraid to give them another chance."

I snorted. Cooper burst out laughing.

Oh God. Did I just do that? I resisted the urge to crawl under the table.

Cooper and Mr. Barker exchanged a look, and Mr. Barked smiled. Cooper nodded and turned to me.

"There's a small museum just outside Peterborough you should visit this week if you haven't any other plans. Gramps knows someone who works there. Told him about a special collection that came in from Ireland, recently. It's been put in storage for now, but Gramps can arrange a viewing for you. I think you'll find it quite enlightening."

I had nothing planned for the next day or so, so I said I'd go. They were helpers, after all. Maybe there was something in the collection that would "help" with my initiation on my birthday.

We'd finished off most of the pizza and salad, so Mr. Barker stood, collected the plates, then placed them in the sink. "Since we seem to be breaking protocol, might I be so bold as to ask to see the doors? The one with the symbols has my interest, as does the one in the garden."

I hesitated to show them the workroom. Mr. Barker seemed quite comfortable in *my* home. *How much time had he spent here with Granny after I moved out? Does he already know about the workroom?* My gut told me not to let them in the basement, but I decided I could show them pictures of the door.

"I can't show you the ones in the house. Those rooms are strictly for family. I'm sure you understand. However, I can show you some pictures. Won't be long." I grabbed my tablet and went downstairs. I took one shot of the entire door, then close-ups of each symbol. As far as I could recall, there was nothing special about the one in Granny's room, except for the fact it existed. No need to take pics of that one. When I returned, I found them sitting in the sunporch off the kitchen.

"Lovely garden. I suspect a wood gnome had a hand in it," Mr. Barker said.

I joined them at the table and passed the tablet to Mr. Barker.

"Very interesting. Some of these symbols look familiar, but I'm uncertain of their meaning. Would you mind emailing them to me so I can research them?"

He gave me the email for the store and I sent them off right away. I had a hunch he'd be up late looking into them. Nothing magickal about that feeling. Anyone with eyes could see his fascination.

"Would we be able to see the one in the garden if you have the time?"

"Of course. It's only just past eight, and the garden looks especially lovely in the evening. *Magickal.*"

FOURTEEN

Granny had loved her garden. She was out there all the time, but I don't know how she managed to keep it so nice. I always saw her enjoying it, never working in it, except to pick veggies and herbs. Never a weed anywhere. Maybe Mr. Barker was right about the wood gnomes. I led my guests through the garden along the path leading to the willow.

The sun had almost settled in for the night, casting eerie shadows throughout the yard and garden. Decorative solar lights hanging on small shepherd hooks activated one by one as the natural light faded. Each fixture was different, but of a similar theme. Some in the shape of grape clusters, others tulip or trumpet-lily shaped, and the colors cycled through pale shades of red, green, and blue. Many were adorned with floral designs, a few had faeries sitting on top.

I turned to Mr. Barker and pointed to the willow. "Over there."

When we reached it, I swept aside the graceful branches and stood back, allowing them to enter. It felt like I held the door to a special realm.

"Oh my," Mr. Barker gasped. "Never once did I think I'd be so honoured as to see a Fae door."

"Pretty cool, Gramps." Cooper held out his phone. "Mind if I take some pics?" He nodded towards Mr. Barker and smiled. "For Gramps."

"Sure, snap away." Cooper wasn't fooling me. He was just as intrigued. Not once did he take his eyes off the door.

Cooper took picture after picture of Mr. Barker crouched by the door, and a thought struck. Ordinary people couldn't see the Fae. Would they see the door in the picture, or just an old man and a tree? I watched while Cooper lay down and took a few shots at ground level.

"I'd like copies," I said. "I'll give you my email before you go. I'd like to frame a pic of the door to hang in the sunporch. I love the gentle arch at the top. The floral carving on it is so intricate, and those teensy hinges… they look like they're wrought iron. You know, I bet Granny put these plants around the trunk for the Fae."

I stepped back and took in the entire view, visualizing some changes.

"Do you think they'd mind some decorations?"

Mr. Barker laughed. "You'll have to ask them."

I smiled. "Maybe I will."

I crouched down and knocked on the door. "Hello? Anyone home?"

We were all laughing when a soft voice said, "How may I help you?"

One by one, we turned and looked down at the door. It was open, just a crack. It had definitely been closed when I'd knocked.

"H-h-h-hello?" I stammered.

"How may I help you?"

"Um, are you able to come out?"

Silence. The door didn't budge. I waved my hand behind me, indicating for Mr. Barker and Cooper to step away.

"Please come out. I live here now and I won't harm you. I'm Francine's granddaughter."

The door opened a little more. We waited for it to open the rest of the way. A tiny woman cautiously peeked around. She wasn't what I'd expected.

I'd been picturing your basic garden gnome. You know, like the statues that sit in the garden looking tacky, wearing that red pointed hat. She stood about six inches high, just like a child's doll, minus the impossibly thin waist, clothed in a simple floral dress.

"We won't harm you," I said.

She looked around me as the Barkers emerged from the shadows. *I'll have to put some fairy lights out here.* The fading sun all but disappeared under the canopy of the willow's drooping branches.

The little lady looked at each of us, spending a minute taking us in. Both Mr. Barker and Cooper stood gaping, but Mr. Barker's mouth slowly closed and he grinned. We seemed to meet with her approval. She nodded once, stepped clear of the door and shut it. Her dress, partially covered with a crisp white apron, stopped just above her ankles. She wore little shoes similar to Dutch clogs, made of leather, not wood. Long, flowing hair hung loose, and she appeared to be about sixty. Kinda hard to tell.

"You really don't remember me, do you?" she asked.

I shook my head. "Have you lived here long?"

"No, only eighty-seven years. Ever since I married. I come from the farm just up the way, over the hill." She smiled and her eyes twinkled. "My family doesn't approve of mixed marriages, so they haven't spoken to me since. They'll come around in a hundred or so years."

She had a slight accent that sounded familiar. Something I'd heard on previous excursions with Granny and Mother. Dutch was as good a guess as any.

"Mixed marriage?" I asked.

"Yes, I married a house gnome. It's just not done, you know."

I didn't know. "So, what's the big deal? He's still a gnome."

She giggled softly. "Francine really didn't tell you anything, did she, or have you simply chosen to forget? Did you know she hoped you'd come back to the family ways? There are lots of books in her collection to help you. Might I suggest you take the time to read them? Study them carefully when you get back from your great aunt's. You won't have time before you go."

"How…?"

"We hear all sorts. Can't keep secrets from us, but we try not to intrude." She looked past me at Cooper. "Any time you feel you need total privacy, just let us know. There are places we can go."

I heard Cooper snicker and tried to ignore it. "That won't be necessary," I said

"I'd heard such beings lived among us, but I never thought I'd meet one. Fascinating," Mr. Barker said. "Unfortunately, it's time Cooper and I took our leave." He knelt in front of the diminutive lady. "It was a rare treat to meet you, ma'am. Thank you for permitting us to see you."

"Francine told me about you, and we've seen you here several times. I've always wanted to meet you, but Francine never called for me in your presence."

"O-oh," Mr. Barker stammered. "Why, thank you." Even in the diminished light I could see he blushed.

"I'd like to ask you something," I started.

"Yes, some new plants and decorations would be lovely. A bench possibly?"

"As soon as I get back from England. Promise."

"Speaking of England, you have arrangements to make, my dear." Mr. Barker groaned as he rose. "If you need any assistance when you return, you know where to find me."

I smiled at the little gnome and wiggled my fingers as a wave before walking the Barkers to their car. Cooper gave me his phone so I could enter my email and cell number. When I returned it, he wrapped his hand over mine, sending a tingle up my arm. Time slowed as he gradually slid the phone from my hand. Our gazes locked. The tingle made its way through my entire body.

"Cooper," Mr. Barker called.

Cooper winked, then helped his grandfather into the car.

When their headlights vanished, I returned to the garden, but the little gnome was gone. Left on my own once again, it seemed as good a time as any to go through Granny's books, as the gnome suggested. I grabbed the book off the chair in the living room and headed to the bookshelf down stairs. While perusing the titles, something moved behind me—the female gnome, a male at her side.

"I'm afraid I forgot to introduce myself. My name is Nenka Lindtwiss. This is my husband Tinkus. You'll meet our son, eventually. We thought you might need some help finding the right books."

"I found one on the Fae earlier. Are there more?" I bent down and held out the book so they could see.

"Oh, that's a very good one. You'll find another one up on the top shelf."

"Thanks. Not to be rude or anything, but why are you here?"

Tinkus took a step closer and cleared his throat. "We've worked alongside your family for generations. My father came over from England with your grandmother. Nenka's family came over from Holland. My parents passed shortly after I married Nenka, and we took over here. We enhance your special skills and help around the house and garden."

I turned to Nenka. "I'm guessing you help with the herbs and stuff like that?" *Did she move my veggies to the sink?* "Could you be the reason I never saw

Granny doing anything in the garden except taking cuttings and picking the vegetables?"

She smiled and nodded. "Don't forget. Top shelf." With that, they turned and disappeared through the door.

FIFTEEN

Before reading any more on the Fae, I needed to protect the house and myself. That presence the day of Granny's funeral initially freaked me out, but somehow I'd convinced myself it was nothing. Maybe my first reaction was correct. After that incident in the garden, that horrid laughter continually rang in my head. For some reason, something wanted me out of the picture. I thought for sure I was a goner. *Not ready to die yet.* Whatever I'd encountered was strong. Granny was sure to have something in her library that would help.

Nenka asked if I'd forgotten. Could years of putting up walls to block my natural skills have actually built a wall around my memories? Anything other than grounding and personal protection seemed to be locked away. *Time for a refresher course.* I perused the stacks and found a row of promising looking books on a lower shelf, below her volumes on herbs. I'd look for the books Nenka mentioned later.

Sitting cross-legged on the floor, I flipped through them, stopping briefly at something for protection against psychic attack. A few pages later, I found the Brigid home protection incantation. They sounded like something a witch would need. *Why does Granny have books relating to witchcraft?* Garlic and sea salt were all that was required for this one. *Isn't garlic for vampires? I suppose it has more than one use.* Both were in the kitchen, so I got started. First, I needed to cut the garlic into small pieces then mix with the sea salt.

Granny designated one drawer in the kitchen for small gadgets, so I dug out the garlic press. It would be more efficient than chopping. Besides, I didn't want to sport another bandaged finger. No specific amounts were mentioned, so my gut would have to guide me. One, no two cups of the salt, one entire garlic bulb. With a little elbow grease, I mixed everything together in the stainless-steel bowl. I picked up the bowl, went out through the sunporch, and began to cast the circle. *Funny how there's such a crossover between our psychic abilities and homeopathy.*

As I called on Brigid for protection, a gust of wind whipped around the corner of the house. *Strange how the salt mixture didn't blow away.* I continued, sprinkling and chanting with each step. The sun had set, leaving me in almost total darkness. No solar lights anywhere except the garden. The moon waned, barely a sliver in the sky. Only managed to complete one side of the house when something blocked what little light reflected off the moon. I didn't think that was supposed to happen. *Did I screw something up? Too much salt? Too little garlic?*

I was half way around when my throat constricted, allowing only short, shallow breaths. *Schist, not again.* Gasping, I picked up my pace, stumbling from lack of breath. The sky filled with black clouds, but only over *my* property. Whatever it was, was strong. Lightening flashed. Hail the size of baseballs fell, but I didn't stop. My breathing grew even more laboured. Several hail stones hit my head, hard, as though thrown. I fell to my knees, almost dropping the bowl of salt and garlic.

The hail pelted my back and neck. One hit me on my side. *What? Hail doesn't fall sideways.* Raising my head, I looked in the direction it came from, half expecting to see someone using the hail like a snowball.

Nothing but darkness.

No hail fell anywhere except around me. *Schist.* Out of nowhere, one extremely large hailstone flew towards me, hitting me square in the face. My glasses knocked off and my head spun when I tried to stand. I fell, vision blurred, and not just from losing my glasses. Somehow, the circle had to be completed. I crawled over to the foundation, resting for a moment, sprinkling a small circle of salt around me.

"Granny, please help me."

The scent of rosewater filled the space around me. A warmth enveloped me, giving me strength.

"Thank you."

Bracing myself against the wall, I rose to finish the circle. That evil presence surrounded me, stealing my breath. Exhausted, I dropped to my knees and crawled the last few feet, croaking out the final lines.

"Protect this home from evil spirits;

Protect this home from evil people with bad intentions;

Let me and my family be safe;

Brigid, hear my voice and protect this home;

Blessed be."

I crawled over the threshold of the sunporch, exhausted, and dragged myself onto one of the wicker chairs, using the table for support. My arm gave out and my face smacked against the table.

There is no way I can fight this on my own. I needed help. This was way out of my league. Someone stronger, more practiced, would be able to deal with this thing. That someone wasn't me. *What else can I do meanwhile? Think. Who are the Celtic gods? Which one could protect me? Epona? No, she protects horses. Morigan? Nope, she's a war goddess. Damn. Concentrate, Marcy, you know this. Tear down that damn wall. An angel possibly?*

I snapped my fingers. *Archangel Michael!* I didn't have the right colored crystal with me, but there was no time to run upstairs. I lit one of the white candles that always sat on the table in the sunporch.

"Dear Archangel Michael, please surround me and my home with your royal purple light. Please dissipate and ward off any negative energies attacking me. Blessed be."

Hail pounded on the roof and bounced off the ground. It did a number on the garden, too. A loud roar of thunder came out of nowhere. I jumped and bashed my knee against the table.

Then, just as suddenly as it started, the hail stopped. The clouds disappeared. The air no longer suffocating. My breathing and heart rate returned to normal. The protection had to hold long enough for me to fly to England and ask Great Aunt Priscilla for help. I had a feeling whatever it was would eventually find a way through the barrier.

Bruised and muddy, but satisfied the protection was working, I headed into the house and back down to the work room. Nenka wanted me to check the top shelf. Hoping it would be something to guide me, I dragged my battered body to the hall and pressed the magick button.

I stood on the landing clenching the rail. *Can it wait?* My legs wobbled. The last thing I wanted was to land in a heap at the bottom of the stairs, possibly breaking a bone.

Maybe it can wait.

No. Nenka must have mentioned the book for a reason.

I started my descent, taking my time, pausing on each step, until my feet touched the earthen floor. *Maybe I should grab some herbs. Help heal the bruises before they take root.*

I stumbled to the table, leaning against it while checking the supplies. Everything was already dried—I needed fresh. *Not what I came down for, anyway.*

My legs grew steadier as I moved to the books. The top shelf was out of reach, but I noticed a little kitchen step-ladder folded and leaning against the wall beside it. Even with the ladder, the top shelf was just a tad out of reach. Stretching my arm to move the books hurt like the dickens, but Nenka said to check the top shelf as though she knew whatever I needed sat waiting for me.

I spotted something half hidden and removed the books hiding it. My fingers gingerly wrapped around an ancient scroll. The ladder wobbled as I hurried off, eager to see what the scroll contained. My hands trembled. I removed the dark blue ribbon and unfurled it across the table.

It felt odd. Not like normal paper. Maybe velum, but since I'd never touched velum, I wasn't sure. Across the top in large loopy script was written *The Celtic Triumvirate*. Below it, someone had carefully printed out what looked like instructions. The letters weren't as fancy as the title, but it was still a challenge to read. I skimmed over it, trying to pick out the important info.

Triumvirate. Three of something. A quick glance and I saw three separate sections.

The first one was titled The Warrior. Stuff about cleansing the mind and body, and shielding, both mentally and physically. Mother tried to teach me after the episode with Missy and the delivery truck. It also mentioned sacred vows and a warrior name. I read that part carefully. Apparently, one has to write their own vows for this, too. Sounded to me like a wedding or something. I'd have to remember to ask Aunt Priscilla about the name thing, but I doubted I'd need to worry about that for quite some time.

The second section was The Shaman. A healer assisting others. Sounded a lot like Granny and her potions. Mother too, in a way. A lot of her readings helped people. Healed them mentally. Of course, some of them just wanted to contact dead relatives to locate something valuable, or find out when they would meet that tall, dark, handsome stranger. She occasionally sold potions to them, made by Granny. Love potions mainly. Harmless stuff. Mostly just water infused with herbs and dried flowers. Lots of lavender and rose concoctions.

Have I been cheating myself, and others, by burying my skill? One time a new client of Mother's came in, crying and anxious, almost hysterical, but by the end of the reading the lady was smiling, calm. *How many people could I have helped over the years?* Despite the terror I just went through, I found myself smiling, my hand shaking a little less.

The last section was for The Druid. Advisors of some sort. I had a feeling it would take a long, long time to get to that stage. As I put the scroll down, I realized my hands had stopped shaking.

I'd spent all my adult life refusing to grow up, ignoring my natural born talents. Lately, my brain, my way of seeing things, had shifted ever so slightly. I was finally beginning to take my life seriously, and now someone or some *thing* was trying to take it away. Literally — take away my life! *Not a snowball's chance I'm going to let that happen.* Unfortunately, I had no idea how to properly protect myself. What I'd done so far was little more than child's play. Simple shields and protections that anyone could do.

I could read all I wanted, but sooner or later, I was going to have to fight back. I slumped over the table. Reading and doing were two totally different things.

Slamming both palms down, I sat up straight. *I'm an Adhamh, damn it! We don't quit. Temporary lapse maybe, but that ends now.* I yawned. *Well, maybe it ends in the morning.* Exhaustion crept through me.

I rolled the scroll back up, re-tied the ribbon, and returned it to its hiding place. *Why did I have to be so childish and stubborn back then?* Because I *was* childish and stubborn… and I hadn't really changed. I needed Mother and Granny, but it was too late. I had to do this on my own.

Or did I?

SIXTEEN

*B*efore crawling into bed, I had to book a flight to England. I dragged myself upstairs, grabbed my laptop, and went back to the sunporch. Since there wasn't any lighting out there, and the sliver of moon didn't help much, I lit more of the candles on the wicker table, along with the candle sconce on the wall behind me. This had always been a special place, more so under the blanket of candlelight. I often sat with Granny enjoying the view of the garden, chatting. The white wicker table and matching chairs were the perfect spot to set up the laptop and look for the cheapest airfare.

The screen seemed blurry. I leaned in. Still blurry. *My glasses. Not looking for them tonight.* Pulling the laptop closer, the letters grew sharper, just. I double-clicked the icon for the browser. *What am I looking for?* I shook my head to clear the cobwebs. *Tickets.* I needed plane tickets. My fingers moved slowly, and I missed the link entirely with the curser. *Come on Marcy. Concentrate.* Finally.

I picked Gatwick Airport. I hated going through London, and it wasn't too far from Auntie P.'s home in Dorking. I used to giggle every time someone mentioned Dorking. *Who am I kidding? I still do. Dorking? Seriously?* Air Canada had a flight with a few empty seats, so I booked my ticket for Wednesday. That only gave me a couple of days to look around the house some more. And I wanted to hit that museum Cooper mentioned, too.

Fighting to keep my eyes open, I shot the e-ticket off to the wireless printer, doused the candles, and headed to bed. I'd call Auntie P. tomorrow and let her know I was coming.

It suddenly dawned on me she could very well be off on a shopping expedition somewhere in Europe. She hadn't mentioned it when I told her about Granny, but we'd both been upset and not in the mood for small talk. I knew there wouldn't be a problem staying with her, or even Susan or Drew, but if she was off somewhere, they would go with her. *No point worrying about that now. Too late to call anyway.*

Back in my room, I pulled a container of crystals from the closet and dug out the largest piece of quartz in my collection. It was the perfect go-to for protection. Tucking it inside my pillowcase, I crawled into bed and fell into a deep sleep.

I slept later than planned, but felt better than I had for the past few days. My head had been spinning since the funeral, and the long sleep cleared my mind. Still couldn't wrap my head around the gnomes, though. I'd worry about them later. First, I went outside to find my glasses. Didn't take long, and luckily, they weren't damaged any more than they already were.

Mr. Barker had sent me an email to let me know he'd already arranged for me to meet someone named Marissa at that museum any day this week. *Just show up and ask for her.* I was curious about what I'd find there, how it would help clarify my life. So, I headed east to the Kawarthas, planning to arrive at the little museum shortly after it opened.

Less than an hour later, a signpost by the road pointed towards a gravel laneway, lined with enormous maple and oak trees. When I rounded the bend, the view took my breath away. A three-story Victorian mansion sat atop a small hill, nestled among pines. Instead of brick, it looked to be of board-and-batten construction, painted white and rust, with a porch wrapping around the front and one side.

A blue jay screeched at me as I stepped from the car and followed a gravel path. A small sign pointed to the front entrance.

The mansion may have been a hotel at one point. The information desk looked like a reservation counter, complete with little boxed compartments on the wall behind. I approached and told the girl I was looking for Marissa. She asked for my name, then picked up the phone and pressed a button.

Several glass cases filled with antique household items filled the front lobby, so I wandered around while I waited. I recognized some items. Hand beaters hadn't changed much over the years, and I'd seen pictures of apple peelers before. Each item had a small tented label in front, with the name of the item typed on it. As I was trying to picture how to use the clothes pleater, everything went funny, wavy, like looking through excessive heat. The A/C was running, so it was cool, but then the sounds changed. Instead of birds singing, cattle mooed. The front lobby shifted to the interior of a kitchen. A tired-looking woman stood at an ironing board using the pleater. She looked up when a couple of little girls ran into the kitchen, giggling, catching her finger in the device.

Oh God. He's in my head again. Where did he get the power to send my mind back in time? I closed my eyes, rubbing at my temples. *Get out of my head! Get out!* I didn't get that same heavy feeling as before. Did I somehow send myself back?

Someone touched my arm. I jumped. When I opened my eyes, time had returned to the present.

"Marcy?"

A young woman about my age, but not as tall, stood beside me. A couple of barrettes held back her frizzy brown hair from a deeply tanned face. She didn't look familiar, but I had a feeling I should know her.

She smiled. "You were inquiring about the new shipment? I'm Marissa Snider."

I blinked a few times, trying to focus. "Yes. I was wondering if I might see it."

"You look a little pale. Are you feeling OK?"

"Yes, I'm fine. Beginning of a headache. It'll pass. Do you have time to show me the items in the shipment?"

"I received an email last night telling me to expect you sometime this week and to help you with anything you need." Her smile widened. "You must have friends in high places."

"A friend at the bookstore knows someone here and made the arrangements for me."

Her eyes moved from my face to the large, uncut emerald in my pendant. "Do you have an interest in crystals?"

Crystals? She had my attention now. Could that be what was in the shipment? "Yes, I've been studying them for years. Kind of a specialty."

She hesitated for a moment. "I've been dying to talk to someone about the package we received last month. No one at the museum has figured them out. Please, follow me."

"Figure what out?"

"It's not an extensive collection, but it is a little strange. There are some old documents with them, too. Covered in symbols that no one here has ever seen."

We took the stairs down to the basement. The well-lit room revealed row upon row of shelves containing collections not on display. *How many of them never made it up to the museum?*

Marissa led me to a table. "Wait here." She went into the maze of shelving and came back with a standard archival box. She set it on the table, put on a pair of white gloves, then handed me a pair.

"You'll have to wear these. Need to keep our oils off the parchment."

She reached in and removed a scroll, much like the one in Granny's basement. She unfurled it gingerly.

"Have you ever seen symbols like these before? They're similar to some Egyptian symbols, which is why they passed it on to me."

I recognized several of them immediately. They were like the ones around the Fae door in the basement. *How much should I tell her?*

"Yes, I've seen these before, but I honestly don't know what most of them mean. I believe they're Faerie symbols."

"You're pulling my leg. Faeries? Like Tinkerbell?" She laughed.

Oh, God. She's not going to take this seriously.

"No, not like Tinkerbell." I let out a deep breath. "The legends of the Fae Folk go back for centuries. You know, leprechauns, gnomes, sprites. Certain people believed strongly in them, still do, in fact, especially in Europe. If you want to be serious about this, I might be able to help you."

"I'm sorry. I didn't mean to offend. I shouldn't have been so quick to dismiss it. After studying so many Egyptian beliefs, I should be more open. What do you know about *these* symbols?"

I pointed to the circle with the three points. "That's called a triquetra. It's for protection. And see this seven-pointed star? That's a Faerie star."

"Yes, we've identified those. What about the rest?"

"Not certain about the others. I haven't really looked much into the symbols yet. I'm more into crystals. You said there were some in this collection. Where did they come from?"

"A former archaeology student that worked here a few summers ago came across them while excavating in Ireland. We helped sponsor the dig, even though we couldn't contribute a great deal. This tiny collection is all they permitted us to have. I'm not allowed to give out any details just yet."

She put the parchment back, took out a small box, and placed it on the table. "They're unique." One by one, she set out the crystals. Each one was highly polished, and intricately carved. I picked up one and held it towards a light. As I moved it around, I could make out carvings.

"Here. It's one of the symbols from the parchment. I'll bet each one has a symbol on it."

Marissa picked up one and looked closely. "You're right. I recognize this one. It's the triquetra."

I leaned over. "You're right. Each crystal has its own special meaning or property. The symbols were probably chosen to enhance the property of the crystals. They would work together to generate more energy. What's the museum planning on doing with them? Will they be on display?"

She shook her head. "Not the parchment. It's too fragile. It'll stay down here where it's safe, but the crystals might go out eventually. They'd make a great Hallowe'en exhibit. We have some items on witchcraft that we were thinking of displaying this year. Get the kids in to the museum."

I groaned. "Hallowe'en display? Witches don't really exist, you know. They were mostly women who knew how to use the properties of plants to heal. People were afraid of them and started connecting the women to bad things happening in their villages." *Did people think Granny was a witch?* "I guess people go in for that sort of thing. Shame to waste the crystals on that, though.”

“Is there anything else you can tell me about them? Instead of Hallowe’en, maybe we could do a display on faeries? I’m sure the curator would go for that. That would bring the children in, too. Blend it with folk lore.”

“I don’t know too much about faeries, but there are several books at the house. My grandmother left everything to me and it’ll take years to read all her books, but I’ve gone through a few on the Fae. There’s quite an assortment of them, not all pleasant.” I laughed, remembering one description. “The boys would probably enjoy the Grogoch. He has bad personal hygiene and is covered in dirt and twigs. If you want, I can come out at a later date and bring the books with me. Or if you’re in Newmarket, you can come to the house.”

Melissa’s smile brightened. “Oh, yes. I’d love that. This is a museum, after all. Even though we’re small, we have the same standards as the big ones. Stick to the facts, or at least the most commonly agreed suppositions. I’ve often wondered how much information the historians and archaeologists have gotten totally wrong. Wouldn’t it be fabulous to travel back in time and speak to—” Missy slapped a hand over her mouth momentarily. “Sorry. I have a habit of rambling.”

I waved a hand, dismissing the comment. “No need to apologize.” My thoughts drifted back to my mother. “It would be nice to have the ability to travel back, even for just a moment. If I find out anything useful, I’ll let you know. Would I be able to look at the parchment again another time? I’m planning on doing some research on symbols soon.”

“Certainly. Any time.” She reached into her pocket and handed me her business card. “Call me when you want to come back. I’d really like to find out more. This is quite different from the type of artefacts we usually display, and we haven't had time to request assistance from a symbologist yet. I'd really appreciate knowing if you find out anything."

"I have a feeling I should know you, but I don't remember ever knowing a Marissa."

"I recognized your name right away. When I was younger, I went by Missy."

"There was a Missy in my class when I was around seven, but she moved away shortly after —."

"The incident with the truck?" she finished.

"Seriously?" Since only my family knew about it, I had no doubt it was her. The picture of the truck and rope flashed through my mind. I fought the urge to cry. That was almost fourteen years ago. *Why does it affect me so much?* Funny about the timing, though. "I never knew why your family moved so suddenly. Thought it was my fault or something."

"Gracious no. It had nothing to do with you. I didn't even know what happened that day for years. We moved because my dad was offered a promotion overseas. I did my postgraduate in archaeology at Cairo University and I've only been back a few months. Too much competition for jobs over there, so when I saw the posting for this position, so close to my home town, I applied right away."

"Thanks for letting me see them. I wish I had more time to examine them, but I'm heading off to England soon and there's so much to do. I would like to come back after I've done some research. It was so nice to see you again. I can't believe it's really you. It wasn't too long after that incident that I became fascinated with crystals. Still am, obviously."

I didn't have any business cards, so she handed me her phone so I could enter my number. We agreed to get together for coffee after I returned from

England, chatting as she escorted me back upstairs. Then she showed me around the rest of the museum. When we returned to the lobby, an antique tall clock chimed.

"Is it one already? Afraid I have to leave. So many things to do before heading to England. I'll be in touch when I return."

Before leaving, I wanted to take a moment to text Cooper. I found a bench under a giant Crimson King maple and made myself comfy. *Why had he sent me here? I learned nothing to help me.* They'd laughed right before mentioning this place. *How could Mr. Barker be so cruel? He was supposed to be my friend.* Upset turned to anger, and I typed one of my typical sarcastic remarks.

Thanks for the wild-goose chase. Not much of a helper.

Helpers indeed. How could I have let Cooper get to me so much? The attraction was all in my mind. He was here to help his grandfather, nothing more.

Just as I was about to hit send, it dawned on me. I wasn't meant to find information, rather, to find Marissa, Missy. Most of my time had been spent alone during high school and my friends from my brief stay at university were more like acquaintances. No attempt had been made to keep in touch with them, either by me or them. I hadn't stayed at any job long enough to make friends. Melissa didn't know about my skill or that I'd been the town freak. *Good place to start making friends.* Since she just moved back, Missy probably needed a friend, too. I smiled, then backspaced and started over.

Txs Coop. Just what I needed. ☺

I hit send, then wandered around the grounds. Behind the museum, a creek ran through a grove of evergreens. The air smelled sweet, cool. The soft babbling as the water passed over the rocks relaxed me. I wandered off the trail, touching each tree I passed. Each had its own energy, even though they shared their life-force through their roots. The trees networked much like the internet super highway. If everyone took the time to connect with it, the planet would be in much better shape.

I let one hand linger on an old-looking spruce. "I'm sorry people no longer care," I whispered. A slight pulsing rippled under my hand in acknowledgement.

A wave of nausea hit me as soon as I stepped away from the tree, followed by a splitting headache. I walked in a circle, looking for the source. "Get out of my head." I screamed the words, not caring if anyone heard. My foot connected with a tree root, sending me tumbling.

"Ow." I rubbed the back of my head and sat leaning against the withered trunk. The headache and nausea began to fade. *The tree is protecting me from him.* I stood, keeping one hand on the trunk, concentrating on my psychic wall. With the energy from the tree entwined around my energy, my wall seemed thicker, brighter.

I hurried back to my car, thanking each tree along the way, certain they all sent energy through their mingled roots. Despite the intrusion from whatever followed me, I wanted to come out here again.

Marissa—someone I actually had something in common with. Definitely friend material. It was time to start tearing down the walls I'd placed around myself. It would be nice to have a friend I could talk to about crystals. Hell, it would be nice to have a friend, period. Reluctantly, I left the peace and quiet and started home.

I needed to phone Aunt Priscilla and explain everything. Hopefully, she'd be able to help me with the ceremony and advise what to write in my vows. I drove through Port Perry and pulled into the coffee shop in Manchester. My thoughts distracted me and I didn't want to end up in a ditch. It wasn't busy and the table in the corner looked inviting.

What would I do if Auntie P. wasn't home? OK, the ceremony sounded simple enough. If necessary, I could probably pull it off. Granny's initiation had been simple, and it was unique to her. That was mentioned in the book. A place special to the person. I'd have to figure out where to hold mine. No reason I couldn't do it in the garden. Maybe under the branches of the weeping willow. But I needed help with the dark presence. So far, I'd managed to stop it from harming me. But how long would it hold?

SEVENTEEN

As soon as I got home from the museum, I phoned Auntie P. It went to voice mail, so I left an urgent message. Needing to do something, I headed into town and purchased a couple of cans of Crocus Petal Purple paint for my bedroom. My phone remained silent, so I called again when I returned from the store.

Still no answer. *Schist. Don't read too much into it. Probably shopping in the city.* I left another message and took the paint upstairs. By the time I moved the furniture, removed the items from the wall, and got the first coat on, it was after six, or eleven in the UK. I didn't really want to disturb her so late, but I needed her help. Someone kept trying to break through my protection. A slight pressure at the base of my neck, then random pictures. The help from the trees faded.

Normally, I only needed to block people's thoughts, and that didn't require much effort. Stopping someone from accessing my mind required a skill not yet acquired. The presence was trying harder, but I got the impression it wasn't using much effort. More like teasing.

A deep, guttural laugh echoed in my head.

What does it want? No, not it, he. I was certain the presence was male. That laugh didn't sound at all feminine. Random pictures continued to float through my mind, but I didn't recognize any of them. I could tell it was the same presence I'd felt at the cemetery and a few times since, and was certain he could have broken through my block with no effort at all. Was he testing me? *How am I going to explain all this to Aunt Priscilla?* I couldn't wait until morning to speak with her. She answered the phone immediately.

"Hello, Marcy, dear. I'm sorry I missed your calls, but I let the battery die."

"Hi Aunt Priscilla. I'm sorry to call so late, but I'm afraid I need your help."

"I know dear. I don't know why I didn't think of it when you called about Francine. Your twenty-first birthday is soon, isn't it?"

"Yes. But that's not exactly why I'm calling."

I gave her a quick run-down on the events, barely pausing to take a breath. "And I don't know what to do. I've put up a shield around the house, but I don't know how long it will hold."

There was silence on the other end of the line.

"Aunt Priscilla?"

"Yes, dear. Just thinking. What shield did you use?"

"One I found in a book of Granny's." I filled her in on the details.

"That should hold for quite some time. It's meant to protect for as long as you live in the house. You always had a stronger sense of intuition than the rest of the family. Do you feel like you're in danger?"

"No, not at the moment," I lied. "I get the impression he's testing or maybe teasing me, but I can tell he's very strong. I feel more uncomfortable than anything else. I know I should have asked first, but I'm coming over on Wednesday. Can you put me up? I have so many questions."

"Always have a room for you, you know that. I was wondering, would you mind bringing over Francine's amulet? I'd really like to have it as a keepsake."

Granny had the most beautiful amulet. Silver, with a piece of raw lavender in the center under a thin cap of clear crystal, surrounded by an etching of ivy. The hospital had given it to me with the rest of her personal things. I could totally understand why Auntie P. wanted it. I'd felt the same way about Mother's. I was so relieved when I found it. I wouldn't be able to wear it, as it was tuned to her essence, but I could keep it safe.

"Sure, no prob. So, are you able to help with my initiation? I mean, is that allowed?"

"Certainly, Marcy. We're family. It's a shame your mother and Francine can't be there, but it's not a requirement. You can even do it on your own."

"No, I definitely don't want to do it alone."

"We'll discuss it when you arrive. Don't fret. You'll be fine."

Auntie P. seemed reasonably satisfied I wasn't in immediate danger, so we chatted for a few more minutes before hanging up. I hoped my cousin Drew could fly back with me. She'd gone through her ceremony a few years earlier. I didn't know her all that well any more, but we'd got along OK when I visited on trips with Mother and Granny.

Remembering what Mr. Barker had said about males not being common in families like mine. my thoughts turned to the boy in the photo I'd found earlier. I went into the front room to retrieve it before making dinner and sat it on the kitchen table while warming up the leftover pizza. I couldn't stop staring at it. The boy had a strong resemblance to Granny and her sister.

Someone had written on the back of the photo: *Francine, Priscilla, and Montgomery.* Who named their kid Montgomery? The name was bigger than the kid. Probably called him Monty. Who the heck was he? He looked like family, but how could that be? *I'll have to ask Auntie P.* Maybe I'd also ask about my father. Any time I'd asked Mother or Granny, they'd changed the subject. Now that I was almost twenty-one, hopefully someone would tell me something useful.

I hadn't thought much about it before, but Aunt Priscilla's husband was never around, and I couldn't recall ever seeing a photo of him, or my grandfather, for that matter. What was it with the women in my family? Couldn't anyone hold on to a man? I needed to find out about our history. I knew the library had subscriptions to a lot of databases, and I remembered seeing Ancestry listed on their website. Maybe I could find out something there.

I finished up the pizza, and spent the rest of the evening doing what I loved best, reading. All night. Until I could barely keep my eyes open. Even after finally falling asleep, I tossed and turned, waking numerous times. Someone definitely wanted my attention.

A voice from somewhere outside called my name. It wanted me to leave the ring of protection, but I had no intention of making it easy for him to do whatever he was planning. The house protection must have been working, as I no longer felt anyone probing my mind, and no headaches started.

In the morning, I had three cups of my favourite Snickerdoodle coffee, grabbed my tablet, and headed to the local library.

Twenty minutes later, I found a vacant computer and logged on to search for my family name—Adhamh. It was Celtic for earth. I got a few hits. By a few, I mean three. The first one I looked at was a marriage record for Annabelle Adhamh. The dates were reasonable for Granny's mother. It gave me the name of her husband—Paul Cannon. The next one was a census record. Same names. The last was a death record for Paul Cannon. Seven years after the marriage. *There's that number again. I'll have to look into that while I'm here. The library should have numerology books I could check out.* After compiling quite the list of questions, I turned my tablet on and started making notes so I wouldn't forget to ask Aunt Priscilla anything. Tomorrow I flew to England.

⁂

After one brief delay, the plane finally got clearance to take off. It'd been years since I last flew anywhere and forgot about the change in air pressure. I pressed my palms against my ears in a futile attempt to pop them. The pressure behind my eyes was new. That definitely never happened before.

Schist. I rubbed my temples, willing it to go away. The plane continued to climb, finally levelling out. The pressure behind my eyes faded. Could it simply have been an effect of ascent, or was I now out of reach of *him*? I plugged the earbuds into the console, tuned to a soft-rock station, and drifted off into the most restful sleep I'd had in weeks.

Once I cleared customs, I turned on my cell to connect to the airport Wi-Fi then headed to baggage claim. This would be my first time travelling alone. I missed Mother and Granny even more. At least I had family here. While waiting for my suitcase, I sent a quick text to Cooper.

Arrived safe & sound.

Enjoy yourself. ☺

Bag after bag wound around the carousel. I two-stepped around a couple of guys as they dragged their golf bags off, almost clubbing me with them. I listened to the voices, trying to identify different accents and languages. So many people travelled from all over the planet.

One by one, the bags thinned out. *Where's mine?* Even though it was a basic black suitcase, it was covered in stickers, and I'd wrapped several brightly colored ribbons around the handle. Normally, most things just washed over me as I had a pretty long fuse on my temper. Today, it got shorter and shorter. The bags stopped dropping onto the conveyer belt and mine was nowhere in sight. The flight was direct, and I'd arrived at the airport in plenty of time to have my suitcase loaded. *Where is it?* Finally, one final drop and there it was. Figures. After heaving it off the conveyer belt, I started my trek to passenger pickup. It seemed as though half the planet decided to use Gatwick today.

Families lined the area, waving, holding signs, but they were all strangers. *Did they forget I'm coming today?*

Someone called my name.

I looked around, trying to find a familiar face. It's a good thing everyone in my family was tall. At the back of the throng of people, a pair of arms waved furiously. *Drew.* They didn't forget. I blinked away tears. I hadn't realized just how much I missed my family.

"Sorry," I said as I ran over someone's foot with my bag. *Not really.* I shoved my way through, finally breaking free from the crowd.

Auntie P. stood tall and refined in the passenger pickup area, but Drew squealed and ran over to me. I couldn't recall ever being hugged so tight. I hugged back, reluctant to let go.

Drew released me. "It's been too long, Marcy. I've missed you." Unlike her grandmother's harsh cockney-like accent, Drew's voice was soft, almost melodic.

Not one to let an opportunity go by, I said, "Planes go both ways, ya know."

The look on her face was priceless, and she stammered for a reply.

"Kidding. I've missed you, too. I think you were getting ready to go to university last time I was here." I turned to Aunt Priscilla. "Auntie P. You haven't changed a bit." Tiny white lie.

Her strawberry blond hair contained a little less strawberry and a bit more extremely pale blond. She still stood like royalty and projected a "don't mess with me" look. I gave her a quick peck on the cheek.

"Don't doddle now. Put your bags in the boot and get in the car." She tried to sound stern, but the familiar twinkle in her eyes gave her away.

"Where's Susan?" I asked.

"Mum stayed home." Drew took my suitcase. "She's continuing the search. We can't figure out what's been stalking you."

Didn't they know either? *Not a good sign.* I tried not to let the disappointment show. If they couldn't figure it out, the consequences weren't something I wanted to think about.

The drive to Dorking, *snicker*, was quick. I knew Drew had completed her business degree, but I was surprised to find out she'd quit her job and now ran her own business. Well, not surprised so much as jealous. No, envious. Drew had her life together. My own fault for letting my life slide. I should've kept in touch.

"You have a jewellery shop, eh? You're so lucky to know what you want. I'd love to work with those beautiful gemstones, but I'm afraid I'm not exactly crafty. I can't imagine how you can come up with so many original designs."

"You'll find your talent soon enough. Don't overthink it." She bumped my shoulder playfully with hers.

I hope she's right. It was time I put down some roots.

The countryside was quiet, relaxing. I'd been the only one to dare move into the city, but I didn't really feel comfortable there. The further from the airport we went, the greener the landscape became. Houses were more like cottages, with lovely little gardens and hedgerows. I'd forgotten how much I enjoyed visiting.

"Emerald is your stone?" Drew asked. "The one you're wearing is beautiful. I have some lovely stones I could work into your amulet. Have you decided on a design yet? I insist on making it for you."

"No, I haven't decided on anything. A willow tree maybe?" *Where did that come from?*

"An earth symbol. Good. I have several small emeralds I could place at the tip of each branch."

Why did I pick the willow? I felt at peace standing under the one in Granny's garden. My garden. Yes. A willow tree amulet would be perfect. My ceremony under the willow, wearing a willow. Drew was really getting excited, already figuring out a design. Her fingers flew as she sketched it out in the air. Almost as fast as Auntie P.'s driving. Good thing there weren't many cars on the road. I jumped when Drew touched my arm.

"And I have a teardrop-shaped stone that would fit in the trunk. I can't wait to start. My gift to you."

When we finally arrived at Auntie P.'s, it was much as I remembered. Her place sat at the end of a row of houses, surrounded by a short brick wall. A deep green front door greeted visitors, and a stone walkway led around back. I pictured a younger me sitting on the bench in the bay window, listening to the birds.

As soon as she parked the car, I took my bag upstairs. Drew dug her sketchbook out of the oversized tote she called a purse, and went into the garden to draw my amulet. Auntie P. had emptied a couple of drawers for me and made space in the closet. I'd brought a few crystals along and placed them on the dresser beside a picture of Mother and Granny. Auntie P. thought of everything. I removed my multi-gemstone bracelet and hung it on the corner of the frame. The lone dress I'd packed went into the closet. It looked as lonely as I felt.

As Auntie P. requested, I brought along Granny's amulet, which I'd placed inside a small velvet pouch. That went into my jeans pocket. Ever since landing, my mind felt a little vacant. *It didn't follow me.* I picked up the picture and twirled around the room. "It's gone, Mother, Granny." I whispered. "It's finally gone."

When I settled, I started downstairs to join Drew and Auntie P. in the garden. As I passed Priscilla's bedroom, I glanced in. On top of her dresser beside a statue of Archangel Michael was a picture that looked similar to the one Granny had. *Interesting.* Auntie P. and Drew were still talking in the garden, so I went over to the dresser to get a better look.

It was from a different angle, but it had definitely been taken about the same time. Granny, Priscilla and the boy, Montgomery, sitting on the steps of a porch. Auntie P. had the photo on her dresser, yet Granny hid it in a drawer. *Who was Montgomery and why had Granny kept the photo, but never displayed it?* I left the velvet bag containing Granny's amulet beside the statue, then went back to my room, grabbed my tablet, and joined them in the garden. I turned on the tablet and found the pic I'd taken of Granny's photo.

"Who's Montgomery?" I asked as I slid the tablet in front of Priscilla. "And please don't tell me I have to wait until I'm twenty-one to find out."

EIGHTEEN

Drew snickered. "May as well tell her now. It really doesn't have anything to do with her birthday, and she'll be back in Canada by then, anyway. What harm will it do? She should know."

Aunt Priscilla wasn't quite as amused as Drew. She reached over, picking up the tablet.

"Montgomery," she whispered, gently touching the screen. Her eyes glistened. Was she actually going to cry?

"Montgomery was my baby brother. We don't speak of him."

"Was? Is he dead?"

"I honestly don't know, dear." Auntie P. smiled, but it was a sad smile. The twinkle in her eyes faded. "He was such a sweet little boy, but he changed when he turned seven. He'd say the most dreadful things and would hurt people and animals for no reason. Actually seemed to enjoy it."

She paused and shook her head. "One day, he was just gone. Francine and I asked where he went, but no one would tell us. Since all his things were still in his room, we assumed he had died. No one was looking for him and they would have if he was missing. As a matter of fact, you share your birthday with him."

She wouldn't tell me anything more. I had a great uncle. Dead or alive, I had an uncle. But what had happened to him? I wanted to ask about my father and grandfather, but I could sense Auntie P.'s melancholy. *Maybe I can get some info from Drew later.* I had a week and a half. Didn't want to piss 'em off my first day with a million questions.

After hearing that little Monty had disappeared, I wanted to find out what had happened to him, along with the rest of the men in our family. I did some quick figuring in my head. Great-grandmother's husband would have died shortly after Montgomery was born. I'd never even seen my father. Was he dead, too? Or did he just desert us? More questions without answers.

Aunt Priscilla got up. "Susan's preparing lunch for us. We can continue the conversation over there. Drew, text your mother to let her know we have Marcy and will be over shortly. I'll just grab that book I found. Won't be but a tick."

As soon as she went inside, I turned to Drew. "What is it with the men in this family? They either die or disappear."

Drew shrugged. "It's just the way our kind are. Once we've had our daughters, well, we just don't need them."

"Sounds like the queen bee. The males die after sex. Or a Black Widow Spider. Wait. No, not a Black Widow. Don't they eat their mate? Eww. Not exactly a pleasant thought."

"Let me ask you this. Have you ever had feelings for a guy other than as a friend?"

"No, I guess not." Then I thought about Cooper. "Well…."

Drew sat up straight. I thought her jaw was going to hit the table. "No! It can't be. It just doesn't happen in our family. Are you certain?"

"No, I'm not at all certain. Oh, sure, I've had boyfriends, but they weren't anything special. Good for some fun weekends away and parties. You know how it is. But I never had the same feelings the other girls at school did. At one point I even thought I might be gay, but I wasn't attracted to women either. Just assumed I was one of those women destined never to marry and end up with twenty or thirty cats." I laughed, but Drew didn't join in.

"Cooper is different. He makes me feel… I can't describe it. It's like nothing I've ever experienced before. He pops into my mind all the time. There's something mysterious about him. He gives off a very strong aura. That's probably all it is."

"Gran needs to know about this. It might affect your ceremony. I don't know what it means."

"It can wait. I'm hungry and Auntie P. is calling us. Let's get going to your mother's."

The three of us walked over to Susan's and spent hours catching up. Once we had swapped all the gossip, I brought up the real reason for my visit, and things got serious. Auntie P. opened the mysterious book she'd brought over and Susan produced a few of her own. Auntie P.'s book got my attention. She'd wrapped it in a piece of white velvet and tied it with a black ribbon. Susan lit a blue candle, then Auntie P. opened the book. It was a stark contract to the newer books Susan had.

"We know of a few ancient shields that should help. Ones our ancestors used to ward off demons." Susan held her hand up. "Don't ask. I'm sure they're powerful enough to help with whatever's going on at your place. Some are personal shields, others for your home and property. It would help if we knew what we're dealing with."

"As soon as I figure it out, I'll let you know. Right now, I'm more than a little interested in those demons you just mentioned. If I have a demon after me, I have a right to know."

Demons? Holy Heliodor. My stomach churned, ripples of nausea turned to waves. I bolted to the can. Susan stood in the hall, waiting for me to come out.

"I'm sorry, Marcy. I didn't mean to scare you or be so dismissive. I forgot you've not been training all these years, and that's not a dig at you. We all respect your decision."

She wrapped her arms around me. "We're glad you're back, though." Looping her arm through mine, she led me back to the table. Auntie P. and Drew looked worried.

"I'm fine. I tend to get sick when overly worried. Please explain everything, so I know what I'm up against."

Susan settled in her chair. "Back in the day, and I'm referring to hundreds of years ago, it was routine for demons to be called forth. Contrary to popular belief, not all demons are wicked. Some aided people in gaining wealth or power. Since several of the things they granted fall under the seven deadly sins, they became demons to Christians. Don't get me wrong. Some nasty creatures do exist and get called up from time to time, frequently by accident."

I interrupted the lesson. "Whatever's after me definitely falls under the nasty category, but I don't believe anyone called him. Don't ask me why, but I think he's acting on his own. Just a gut feeling."

Drew patted my hand. "We'll figure this out."

We spent the rest of the day going over the correct gemstones and chants essential for the shields, and making sure I could gather the necessary items.

I was wearing down, so I said my good-nights and took the house key from Auntie P. The walk back gave me time to reflect on what I'd learned. *Why would a demon latch on to me?* At least I hadn't felt him since leaving Canada. Unfortunately, I couldn't stay away forever.

As I wondered along the empty moon-lit streets, my gaze turned to St. Martin's church. When we drove in from the airport, I'd asked about it. Drew told me it had one of the tallest spires in England. Curious, I detoured through the yard and walked around the Victorian building. Moonlight shone through the stain glass windows. It was beautiful. A slight breeze raised bumps on my arms, so I hurried around the church and back to the street.

By the time I got back to the house, exhaustion consumed me, and I fell asleep as soon as my head hit the pillow.

❋ ❋ ❋

Next morning, Drew came over early and joined us for breakfast. Auntie P.'s kitchen was narrow, so we moved into what they referred to as a reception room and set the table. Unlike Granny, Priscilla preferred the modern look and had a cross-legged walnut table, surrounded by six dark grey velvet chairs. Unlit logs sat in the brick fireplace, partially obscured by a steel screen shaped like twigs, with golden butterflies sitting on several of the branches. Auntie P. finally finished preparing breakfast and joined us, carrying a tray overloaded with eggs, toast, and a teapot. I wanted to know about the guy thing, but decided to wait until we'd finished eating before asking.

After devouring a second helping of eggs, I sat back in the chair. "Even though it's been years since I've been here, it feels like home."

Auntie P. smiled. "I'm glad. You're family. This will always be a second home for you. Never forget that."

We sat in comfortable silence for several moments. *Now or never.*

"Aunt Priscilla, I have a question and I'm not exactly sure how to word it, so I'll just say it. Where are all the men in this family? My father, grandfather, your husband, your son-in-law. I've never once seen so much as a photo of them. Why don't the men stick around?

Auntie P. froze, tea cup almost to her lips. She just looked at me. I glanced over at Drew, who sat there smiling. She gave me one of those "you had to ask, didn't you" type of looks.

I turned back to Priscilla. "I know Granny's father died seven years after he married my great-grandmother. But no one would ever tell me what happened to my grandfather or my father. I don't even know if my father is dead, or just up and left us. And, now that I think about it, why do we all have the same last name? Is there some sort of tradition that the women keep their maiden names after marriage? What's the deal with that?"

Aunt Priscilla put the cup down. "I know you have many questions, Marcy, but some things will just have to wait until after your birthday. What I can tell you is that it's a tradition that we retain our maiden names. It wasn't common in my day, but it's not such a big issue now. Actually, you probably don't even have to bother with all the hassles of getting married these days. What I can tell you is that both your father and grandfather have passed over, as has my husband and Drew's father. You'll just have to be patient for the details."

"There's something you need to know, Gran," Drew said. "Marcy fancies some bloke. I didn't think that could happen to us."

"Fancies? Romantic feelings? When?"

I'm pretty sure I turned red from top to bottom as heat emanated from every pore in my body. I wasn't used to discussing personal things with anyone. I thought I'd been close to Mother and Granny, but we'd only talked about day-to-day things.

"I don't know, Auntie. Um, there's this guy. The grandson of the man who owns the bookstore I go to all the time. Thoughts of him pop into my head at the strangest times. And, um, did I mention they're helpers?"

Auntie P. cocked her head. "A helper? Interesting."

"Yes… Problem I'm guessing?"

"I don't know. I don't think so, but I'll have to check." Aunt Priscilla was talking more to herself than to me or Drew. "I recall reading something once about one of our kind mating with someone similar to a cuideachaidh, but it was a long time ago. I'll have to find the right book and talk to some of the elders."

Talk to the elders? About me and Cooper? Or was it more? I thought back to the events of the past few weeks. The symbols in Granny's recipe book. Similar ones around the fae doors. Granny's holistic remedies were spells. The wall I put up to keep out other's thoughts didn't involve my psychic abilities. Was it a spell? No. Not possible.

I looked around the table at Drew and Auntie P. My heart rate rose. They wouldn't have kept me in the dark all these years, would they? Impossible. Pressure built in my shoulders and neck. I bit my lip to quell the rising anger.

"Um, Aunt Priscilla?" I hid my shaking hands under the table. "I found Granny's journal and read a little.

My voice quivered.

"Please tell me I'm crazy for thinking this, but… are we witches? I know we're Pagan and we have psychic abilities, but are we actual honest-to-God witches?"

Priscilla's eyes twinkled brighter than usual as she smiled. Did Auntie P. think this was funny?

"Yes, dear. We're witches. A form of Celtic witch, to be precise. Actually, we traditionally followed a less well-known coven called Dianic Wicca. Our ancestors worshiped the goddess Diana, so it was female-centred. Even though many aspects have changed over the decades, we lost the ability to have romantic feelings several generations ago."

My jaw dropped. "You're joking, right?" Auntie P. rarely joked. The chair fell back when I stood.

"No way! No freaking way." I paced back and forth across the living room. "It's not bad enough my ability to foretell the future branded me a freak. Could you imagine if they knew I was, no, am, a witch? They'd have dubbed me one of the *Charmed* sisters." I sat on the bench in the bay window, knees up, and tightly clenched them in a bear hug.

"We aren't the same as the witches on TV or in the movies. Yes, everyone in our family is psychic, but that doesn't make us witches. We have other powers, although we can't turn people into toads." Auntie P. tried to explain, but I wouldn't let her finish.

"No. No. No. Witches aren't real. Why are your lying to me?"

Drew came over. "Marcy—"

I pushed her away. "Don't touch me. Don't even talk to me. Either of you."

I bolted for the door.

For the next half hour, I stomped around the neighborhood, questions zipping through my mind. Eventually, my pace slowed, my thoughts came together.

Thinking back, some of the things I'd seen Mother and Granny do should have clued me in. Some of what appeared at the time to be blessings were actually more like spells. And the thought had crossed my mind on more than one occasion.

I stopped abruptly when I recalled the words spoken before my rude departure. *Time to return and grovel.* First, I needed to figure out where I was. Fortunately, I'd found time to pick up a SIM card for the UK, so I called up Google Maps UK and plotted a path back to Auntie P.'s.

Both she and Drew sat at the table, enjoying a second, or possibly third, cup of tea.

"I'm so sorry for everything I said to you both. It's no excuse, but it has been a rough few weeks. It's not your fault I know so little about my heritage, and I truly regret taking it out on you."

Auntie P. took a sip of tea. "You would've learned more about us when you reached your 16th birthday if you hadn't turned your back on us."

Ouch. I knew my family wasn't happy that I didn't want to learn, but did she really have to rub it in?

"OK, I deserved that, and more. I came here to learn. May as well get started."

"As I said, some traditions have changed a little over the centuries." Auntie P. cleared the dishes from the table. "You know how it is. Someone forgets to pass on a little bit of information, or it gets changed a little, either accidentally or on purpose. Some things were changed to keep up with the times, but the core beliefs have never been altered. We still hold rituals in honour of the seasons, the Sabbats, and to celebrate auspicious moments in pagan history. Are you familiar with the Celtic cross?"

I nodded.

"Picture it in your mind. The top of the cross is Calas, the earth, at midnight. The right arm is Fluidity, the water at sunrise. The bottom is Breath, the air at noon. The left arm is Uvel, fire at sunset, and the center is Nwyvre. The Devine spirit, or soul, is the sum of all the parts."

"Nwyvre. You mean God?"

"No, not exactly. The Devine Sprit refers to the faeries, sprites, leprechauns, and other Fae creatures."

"Oh, like the gnomes at Granny's house?"

"Yes, in a way. They're part of our culture, our heritage. And before you ask, we don't have any living here. We connect with them in the forests and meadows. We have special places that no one knows about. If anyone accidentally stumbles across them, they wouldn't know it as they wouldn't be able to see them. Only our kind can see where they live. Nwyvre is more like our energy. If you read the old texts, often Nwyvre is depicted as a dragon. Now, I need to speak with the high priestesses in the area to find out about mating between our kind and the helpers."

"Whoa. You're getting way ahead of things, Auntie P. I hardly know the guy and don't know how I really feel about him."

She finished putting the dishes in the sink, then scurried off.

I turned to Drew. "So, did I break some taboo or something? Are we only supposed to take up with certain types? And did she say mating? What are we, animals? Makes it all sound so, I don't know, impersonal. Besides, we're just friends, barely. I've met him a grand total of twice and she's already got me in bed with him."

"Hmm, looks like you've stirred up something. There's a lot we need to tell you before you go back home, but there's much more that you'll need to learn once you turn twenty-one. How's about I fly back with you and stay for a bit?"

"Oh, Drew, would you? I was going to ask, but wasn't sure if you could. You've got a business to take care of, and we hardly know each other anymore. Strange though, I feel like we haven't been apart that long. Like we're connected."

"In a way, we are. That's one of the things you'll find out about later, but based on Gran's reaction, I have a feeling some of the rules will be broken over the next few days. My intuition isn't as strong as yours, but it's better than Mum's or Gran's, and I'm certain there's something about that bloke that you'll need to know before you leave."

We left Great Aunt Priscilla with her nose in a book while talking on the phone to one of the elders she'd mentioned. She mumbled something about a mating between one of our kind and a helper a long time ago. *Mating*. She made everything seem so detached and unfeeling. I definitely didn't feel detached when I thought about Cooper.

NINETEEN

After the breakfast dishes were washed and put away, I walked with Drew to her shop to check it out. She conveniently lived above her store. She wanted me to go through the emeralds she had in stock and pick out the ones that resonated with me.

Like so many places in England, the town was centuries old, surrounded by hills. The buildings reflected the different periods in time. Sometimes the change in architecture blended with the old, other times it looked like a blight.

Her shop was amazing. The three-storey building had a cute little black wrought-iron fence around the front, stopping people from stumbling into the gap that let a little light through the basement window. The main floor had a rounded bay, which accented the arch over the front door. Two more smaller windows sat near the roof. Probably a tiny attic area. Drew certainly had a lot of room.

Simple pendants and polished gemstones dangled in the front display window, sending a rainbow of color in all directions when the sun hit. I turned to see if they were visible on the buildings opposite. Her shop sat on High Street, not far from the White Horse. The multitude of colors just reached the side of the tavern before the sun shifted. For a short time, a beautiful display danced on the stark walls of the White Horse.

"I often get people from the tavern coming by to look in the window, curious about the vibrant show of color. Doesn't look like anyone noticed it today." Drew pulled out a key-chain dripping with tiny crystals and unlocked her door.

"I didn't realize I knew so little. Mother tried to teach me loads of things, but I hadn't paid much attention. Granny made sure I knew at least the basics of natural medicines. I guess they concentrated on their specialities, planning on teaching me our history as I got older."

I plunked down on the chair in front of what looked like a workstation. My head spun. There was so much to learn, and it sounded like it would never end. My eyes moistened. *No! I will not give up.* I pushed the chair back, spinning around to face my cousin. She shook her head and smiled.

"Ok, where do we start? I quit my job so I have all the time in the world. Well, at least all the time in the next couple of weeks. I was the Queen of Cramming at school." My fingers drummed on the tabletop. "I can do this. I don't suppose there's a primer or something?"

Drew laughed. "No, no primer, and no need to panic. Knowing everything isn't necessary for your ceremony. It's not like there's going to be a test. You just need to know enough so you can decide what you want to do. You already know more than I ever will about crystals. Candle magick will be an asset. Are you comfortable with that?"

I shrugged and wiggled my hand. "So-so."

"Great, we'll start there. I'll weave in a bit of our history as we go, and there are plenty of books and journals you can read, along with a variety of things we can practice. I can also introduce you to other witches in the area. And then there's the internet." Drew opened a drawer in the table while she spoke, and pulled out a cloth, smoothing it out flat across the table top.

"Seriously? The internet? Isn't all the stuff online total crap?"

"There's a website that requires special access. Not available to the general public. You'll never find it searching on Google. And I'm certain Mum will let you read some of her books while you're here. Make as many notes as possible, and I might even be able to convince Gran to let me take one in particular back to Canada when we leave. I don't know if your mother or grandmother had one like it, and since you need a crash course, this book has most of what you should know before your ceremony. Have you picked a place yet?"

I nodded. "Yes. There's a lovely old willow in the back garden. I feel so at peace when I'm near it. Oh, did I tell you there's a Fae door in it? That's where I met Nenka, the female gnome. It's the perfect place for my initiation."

"That's why you chose a willow for your pendant. If that's where your initiation is, the pendant will be much more powerful."

Drew went into the back and returned with a tray of emeralds.

"Here, pick out about a dozen. The tree in the pendant will be about two inches high, so look for round emeralds, about one or two centimeters. There's a gauge in the tray."

She placed a teardrop shaped emerald on the cloth.

"This will be in the tree's trunk. I finished the sketches, so I'll start making the mould while you find the stones. I'll have it ready before we leave for Toronto."

Drew pulled a chair up to the other side of the workstation and laid out the rubber moulding compound and a brick of wax. While she prepared her materials, I swiveled the chair, taking a closer look at her goods. A counter along the east wall contained several shelves of loose gemstones, grouped by color. I recognized citrine, emerald, garnet, but without a closer look, the others could be almost anything. Beside that was a display of books. I couldn't read the titles from my chair, but I could see pictures of crystals on some covers. One book had a picture of a lady doing yoga. There were candles of all shapes, sizes, and colors on the opposite wall, along with incense and holders. A little bit of everything to help relax and clear one's mind. Turing back to Drew, I watched as she carved out the shape of my willow tree. I was amazed at the speed of her hands as she whittled the wax away, not making one mistake.

She looked up, grinning. "Don't mind me, just sort through those emeralds."

"It's all so fascinating. I've never seen anyone make jewellery before. Not from scratch, just setting stones. I wish I had a skill like yours. I can't even draw a straight line with a ruler."

"You've got your own skills. Think about what you enjoy doing. I've always drawn, so I explored that. A little witchy-poo hocus pocus and voilà. We can't conjure up skills we don't have, though. No waving a wand and suddenly being able to compose like Mozart or anything like that. We can just enhance whatever natural skills we have.

"After your initiation, you'll have to explore areas outside your previous learning. It's natural for your mother and grandmother to teach you their skills, but we need to expand your education considerably. I can stay with you until your birthday, but I can't close the shop indefinitely. We'll set up a schedule and after I return home, we can video chat once a week or so."

"I guess my education will continue for quite some time."

"Yes, if you consider the rest of your life to be 'quite some time.' You can stop learning if you want to, but why limit yourself? My mum and Gran both still try new things from time to time. It can be hilarious watching them fail over and over. They eventually get it, but they get so frustrated. You wouldn't believe some of the words that come out of their mouths."

Drew went back to carving the wax, and I picked and measured stones until I had an even dozen.

"Done. What next?"

"I have to finish the wax and make a rubber mould so I can pour the silver. You don't have to do anything."

I moved around behind her and peeked over her shoulder. She'd carved out the shape of the willow. It was fairly thick with small lines giving the appearance of bark. It looked pretty damn good.

"I just need to carve out the spots where the stones will be mounted. You can explore the town, or head back to Gran's to see if she's found what she was looking for."

The little silver bell over the door tinkled and a couple of teens wearing Terminal Gods tees came in, goth makeup to match. Drew put down the wax and went over to help them. I waved goodbye and went out to explore what Dorking had to offer. I figured it was too soon for Auntie P. to have found what she was looking for.

I wandered along High Street and veered off at West, noticing a sign on the side of a building pointing to the Museum down a lane. I've always enjoyed local histories, so I decided to check it out, disappointed to discover it was only open on Thursdays, Fridays, and Saturdays. Another sign mentioned the South Street Caves. Exploring them would have to wait for another day, but I could ask Auntie P. what they are.

Heading back out to West Street, I went into Gorgeous Gertie's Vintage Emporium, then to Shabby Chic Country Living. I loved those types of stores. Shabby Chic was jam-packed with furniture, pictures, bottles. I even found a pair of twelve-inch plaster angel wings. The perfect gift for Auntie P. as an apology and thank you. She was being an angel, after all. I strolled around town for over an hour. It felt good to relax and not think about anything. I'd even forgotten about the dark presence back home. Occasionally, I thought I could sense someone or something watching me, but I didn't feel at all threatened, except by my feet.

It'd been ages since I'd done so much walking, and I hadn't brought the proper footwear. Across the road, I spotted a bench. Hobbling over, I plunked down and removed my sandals. Blisters had popped up on both heels, and my left big toe. *Crud*!

I remembered passing a store called Shoerite. They probably had something more appropriate for walking than my cheap sandals. One of the blisters started to bleed by the time I got there, but the clerk was kind enough to provide some bandages, or *plasters* as she called them, enabling me to head back to Auntie P.'s house on Myrtle Road with a bit more comfort.

As expected, Auntie P. had her head buried in a book. *Guess that runs in the family.* I found her in the back garden sitting on the bench under the shade of the trees lining the west side of her yard, surrounded by books, and jotting things in a hard-covered journal. I plopped down on the grass in front of her.

Priscilla smiled. "Did you enjoy your walk, dear?"

I nodded. "I found a museum, but they aren't open today. Also saw a sign for the South Street caves. What are they?"

Auntie P. chuckled. "Part of an old legend. They were used by the local witches, apparently. No one's found any evidence, but people keep searching."

"Maybe I can find time to check it out before I go home." I pointed to the books. "So, find anything interesting?" I asked.

"Yes and no. None of the elders could recall anything specific. There is some mention of the joining in these books, but the problem is, it happened over four hundred years ago. They passed the story down from generation to generation in the form of a ballad. Each of these books has a different version of it. Have you ever played telephone? You know, that game where someone whispers something to one person, who whispers it to the next? By the time it gets back to the first person, it doesn't resemble the original sentence."

"So, there's no way to know what happened, or if the story's even real? Is it an urban legend? You know, a myth?"

"No, I don't believe it's a myth. Ballads are generally based on fact. The problem is trying to determine which parts are true. Each version has the same basic information. A Celtic witch mates with a seeker. What you call a helper. The union produces a daughter. The most beautiful in the land. Her powers develop at a very young age and are more enhanced than anyone else's. Some revere her, others fear her. According to the ballad, she becomes the High Priestess of the largest and most powerful coven and falls in love. Unfortunately, there's nothing about what happened to her parents, and it's never happened again."

Auntie P. didn't once look at me as she spoke. I got the distinct impression there was more, but I wasn't going to press her.

She gave me one book, open at the ballad. I read it over, trying to find some clue to tell me why I had romantic feelings when no one else in the family did. It was just a story as far as I could tell.

Why can't I be like everyone else? I wiggled the book she'd handed me. "Thanks, Auntie P. I'll read through it tonight." Slamming the book shut, my shoulders slumped, my head hung. An explosion of tears fell.

"Why did I have to be born a freak?"

Auntie P. leaned down and patted my shoulder. "You're not a freak, dear. Never think that. You've been given a special gift. While most people take love for granted, our kind are not so blessed. If one of our kind married a helper, it's highly possible they could have a very special child. A child from such a union could achieve the Celtic Triumvirate and become the youngest High Priestess ever."

"You said this child was High Priestess of a coven. I thought we had no coven."

"Not now, but in the past. There's so much history for you to learn. I wish you could stay longer."

I got up, sat on the bench beside her, and wrapped my arms around her shoulders. "So do I. Drew said she'd fly home with me and stay awhile, then set up some sort of schedule so we could video chat. Sounds like I'll be learning forever."

"While you're here, I thought it would be interesting to assemble everyone like us in the area. We haven't had a gathering in such a long time. It's a perfect opportunity for you to meet others like us. It's a fun time for everyone."

"Won't people notice a large group of witches descending on the town?"

"That's the fun part. It'll be a fair that everyone can attend. We used to do it annually, and I'm not sure why we stopped."

"But won't that take a long time to organize? Don't you need a permit?"

Auntie P. waved her hand, dismissing the question. "I know one councillor. Permit won't be a problem."

Priscilla pulled a small book from her pocket. "Here, read this. A long time ago, one of our ancestors wrote down all the stories she could remember. It will give you a sense of our history. I have a good idea what books you'll find in your grandmother's house and I can let you read some of mine while you're here. Did Drew tell you about the website?"

I nodded.

"Good. It's such a wonderful resource. I just love all the technology. It's like a new kind of magick. Even has a chat board. I've made some wonderful friends from all over the world."

I thanked her again for the books, promising to read both later tonight. After giving her a quick peck on the cheek, I headed to my room and settled into the rocking chair by the window to re-read the ballad. The handwriting was fancy script and a little challenging to read. Too bad someone hadn't thought to type it up. I turned to the first page.

> *Beware the night the moon is full,*
> *The White Witch rides her steed.*
> *All young men will feel her pull,*
> *If this warning they do not heed.*

TWENTY

Saturday morning, I decided to take a break from reading and venture out. No way I was going to attempt driving on the other side of the road, so Drew lent me her bicycle. Maybe a trip out of town into the wooded areas would be nice. Who knew what mysterious things were hidden from mere mortals?

I stuffed some snacks and water in my backpack and took off down Myrtle, weaving my way through the streets west-ward, out of Dorking. I left late enough so the traffic was light, avoiding most of the rush hour. My mind wandered as I imagined what type of festival Auntie P. could put together in only two days.

The summer solstice was on Sunday. Litha, we called it; mid-summer to Auntie P. and her family. I hadn't celebrated it properly for years. Even after I gave up the craft, I still went to the solstice dinners with Mother and Granny, just not the celebrations that went with the day.

It would be nice to attend the festival, celebrate properly with family and others of our kind. *Our kind.* That was going to be a new experience. My emotions kept flipping between excitement and fear. Yes, I wanted to meet others like me, but so afraid they'd look down on me. For years I'd ignored our traditions and had no idea how to use my skills.

I finally reached a wooded area and slowed down, looking for a trail. My spidey-senses kicked into high gear. *Could there be Fae nearby?* A slight change in the ground cover caught my attention. The weeds and wildflowers were broken, trampled, the earth visible. *A deer trail, possibly?* I leaned the bike against a tree and listened. Birds chirped, and something else. Softer. Whispering.

"Hello? I won't harm you." I said and giggled as an old movie line went through my mind. *I come in peace.* The whispering stopped, but no one came forward. I shrugged and followed the trail. The canopy from the trees blocked most of the sun, making the air cool, but not cold.

Rustling came from just off to my right. Was I going to see an English faerie of some sort? Nope, just a red fox, and a beautiful one. We made eye contact and I swear it nodded at me before crossing the trail, disappearing into the brush on the other side.

I walked a little farther, enjoying the solitude, when I heard a voice—this time louder than a whisper. "Over here."

I didn't sense any danger, so I carefully wove my way through the trees in the general direction of the voice.

"Almost."

This time it came from my left. I walked a few feet and spotted a small hill covered in some sort of ivy. I looked around but couldn't see anyone, so I set my pack on the ground and went over to the hill for a closer look. I suppose hill was a bit of an exaggeration. It was more like a mound. I've read plenty of history and seen enough episodes of *Time Team* to know there are mounds all over Great Britain hiding ruins of castles, keeps, and even burials, so I was more than a little curious.

I knelt down and moved the ivy around, careful not to do too much damage. I apologized to it as I pulled some out by the roots. I hated damaging plants, but sometimes it was necessary.

"Left," a tiny voice said.

This time, it seemed to be inside my head rather than an actual voice. *Who or what am I communicating with?* I shifted over a few feet and fell forward. I put my hand on the mound.

I bit my tongue when my jaw connected with the ground. "Ow." What I thought was ivy-covered dirt was actually an ivy-covered hole. I retrieved my backpack and fished out my flashlight and phone. I need to take some pictures to show Auntie P. and tag the location with the GPS app. The opening wasn't large, forcing me to crawl in. I was glad I'd put on capris instead of shorts, else my knees would've ended up full of cuts and scratches.

Shining the light in front of me, I was shocked to see a tunnel that seemed to have no end. Then again, my flashlight was small and didn't cast a long light. Part of me wanted to forget it. I'd expected a cave, not a possible labyrinth. But something led me there for a reason. *Maybe it's not that big.*

I directed the beam upward. The ceiling rose higher a little farther along. Why had the voice directed me here? *It is a trap?* No, I felt no threat. No malicious energy enveloped me. I cleared my mind and reached out, feeling around for anything. Nothing but pleasant feelings. Somewhere nearby were Fae, but they weren't revealing themselves, at least not physically.

My heart ached as I longed to tell Mother and Granny I might have found the long-lost caves. At least I now had someone to talk to about this type of thing. Over breakfast, Auntie P. told me the caves in town were only a tiny portion of what they were rumoured to be. Just a few tunnels dead-ending after a short distance. Our ancestors had used the full extent of them for centuries. Unfortunately, the main sections of caves had been out of use for decades, and no one could remember where the hidden entrances were. Guess I just found one.

As I crawled deeper, the ground sloped downwards slightly. After a couple of minutes, I was able to stand and stretched out my back. Still couldn't see an end. I made my way out, grabbed my backpack, and crawled back in, pushing it in front of me as I went. I opened the compass app on my phone. The tunnel curved, and I needed to know where it might head. As I made my way deeper, pressure built in my head. Since I'd never explored a cave, I had no clue if it was a normal reaction. I certainly didn't want a headache. Not now. *Maybe I should go back and get Auntie P.*

Another voice. "Keep going, Marcy."

It was different from the last one. Deeper. A little further wouldn't hurt.

I shone the light mainly on the floor, unsure of my safety. If this was part of the cave system Auntie P. mentioned, there shouldn't be any holes to fall into, but it'd been decades or centuries since they were used. Back then they would only have had candles to light the way, so there likely weren't any hidden booby-traps. But now, who knew? Too dangerous if part of the floor was missing.

Slowly, I shone the light away from the floor and let it creep toward the ceiling. Something was attached to the wall, just far enough away to make it impossible to see clearly. The shadow it cast looked like a human arm. I froze. *What if there are booby traps? Should I go back? No, just a few more steps.*

I took another step and stopped again, sweeping the ground with the light. Nothing seemed out of place. One more step. I directed the light to the thing on the wall. *Is that what I think it is?* Another step. A torch. *Nothing sinister about that.* Too bad I didn't have a lighter or matches.

As I shone the light around, more torches lined the walls. They looked quite old. *Funny, there didn't seem to be cobwebs on anything.* And I hadn't noticed any bugs or spiders. Was Auntie P. wrong about no one knowing where the tunnels were? I checked the compass. The tunnel seemed to go in the general direction of Dorking. *Could this really be one of the hidden entrances?*

The tunnel was narrow enough to allow me to touch both walls. I tucked my phone in my pocket and stood in the centre, one hand on each wall. Energy flowed into my right hand and up my arm. Slowly, at first, as though testing me. A tingle crept into my core, swirling around, making me nauseous. It felt alive, but not sentient. Afraid what would happen if I broke the bond, I stood still for several minutes. The energy went into my head, increasing the pressure I'd felt continuously since entering the cave.

I tried to move, but couldn't. The pain in my head increased. I squeezed my eyes tight as the pain intensified. A battle raged inside my mind. The pressure became too intense. My eyes watered. Then it was gone. The energy moved into my left arm and hand. The walls of the cave glowed.

"Welcome."

The voice echoed through the tunnel. Soft and melodic. I felt protected.

"Th-th-thank you. Who are you?"

"We are everyone. We have been alone too long and are weak, but we will protect you from him."

Whoa. Protect me from *him?* The headache wasn't from pressure changes. He'd found me. Why hadn't I felt his presence?

I pulled my hands off the wall. An electric charge crackled as the connection broke. The flow faded, leaving me in darkness again. Unsure what to do next, I sat cross-legged in the middle of the tunnel, allowing the blackness to devour me.

I really only had two choices. Go back or go ahead. It would be more fun exploring with someone. *And safer.* But I was already here. Unfortunately, so was he. But I had a protector. *Or was that protectors?* The voice said *we.*

Reminded me of the Borg. No. Bad example. This presence said they'd protect me, not assimilate me into their collective.

She did say they were weak. *Hmm, how much protection could they give me? Anything is better than nothing, I suppose.* They won the battle in my head, and it seemed to be holding.

The deep voice came back. "Go ahead."

"Bugger off," I yelled. It echoed down the tunnel. I slid over to the wall and leaned back. The flow returned, barely. *Had I pissed it off?* I fished out my cell and illuminated the surrounding area.

"I didn't mean to break the connection so abruptly. You started me. I'm sorry if I hurt your feelings, or broke a taboo or something." The glow pulsed, but no one spoke.

I scrambled to my feet and continued on, wanting to find whatever was at the end. The deeper I went, the heavier the air grew. It wasn't musty smelling, but it was rather humid. My skin became damp, not quite sweaty.

After another fifteen minutes, I came to a fork in the tunnel. The compass showed one led the general direction towards town, the other went west-ward.

If I took the fork seemingly leading to town, I'd be able to find out where another entrance might be. *'Course it could lead to a dead end. What was west?* I pictured the Google map I'd called up earlier. South Downs National Park. *No, maybe another day.* I didn't want to get lost in there. *Into town it is.*

I no longer had any bars on my phone, so I couldn't tell Auntie P. where I was or what I'd found. After a brief stop for a snack and drink from my pack, I continued on. The tunnel grew narrower, but thankfully I had plenty of headroom.

As I moved the flashlight around, scratches on the wall caught my attention. Stepping closer, I realized they weren't scratches, but symbols engraved on both sides of the tunnel. Most were partially filled in with dirt accumulated over the centuries. I used my stubby nails to clear them as best I could. Pentagrams, witches knots, quarter moons, triple moons, the Eye of Horus, and some I didn't recognize. I continued on after taking numerous pics. A little past the fork, I found an alcove. A rather large one. In the centre stood a stone altar. Again, no bugs or cobwebs. Took a few more pictures, then went in for some close-ups of the altar, remnants of wax still visible.

As I walked around, breathing became difficult, but not like in the cemetery. No one tried to suffocate me this time. *Probably just bad air trapped inside and not him.* Since breathing was easier in the tunnel, I exited the alcove, but slowed my pace, not wanting to pass out. *Should be near the end by now.* It felt like I'd walked for hours. The air was still cool, but had become heavier—my breathing laboured. *Should I keep going or turn back?* I needed to rest first, so I sat on the dirt floor with my back against the wall and closed my eyes.

When I woke I checked the time on my cell. *Seven-thirty! My God, I've slept all day.* Or had I passed out? I started to get up and almost keeled over. I desperately needed to get out of the tunnel and away from the thin air.

I drank more water and started to crawl back the way I'd come. My palms hurt and bled from the tiny pebbles and grit on the tunnel floor. My arms moved like jelly. Beads of sweat dripped off my hair, stinging my eyes. *Have to get out.* When I reached the fork, I couldn't remember which way to go. I closed my eyes and concentrated. *Which way? Left. No, right. I need to go to the right.* I crawled for what seemed a lifetime, then my arms gave out and I tumbled into the alcove.

I stopped rolling when I collided with the altar. I leaned against it and rested. Deep breaths. The air felt heavier than before. I fought to remain conscious. My mind wandered. *Did they do sacrifices here? Maybe I'll be next. No! I will not die in here.*

Using the altar to steady myself, I got to my feet and stumbled back into the tunnel, tripping over my pack. *Schist. Back to crawling.* Too weak to drag it along, I finagled my pack onto my back and continued in the direction I hoped led to the way out.

TWENTY-ONE

Gradually, my breathing got easier. I could stand without becoming dizzy. A slight breeze raised the hairs on my arm. A little light glowed ahead, but the ceiling sloped downward, causing me to crawl again. I threw my backpack ahead of me, wiggled out, then sprawled on my back, gulping down the fresh air.

When I felt rejuvenated, I checked my phone. Message after message from Auntie P., Susan, and Drew filled my screen. I sent a quick text and dropped the phone beside me. Despite sleeping the day away, my entire body sank to the ground. *Where did I leave the bike? Can I even pedal it?* Somehow, I needed to re-charge. Too bad I didn't have a cable I could plug into a tree.

I smacked my forehead. *The trees! Earth energy.* I dragged myself over to the tallest tree. Old tree, stronger energy. I leaned against it, wrapping my arms as far around it as possible. Nothing at first, then a slight pulse, and another. Each one stronger than the last. It felt like the tree moved with each beat. For ten minutes I stood, absorbing the energy, finally feeling strong enough to let go.

"Thank you."

I picked up my pack and cell, then looked around. I couldn't remember which way I came in.

"Follow me."

I turned. A fox peeked out from behind a clump of wildflowers. It walked a few feet, then turned and looked at me. I followed it for about five minutes and spotted the bike leaning against a pine.

"Thanks." I waved at the bushy-tailed red fox as it slipped into the underbrush.

Part way home my legs gave out. I called Auntie P. to come get me.

I sat by the side of the road, watching for her car. The sun had dropped behind the trees, leaving me in partial darkness; there were no streetlights on this stretch of road. A few cars went by, one stopping to ask if I needed a lift. After that, I moved farther off the roadside and hoped I'd spot Auntie P.'s car before she drove past. Somehow, she managed to see me and honked, did a U-turn, then pulled up behind me. She flew out of the car as I struggled to my feet.

"Marcy, how could you go off and not tell one of us where you were going? This is a nice, peaceful area, but anything could have happened to you."

She grabbed my shoulders, forcing me to look at her. Worry lines marred Auntie P.'s normally smooth skin. Sparks of anger flashed in her eyes. "What if you'd been struck by a car? You had us all worried. Promise you'll not go off again without telling one of us where you're going." She pulled me close.

I couldn't recall ever having a finger wagged in front of my face with such force. "Sorry," I mumbled into her shoulder. "I couldn't get a signal."

Auntie P. gave me a squeeze. "I'm just glad you're OK." She helped stash the bike in the back, and I climbed into the passenger seat, wiggling around trying to avoid the lumps. She really needed a new car. Auntie P. was still talking when I fell asleep. She nudged me awake after pulling into Susan's driveway.

Drew retrieved her bike from the back of the vehicle, then the questions started. I held my hands up, waving them slightly, trying to get everyone to stop talking.

"You're not going to believe what I found. But first, I need the bathroom and food." I dropped my backpack and made a bee-line for the can.

When I joined them in the kitchen, Susan made me a bacon and egg butty. Between bites, I told them about the tunnels and altar, and showed them the pictures. "It was the strangest thing. A voice guided me straight to it. Could one of the Fae have reached out to me?"

"Why you?" Drew asked. "Nothing personal, cuz, but we've walked through there lots of times. Why not guide one of us?"

I shrugged.

"You said the tunnel branched to the west? Interesting. There are stories that one of the tunnels ran west directly to Stonehenge." Auntie P. tapped her fingers on the table. "If the tunnels have been sealed all these years, it's no wonder the air is thin. You're lucky you didn't pass out permanently. How could you have been so careless? Please promise me no more excursions alone."

I nodded. "No worries on that score. It's too easy to get lost or hurt, and there's no cell service down there." It suddenly dawned on me just how stupid I'd been. And selfish. Again. Not once had I considered anyone when I went off on my journey. I'd ventured into unfamiliar woods, and hadn't the foggiest clue what wildlife was in the area. What if the cave collapsed? My body would've never been found. No harm this time, and I had made a great discovery.

I remembered the festival Auntie spoke about. "Can we use the tunnel and alcove for part of the festivities Sunday?"

"No, it won't be safe. Besides, we need to hold the festivals outside. I'll spread the word, though. If you can show me where it is, I can arrange a safe trip in to check it out."

"I have a GPS reading. I'll text it over to you." I turned to Susan. "Thanks for the sandwich. I was famished. I'll have to treat you all to dinner one night. Anywhere you want to go."

"I won't turn down a free meal." Drew waved her hand in the air. "I vote for the King William."

"I think it's time to get you home." Auntie P. rose from the table. "You need to take it easy."

When we got back to Auntie P.'s, she started calling people to tell them about the tunnel, occasionally giving me one of her "stupid girl" looks. It was too early for bed, and I had slept most of the day, so I wasn't tired. Not one to pass on an opportunity to read, I picked up the hand-written journal on the history of Celtic Magick and soon became lost in another world.

Without even being aware of it, I discovered I'd been following some of it all my life. The Celts had a strong love of Mother Earth and I'd always had an overwhelming feeling of serenity and belonging when out enjoying nature. I often explored the woods around Granny's house as a child, usually barefoot. Somehow, I never came out with scrapped feet. While Granny seemed to be in tune with her herbs and plants, I felt connected to the trees, imagining I could communicate with them. *Maybe I hadn't been imagining it. Had it been the Fae guiding me to the opening in the mound, or the trees?*

I turned each page with care. The book was bound with a dark brown leather cover; a large embossed pentagram sat in the centre. I ran my fingers over it, tracing each line. Instead of being cracked and wrinkled, the leather was soft and supple.

As I read, I gasped as memories swirled around my mind. I recalled Mother telling me about the importance of the four elements and being in touch with nature. As I continued to read, one point hit close to home. In order to practice Celtic magick you need to suspend disbelief. The corners of my mouth rose and I laughed. An early lesson with Mother popped into my mind.

We were in the garden where a vine grew along the fence. Mother told me to ask the vine to move as it was covering a piece of outdoor art that hung on the fence. I tried over and over but nothing happened.

She asked me if I believed the vine could hear me. Naturally I said no, it was just a plant and had no ears. She explained how plants are living things that had many of the same feelings as people. That made perfect sense to a seven-year-old, so I concentrated and tried again. I watched in amazement as the vine shifted and moved away from the wrought iron quarter-moon. Now it wasn't so much disbelief as choosing to ignore. I suppose it amounted to the same thing.

My eyes became sore and drifted shut. *I suppose I needed a proper rest.* I shoved a piece of paper in the book to mark my place, then trudged up to my room and settled in the chair by the window. Removing my glasses, I reached over and dropped them on the bed. After I returned home, I'd need to make an appointment to get my eyes checked. The tiny screwdriver was almost worn down from my constant tightening of the screws, not to mention the screws were almost threadbare.

Closing my eyes, I leaned back in the chair. The sounds of birds chirping calmed my mind. Their songs faded as I drifted off. I jumped when my phone buzzed. I picked it up and read the name. *Drew.* She wasn't surprised to hear I'd been reading again.

"Has your head exploded yet?"

I laughed. "Not yet, but I think it might if I don't stop reading soon."

"Ok, time for a distraction. Have you set up your altar yet? You really shouldn't use your grandmother's."

I leaned back in the chair and stretched out my aching back and shoulders. "My altar? No, I hadn't given it much thought. It's weird how I can't remember much when it's only been about seven years since I put all this behind me. Both Mother and Granny taught me ever since I was old enough to understand. Probably before I understood. I think some of the games we played were actually lessons."

"It is rather peculiar. At least it's coming back in dribs and drabs. Maybe talking about it will help. You must have had an altar. Tell me what you remember."

I nodded and closed my eyes, trying to picture my old room. I could see the large poster of the full moon that hung on one wall. My eyes drifted down. I saw my altar and laughed.

"You remembered something? What's so funny?"

"My athame. It's an antique knife that I found on one of the annual trips I took with Mother and Granny when I was about ten. We went to Germany that year. The knife has a beautifully engraved silver handle and sheath, and caused a bit of a delay going through customs. We showed them the paperwork that came with it, and once they understood it was a collectible antique, they finally let us through. Can you imagine if they knew it was a ritual knife for a witch's altar? I must have known we were witches. Why else would I have an altar?"

"No reason I can think of, Marcy. Do you remember where your items are?"

"When I decided not to pursue our craft, I packed everything into an old steamer trunk and it went into the attic. That's the last time I saw it. At the time, I was glad to see the back of it. After Mother died, Granny cleared out the house and sold it. I wasn't really thinking straight and didn't want anything except my crystals. I can't imagine Granny would have tossed anything of mine or Mother's. It's probably all in Granny's attic. I mean, *my* attic. Can't get used to the house being mine now. Anyway, that's one place I haven't explored since moving in."

"I can pretty much guarantee Francine would never throw away sacred items. We'll have a look for it when we get back to your place."

We chatted a bit longer, then ended the call when I started yawning. I wanted to help Auntie P. make the festival arrangements, and needed to be wide awake. She was royally pissed at me. I needed to redeem myself.

TWENTY-TWO

I forgot to pull the curtain when I went to bed, so the sun shone through my window, almost blinding me. I glanced at the time, then threw the covers off. It was almost 11:00 a.m.! I couldn't recall the last time I'd slept that late. After a quick shower, I threw on a t-shirt and shorts and made my way to the kitchen for a much needed cup of coffee.

Auntie P. sat on the sofa, talking on the phone, again, making arrangements for the mid-summer gathering. *Is she still pissed off with me?* Somehow I'd have to find a way to fix it. I'd hoped she'd let me help with the planning and had left something for me to do. She finally put the phone down and turned her attention to me.

"How are you feeling this morning, dear? No side-effects from yesterday?"

I plopped down beside her. "Other than sleeping in, I feel perfectly fine. Is there anything I can do to help with the planning?"

She flipped the pages of the notebook she'd been scribbling in. "It's pretty much all in hand, but there are supplies you can gather." Priscilla tore a blank page out and wrote a few lines before handing it to me. I skimmed through what she'd written.

"It's going to be so much fun. Do you think the entire town will turn out?" I asked.

"Slight change of plans. We're going to keep it private, but there will be enough of our kind to make it feel like the entire town showed up."

"If it's just for us, where will you have it? It doesn't make sense to have it in a hall."

Auntie P. shook her head and smiled. "No, that would never do. Can't have these things indoors. One of my friends will host. We've had celebrations there before. And I have a surprise for you. Tonight will be an early one, as we're getting up before sunrise."

I groaned. "Wonderful surprise, Aunt Priscilla. Might I be so bold as to inquire why?"

"We're driving to Stonehenge for the solstice sunrise. It's one of the few times the public is allowed to go right up to the megaliths. We'll have to be there at least an hour early as the line-up will be horrendous."

"I'm afraid to ask, but when is sunrise?"

"A little past four thirty. We'll just be coming out of a new moon, so it's a good time for a fresh start."

"Why bother going to bed at all? May as well just stay up."

"It's going to be a full day tomorrow, so we'll need some rest. I suppose we could go tonight and sleep under the stars. That way, we wouldn't have to get up quite so early."

"Are you serious?" Much as I enjoyed the outdoors, sleeping with bugs and possibly wild animals wasn't high on my to-do list.

Auntie P. nodded.

"Well, it might be fun. Will Susan and Drew agree?"

"Oh yes. We've done it before. I have a friend a little north of Stonehenge who allows a few of us to camp out on her property."

That settled, Auntie P. gave me a list of places to collect the items for the festivities. Based on the list, crafting was involved.

Even though I hated driving on the left, I borrowed Auntie's car and carefully made my way to the store. A few people honked at my slow driving, but most were tolerant. I picked up a couple of cases of water, crafting wire and glue, then spent most of the day driving around, gathering moss and wild flowers. Apparently, it didn't matter what species, as long as they were colorful and at least twenty-five per cent of the blooms were yellow.

I picked some from her garden that I knew wouldn't be easily found in the wild: monkshood, which is poisonous but has beautiful purple blooms, white carnations, lavender, astilbe, and snapdragons. I found the rest growing wild outside town, where Auntie P. told me I was allowed to pick them. Phlox grew on the hillsides, mostly pink and white. I didn't know many of the others, but I ended up with three bushel-baskets full of floral rainbows, heavy on the yellow.

Shortly after six that evening, I helped Auntie P. put sleeping bags and snacks in the car, along with a change of clothes. Then we picked up Drew and Susan and headed towards Stonehenge. Even though it was only a two-hour drive, we stopped at Basingstoke to eat. Drew told me they'd started that tradition years ago.

I picked the Fur & Feathers solely based on the name. The place was packed. Several patrons mentioned the Henge as we walked to our table. A few people came over to say hello, and I assumed they were witches, but didn't ask. Some of them were camping out at the same place as us.

After dinner, we took a stroll through town.

"Did I ever make the trip with Mother and Granny? I don't recognize anything."

"No, dear," Auntie P. answered. "They never came in the spring. They seemed to prefer early fall."

I thought I heard people talking behind me several times, but when I turned, no one stood anywhere near. "Why is my block not working? How are they getting through?"

The three of them exchanged a look I couldn't quite decipher. Surprise? Susan smiled and turned to me.

"Now that you've accepted your heritage, you'll begin to experience things. Exactly what thing is still to be discovered. As a child, you never exhibited any one particular skill. We'll help you with that while you're here."

"I take it that's unusual? Not leaning towards something, I mean."

They all nodded.

"So, everyone was right. I am a freak, just not in the way they meant." I laughed to lighten the mood, but it didn't work.

"Time to get back on the road." Auntie P stood. "Claim our spot on Izzy's lawn."

When we arrived, the field beside the house was full of sleeping bags and tents. The air felt electrically charged. Auntie said I'd meet most of the witches tomorrow at the gathering, so she didn't bother with introductions. I was eager to see what would happen tomorrow.

I couldn't understand why Granny and Mother never seemed to socialize with any other witches. Back home we had a wiccan store close to town, so obviously there were other witches in the area. I remembered seeing a poster in their window once listing some workshops. *Mental note to self: sign up for one.*

As the sun drifted closer to the horizon, the chatter faded away. An early sunrise meant an early bedtime. Everyone wanted to be fully awake for the solstice. Even though it happened twice a year, for many, it would be a once-in-a-lifetime event. Sleep could be had later.

I shared a tent with Drew and we chatted for a while. Since she lived so close, the summer and winter solstices were nothing new for her.

"Don't you ever tire of seeing it?" I asked.

Drew laughed. "Once you witness it, you'll know the answer. It's beautiful beyond compare, not to mention both magickal and mystical. Time to get some sleep. Plenty of time to chat after."

✵ ✵ ✵

Several hours later, bells jingled and buzzers hummed from alarms numerous people had set on their phones to signal the start of the new day. I rubbed my eyes, then gave Drew a poke. "Time to get up. How did you manage not to hear all those phone alarms?"

Drew shrugged. "Heavy sleeper. I need two alarms set to get up in the morning."

Shadows moved around outside, so I crawled to the opening and poked my head out. Auntie P. and Susan were already packing their tent. Then I saw it.

The faint hint of a golden halo at the edge of the horizon. An amazing sight. I couldn't take my eyes off it, stumbling as I moved to join the line of people at the portable toilets that Auntie P.'s friend provided. A sudden jolt of sadness hit as I thought about all the things I'd missed because Granny and Mother never participated in such things.

Breakfast was a power bar, no coffee. I supposed I'd cope, just this once. We managed to get out early enough to stay ahead of most of the traffic, but by the time we parked, the in-coming line of vehicles was so long I couldn't see the end. We joined the line at the gate, waiting for security to open it up.

Several ladies dressed in ceremonial robes approached and everyone allowed them to get to the head of the line. The guard finally let us in. We followed the robed ladies through the tunnel under the road and towards the Henge.

I gasped out loud when it came into view. The sight from across the motorway wasn't quite the same as being right up alongside the gigantic stones.

The barrier around the Henge was gone. We passed through the stone giants and headed to the centre. People entered from all directions. Thousands came to witness the summer solstice at the most magnificent location on the planet. Some brought crystals and candles and set up small altars, us included. The robed ladies set up a larger altar at the centre. I watched as they assembled their items around a good-sized piece of quartz—a small mound of earth, a white candle, a chalice of water, and a feather. Ours was similar. Silently, we said our blessings, then the crowd moved to the eastern side of the sacred temple to wait for the sun to take its place above the Heel Stone. Gradually, the sun rose higher as the Lord of the Day left his lover, Mother Earth, and took his place in the sky.

One of the ladies wearing robes invited us to be part of their circle and join hands—another of Aunt Priscilla's friends. She led us in blessings to heal Mother Earth and asked for peace. The four directions were honoured and the circle cast. The ceremony began.

A lady in a lavender robe removed the chalice from the altar and passed it around the circle. We each took a sip, then she poured some on the ground, an offering to the Goddess. Auntie P. told me it was a Druid healing essence.

I closed my eyes and listened. My skin tingled from the energy in the air radiating off the participants and the sacred stones. The kee-kee-kee of a kestrel signalled the end of the ceremony. It circled three times, screeched again, then flew off. Before leaving, we made our personal offering to the Goddess. The energy was still high, and I didn't want to go, but our time was up. We headed back to the car-park in silence and followed the long procession as everyone headed back to their homes, hotels, or local restaurants. We were half way home when Susan broke the silence.

"So, what did you think, Marcy?"

I'd spent most of the drive back staring out the window, still absorbed with the ceremony. Drew nudged me.

"Earth to Marcy. Mum's talking to you."

"What? Sorry. I can't get over how amazing that was. What is it you say? I'm gobsmacked. It was the most spectacular and spiritual thing I've ever experienced. I want to come back for the winter solstice. No camping though."

"I'll have a room ready for you," Auntie P. said. "You know you're welcome any time." She paused briefly. "You can make the room your own, if you want."

I glanced at the rear-view mirror and saw Auntie looking back at me. My heart swelled. She'd forgiven my earlier outburst. Drew reached over and squeezed my hand. I had a family again. In heart, not just by biology.

"Nothing would make me happier."

We had a proper breakfast and several cups of coffee when we got back to the house. I'd have to stock up Auntie's cupboard with Snickerdoodle. As soon as the dishes were cleared, we prepared for the gathering later in the afternoon. One of Auntie P.'s friends had a small farm, so she had plenty of room for the event.

Susan and Drew got in Auntie's car and I handed them each a basket of flowers. I sat with the third one in my lap and we set off.

A few cars already sat parked along the long driveway. Like my home, a lot of the property was tree covered. Auntie's friend had a garden three times the size of Granny's. A couple of dairy cows and some goats grazed by the side of her barn. Something grew in a field behind the house, but I couldn't tell what. Probably grain for the livestock.

Auntie P. led us down a trail through the trees. We must have looked like we were heading to a funeral with all those flowers. Tucked away from prying eyes sat a clearing with a large earthen circle in the centre. Bamboo tiki torches lit up the area, candles waiting to be lit. Several small statues of faeries and animals had been placed haphazardly around the clearing, along with wind chimes and bronze suns hanging from shepherd hooks. I could already picture what it would look like after the sun set.

As soon as I had a moment, I planned on texting Cooper. First, I'd need to ask if I'd be allowed to tell him, or anyone, about the gathering. At least the sunrise at Stonehenge wouldn't be taboo. Maybe I could invite him to come over with me for the winter solstice, assuming we were—what? Dating? That would certainly make Auntie P. happy.

"Watch out!"

I stopped day-dreaming when Drew hollered. I was headed straight for a rose bush.

"Do watch where you're going, dear." Auntie stood beside Drew. "Don't want an injury before the fun starts. And you don't want to know what my friend would do to you if you ruined her prize roses." Her eyes twinkled, but I don't think she was kidding.

At the far end, someone had set up several tables like workstations, each covered with a floral tablecloth. Gwendolyn, the owner of the property, instructed us to place the baskets on one of the empty tables.

I wandered around, checking to see what was on the other tables. One had small pieces of fabric, lace, and dried lavender. Another had crafting wire and dried herbs. Excitement bubbled inside me as I tried to decide what to do first. I felt like a little kid at camp.

One by one, people arrived, some with drums, a few with tents or canopies. I helped one older lady struggling to get her canopy set up. She introduced herself as Elspeth.

"What will you be doing at the festival?" I asked.

"Why, fortune telling, of course." She pointed to a girl who couldn't be more than sixteen. "Sara does tarot. Since you were kind enough to help me, you can be my first reading of the day. Have you had your palm read before?"

"Never." A feeling of dread grew in the pit of my stomach.

She reached over. "Give me your right hand." I extended my right arm, palm up. Her hands were soft despite her advanced age. A stark contrast to her wrinkled face. Elspeth leaned close, turned my hand slightly, gasped, and let go. You'd think my hand had suddenly caught fire or something. I didn't like the look on her face.

My feeling of dread turned to panic. I had no doubt she was legit. No one here would be a fake. Part of me wanted to know what she saw. Most of me wanted to bolt, afraid to hear what she read.

Trying to keep it light, I asked, "No tall, dark, handsome stranger?"

Reluctantly, she took my left hand, then my right again.

"Who are you?"

TWENTY-THREE

Elspeth's eyes widened. I lowered my wall slightly to tap into her feelings. Whatever she saw didn't frighten her. She radiated surprise and puzzlement.

"I'm Priscilla's grandniece. Her sister Francine was my grandmother."

"Ah, you're an Adhamh." Not a question, a simple statement of fact.

"Yes. Does that make a difference?"

Her brow wrinkled. "You do know your family history, don't you?"

I didn't want to get into it with a stranger, so I kept my answer short. "No. That's partly why I'm visiting. What did you see? Something bad, I'm guessing?"

"No, not bad. You've been given an amazing gift. I was just startled by it."

"Marcy?" I looked over and spotted Drew watching us.

"Coming." I answered, then turned back to Elspeth. "Thank you for the reading."

"Wait. I need to see more."

"My cousin needs my help. I'm sure I'll see you later tonight." I scurried away before she could say anything else.

Drew stood beside one of the tables, setting up the items she'd brought from her shop. I hadn't noticed she'd brought along a box, so I hurried over to help unpack.

"I wondered where you'd gotten to. I thought I'd help people make some crystal pendulums and simple pendants. Want to be my assistant?"

I nodded eagerly. "For sure. Sounds like fun."

A steady stream of witches, and I assumed warlocks, joined the activities, trickling down to the occasional stray by late afternoon. Several deposited their kids at Drew's table for some free babysitting.

I spent part of my afternoon explaining the powers of various gemstones and crystals to the children so they could pick just the right one before having Drew help them assemble their items. When it slowed down, I wandered off to the other tables.

My phone had dinged when we first arrived, but my hands were full carrying our contributions to the clearing. As I made my way around the grounds, I checked my messages. My heart fluttered when I saw who sent them. Cooper, asking how my training was progressing. Since there wasn't any Wi-Fi in the field, I'd have to wait to get closer to Gwendolyn's house or back to Auntie P.s before replying.

I stopped at one table and made a lavender cachet, then helped make a huge sun wheel wreath at another. Now I knew why I had to get so many yellow flowers. The wreath took up most of the flowers and moss I had collected.

Throughout the afternoon the drums sounded, people sang, and danced. I tried to join in. None of the songs sounded familiar. Nailed the dance part, though. The rhythm of the drums sped up, my body instinctively keeping pace. My mind cleared, allowing the energy from everyone to flow through me. I continued, totally oblivious to the sudden silence. It wasn't until I found myself on the ground in a heap, surrounded by a dozen or so people, that I realized the music had stopped. Susan pushed her way through.

"Marcy, are you OK? What happened?"

I shrugged. "I was just dancing. Can't remember most of it. The beat of the drums mesmerized me. Guess I wore myself out. It's been a long time since I danced like that. I totally zoned out."

Auntie P. and Drew burst through the ring of bodies and joined Susan at my side.

"What happened?" Drew asked.

Susan answered before I even had a chance to open my mouth.

"Marcy just got caught up in the moment. She danced along with the drums, even after they stopped. If I didn't know better, I'd say she'd been possessed. We all watched for at least fifteen minutes after the drumming ended. That's when the clouds congregated overhead and turned black. Then she just collapsed."

I couldn't believe it. *Susan must be mistaken.* "Did you say fifteen minutes? And what's that about dark clouds?" I looked skyward. "Not a cloud in the sky."

"They vanished when you hit the ground." Susan reached down. "Let me help you up. You can rest under the trees."

My legs wobbled like rubber. I couldn't walk. Drew put my arm around her shoulder and helped her mother get me away from the crowd. I felt like a specimen under a microscope.

Several picnic tables had been put in the shade and were covered with bowls of fruit and vegetables for everyone to munch on. Someone had put my cases of water with them.

As the sun set, the beating of the drums resumed, signalling everyone to gather around the earthen circle. A huge bonfire glowed in the centre. One candle from the tiki lanterns was lit from the fire and used to light the remaining tikis. It was more beautiful than I imagined.

A hint of sun glistened through the trees, casting strange shadows around us, then disappeared for the night. A soft breeze made the tiki flames dance, reflecting light off the crystals in the statues. A small grouping of garden faerie ornaments sat a little east of the circle. They seemed to dance under the flickering light. I wasn't entirely certain it was an illusion.

Before joining the circle, Auntie P. told me to take extra care grounding. "Don't want the drums to carry you off into la-la land again."

I didn't want that either. The four of us joined hands, making the grounding stronger. Several odd looks greeted me as I approached, but no one said anything.

Someone walked around the circle of people with a basket of ribbons, while two more followed with the sun wheel I helped assemble. The sun-bearers went from person to person, stopping long enough for each to choose a ribbon, then tie it to the wheel.

Drew explained. "You make a wish and concentrate on it while holding it in both hands. Imagine your wish flowing through your arms, into the ribbon. Visualize the outcome, then tie the ribbon to the wheel."

I chose a fuchsia one and made my wish. The drums grew louder as the sun wheel made its way around. I felt a tug, but fortunately my grounding kept me still. After the last person tied their ribbon, the wheel was tossed into the bonfire, releasing all the wishes so they could float up to the gods and goddesses.

The wheel crackled as it burned, then one by one the ribbons rose out of the fire, unscathed. My mouth actually fell open as I watched the smoke rise. Instead of the usual grey, a rainbow of color plumed high. I had no clue that type of magick actually existed. Hell, I had no clue about a lot of things.

The rainbow faded, replaced by grey smoke, but it didn't rise. A plume of dark grey rose from the fire and drifted in my direction. The drums fell silent. No one spoke as it slowly floated towards me, then stopped. A solitary tendril reached out. I conjured an image of a pointing spectre, hovering for a moment, then dissipated with a soft puff. The whispering started as everyone stared at me. I could see Auntie P. talking with Elspeth.

Drew leaned toward me. "That's never happened before. I have a feeling word will spread quickly."

"Word? About what?"

"About you, of course. There's something different about you, Marcy."

"I don't want to be different. I just want to be normal. For a witch, that is."

The weird phenomenon with the smoke dulled the mood considerably. The drumming and singing gradually resumed, but no one seemed to be putting their heart into it.

"This is getting way too weird for me." I turned to Susan. "Would you mind if we left?"

"That's probably a good idea. You are looking rather drained."

Auntie P.'s conversation with Elspeth seemed rather animated. Lots of gesturing and head shaking. After about ten minutes, Auntie joined us, and she didn't look like a happy camper.

"What were you whispering to Elspeth about?" As if I didn't know.

"Your future. She told me what she saw."

"Elspeth read your palm?" Susan looked over at Auntie P. then turned to look at me. "From the looks on both your faces, it wasn't good."

"I don't know. She didn't seem frightened by what she saw, just puzzled. Said I'd been given a gift and asked about my ancestry."

"That's what we were discussing," Auntie P. said. "I'll have to pull out our lineage chart and make some inquiries. One of the elders might recall a story or two about her."

"Her?" Drew asked. "Really? Is it possible?"

"Her who?" I didn't like them talking about me like I wasn't even there. "Can someone fill me in?"

"We refer to her as The Ancient One. A powerful witch and our ancestor, the one from the ballad."

❋ ❋ ❋

Auntie P. told us to gather around the dining room table, then disappeared down the hall. She returned with a large roll of what I assumed to be paper. Once again, I assumed incorrectly. It was a hide of some sort. For all I knew, it came from a dragon or unicorn. Not that far-fetched, considering what I'd experienced tonight.

"This is our most prized family heirloom." She closed her eyes and her lips moved as she mumbled something before untying the ribbon holding the roll. Gently, she unfurled the hide. I leaned over to read it. The printing had been done by different hands, but the meaning was clear. This single piece of rawhide contained my family tree.

"This has been passed down to the eldest daughter for generations. My mother was the last to receive it. When she died, it was to go to Francine, but she'd moved to Canada, and requested it stay here with me. As it rightly belonged to her, it will be given to you."

I looked up at my family. Susan and Drew both smiled and nodded. Auntie P. avoided eye contact. It was the first time I'd heard about this chart. Strange that Granny hadn't wanted it. *Could she have had a premonition about it?* I wasn't at all certain I wanted to be responsible for it, not yet anyway. I ran my hand across the chart, hovering over my mother's name before pointing to one name. "It's fine here for now. What about this Ancient One? Tell me about her."

Auntie pointed to one entry near the top. She moved her finger down to the next entry, the one called the Ancient One, careful not to touch the hide. "She's the first one to give birth to a male. The only one we know about until Montgomery. When the male twin was banished, he cursed our family. The women born after that time didn't have the same power as the generations prior. We each have a particular skill that is stronger than others with that same skill, but we no longer have multiple skills, as in the past, except in extremely diminished capacity. We're gradually losing our special strength. The one trait that made our family superior to the rest." She crinkled her nose. "No, superior's not the right word, but you know what I mean."

"We've never truly believed in the curse," Susan added. "But it is possible in another four or five generations we may not have any power left."

My initial thought was *so what?*, but I hadn't grown up immersed in the magick. It was different for my family. More so, as we apparently came from some sort of witchy royalty.

"I've always been afraid to let Elspeth read my palm," Drew said. "Afraid of finding out our suspicions are true." She put her arm around her mother.

"So what did she see in my palm that had such an effect on her? She didn't seem to want to explain, even after I said I didn't know much about my family history. Then Drew asked for my help and I didn't pursue it."

Auntie P. pointed to the Ancient One. "She's the only one in our family we know of who married for love, and the first one to bear twins, and a boy. Now, we find out you may possess those feelings for someone. Elspeth believes you could be the one to restore the old power our family once possessed. A child conceived both in love and with a seeker, or helper, might restore the power of future generations."

"Whoa! I never said I was marrying Cooper. I only just met him."

"But the door's been opened," Drew said. "Step through and see what happens. If not Cooper, someone else. Explore your feelings."

How could I explore feelings I didn't understand? A picture of Cooper flashed through my mind and I smiled. Then I remembered his touch when he took his phone from me in the garden. The tingle that raced up my arm and filled my body. Could he be the one?

"This is all happening so fast. I need to mull it over. It's late and I'm tired. Excuse me."

After one more glance at the family tree, I ran upstairs and slammed the bedroom door. Leaning back, I banged my head against it. "No, no, no!"

The events of the day overwhelmed me. First, the high I felt at Stonehenge, then all the weird shit at the gathering. My legs still ached a little. Susan had said I looked possessed. *Was I? Could it have been my tormentor from the cemetery, reaching out again?* Only a few weeks ago, I decided to return to the craft and now I was supposed to be responsible for restoring my family's dwindling power? Oh, and not to mention I was supposed to be in love with someone I barely knew, and marry him. *Why me?*

TWENTY-FOUR

I spent the rest of the week going over simple candle magick and learning more about my ancestors. And thinking. A lot of thinking. I wasn't opposed to getting married, but was Cooper *the one*? I hadn't really had time to find out. Maybe in a few months I'd be ready, but from what Mr. Barker said, Cooper would be back in Halifax by then.

How could I marry someone living almost two thousand kilometres away? I doubted we'd even have time to date before he returned home. Would I even miss him? The thought of separation left me empty. I pushed it away as there wasn't enough time to dwell on it.

More important was the revelation it was *my* responsibility to fix my family's power issues. Something that enormous would require a powerful witch, experienced and sure of her abilities. That wasn't me. Witch-wise, I felt like an infant.

Drew set up on the dining room table after breakfast. Today, we worked on candle magick. I progressed quickly, or so I thought.

"Concentrate harder." Drew's frustration grew. "You need to see the flame in your mind. Will it to do what you want it to."

Her frustration added to mine. The earlier lessons with incense and crystals came easily. This stupid candle just wouldn't cooperate. I lashed out with my arms to indicate I gave up. Instead, I hit the candle while still attempting to light it. The wick chose that moment to ignite. I watched helplessly as the candle toppled, flame intact. The tablecloth caught fire.

"Marcy, release it." Drew grabbed my shoulders, shaking me. My concentration broke.

Drew grabbed the vase of flowers we'd removed from the table, and dumped it, flowers and all, over the flames.

"I'm sorry. It's just so maddening not to be able to do something so basic. I'll replace the tablecloth before I go back home. Please tell me it's not a treasured family heirloom."

"Don't worry. It's relatively new and inexpensive. I think we should continue this outside."

"Yeah. Less stuff to burn."

If they were expecting me to be their saviour, they were going to be disappointed.

❋ ❋ ❋

A few days later, I led Auntie P. and a small group of ladies from her circle to the hidden tunnel entrance. As there wasn't a car park nearby, everyone piled into three vehicles. I think they had more equipment than people. It turned out to be a good thing I'd GPS'd the spot, as I had no idea which way to go. One tree looks pretty much like another. A little red fox popped out from under a bush and trotted ahead of us. *Could it be the same fox?*

Every now and then, one of the ladies stopped at a tree. She mumbled something, then carved a small symbol on the trunk. Auntie P. told me she was marking the trail, after asking the tree for permission, of course.

Of course. Doesn't everyone ask trees for permission before slashing them with a blade? I thought about that as we followed the GPS and the fox. Trees were living things. They were sacred. I knew enough to know to ask before cutting twigs off. An offering was supposed to be left. The next time she carved a symbol, I watched. Afterwards, she sprinkled something on the ground.

"Granular fertilizer," Auntie P. whispered. "Always leave something it can use. A gemstone is pretty, but won't help the tree much."

We finally arrived at the mound of ivy-covered earth. The fox winked at me, then trotted off. Two of the witches were already peering through the opening. There were eight of us, so we divvied up the equipment and split into two groups. The lady who marked the trees took charge of one group. I think Auntie called her Trish. I was with Auntie and the other two.

Our exploration seemed more like a scientific expedition. We were armed with high powered flashlights, or torches as the Brits called them. *I wondered why they're called torches?* Everyone had tablets or opened the camera app on their phones, and we had a meter that could detect both gas and oxygen levels. It hadn't occurred to me there might be gas trapped in the tunnels. I really needed to start thinking things through *before* I acted.

Trish brought portable oxygen and masks. *Wish I had some of that equipment earlier.* We split at the alcove. Trish's group stayed there, while Auntie's group went to see where the eastward tunnel went. We only got a few yards when it started.

"Do you hear that?" I asked.

"Hear what, dear?" Auntie P. replied.

"It's like… humming. Let me try something."

I took the same stance as before. One hand on each wall. The humming grew louder, gradually turning into a song.

"Do you recognize the song, Auntie?"

"I don't hear anything, do either of you?"

The other ladies shook their heads.

"It's them. They protected me when I found the caves."

I pressed my hands harder. "Do the same," I instructed.

The four of us stood in a row, hands pressed against the cool dirt walls. The symbols that were carved so many years ago glowed.

"Oh, my." I think that was Stella, or maybe Sheila? They were identical twins.

"Do you hear them?" I asked.

Auntie shrugged. "No, but I feel them. They are weak and need our power." She closed her eyes. "Take as much as you need."

The twins did the same. "My arms are tingling," one of them said.

The other nodded. I think she seemed pleased. One by one, we removed our hands from the walls as the tingling ceased. The symbols continued to glow.

"They've been alone for too long," Auntie P. said. "We'll have to start using the cave and tunnels again. Before we leave, we'll put a protection ward around the entrance. No one but a true witch will be able to see it and enter."

"Thank you," a voice said.

"You're welcome," we all said in unison.

Behind us, we heard more voices. Trish came out of the alcove.

"You won't believe —" She stared at the symbols on the walls. "It happened over here, too, I see."

"We seem to have awoken our ancestral spirts," I said.

"About bloody time." Trish smiled and returned to the alcove.

Nothing spectacular happened again, but the walls for the entire length of the tunnel glowed with symbols. Some were familiar, most were not.

We shared the oxygen when necessary and finally hit a dead end. It looked like the back of a wall.

Auntie ran her hand over it. "Feels like oak, and it has a ward on it. Probably can't see it from the other side, unless you're one of us." She knocked on it. "Sounds pretty thick."

I touched the hinges. "These look old. I'm no expert, but I'd guess they were hand forged. They're basically the same, but not quite. And they're held with small spikes, not nails."

The twins leaned forward for a better look. "Considering how old these caves are, I'm not surprised. They must have stopped using them longer ago than we thought."

We looked at each other and shrugged.

Auntie grinned. "Can you imagine the look on someone's face if their wall suddenly opened up? We don't even know where we are. Could be a business or a house. Maybe it opens up into a loo."

We giggled like little kids as the possible locations whipped through our minds.

"Eww," I said. "What if it opens into an old outhouse?" We all burst out laughing.

"Wait," one twin said. "Trish bought trackers." She dug into her bag and rummaged around. "Here." She held up a small item and waved it.

She attached the button-sized device to the wall and activated it. Trish must have had fun shopping for everything.

We turned back and met up with the other group, then headed into town to a coffee shop. Trish pulled out her laptop and opened the tracking software. The blip was a few blocks away at a ladies clothing store. Unfortunately, no one knew the new owner, so we left the ladies to plan how to get in and find the tunnel entrance.

Auntie wanted me to get back to my lessons. The fun had come to an end. It would take a long time to make certain the cave system was safe enough to use. They could explore the other fork in the tunnel without me. Everyone agreed it probably went to Stonehenge. Not a walk I wanted to make, but I hoped the cave would be ready for use when I returned to England.

✳ ✳ ✳

The weekend finally rolled around, and I packed for my return home with Drew. Auntie P. and Susan lent me some books, but they didn't all fit in the single suitcase I'd brought. *Maybe Drew has room.*

I didn't want to leave, even though I knew I had to. Auntie P. would continue trying to figure out what had attacked me in the cemetery after Granny's burial. Hopefully, that wouldn't take much longer.

I left the overstuffed suitcase and walked to the window. Auntie's garden was so peaceful, and we'd had a few pleasant chats under the canopy of the maple. I pulled out my phone and checked the time, calculating the current time in Ontario. Cooper would still be up. I sent a message on *WhatsApp*, letting him know when I should land and that Drew would be with me. I waited several minutes, but he didn't reply. A wave of disappointment washed over me. Maybe he wasn't "the one" after all.

"Are you packed yet?" Drew stood in the doorway, pointing at my suitcase. "Hurry up. We have to leave soon."

I shoved the phone in my pocket. "Can you take those books? My case is full."

"Think so." She grabbed them off the bed and disappeared. I closed my case and went into the hall.

"They fit." Drew came out of her room, case rolling beside her. "Ready?"

The ride to the airport was quiet. Well, except for Drew. She'd never been to Canada and was super-hyped. I barely heard a word.

Not wanting to have a long goodbye, we hugged Susan and Auntie P. at the drop-off, got our boarding passes, and headed to the gate. I ignored Drew as she continued to natter. All I could think about was my upcoming birthday. Exactly one month away. I was scared about screwing up the ceremony, but glad Drew would be with me.

✳ ✳ ✳

As we waited for our bags to appear on the carrousel in Toronto, a sense of unease crept through me. I looked around and spotted someone watching me. A man leaned against the wall, reading a newspaper. Not once did I see him turn a page. The suit he wore fit well and looked expensive, but he seemed out of place at the airport. I didn't get a good vibe from him, so I moved closer to Drew and spoke low enough so no one else could hear.

"Don't turn around, but there's a man watching us. There's something familiar about him."

Drew nodded. "There's my bag."

She walked around the carrousel rather than waiting for the bag to reach us. Drew looked at the tag and shook her head.

"My mistake. Same brand." When she came back, she leaned close and whispered. "You mean that old guy over by the toilets?"

"Yeah. He hasn't moved from that spot and doesn't appear to be waiting for anyone."

"I got a strange sensation about an hour before we landed. Everyone in the family has that, you know."

"Yep. Mother enjoyed that little super power. Granny didn't bother with it much, but if it was something important, she took notice. I'm like Granny. I've always felt it was an invasion of people's privacy, so I shut it out, but this is really strong."

I turned to take another look at him, but he was gone.

"I don't know what's creepier. Being watched or his sudden disappearance. Now I'll be looking over my shoulder all the time," I said.

"I know what you mean. I don't think he was on our flight. He must be waiting for someone."

The crowd around the carrousel thinned as people retrieved their bags. Drew went to the opposite side so we could each survey different areas of the terminal without constantly turning around. Neither of us spotted the man, and the creepy feeling faded. Drew re-joined me as the few remaining bags circled.

"He was looking at us and I'm certain I should know him." I tried to think where I'd seen him. "Who the heck is he?"

"Beats me. Let's just grab our bags and get out of here. There they are. Figures ours are last off the plane."

We got through customs without any issues and grabbed a cab. As we left the city and headed north, the concrete turned into trees and the traffic thinned.

"It's so different over here." Drew looked out her window, then leaned over to peer out mine. "The building are all so new. I forgot you don't have the same history as England."

"We don't have many buildings more than a few hundred years old. Wish we did."

"I'm glad you don't live in the city."

I nodded. "Used to. I think I'm going to enjoy living back here."

The cabbie headed up the 404 and exited onto Davis Drive, then turned north up Woodbine Avenue. My house wasn't much farther. *My house.* Couldn't get used to that. It'd always be Granny's home.

"There it is," I said.

"Oh, it's lovely. You have lots of privacy, but are still near town."

Drew looked around, trying to peer through the wall of trees. "Can't even see the house."

When we turned into the driveway, the hairs on my arms stood up; a chill ran down my back. I looked at Drew. Her brow furrowed and she looked around. She felt it, too. It increased as soon as my foot hit the ground. A wave of nausea hit. I swallowed hard, then paid the cabbie. We hurried inside, locking the door behind us.

"It's nearby," Drew said

"I have the same feeling as at the airport. Who is he and why is he following us?"

An engine revved. We held hands and peeked out the front window. A motorcycle drove by and slowed as it passed the driveway. The nausea returned, then subsided as the bike sped up and drove out of sight.

"He's gone, for now anyway. At least we can tell when he's around. Funny, it's not my normal sensation. Now, I want to see your workroom. Sounds intriguing. So much better than a simple room in the house."

"Sure, why not? If you're going to help me, there shouldn't be any secrets. This way."

We left our bags by the front door. I went down the hall and pressed the hidden button. The wood panel popped open. I turned on the light and led her downstairs.

"Oh. My. God! This is spectacular. It's the perfect place for drying and mixing herbs. It's warm, not damp, and there's no direct sunlight to dry things too fast."

Drew walked around the room, turning every few steps to take in every square inch.

"I'll bet she gave the builders a special potion to make them forget they did this. Put something in their drink or made them a snack. It's absolutely magnificent. And so quiet."

A click sounded behind us. We both turned. The tiny door in the corner opened a little.

"It's OK. You can come out. Drew's family."

Nenka peeked around the edge of the door. She looked at Drew, then me, before stepping out. "Yes, I see the resemblance."

She looked worried, not her happy self.

"What's wrong?"

"I'm not certain. I've had a bad feeling lately. Ever since that man was here."

"Man? What man? When was he here?" I didn't like the idea of someone creeping around my house while I was in England.

Nenka jumped when I spoke, or rather, when I yelled.

"I didn't mean to startle you. It's just that there was a man watching us at the airport. I'm certain it was him who drove by a minute ago. He was here, on the property?"

"Yes. He walked around the house, looking through the windows, and I saw him in the garden. He felt evil." She wrapped her arms around her body. "I've never felt anything like that."

"Where's Tinkus?" I asked.

"Right here," a voice said from inside the walls. A few seconds later, he came through the door. "Nenka is very upset. I've been trying to calm her for days. Been telling her there's nothing to worry about, but she can tell when I'm lying. Something's not right."

"Maybe we can whip up something to calm her nerves," Drew said.

I smacked my forehead. "Why didn't I think of that? There's camomile growing in the garden. I use it all the time. I have a mixture in the kitchen already prepared. Be right back."

I ran upstairs and rooted through the bottles, looking for the potion. I grabbed it and raced back down. One shelf in the basement held an assortment of various sized bottles. Some were the tiniest I'd ever seen. Granny must have made potions for the gnomes before. I put some of the camomile mixture into a little midnight blue bottle and pressed a teensy little cork into the top.

"Here, this should help. Just put some in your tea."

Nenka took the tiny bottle from me. "Thank you, dear."

Before Tinkus led her through the door, she turned back. "Be very careful," she said, then disappeared into the wall.

"Amazing," Drew said. "It's like they're part of the family. The Fae folk we deal with are helpful, but a little distant. Guess it makes a difference when they live in your house and not in the woods. They're absolutely adorable."

"I don't think Tinkus would appreciate being called adorable, but I know what you mean." I stifled a yawn. "It's only just after suppertime, but my body thinks I'm still in England. I'm afraid of sleeping, though. What if he comes back?"

"Maybe you should consider an alarm system."

"Possibly. But that won't help me sleep tonight." I hugged myself as another chill ran through me.

Drew put her arm around my shoulder. "I feel it, too. Faint. You mentioned the Brigid Protection Spell you did around the house. It won't keep whatever it is off the property, but it will keep it from getting inside."

Only slightly reassured, I agreed to get some sleep, but only after checking every door and window was shut and locked.

TWENTY-FIVE

I ran as fast as I could through the dimly lit garden, not caring how many of the precious herbs and medicinal plants I trampled. I had to get to the woods beyond my property. Stopping in the shadow of an old oak, I turned to see if he followed me. As the clouds moved away from the half-moon, I saw him pace the patio, trying to figure out which way I'd gone. He looked my way. I made myself as small as I could. He turned his head left, then right. Seeming satisfied I wasn't in the garden, he started around the house.

Standing, I took one step back, tripping over an exposed root. I went down with a thud, twigs snapping under my butt. He turned around. I scrambled to my feet and ran. His footsteps closed in, each pounding like thunder in the stillness of the night. Finally, I reached the woods and called out for the Fae folk to help me, but it was too late. My nightgown snagged on a branch. I struggled to free myself. A hand grabbed me and threw me to the ground, tearing the sleeve. I rolled over on my back to see who it was. He stood over me, laughing, then knelt beside me, placing his hands around my throat.

I woke, gasping for air; sweat beaded on my forehead. The dream felt so real. I turned on the lamp on the nightstand and looked at the antique mantle clock. The hands sat at 3:21. I swung my legs over the side of the bed and sat hunched over until my breathing returned to normal. My legs ached as though I'd run a marathon.

Stumbling, I made my way down the hall and into the bathroom. Without bothering to switch on the light, I found the sink and splashed cold water on my face. There wasn't much moonlight coming through the window, but when I raised my head, I caught my reflection. Something wasn't right. Reaching behind me, I switched on the light, gasping when I looked back in the mirror. The sleeve of my nightgown was torn. And my neck! Bruises that looked like finger marks circled my throat. Something in my hair caught my attention. I reached up and touched it. It crinkled. *How did I get a partially dried oak leaf in my hair while sleeping?* I let loose with an ear-piercing scream.

Drew came running down the hall when she heard me scream. "Marcy! Are you all right?"

I held the oak leaf towards her. "How…?"

Drew reached for my torn nightgown. "That must have been a nasty nightmare. Come downstairs and we'll chat until you feel better." She lead me down to the kitchen and made a pot of camomile tea. Between sips, I told her about my dream. My nightmare.

"I was awake before you screamed and felt his presence again. I've never experienced anything like it. It seemed as though someone shrouded me in a heavy blanket, making it difficult to breathe." Drew held the leaf in her hands. "He must have strong powers to invade your sleep. Leaving marks on someone is not uncommon in dream invasion, but to bring back something physical. Wow, that's special. I've never heard of that before."

"Well, I don't feel special. Who the heliodor is this guy? What does he want? Why me?"

"Did you see his face?"

"No. He stayed in the shadows. When he caught up with me, the moon was behind him, so all I saw was his outline. But his hands…." I closed my eyes to try and get a better picture of them. "It doesn't make sense. He chased me and pretty much kept up with me, like he was my age, ya know? But the hands around my throat were old. I can still see them as they came toward me. Wrinkled and covered with age spots."

"Dream invasion is not allowed in our circles. And to be violent, that sounds like dark magick. I need to call Mum. Maybe she can speak with Gran and figure something out."

"It's three thirty in the morning, Drew. I think it can wait a few hours."

"You forget, there's a five hours' time diff. They're probably having breakfast. Finish your tea and go back to bed. I'm sure you'll be safe. I can tell he's no longer around."

I felt violated, but Drew was right. Whoever it was, wasn't around any longer. But if he'd been in my dream, how could Drew detect him? His physical body had to be near. At least I think it did. I hadn't seen anyone at the cemetery, but there was that man at the airport and someone on a motorcycle. Did the dream invasion mean I'd not been entirely successful with the protection around the house? I didn't like the thought of that and planned to fix it with something more powerful, but what?

The soothing tea helped calmed my nerves. Camomile never had that effect on me before.

"Drew, did you add a little hoo-doo to my tea?"

She looked up from the laptop and winked, but admitted nothing. I headed back to bed, already half-asleep from whatever she'd added to my tea, and left Drew to Skype across the ocean.

✸ ✸ ✸

A few hours later, I dragged myself into the kitchen just as Drew closed her laptop. From the empty pods on the counter, it looked like Drew had more than one cup of tea. There were empties for Numi Organic Rooibos Chai, Aged Earl Grey, and one Higgins & Burke Tame Dragon. I grabbed my usual Snickerdoodle, fumbling to get it in the machine. If I didn't know better, I'd say I had a hangover. Didn't want to know what that extra ingredient Drew gave me was. While I waited for my coffee cup to fill with my morning energizer, I turned to Drew.

"You haven't been on Skype all this time, have you?"

"No, been on and off a few times. I called Mum and told her about your dream invasion. Only chatted a few minutes. We rang off so she could talk to Gran about it. I browsed that website I told you about to see if anyone ever posted anything about dream invasion. Nothing. Nothing at all, which doesn't surprise me. The site is for our kind and we don't use dark magick. Besides, people can't discuss stuff like that on the chat boards. It's one of the rules."

I grabbed my freshly brewed Snickerdoodle, inhaling the mixed scents of vanilla and cinnamon, and joined her at the table.

"So we're going in blind with this then?"

"Not completely. Mum called back a bit ago. Gran found something. Unfortunately, it was just a reference, so we'll have to do some research on our own. We don't have any books on the dark arts, and I doubt very much that you'll find any info here. We'll have to find it ourselves and be very careful. We'll need double protection before we even start. Can your helper friend find what we need?"

My helper friend. Mr. Barker, or Cooper? My stomach did a backflip when I thought about Cooper. It was unsettling, yet nice. But how could I think about a relationship with him or anyone else? I needed to sort out who and what I was. And now we were heading down a road we had no business travelling.

I twirled my cup a few times, thinking about what Drew had said. *Do I want to get mixed up with anything dark?* This was getting too freaky, even for me.

"Drew?" I looked up at her. "I'm scared."

She reached over and placed her hand over mine. "Me too, but we have to do something. Whoever this guy is, he's powerful. He's already hurt you more than once, and has to be stopped before it gets more serious."

Drew sat back and reached for the notebook sitting beside the laptop. "I made a few notes from websites I found. Several mentioned the grimoire Gran told me about."

"Wait, what? A grimoire?"

"It's a book of spells, in this case dark magick. Even the name is spooky: *The Munich Manual of Demonic Magick*. Even saying the word demonic gives me the willies. We need to find something like that, and soon."

"I don't want to experience anything like last night again. Scared or not, we have to try. I guess it wouldn't hurt to ask Mr. Barker. He does seem to be able to find things fast. He doesn't open for a couple hours, though. Let's have breakfast, then we can work on some protection spells, talismans, and amulets."

I made a couple of omelettes, and once the dishes were done, we went down to find any protection spells that were in Granny's library. We assembled the necessary items, listing those we had to buy. By 10:00 a.m. we had a pile of a dozen or so books and a fairly long list of necessary supplies. Mr. Barker's book store was just opening, so we set off to see if he could find what we needed.

Drew went over the list on the drive into town, mumbling to herself and changing a few quantities. I found an empty spot near the splash pool beside the community centre.

"Oh, that's lovely," Drew said. "I wish we had time to cool off in it."

"Plenty of time for that later. Come on. The store's just off Main Street."

We crossed at the lights and walked a few feet up a small side street. Mr. Barker's bookstore was in one of the older buildings in town and even had an historical plaque on the wall. A little bell tinkled when I opened the door.

"What a quaint little shop." Drew walked to the closest shelf. "I'm surprised a small town has a bookstore like this."

She pulled a book off the shelf. "A first edition Dickens. I wouldn't think an antique book store could survive in a small town."

"It's a good thing for me I have another source of income."

Drew turned around. "You must be Mr. Barker."

He smiled and nodded. "I guess I must be. Marcy, are you going to introduce me to your beautiful friend?"

"This is my cousin, Drew. She flew back from England with me."

"From your accent, I'd say Surrey. Been there many times. Now, what can I do for you lovely ladies?"

"We're looking for a book. One of your special orders," I said.

"Let me lock the door so we aren't disturbed. Cooper's running some errands for me, and my part-time help doesn't come in until one. We'll have to talk out here so I can watch for customers. What are you looking for? Something on crystals, maybe? Or herbal medicine?"

My body sagged when Mr. Barker said Cooper wasn't in. Could I actually be disappointed I wouldn't see him? Maybe. I needed to concentrate on one thing at a time. Protection was my number one priority.

"No. This is totally different." I bit my bottom lip. "Um, we need a dark magick grimoire, or something like that."

Mr. Barker's skin became translucent. He didn't really have a rosy completion to start with, and it surprised me how much paler he got.

"Marcy, are you certain you want to go down that road?"

"No, I'm not sure at all, but I have to. Someone is stalking me and I need to find some way to fight back. Drew's already called her mum and Gran, so we have help. We'll be careful."

"I don't know…" He looked up at the ceiling, thinking while fiddling with the bottom button on his cardigan.

Maybe this wasn't such a good idea after all. Unfortunately, we had no other option. I completely understood his hesitation.

"I didn't want to show you this, but I have no choice." I reached up and removed the silk scarf that I'd wrapped around my bruised throat.

"Someone attacked you?" He grabbed my shoulders, finally making eye contact. "Call the police. Let them deal with it."

"I can't. He did this in my dream."

His hands dropped and he stepped back. "Dear God. Dark magick. I know what you need, but it's dangerous."

"My mum and Gran will guide us," Drew said. "We have to figure out what he's doing so we can put up the right protection. If it's not strong enough, he'll continue getting through, and Marcy might not be so lucky next time."

"I believe I know where to locate what you're looking for, but I hesitate to procure it. Anyone untrained in the dark arts dabbling with such things can conjure up all sorts of evil. Uncontrollable evil."

I walked over to Mr. Barker and placed my arm around his boney shoulders.

"I've known you for years, and I consider you a friend and confidant. Family. You know I'd never do anything without fully understanding everything. We're not doing this alone."

A knock on the window interrupted us. A well-dressed man pointed at his watch, then the door. Drew was closest, so she unlocked it. It barely clicked open when he pushed in, the knob hitting Drew on her hip. She glared at his back and swore. He checked the time again and gave Mr. Barker a dirty look before heading to one of the shelves. Something about him gave me the creeps.

He seemed to know what he was looking for. The man grabbed a book, then came back right away. As he passed me, he gave me the strangest smile. A smile that got my spidey-senses tingling. The corners of his lips curved up, but the smile never reached his eyes. He stopped for a few seconds, then went to the counter to make his purchase. Drew locked the door as soon as he left. She turned towards me and we both stiffened. In unison, we said, "He's nearby."

"Who's nearby?" Mr. Barker asked.

I touched my throat. "The man who did this."

"And you both can feel his presence? Amazing."

"Please, Mr. Barker. Can you get the book? We need to know how he's doing this so we can fight him.

"I'll make my inquiries. It won't be cheap, but I'm certain I can get what you need in a day or two."

"I'm not bothered about the cost," I said.

I could tell he was genuinely concerned. Normally, Mr. Barker was cheery, but he hadn't smiled once since I removed my silk scarf. Why would he? It wasn't funny. *What am I getting myself into?*

We thanked him and Drew unlocked the front door, opening it only a few inches at first. "Can you feel it?" she asked.

"It's faded, but it's not gone."

We stepped out onto the sidewalk and looked around. People went in and out of the shops, but the old man from the airport was nowhere to be seen.

"You know what?" I said, as we waited for the light to turn green. "The feeling was strongest when that guy came into the shop, but I didn't sense anything *from* him."

"If this mystery man is into dark magick, he could have taken temporary control of that man to find out what we were up to."

I raised an eyebrow. "How do you know so much about black magick?"

"Don't worry cousin. I don't practice it, I've just read about it." She opened the passenger door and slid in. "When reading up on our magick, it's frequently mentioned. Sort of a 'don't do this' type of thing."

"Sure, whatever. Next stop, Sharon. I know a store where we should be able to get everything we need to protect ourselves and hopefully fight back. It's called the Garden Witch."

There were so many things we needed. I needed. A general protection amulet or evil eye bead just wasn't gonna cut it. One of the items we had to get was a hazel branch. I could snip one off the tree at the back of the property. Good old Granny. She always grew or bought plants that had a purpose. If only she'd known how handy that hazel tree would be.

The feeling of the creepy old guy died off, so we felt safe driving out. Something told me we needed to be quick, though. I wanted to enhance the protection around the house and as much of the property as possible. Especially the Fae door on the willow. I had plenty of crystals, but we'd need blue gemstones for most of the protection spells. Lots of them. I drove as fast as I dared up Leslie Street. Fortunately, it wasn't far.

By the time we finished buying crystals, gemstones, incense, oils, and candles, the store seemed rather empty, but the owner was quite happy. In addition to blue gems, we needed items in red and black, too. Dried heather and lavender weren't a problem as I had plenty, both in the garden and hanging in the magick room. They had an extensive selection of dried herbs, so if I needed something that wasn't growing in the garden or already dried, I knew where to go. I picked up a workshop flyer while I was there.

We hurried back home, and while Drew got everything ready downstairs, I went out to the hazel. I asked the tree for permission to take a branch, then left a small offering at its base. I sprinkled some fertilizer around the trunk and placed a small black onyx beside it. The fertilizer was a gift for the tree, something it needed. The stone wasn't necessary, but black helped absorb or fight negativity. If I could, I'd place a ring of them around the entire perimeter of my three acres.

I circled the tree, searching for the perfect stick. Not too long, not too thin. My eyes were drawn to a branch just above my head. One solitary twig grew down, pointing at me. It was perfectly straight and thick enough to use to draw the protective circles in the ground around the house. I gently snipped it off and thanked the tree.

Before I could get the snippers back in my pocket, a sharp pain hit my temples. I dropped to my knees and tried rubbing the pain away. The throbbing moved behind my eyes, blinding me. *Him.*

The man from my nightmare. The man at the airport. How did he cloak his presence? I struggled to think, to clear my mind, and get past the pain. The hazel stick! I tried to remember one of the protection spells. Fighting the increasing pressure in my head, I slowly drew a circle around me and repeated one of the chants. Or was it a mish-mash of several chants? I just hoped it worked. I crawled around, barely able to complete the circle. The pain was unbearable. I tried to scream, but no sound came out. My eyes watered. My vision blurred until darkness took over.

Next thing I knew, Drew was shaking me and calling my name.

TWENTY-SIX

"Marcy, what happened? Are you all right? My God! You're so pale."

I tried to sit up, but was too weak. My head spun, my vision blurred. At least the pain was gone.

"I think I'm OK. I'm not really sure what happened. It was horrible. I've never felt anything like that. Give me a minute and I'll be fine, I think. Just let me rest a moment."

"You're not resting out here. Let's get you inside."

With Drew's help, I slowly got to my feet, still clutching the stick. Blood covered my palms where my nails had dug in. I couldn't recall clenching my fists so tight. Clinging to Drew for support, we started back to the house. I stopped suddenly, almost toppling Drew.

"Oh, wait a minute." I turned and looked around, then took a step and almost fell over when I reached for the snippers. Drew gave me one of those "seriously?" looks. I gave a weak grin and shrugged.

"Old habits die hard. Granny would kill me for leaving a tool outside."

Drew rolled her eyes. "Come on. We need to get you inside in case he comes back."

She helped me down to the magick room. I sat on the bench by the table while Drew blessed one of the crystals we'd just purchased. It already had a hole drilled in it, so she hung it on a blood red silk cord, also one of today's purchases. She held it over a cone of wisteria incense for protection against evil, then hung it around my neck.

"We need to place a protective seal on all the windows and doors," Drew said. "Tomorrow we can start on the property. The Brigid Protection spell should've worked. Whoever is doing this must be extremely powerful to get through it."

"The Fae door. We need to protect that now. I hope there aren't any others outside. I'll have to ask Nenka or Tinkus. Strange they're not around. They must have felt him too."

I searched the shelves for peppermint oil and dabbed several drops on my temples, hoping to ease the headache that lingered. With shaking hands, I wove a tiny wreath of lavender, heather, and hyssop, combining dried and fresh, then blessed five gemstones to protect against negative energy—Chrysoprase, Black Onyx, Topaz, Citrine, and Jet. The wreath looked like it'd been run over, but that didn't matter. As long as it worked.

We rushed out to the willow. Drew fastened the wreath to the door with a tack while I placed the five gemstones in a circle around the base of the tree. I brought the hazel stick and drew a circle enclosing the willow trunk and the ring of stones, repeating one chant in Granny's books.

> "Protect us from all that is harmful,
>
> Repel the evil that is sent to me
>
> This shield holds back all negativity,
>
> As I will, so mote it be."

I looked over at Drew and grinned. "Double circle, double protection, right? Now, let's get out of here and safeguard the doors and windows."

By the time we finished blessing and enhancing the protective properties of the crystals and gemstones, working with the lavender, heather, and other plants, and placing them around every opening we could find, it was after 1:00 a.m It wasn't until we'd finished. I realized my headache had vanished and my hands no longer shook.

Both Drew and I could barely keep our eyes open. Once I stopped moving and finally sat, all the energy drained out of me. I think I set a new record for energy depletion. I yawned first, then Drew.

"That should do for now." She flopped beside me on the sofa in the living room. "He's more powerful than I imagined, so we'll need to do more research. I'll call Mum in the morning and see if she can think of something else we can do. I can't believe he managed to sneak up on you like that. I didn't even feel him at first. It's a good thing you were able to put yourself inside a protective circle."

"Will what we've done so far stop him from invading my dreams again? It there something else I can do?"

"Didn't I see a dreamcatcher around here somewhere?"

"Hanging in the sunporch. It's a real one, not mass produced. They're made by a First Nations gentleman who lives nearby. I've been meaning to pick up another. They're so beautiful."

Drew scurried to the sunporch and came back with it. "This will be more useful hanging over your bed. It's called a dreamcatcher for a reason, you know. Get your sage and smudging bowl."

I lit up the white sage and let the smoke permeate all around the dreamcatcher. Drew carried it up to my room while I followed behind, smudging the hall and then my room. Drew tied my dreamcatcher to the headboard, and I fanned the smoke around the bed, then placed the bowl and sage on my dresser. I knew it would burn itself out by the time I fell asleep.

Drew went to her room. I changed and crawled into bed. The entire house had a peculiar, but pleasant scent, with the mixture of the dried flowers and incense. I inhaled deeply and fell asleep almost immediately. Next thing I knew was outside again, back by the hazel tree.

I woke the next morning fairly well rested. All the protection spells and assorted wreaths and gems seemed to have worked, for now. I looked at the clock. *Almost eleven.* I laid back and closed my eyes. *Coffee!* I sat up and inhaled. *And bacon! Drew must be up.* I scrambled out of bed and put on the jeans I'd discarded on the floor, then pulled a clean tee out of the drawer. When I walked into the kitchen, Drew sat at the table with a plate of scrambled eggs and bacon.

"I got up about thirty minutes ago. Guess yesterday's excitement wore us both out. I made plenty of bacon. Didn't know how you liked your eggs."

I walked over to the stove and picked up a piece of the bacon. Barely warm, but crispy. I stuffed it in my mouth and grabbed a paper towel to lay the rest on to absorb the grease. I decided on an omelet and crumpled up some of the bacon, dropping it into the mixture. The rest of it went into the microwave to warm up. When everything was ready, I took my plate and the remaining bacon to the table.

"You look well rested. No dreams?" Drew asked.

"I had one, but it wasn't as bad as the other. That man was there, but he stayed away. He approached me, but stopped at the edge of the property. I stood under the hazel, pretty much in the same spot where you found me. He put his hand out, as though reaching for me, but pulled back. He reached out again and grinned. Not a pleasant grin, either. Gave me the willies. Then he laughed. I think he was surprised, amused even, that we put up more protection. I have a horrible feeling he'll be back with something to combat it. I didn't feel at all threatened this time, so I slept surprisingly well. Hopefully, Mr. Barker can find what we need."

"If this guy is older, he'll have a lot more practise and will be much stronger than either of us. He probably thought it would be as easy as the first time, so wouldn't have been prepared to fight any spells."

"I can't get over how familiar he looks. I got a better look at him this time." I gestured with the last piece of my bacon. "I remember a mark on the left side of his face. I think it's called a port-wine stain. But I don't know anyone with that type of mark. I don't think he's as old as I first thought. Maybe in his sixties."

"At least we have something to identify him by," Drew said.

I picked up the dishes and took them to the sink to wash them. Drew picked up the tea-towel to dry.

"Tell me, did you really not have any clue we were witches?"

"It never occurred to me we were anything other than psychic. Yes, it crossed my mind once or twice, but I figured it was my imagination. Who believes in witches? The premonitions were pretty cool at first.

"I remember once when I was in grade six or seven, I went to the store with mother and we were in line behind this old lady. That day, my perception of our skills changed. I appreciated them more. This lady kept putting items aside because she couldn't afford them. She was rummaging through her purse, looking for change, and had pulled out an envelope. Mother looked at the name and address, then pulled me out of the line. Mother had tapped into her and she whispered to me that the lady was struggling and very hungry. We picked up the things the old lady had put aside and got some fresh fruit and veggies. Enough to last a few days without spoiling."

The memory of that day was still fresh in my mind, and I stopped to compose myself. I pressed a finger to the corner of my eye, stopping a tear. I looked over at Drew and she smiled at me, waiting for me to continue.

"Go on. What did you do?"

"We boxed up the extra groceries and Mother wrote on a card. It's funny that I remember that day so well, but can't recall what she wrote. Something about a guardian angel. That's the day I realized our special skills could help people, and not just be 'an invasion', as Granny called it."

"Yes, it's always nice when we can help others, especially without them knowing."

"The lady was walking, pulling a bundle-buggy, so we got to her house before she did. Mother parked at the corner and I carried the box and left it on her front porch. The neighbor saw me, so I winked and put my finger to my lips. She looked at me like I had three heads, but went back to her garden."

I cleared my throat as the words caught. I still held the first plate I'd started washing. I rinsed it and handed it to Drew.

"I can only imagine what the neighbor thought. I know I'd be curious," Drew said.

"I ran back to the car and we sat waiting for the lady to come home. Eventually, she came around the corner and slowly made her way up the walk to the house. We watched as the neighbor came over and helped her into the house with the box of food."

My voice wavered. I choked back the tears. I couldn't continue. Drew reached over and put her hand over mine.

"That was so nice. Our family has always been able to tap into people, but your mother and gran were exceptionally good at it," Drew said. "You have it, too. Your side of the family is better at that than ours. I think it has something to do with our dwindling powers."

"That's not the best part. A few weeks later, I was at the Dairy Queen and a lady approached me. She looked familiar, but I couldn't place her until she said, 'It was you, wasn't it? The girl who left the box of food.'

"It was the neighbor who saw me put the box on the porch. She told me that until that day she hadn't realized her neighbor was struggling. She helped put the groceries away and couldn't believe how little food there was. She'd lived there for two years and didn't even know the lady's name. Only knew the neighbors with kids the same age as hers. Said she spoke with some of the mothers and they organized a senior neighbor watch. Seems there were a lot of elderly people in their area. They started checking on them, helping them with chores and sharing veggies they grew in their gardens."

I forgot about the dishes in the sink. It was more important that I told Drew my story.

"I ran home afterwards and told Mother. We sat and cried for ages. Imagine. One box of food ended up helping an entire neighborhood. I felt so proud and opened myself up more after that. It's such a wonderful feeling to help people. Until just before high school when I shut everything out, but it's time to open up again."

I couldn't stop the tears any longer and they flowed down my cheeks. Drew started crying, too. We stood in front of the sink, hugging each other for several minutes.

"I wish I could tap into people as easily as your family," Drew said. "I have my own special skills, though. I enjoy being able to help people with my jewellery. Crystals and gemstones are something we have in common. We can combine our knowledge and, together, we can fight him. We *will* win."

TWENTY-SEVEN

We eventually stopped blubbering and got back to reality. Time to continue my crash course in magick. I already had the crystals down pat, and was half-way decent with the herbs, but I'd let my psychic abilities go dormant after all the issues in high school. One thing I had no inkling about was casting spells, so Drew decided to combine my lessons. The mall was as good a place as any, and one of the few spots open on Canada Day.

We headed straight for the food court and sat off to the side. "I want you to relax and open your mind." Drew kept her voice low. "Let your thoughts mingle with everyone else's."

I dropped my wall and let it all in. For about five seconds.

"Holy Heliodore, Drew. Why didn't you warn me?"

She grinned. "The noise can be a tad loud until you get used to it."

"A tad? That doesn't even begin to cover it. Imagine the loudest storm you've heard, add the roar of voices when hundreds of people are talking at once. Then multiply it by a gazillion."

"Don't be such a drama queen, Marcy. You're just not used to letting other's thoughts in."

I cradled my head, trying to keep it from splitting in two. "Not exaggerating, cuz."

Drew reached across the table and touched my arm. I looked up at her.

"My God, Marcy. You're pale. You're much more sensitive than I thought. Relax. We'll try again in a few minutes."

With my wall back up, it didn't take long to recover. "I'm ready."

"Are you certain?"

I nodded.

"This time, let your wall down a bit at a time. Try to control who you let in. Look around and zero in on just one person. Concentrate on that person *before* you open up."

I was skeptical, but what the heck? Couldn't be any worse. Looking around, I saw a man sitting alone. I stared at him and concentrated. Everyone else disappeared from my view, kind of like tunnel vision. All I saw was this one man, framed in darkness. I opened my mind, a little slower this time, and felt sadness, sorrow. He was thinking about a woman and child and I saw what he remembered. A picnic one sunny day. Then the cemetery and two graves. I gasped and closed my mind.

"Oh Drew, I don't think I want to do this." I told her what I saw. "This is why Granny didn't use that particular skill."

"Strange that you actually saw his memories. You should only be able to pick up on feelings."

"Is that what my tormentor is doing? Am I just as bad, invading someone's mind without their consent?"

"It's not the same. Fine line, though. You aren't doing anything malicious. Remember what you told me about the lady your mother read at the store? With practise, you'll be able to tell who needs help and avoid sad memories. I agree it is a form of invasion, but you just need some fine tuning. Let's go find somewhere we can light the candles and incense and practice some spells."

When we left, I made a point of passing the man's table and smiling at him. I wanted to hug him and tell him everything would be OK, but that would be just plain weird.

"Let's go to Fairy Lake. People BBQ there, so a few candles shouldn't be an issue. We can sit on the grass out of the way of the festivities."

"Fairy Lake? How appropriate."

Parking was at a premium. The Canada Day activities were underway, and the park was packed with happy families, dogs, and couples.

Drew had assembled what she considered "the basics" and put them in a lovely multi-colored tote I bought years ago. She'd packed several different crystals, herbs, candles, a small glass plate, matches, a notebook, pen, and one of Granny's books. Everything but a blanket to sit on.

Quite a few people wandered along the Tom Taylor trail with their strollers and dogs. An elderly couple sat on a bench in the shade enjoying ice cream cones; hers vanilla, his strawberry. Little kids ran around while parents watched and took pictures and videos.

We crossed over the bridge and veered off the trail to the grassy section on the west side of the lake, putting a little distance between us and the loud music coming from a portable stage. For some reason, that spot never seemed to have people on it, just the odd Canada Goose or duck. We'd have to be careful where we sat.

Drew pulled her collection from the tote, and I arranged it on the grass. I set the glass plate in front of me and placed a white candle on it. The crystals were lined up along the left and the herbs on the right. Drew handed me the notebook, along with the pen.

"You need to write down your spells. Once you figure out what works, you can copy them into your own Book of Shadows. First things first. Time to ground."

We stood side by side, arms down. With the first deep breath, I imagined roots sprouting from my feet and going into the earth. Second breath, I imagined a white light flowing up through my body. Third breath and the light exited from the top of my head and cascaded down and around my body. We were ready to begin.

Drew and I sat cross-legged in front of the items assembled on the ground. I lit a match, picked up the white candle, and held the flame briefly under it to melt the bottom, before sticking it to the plate, barely managing to light the candle before the flame reached my fingers. I glanced around. No one paid us any mind.

"So, what's first, oh Great Master?"

Drew rolled her eyes. "OK, little padawan, concentrate on the couple eating their cones. The people are more spread out, so it shouldn't be as bad as it was in the mall."

I closed my eyes and pictured them. They got closer and closer until I was inside her head.

"Oh my." I opened my eyes and turned to Drew. "She's upset because she lost her wedding ring. She told her husband she took it to be cleaned. Can't bear to tell him the truth."

"That's easy. Simple location spell. Must be one in your grandmother's book. You just need to tweak it to fit you. Use the basics and add intuition." She flipped through the pages for a moment. "Here it is. Start with four blue candles and some jasmine. That's all."

"Wait, if we can do location spells, why can't we find that book Mr. Barker is getting for us? Why use helpers at all?"

"Big diff between these simple spells and what he does. All we're really doing is uncovering memories that the person didn't realize they had. If it works, she'll recall exactly where she last had it, and be able to locate it easily."

I thought for a moment. "OK, I guess I understand. I need the rose quartz. It's a wedding ring she's lost, so what better to use than the love stone?"

I placed the blue candles around the white one. Each represented north, south, east, and west, as well as air, water, fire, earth. I held the rose quartz in my right hand and concentrated. After a few minutes, I visualized the ring. She'd placed it in the jewellery box while putting on hand cream. I could hear her doorbell. She went to answer it and didn't notice the ring slip through some loose stitches. It was caught in the lining of a jewellery box. I tried to send my thoughts to the lady, then put out the blue candles.

"Now I guess I cross my fingers. I've seen them in the coffee shop, so maybe I'll bump into them again. Hopefully, she'll have the ring on her finger. The spell felt complete." I jotted my little spell, as Drew had instructed.

We spent the next few hours reading people and casting simple spells. Mostly missing items or arranging for old acquaintances to cross paths. I felt confident, and Drew seemed satisfied with what I had accomplished.

"Marcy."

"What?"

Drew looked puzzled. "What?"

"You just said my name."

Drew shook her head. "Nope. Must be hearing things." She pointed to a group of teens walking across the nearby bridge. "Probably just misheard one of the girls."

As we packed up everything, I heard it again.

"Marcy."

This time louder, and it seems to come from inside my head. *Schist.* I tucked a piece of crystal in my pocket and strengthened my wall.

"What are you mumbling about?" Drew asked.

"Feeling a little drained, so I thought I'd better fortify my protection. Keep all the voices out."

"Good idea."

If only she knew.

I headed for the path. "Let's grab a coffee and something to eat before heading back home. Cardinal Press Espresso Bar is open today. The owners are really nice and the place has several books in the back. Besides, they make a mean quiche that's available all day."

We strolled through the park over to Main Street. The road was still blocked from the First of July parade, resulting in a crowd of people stretched from one sidewalk to the other. The coffee shop was packed, but I snagged a spot in the back while Drew placed our order. I fiddled with my phone while I waited.

Part of me wanted to text Cooper to update him on today's training. The rest of me felt like an embarrassed teen, totally lacking any shred of confidence. Most of my dates in college were one-offs. Occasionally, a second date took place, but not often. Not that I really cared. I'd felt nothing for any of them. Cooper was different, in more ways than one.

"This is nice." Drew looked around after we sat. "Such lovely paintings on the wall."

"I come here often. It's not unusual to see people working or having meetings back here, and the owners are great at promoting local artists of all types."

Drew pointed at my phone. "Who're you calling?"

"Texting. No one."

She raised an eyebrow.

"Cooper. He's always on my mind. And Auntie P.'s comments about marriage keep running through my mind."

Drew took my phone and read the unsent text. "You're not declaring undying love for the bloke. It's just a casual conversation." She hit send and gave the phone back.

"I can't believe you did that." I smiled. "Thanks."

My phone dinged and I glanced down. "Thumbs up from Cooper."

Our food was ready, so talk of Cooper stopped as we dug in. Hunger satisfied, we headed back home.

We were almost at the car when a sharp pain behind my right ear caused me to stumble. Drew grabbed me before I fell.

"He's here. I can sense him. Are you OK? You look pale." Drew held me steady.

Sharp, vice-like pain behind my eyes blurred my vision. I fought to keep them open as I tumbled onto the passenger seat.

"He's trying to get inside my head again."

Drew took my keys. She fumbled trying to find the ignition. After a few near-misses leaving the parking lot, we raced home. She mumbled *right side, right side* over and over. If I wasn't in so much pain, I'd have laughed. It was the first time she'd driven over here.

By the time we pulled into the driveway, I was almost unconscious. Drew spoke to me as she struggled to get me out of the car, but her voice came from far away. I fell out the door. The pain from the gravel digging into my knees almost brought me out of it. The vice inside my head tightened. White spots appeared when I cracked open an eye. Instead of trees and my house, I saw colorless blobs.

I had a vague recollection of Drew helping me inside and down to the basement. I heard her rummage around, talking to someone. Probably Nenka or Tinkus. I slumped on the bench beside the table, head cradled in my arms.

Once more, the vice-like grip tightened. My head exploded as he took me away.

I was outside again. The pain gone. I stood in total darkness. I waited for my eyes to adjust so I could see where he'd taken me. Nothing. Absolutely nothing. No shapes. No sounds. Just a whole lot of nothingness.

"Thought you could block me, *little one?*"

I jumped at the sudden voice behind me. It was little more than a whisper, but it sounded loud in the silence. I twirled around. No one there.

"You're not strong enough." His voice mocked me.

I turned towards the voice. Again, nothing but emptiness. Now that the pain had diminished, I became annoyed and pissed. I stomped my feet.

"Show yourself. Only a coward hides from a *little one*. What are you afraid of? Me? Am I more powerful than you'll admit?"

Silence.

I waited, arms crossed. A figure emerged from the darkness. He stood tall and slender. I guessed him to be in his mid-sixties at the very least, but he moved like a much younger person. His grey hair and wrinkles the only clues as to his age. And the port wine stain. Why did he seem so familiar? I didn't know anyone with that type of mark, but I'd seen it somewhere recently.

"What do you want from me? I've done you no harm. I don't even know you."

"You're one of them. An Adhamh." He practically spit out my name. "Your mother didn't know me, but the look on your grandmother's face before she collapsed was priceless. Francine hadn't seen me in years, decades, but she knew. Much more satisfying when they do."

"My mother? Granny? More satisfying?" His words swirled around my head for a bit, then it sunk in. "Are you saying you had something to do with their deaths?" I remembered Granny's words before she died. *He's not dead. Is this who she referred to?*

The man stood silently for several minutes, a slight grin on his face. "Yes, it's better when they know. I'll let you figure it out, but don't take too long. I don't like to be kept waiting."

He raised his right arm and held it towards me, palm open. He closed his hand as he backed into the darkness. My insides twisted, sending an excruciating pain throughout my body. The room spun. I reached out to steady myself, but found nothing, falling sideways. I curled up in a ball, trying to rock the pain away.

I could hear Drew. I was back in the basement. My gut wrenched and a thick, dark burgundy liquid spewed out. An endless stream covered the table, slopping onto the floor. My energy was spent by the time it finally stopped. I looked around. Everything was covered in what? Blood? The table, floor, walls, herbs. Even Drew and Nenka.

I tried to stand. The splash as I hit the floor was the last thing I remembered.

TWENTY-EIGHT

I opened my eyes a crack. Nenka stood on the table, leaning towards me. "Marcy, are you all right? Please don't be dead."

The pain had eased up, but the light bothered my eyes. Propping my elbows on the table, I cradled my head in my hands.

"The table! It's clean. Did I imagine it?"

"No, it happened." Drew came around the table and hugged me. "I've never been so scared in my life. I thought you'd died."

My eyes adjusted to the light, and I looked around. The mess had been cleaned up. Except for Drew and Nenka. I looked down at myself and almost puked. My clothes were soaked in whatever came out of me. And the smell. No wonder Drew thought I'd died. I gagged. The motion sent a flurry of pain through me.

"It hurts so bad, Drew. What happened? How long was I out?"

"Couple of hours. I can mix you some peppermint if you feel queasy, but you should see a doctor."

"And tell him what, exactly? No. I'm sure Granny has a recipe in one of her books. I'll be fine. How did you clean up so fast?"

"Tinkus mostly. House gnomes are quite useful for cleaning up messes. I think we both need a shower. Maybe a soak for you. Add lavender oil to the water."

I didn't feel strong enough to move yet.

"I think he had something to do with Mother's and Granny's deaths. He didn't come right out and say so, but when I asked him, he said 'it's better when they know'. Granny recognized him, apparently. Now, he wants me to figure out who he is. Then he's going to kill me if I can't figure it out. I'm certain he'll still kill me. I lose either way."

I slammed my palms on the table.

"How am I supposed to figure out who he is? He looks familiar, but I'm certain I've never met him. That mark on his face is quite distinct."

"Maybe we could try a séance. Ask your grandmother who he is."

I glared at Drew. "Very funny. This is serious. That bastard wants to kill me."

"I'm very serious, Marcy. Your mother was a fortune teller. She conducted séances and could connect with those in the other realm. Maybe you can too."

"I really wish Mother had forced me to learn all this."

"That wouldn't have worked," Nenka said. "If you don't believe with your heart, the magick won't come. You knew us as a child, but that was before you stopped believing, stopped learning. Then you could no longer see us. That may be why you don't remember us when you lived here after your mother passed. We didn't hide from you, you just didn't notice us. You blocked everything, but when your grandmother died and you decided to learn the family ways, you unlocked that part of your mind."

"OK, I'm beginning to understand. So, I could see the Fae doors and you when I was little? I believed until I was about twelve or thirteen. That's when the teasing started and I shut it all out."

Nenka's eyes twinkled as she smiled. "When you decided you didn't want to learn any more of your family ways, you may have inadvertently given yourself a forget spell. Now that you're learning the craft again, it may wear off."

"I put a spell on myself without even trying? That's a frightening thought." I shuttered as that sunk in. Control would be essential in my training.

"That's why you need a teacher," Drew said. "It can be very dangerous if you don't know what you're doing. You don't mess with magick, or Ouija boards, for that matter. Too many things can go wrong. A lot of people think those boards are just a game, not real. Most times it's harmless, but sometimes they hit the right combo with their questions or chants and bad things happen."

I nodded. "I've heard that. Mother and Granny both steered clear of Ouija boards and would never let me have one. I remember I was shopping with Mother and we went into a store that carried them. When we walked past them, she wrapped her hand around her pendant and whispered something. I assumed it was a Pagan version of how a Catholic crosses themselves."

Drew shrugged. "Something like that. She could have been saying a protection spell or even a blessing. You're looking much better, by the way. Pain gone?"

I wiggled my hand. "More or less. I can still feel it, but it's manageable," I lied. "I can function. We need to find stronger protection, though."

"As long as you're better, I'll leave you with your cousin. The garden doesn't take care of itself. And I need to replace most of the herbs."

Nenka's furrowed brow smoothed, and the twinkle in her eyes grew bright again. She hopped from the table to the bench and down to the floor. She stopped long enough to rub her knees before disappearing behind the little door. I made a mental note to rig up some sort of ladder so she could get on and off the table easier, and mix up some herbs for her joints. She really was a dear.

I turned my attention back to Drew. "So, any suggestions?"

"I texted Mum. She and Gran are going to email some stronger protection spells and directions for more powerful charms and amulets. Hopefully, they find something soon."

"I'm ready to clean up."

"Good idea." Drew wrinkled her nose at the stench radiating off us. "We should leave our clothes down here to avoid dripping through the house."

Nenka disappeared through the Fae door while Drew and I stripped down to bra and panties before heading upstairs. It took me twice as long as normal. Each step sent an excruciating pain through me. Drew said nothing, but the look on her face told me she knew it was worse than I'd let on.

As instructed by Drew, I took a bath and poured lavender oil in. It didn't help the pain much, but I came out more relaxed. Maybe I *should* seek a doctor. I'd have to ask Auntie if witches went to medical school. I could certainly use a witch-born doctor right about now. A regular doctor wouldn't be able to diagnose or treat me. The sudden release felt good despite the pain it caused. Drew had already returned to the basement by the time I dragged myself down. She sat at the table mixing herbs.

"Hopefully, this will ease some of your discomfort." Drew handed me a jar and told me to drink.

It tasted awful, and it only eased the pain slightly.

I thought about what my mystery psycho said. He wanted me to figure out who he was first. *First.* I shuttered at the thought of what he might be planning.

"OK, let's think this out." I shook my arms and hands, trying to calm myself. It usually worked, but not this time. My anxiety was too high. "He indicated he wants me to discover his identity. I also got the distinct impression he was responsible for both Granny's and Mother's deaths. Granny's death certificate says heart attack. That never felt right, but the police didn't bother with an investigation. I need to get my hands on the police reports from Mother's accident and find out the details. No clue how. Most importantly, I need to stay alive. At least that's something I can work on, with your help."

Drew got up and walked over to the shelves where Granny had stored her dried herbs and oils.

"I can help with the police reports." Drew pulled a few bottles off the shelves, checking the hand-written labels. I watched as she went through bottle after bottle, finally settling on calamus root, licorice root, bergamot, and castor oil.

"I'll whip up a simple potion that will make the police give you access to the records without any fuss."

"And just how am I supposed to get a cop to drink a magick potion?"

"No, not a potion that you drink. You wear it like perfume.

"Seriously?"

"Seriously. Now get me an empty jar and the mortar and pestle, then light a white candle."

I did as asked and rubbed my temples as I watched her crush the herbs and mix them into the oil. Drew finished in less than ten minutes. Carefully, she poured the contents into the small, deep-purple jar I'd found, then sealed it with a cork. It was impossible to tell there was anything inside. When she handed it to me, it warmed my hand.

"Why is the bottle doing that? You didn't heat anything."

"It's the magick. You must have noticed it before when you helped your grandmother mix up her potions and medicines."

I shrugged. "Never really paid that much attention. Maybe I just forgot. If I put a spell on myself, I hope it wears off soon. Isn't there a counter-spell I can do?"

"Probably, but unless you know exactly what you said, it's a little difficult to reverse it. I'll ask Gran or Mum next time I contact one of them. Meanwhile, why don't you see if you can get a look at the police report on your mother? I'll work on dinner while you're gone and check to see if Mum has sent any information on more protection for you."

"Sure, why not? I've got nothing to lose. Fingers crossed."

I slipped the little bottle into my jeans pocket and we headed upstairs. It was just past three-thirty, so I had plenty of time. It's not like the police station ever closed. I was hoping it would be busy so the officers would be distracted, just in case my special perfume didn't work.

The drive into town took longer than usual. The pain in my gut jabbed every time I turned to check traffic. Fortunately, rush hour hadn't hit high gear. I found a parking spot near the station and walked to the building. The original jail still stood and was in use, but a few years ago, they built an addition. The architect did a fabulous job blending it in. From the outside, it looked very similar to the old jail, except the bricks weren't exactly the same color. I remembered Granny telling me they used bricks from a building that had been destroyed. I'd never had occasion to go into the new building, even though I'd passed it many times.

I walked past it again and kept going. After my third pass, I stopped and turned around. If I didn't go in now, I never would. One step at a time, I climbed the half-dozen steps leading to the front door. Even though it took less than thirty seconds, it felt like an hour. I grabbed the door when someone came out and walked inside.

The brightness took me by surprise and hurt my eyes a little. It wasn't noisy, but there was a constant buzz from the voices, so I threw up my wall. I pulled the bottle out of my pocket and dabbed some of the potion behind both ears and on my wrists, then walked up to the front desk, fingers crossed it wouldn't be a woman on duty.

"Excuse me," I said. The male officer looked up.

"Um, is there someone I can talk to about maybe seeing an old police report?"

He had a slightly confused look on his face, and I thought he was going to tell me to leave. He sniffed the air and cocked his head, noticing the bewitched perfume.

I waited.

He smiled.

"Certainly, Miss. I can assist you. What is the nature of your enquiry?"

"Well, I'd like to see the report on my mother's car accident. It happened a while ago. Back in 2009, in May.

"It's closed then?"

I nodded

"Everything's been digitized. You'll have to fill out a Freedom of Information form. I can give you the website."

My heart sank. It'd probably take months to receive the information. "Are you certain there's nothing here?"

"Sorry, Miss. I can look up the case file number for you. What's your mother's name?"

I gave him her name and repeated the date of the accident.

"Well, that's interesting." He scratched his head.

"Please don't tell me her file is missing or sealed or something."

"Says here the box is still in the evidence locker, even though everything's been scanned. Closed cases shouldn't still be here."

Could my uncle's magick be responsible for the oversight? "Would I be able to go through it?" I crossed my fingers and toes.

He shrugged. "Don't see why not."

He picked up the phone and called someone, asking them to pull the evidence box. I hadn't thought about a box. What would I find in it? I wasn't sure I wanted to know. I'd only planned on reading a report. Despite the temperate air in the building, a sudden chill wrapped around my body. I didn't know how bad the accident had been. Could I handle graphic pictures or blood-stained items?

He hung up and directed me to a room in the basement.

My finger hovered in front of the elevator button. I wanted to bolt out of the station, but my feet wouldn't move. *I have to do this.* I stabbed the button and the doors whooshed open. Two levels down, I exited. There were plenty of signs on the walls, so I had no trouble finding the room.

I signed in and left my bag with the officer in charge, as well as submitted to a quick scan with the police version of a magick wand. Satisfied I wasn't a threat, she found the box and told me to sit at one of the desks. The box had a bit of weight to it. I figured anything personal had been given to Granny. I smiled as I pictured Mother's amulet, now lying on my dresser. It's not like it was a major crime, so there shouldn't be tons of evidence, so why so heavy? I lifted the lid and peeked inside.

Relief swept through me—no blood-soaked clothing. Maybe it wouldn't be so bad after all.

A folder sat on top of something. I removed the file and discovered a couple of plaster casts of tire marks. I left them in the box and opened the folder. Quite a few photographs of the accident scene spilled out. No one had ever told me exactly what happened to her, so I wasn't prepared for what I saw.

Mostly close-ups of the tire marks in the grass, and several shots of the road leading to the place she went through the wooden guard rail. They showed nothing but broken timber and tire indentations in the grass. And numerous shots of the car, from all angles, distant and close-up. I gasped when I came to the one with my mother still inside. Bile rose, burning my throat. I quickly turned it face down. I cried uncontrollably.

The officer came over and placed a box of tissues on the desk, then went back to her post.

No wonder no one had told me much. It was difficult now. I couldn't imagine how I would've reacted back then. I was only fifteen. I let the tears flow until I was cried out. I didn't want to look at any more pictures, so I read the reports.

There had been no indication of her trying to avoid an animal or other vehicle. I thought back to the picture of the road. *No skid marks.* She hadn't braked for anything and the road was dry.

The mechanic's report said nothing was wrong with the car. The coroner's report showed no alcohol or drugs in her system, and no sign of any health issues. Absolutely no reason for her to veer off and break through the barrier. It appears as though she just drove off the road. The conclusion, driver error, possibly suicide.

Mother was an excellent driver. Never any tickets. She always drove the posted limit, slower in bad weather. Maybe there *was* a more magickal reason. I put the folder back in the box and returned it to the cop at the evidence locker.

TWENTY-NINE

As I walked into the house, music floated from the kitchen. I stopped at the doorway and watched as Drew bopped and wiggled to the punk beat. Her phone sat on the counter, connected to a small Bluetooth speaker. She prepared a chicken while listening to her favourite group, *The Kinks*. When Dew finished, she picked up the roasting pan and turned around to put it in the oven. She almost dropped it when she spotted me. Her surprise quickly changed to giggles.

"Did you enjoy the show? Just how long have you been standing there?"

"Only a minute. Don't quit your day job."

She stuck her tongue out and put the chicken in to cook, then sat at the table. "Sit. Tell me what happened. Did you get the report?"

I told her everything I found and started to cry again when I got to the part about the photo of Mother in the car. Drew said nothing, just reached across and squeezed my hand. There wasn't really anything she could say, and the gesture made me feel better. Not so alone.

"So, did you hear back from your mom about more protection for us?" I asked, once composed.

"Yes, she gave me a few suggestions. She spoke with Gran, who provided a short list of books to check. Said she was sure you'd find copies here. I haven't looked yet. We can do that after dinner. Mum suggested a recall spell for you, but she wasn't certain it would work. It would help if you knew what you said to yourself."

"I was a teenager. I probably said something like 'I wish I wasn't a witch' or something equally stupid. Maybe I *had* known we were witches. At least I'm picking up things fairly fast."

I pushed my chair back from the table and stood. "Why don't you see if you can find those books now? Probably on one of the shelves downstairs. I'll go to the garden and pick some veggies and make a salad. Then we can go through the books while waiting for dinner."

"Sounds like a plan."

Drew went searching while I gathered up enough veggies to last a few days. I made a salad without wounding myself, then cleaned off the string beans and put them in a small pot of water. I put the beets on straight away as they took forever to cook. I was just opening a bottle of wine when Drew returned with three of Granny's books and the laptop.

We sat quietly, reading through the old tomes. If one of us found something of interest, Drew made notes on the computer. I got up occasionally to check on the beets, then put the beans on. We were less than halfway through the books by the time the chicken finished cooking. We chatted about this and that, trying to temporarily distract ourselves from my problems, and consumed a second bottle of wine.

"So, are you going to go out with him?"

"Who? Oh, you mean Cooper? He hasn't asked me. Besides, I'm a little pre-occupied here."

"You could use a distraction. Why don't you ask him? Women have been known to make the first move, you know."

"Yes, I'm well aware of that fact, thank you. I would like to see him again, though. I'll think about it."

Thankfully, my cell went off. I smiled when I saw who it was. "Hi, Mr. Barker. Putting you on speaker."

I sat the phone on the table so Drew could listen in.

"I found a book that I think may help you. Unfortunately, it's rare and extremely expensive. Seven-digit expensive."

My heart felt like it dropped to my feet. I needed to have some idea of what I was up against. There was no possibility my mysterious tormentor was ever going to tell me how he got through my protection, so that book was my only hope. Granny left me well-off, but a seven-digit price tag?

"Thank you for trying, Mr. Barker. I appreciate your help."

"You didn't let me finish, my dear. The owner of the dark grimoire is an acquaintance of mine. Known him for decades. He's agreed to let you look at it. I have the book here now. The only condition is it doesn't leave my possession. He's allowing me to have it for three days. Can you come to the store tomorrow?"

I gave Drew two thumbs-up as I wiggled in the chair. "Oh, yes! Yes, yes, yes. We'll be there first thing. Thank you so much."

Drew watched my changing expressions as my hopes rose, dropped, and rose again.

"He has the book. I can't believe it. We may actually be close to ending this nightmare."

"Did you notice the tone of his voice? We have to be very careful. It'll have to be kept under as much protection as possible. The magick it holds can be very dangerous."

"We only have three days. I want to be there tomorrow as soon as he opens up the store."

Drew thought for a moment.

"We'll need help from Gran. I'll send her an email tonight and ask her if she's available tomorrow. If she's busy, I know she'll change her plans. She'll be able to help us find the protection we need."

We went back to the kitchen to clean up, then finished off the wine while making plans for the morning. Discussion of the grimoire staved off the effect of the wine, and Drew became unusually quiet. I didn't need to be a mind reader to know she was just as nervous and scared as me. But we had no choice.

The spells in that book were not intended for newbies, like me. *What am I getting myself into?* Auntie P. had emailed a list of items to take with us when we looked at the book. I printed it before heading off to bed.

My sleep was undisturbed by the man I'd dubbed Mr. E.—E for evil. It was not a restful slumber, however. I tossed and turned most of the night, thinking about that book and what it might contain. I was uncertain if the grimoire would be at all helpful. Once, I was awakened by what I thought was a scream, but the house was silent.

I finally got up around six thirty, went downstairs, and popped a Snickerdoodle pod in the coffee machine. I sat enjoying the stillness of the morning, listening as the birds gradually started their morning routine. The songs from robins, sparrows, and others I couldn't name drifted through the screen in the kitchen window.

The robins and sparrows were always early risers, followed by the jays and cardinals. I filled the feeder while waiting for the coffee to brew. The birds wasted no time getting to it. Several landed on the feeder as soon as I closed the flap on the top.

I walked back to the house and turned to watch for a moment. A half-dozen already sat eating. I watched as they flitted from the branches to the feeder, down to the ground and back again. One lone squirrel rooted around under the feeder, picking through the seeds spilled as the birds competed for the food. One robin had gone to the birdbath for a quick drink. I left them to their morning meal and went back in to savour my coffee. Drew came down as I washed out my mug. She looked exhausted.

"You look like something the cat dragged in, assuming I had a cat."

Drew sat at the table without speaking. She just stared at the wall. Something was definitely wrong.

"Are you worried about the book?" I had a terrible feeling it was much worse than that.

"What?" She seemed startled. "The book? Oh, no, not that. I suppose I should tell you. Promise you won't tell Mum or Gran."

"If you don't want me to say anything, I won't. What is it?"

Drew seemed a little better, but only just. "He visited me last night. That man. What was it you called him? Mr. E?"

"Holy Heliodor! Are you all right? Did he hurt you?"

"I'm fine. It was only for a moment. To tell you the truth, I'm not completely certain it was him and not just a dream. What he said was so creepy, though."

"What did he say? You have to tell me." I held my breath, hoping he hadn't threatened her. *What did I drag Drew into?*

"It was only one sentence. Actually, only two words."

Drew hugged herself in an attempt to calm down. I waited until she was ready. Finally, she turned and faced me.

"You're next."

"I'm next? Next what?"

"No." Drew took my hand. "That's what he said to *me*. He's planning on coming after me, too."

THIRTY

I leaned back against the table, reeling as if slapped. I'd put her in danger. First Mother, then Granny. Now he was planning on killing me, then Drew. I didn't want to say anything, but I wondered if Drew's mother and grandmother could be next. From the look on Drew's face, I had a hunch she thought the same. I wasn't sure if it was a good or bad thing that high emotional states seem to hinder my ability to read people, especially family. Enough was enough.

"Whoever this jerk is, he's determined to destroy our family. We have to find some way to stop him," I said.

"This sounds like some sort of vendetta." Drew leaned forward, rubbing her temples. I could almost feel the lingering headache that always seemed to accompany *his* visits. "I don't recall ever hearing any stories like that, though. As far as I know, we've never had any issues with anyone. Especially not a dark witch. I'll check my email and see if Gran sent any more info."

"You get your laptop and I'll start breakfast."

Since today was not a day for a leisurely meal, I rooted around the freezer for the box of frozen waffles and put a couple in the four-slot toaster. I got the maple syrup from the fridge, real maple syrup direct from a local sugar bush, and poured some into a small container, then placed it in the microwave. Call me weird, but I like warm syrup on my waffles and pancakes.

The toaster popped up as Drew returned. I put the waffles on plates and put two more in the toaster, then put a tea k-cup in the Keurig for Drew.

Great Aunt Priscilla was available, so Drew Skyped her. We took turns eating and talking, filling Auntie P. in on the latest news—all except the bit about Drew's night-time visitor. When asked about a vendetta; she hesitated. Was she thinking, or trying to figure out a way to break some bad news?

"Gran?" Drew asked. "What is it? Is there someone who has bad feelings towards us?"

"I remember my great grandmother telling me a story about someone." Auntie P. hesitated as she thought.

I tried not to laugh. She made the funniest faces. Her head bobbed, and she scrunched her face, her eyes practically closed. She even smacked herself on the forehead once. I guess she thought that might help loosen her memory. Suddenly, her eyes popped open, and she almost fell out of her chair.

"I've got it. It goes way back. Remember the ancestor who fell in love? The one you seem to take after? The one who had twins." She leaned closer to her computer screen. "I can't recall too much, but the boy was pure evil, according to the lore. All I recall are vague memories. Something happened and he turned on his family. After they banished him from the area, no more was said. At least, I don't remember hearing any stories of him returning. No mention of a vendetta or curse or anything like that. Just the one bad ancestor. I'll ask around. See if anyone knows of other tales. Someone in the area might recall hearing about it. If your mother was still alive, she could help."

That took me by surprise.

"Help how? Did she know the stories better than you?"

"Oh, probably not. It's her talent I'm referring to. You do know the fortunes she told were real, don't you?"

"Yes, Aunt Priscilla." I tried not to roll my eyes. "I know that. She was very good. Even the skeptics admired her skill. How would that help? Do you think she could contact your great grandmother or something? I thought only those who passed in the last ten years or so could be contacted. Aren't the really long-passed already gone?"

"Oh, pish-posh. That's total rubbish. Your mother wasn't an ordinary medium. Her power was quite strong. What about you? Have you tried to contact anyone from the other side?"

"Me? No. It never occurred to me. Honestly, I haven't even tried to figure out what my specialty is."

"We can work on that later today," Drew said. "Might be a fun distraction."

"Sorry I couldn't be of more help, luv. Call me and let me know how it works out. Oh, and double, or even triple, your protection. Please be careful."

We ended the call, and I leaned back in my chair. *Could I be a medium?* I put all this behind me before my training with my mother got that far. I suppose it's not unreasonable to assume I may have inherited that particular skill set. *What the heck. I have nothing to lose.* Either it worked or it didn't.

I fiddled with my empty coffee cup. "OK, cuz. We know one person from what, a few hundred years ago, that wasn't particularly nice. Does that help? My gut is telling me it's pertinent. What now?"

Drew shrugged. "I have the same feeling. We should find out if you have your mother's skill. I've never had the knack. Neither does Mum nor Gran. I know someone who may be able to help guide you. You really need to expand your circle of friends. Your family was way too isolated here. I never understood why."

I almost replied with *don't know, don't care*, but I did care. Whatever the reason for the lack of witch friends, I suppose I'd never know.

"I promise I'll find some little witchy friends. Not a top priority at the moment. Can you call your friend and see if she'll help?"

"He, actually. Loki. It's his stage name. His real name is Randy. A bit of a showman. While your mother is low key, Randy is a total nutbar. He really is quite talented, though. He puts it all on for the punters. They love it. Outrageous outfits and all. Like in the old movies. His private bookings are normal though, but he's always busy. I'll text him now and tell him it's urgent." Drew sent the message and put her phone aside.

I called up the picture of Mother and her siblings on my tablet. "We need to find out more about our great uncle Montgomery. Follow the evil, so to speak. My gut tells me there's a connection. We have a distant ancestor who was banished because he wasn't exactly Mr. Nice Guy. Turns out we also have a great uncle who mysteriously disappeared at a young age. Did he die, or was he sent away? Was he also evil? Could it be that any time one of 'our kind' has a male child, he turns out bad? I think you need to contact your Gran again and ask her what else she remembers about him. Maybe we can find a connection."

"I'm not sure Gran knows anything else. All she ever told me was that he existed. She obviously doesn't want to talk about him."

"Well, it's not exactly a secret, and weird things are happening, so maybe she'll tell us about him. I wonder if our moms knew? Go on, ask her. The worse she can say is no."

Drew picked up her phone and sent a short text. She barely put it back down when I saw a Skype request on the laptop. It was Auntie P.

"Why are you still asking about little Monty?" Aunt Priscilla bristled. I couldn't read the look on her face. Was she worried or suspicious?

"I'm just curious, Auntie. As you said, our kind don't have male children. Is it a coincidence that the only two boys we know of in our family both vanished? Forgive me for asking, but was Montgomery really that bad as a boy? You mentioned he'd harmed animals." I bit my lower lip. I could tell by the way she fidgeted she was a little uncomfortable with the question.

"Please Auntie. It's important. Both Drew and myself feel there's a connection. What can you remember about him?"

Priscilla closed her eyes and rubbed her forehead. I didn't want to push her too hard, so I let her have all the time she needed.

"He was a few years younger than me, but I was ten when he left, or disappeared, so I do have some clear memories. Since no one ever spoke about it, we always assumed he died. I do recall a few incidents that I won't go into. Needless to say, he wasn't an angel. Cruel would probably be a better description, so yes, he really was that bad."

She had a hurt look in her eyes, so I wasn't going to probe further.

"Thanks Auntie P. I'm sorry to dredge up bad memories, but I really needed to know. Two males born, both evil. One banished, one vanished. Is there a connection?"

Auntie P. looked startled. "Connection? Monty's been gone for decades. He'd dead. I'm certain of that. I'd sense him if he was still alive."

I knew the sensation she spoke of. We could tell when others like us were around, but the feeling was different for family.

Once again, we said goodbye. My mind raced. I looked over at Drew and saw her texting someone. When she finished, she sighed.

"I feel awful having Gran tell us her brother wasn't nice. I texted Mum and asked her to go over and talk to her. Gran probably needs a shoulder after that. Even if she doesn't talk about it, she'll probably feel better just having someone with her."

"Good idea. I feel bad too, but it was necessary."

I called up the scan of the old picture of Granny, Auntie P., and Montgomery I had on my tablet and zoomed in on the little boy.

"Holy Heliodor! Drew, look at this."

THIRTY-ONE

I angled the tablet so Drew could get a better look. "When my tormentor paid you a visit last night, did you see his face?"

"Yes, briefly," she said.

I pointed to Montgomery.

"The port wine stain. It's identical to Mr. E's. Could it be possible he's alive? Is it our great uncle who's doing this? But why?"

"He must have been given away. Maybe he's punishing our family for doing it? His parents are long dead, so maybe he's taking it out on the rest of the family. But how would he have known about us? Aren't adoption records supposed to be sealed or something? How would he know who his birth family is? And who would have taught him the dark magick?"

I shrugged. "Beats me. Private Investigator maybe? Spell? However, he found us doesn't really matter. All I care about is how to deal with him and prevent him from killing me. Us. We have to go through the book that Mr. Barker found. He'll be open soon, so we can head over and look."

"Not so fast." Drew held my arm. "One thing I do know about these dark spell books is the need for extra protection, as Gran said. She sent that list for a reason. It's too easy to say or write something from the book and have it latch on to us. Could be as bad as mis-use of a Ouija board, or accidentally opening a portal by leaving a closet door open."

I had to laugh at that last comment. "The closet door is something I remember having drilled into me. I never understood how an open closet door can create a portal without a chant or spell. However, it's something I've always followed, just in case."

"I don't fully understand it either, but why take a chance? Anyway, we'll have to take a few things with us. Standard things, like white candles and incense. Probably wouldn't be a bad idea to take a bundle of cedar to smudge before and after."

"I'll get that engraved wooden box I bought when we went on the shopping spree for crystals, candles, and all the other protection items. I think I'll also grab the black tourmaline bead bracelets I bought. They're supposed to repel evil. I bought two, so we can each wear one. Funny how at the time something told me to get an extra. Must be that Spidey-sense kicking in again."

"I'm glad you can maintain your sense of humour, Marcy. It can help keep you sane. Just don't get cocky."

I placed my hand on her forearm. "Don't worry, cuz. I'm deadly aware how serious this is, pun intended. If I don't joke, I know I'll just hide away and wait for the inevitable to happen. Let's get ready."

I went upstairs and took the box from the bookshelf to my room. When I purchased it, I had no idea what I was going to do with it. I was just drawn to it. The box was only two inches deep and a little smaller than a shoebox. Whoever made it did beautiful work. All four sides were engraved with ivy. One long continuous stem that had no beginning, no end, with tiny symbols hidden among the leaves. If you didn't look closely, you'd never know they were there. The top had a pentacle in the centre, framed with a Gothic-looking border. Each corner of the frame had a triquetra. The entire box was stained dark brown, and on the inside, the bottom was lined with deep-red velvet.

Drew had already gone downstairs to the hidden workshop. I joined her and noticed she'd gathered two slender four-inch candles, two plain cubed silver holders, dragon's blood incense, and an incense burner. I went over to the cabinet against the wall and opened one of the small compartments where I'd stashed the two bracelets. I'd returned Mother's amulet to the drawer earlier to keep it safe. I picked it up and held it to my lips, whispering for my mother to guide and protect us. I gave it a quick kiss and put it back. Grabbing the bracelets, I slipped one on my wrist, then handed the other to Drew and put everything in the box. Drew took a bundle of freshly dried cedar from the line and put it in the box with everything else.

"We need a plate or dish, and a feather for the smudging. What did you do with them?" Drew asked.

I smacked my forehead. "They're still in my room."

Drew took the box out to the car while I bolted upstairs. Once outside, we added the feather to the box. I slipped the bowl into my bag.

✳ ✳ ✳

My stomach did back-flips as I reached for the doorknob. *Are we doing the right thing?* Mr. Barker looked up at the sound of the tinkling bell that hung over the door of his bookstore. It was the first time he didn't smile when he saw me.

"What's wrong?" I asked him.

"I'm worried about you. That book is not something to be taken lightly. Won't you reconsider?"

I shook my head. Even though we'd both grounded before leaving the house, I took a deep breath and re-set my roots. I noticed Drew grounding as well. The aroma of Mr. Barker's tea helped calm me, even though I didn't see it anywhere. A combination of camomile and vanilla.

"We need to figure out what Montgomery is doing and how to fight it. This book is our only hope. We both appreciate your concern, but we don't have a choice."

He looked puzzled. "Who's Montgomery?"

"This morning, I finally figured out who it is that's tormenting us. It's Granny's little brother. I'm certain of it."

"Brother?" Mr. Barker's brow creased, but he didn't ask any questions. The look of concern and puzzlement increased, though.

I wanted to ask him about it, but there wasn't time. "The book?"

"It's in the back. Follow me." Mr. Barker led the way.

We followed him into the room he used for his private transactions. When he opened the door, both Drew and I burst out laughing.

I gave him a quick hug. "You don't do things by half, do you, Mr. Barker?"

He had a huge white candle sitting in the centre of the table, the dark grimoire placed in front of it. The candle had to be at least six inches in diameter and about a foot and a half tall. A lighter sat beside it.

"That's what we forgot," I said. "No lighter." I turned to Mr. Barker. "I'm glad you set this up, but we came prepared, almost. I can't believe we forgot a lighter or matches."

Drew set my engraved box on the table and set up. Our candles were dwarfed by Mr. Barker's. She placed one on each side of his.

"Is it all right to burn incense and cedar?" she asked.

"Certainly. I don't have any or I would have put it by the candle. I guess I figured a large candle might make up for it. I'm glad to see you've thought about this so thoroughly. It makes me feel a little better. I still don't like it, though."

He noticed my bracelet and half-smiled. "Good luck."

"They'll need more than luck." Cooper stood in the doorway, looking more concerned than his grandfather. He walked in and placed a tray with a full tea service on a small table by the comfy chairs. "One of Gramp's special blends to ease our worries and boost your strength."

Cooper placed a hand on my shoulder, sending a surge of electricity through me. The corner of his mouth curved up. He felt it, too.

"Save it for later." Drew removed Cooper's hand and pushed him towards the door. It closed with a soft click and we were left alone with the book.

Drew lit the ginormous candle, then we grounded again. She used the large candle to light our two tiny ones and the incense. I picked up the lighter and held it to the cedar bundle, then walked around the room fanning the smoke with the crow's feather, saying a prayer to Archangel Michael as I walked. I circled the room several times, starting at the walls and going in smaller circles until I reached the table. I stood in front of the grimoire and fanned the smoke over it repeatedly, just to be sure.

"OK, let's get this show on the road." I set the cedar aside.

We put the chairs side by side, sitting with the book between us.

"Are you ready?"

Drew shook her head. "No. Are you?"

"No, but we have to do this. It's now or never."

I took a deep breath and reached out. I froze when my hand was about an inch from it. "Can you feel that?"

Drew extended one hand towards it. "It's very powerful. We need to take care. Don't read anything out loud. Whatever notes we make must be just brief points. We can't copy anything word for word."

I reached out, pushing past the energy radiating from the book, and opened the cover. The aged leather wasn't hard or cracked. Someone had taken great care to preserve it. I turned the pages, making sure not to damage them. The script was old and difficult to read. Page after page of dark spells. One section was devoted to death spells.

"This can't be right." I pointed to one item. "Goofer Dust?"

"I've heard of that. It may sound funny, but it's meant to kill. Skip over that section. It gives me the creeps."

I flipped the pages as fast as I dared, careful not to tear them.

"I wonder if he's been using something like this?" I pointed to Astral Binding and started to read.

"Place a circle around the victim—"

"Stop!" Drew placed her hand over my mouth. "Don't read them."

The candles flickered. The light fixture crackled.

"Did I do that?"

Drew picked up the cedar and waved it over the book. "Please be more careful. This isn't a joke."

"Sorry. Forgot. We've been looking through this for ages. I need a break."

I sat in one of the comfy chairs and removed the cozy from the teapot. "Tea's still warm, and it smells amazing. Not what I could smell when we first arrived."

Drew joined me and I filled two cups. She took a sip. "This is amazing. I don't recognize any of the flavours, but I do feel better."

The light flickered. "Schist." We swore in unison.

"I didn't even complete one sentence. How could I have activated anything?"

"It's dark magick. Even though you didn't read it all, you were thinking of his attacks, weren't you?"

I nodded. "Michael?"

Drew agreed. We said another prayer to Archangel Michael and asked for protection.

The candles went out and the ceiling light exploded. The door opened and both Mr. Barker and Cooper rushed in.

"All the lights went out." Cooper made his way to me. "What happened?"

Drew wrapped her arms around her body. "The grimoire is stronger than I expected."

"You need to fill the room with natural light." Mr. Barker hurried over and almost pulled the curtains down as he opened them.

Drew went to the table and picked up the cedar. "I'll cleanse the room again. We should be all right after that."

Mr. Barker reluctantly headed for the door. Cooper squeezed my hand. For once, no jolt of excitement ran through my body. Only warmth.

"I'll reset the breaker, Gramps." Cooper slowly released my hand and followed Mr. Barker.

Once they'd shut the door, Drew and I resmudged the room, extra heavy over the book, and said another prayer to Archangel Michael. *He must be sick of me by now.* The atmosphere became lighter almost immediately, so we focused on the grimoire again. About three-quarters of the way through, we found it.

Mind Invasion Spell

"Looks like it's mainly concentration." I looked over at Drew. "The only ingredient is black salt. How do I open my third eye?"

"I can help you with that. It's not something you can learn overnight. I'll have to ask Mum about the salt."

I opened the notebook I always kept in my bag and jotted down what seemed relevant. Drew watched, nodding her approval. She pointed at a few things, then we continued looking through the book to see if there was anything else significant. A counter spell would've been nice.

Satisfied we had found everything, I closed the book and picked up the smoldering cedar to smudge the room again. We thanked Archangel Michael and extinguished Mr. Barker's candle, then our two. There wasn't much left of the ones we brought. Everything went back in the box, and I carried the bowl and cedar out into the store. My hand shook so much I almost dropped it.

"I'm getting a headache. Not a Monty one," I quickly added. "I need to sit a moment."

Drew took the bowl of cedar and I dropped into one of Mr. Barker's wing-backed reading chairs. "I believe it's an effect of whatever you almost conjured up in there. Those old grimoires are extremely dangerous. I just hope nothing attached itself to you."

"If you're trying to cheer me up, you've failed miserably." I tried to smile, but the little effort that took made my head hurt more. "How can I tell if I have an unwanted hitch-hiker?"

"I know someone. I'll call her now." Mr. Barker picked up the receiver on the antique telephone at the front counter and dialed.

My headache was gone by the time she arrived. A demonologist, Mr. Barker called her. She was old, her face covered in deep wrinkles. Mr. Barker introduced her as simply Mihaela, from Romania. *Great. A demonologist from what used to be Transylvania.*

I'm not entirely certain what she did, but she seemed positive nothing had attached itself to me, or anyone else. I think she spoke in Latin. She did pick up on the back room, and I know Mr. Barker didn't mention that on the phone. Whatever I'd brought over hadn't come completely through.

Before she left, she gave me her card. "You are special woman. Much power. There is black aura following you. Be very careful." She nodded towards Mr. Barker, then headed out the door.

"A black aura? Following me? How can an aura follow me?"

No one answered.

"I know she's a little," Mr. Barker wiggled his fingers. "Odd. But she's good. Don't hesitate to call her if anything bad happens."

"Anything bad? Other than having my mind invaded and being astrally transported somewhere else?"

"You know what he means." Drew put her hand on my shoulder. "At least we now know who's doing all that."

"Yeah, yeah. I get it. If I suddenly start speaking in tongues and my head turns backwards, she'll be the first one I call."

"It's no joke, Marcy." Cooper knelt in front of my chair. "Anything can happen."

"Don't mind my cousin. It's her way of dealing with things. You'll get used to it."

I looked down at my feet, feeling like a scolded child. "Sorry. It's so overwhelming. I think I can deal with Montgomery with a lot of help from my family." I looked at Cooper and Mr. Barker. "You two included. But the thought of a demon attachment is too much."

I stood and paced around the book stacks, shaking my arms in an attempt to settle my nerves. It didn't work. I couldn't concentrate.

"Can we go home now, Drew?" I turned to Mr. Barker. "Thanks for your help. Thank your friend, too, for the loan of his book."

"Good luck, girls. And be very careful." He glanced at the cedar bundle. "Do you mind leaving that here?"

He was definitely worried about that book, and I didn't blame him.

"Certainly. Better safe than sorry."

He took the saucer out from under his teacup and handed it to me. I slid the cedar out of the bowl and onto the saucer, took it into the back room, placed it in front of the book, and re-lit his candle. I let him know it was burning so he could keep an eye on it, then Drew and I headed back home. The worried look on Cooper's face broke my heart.

THIRTY-TWO

As I drove home, Drew checked to see if her medium-friend replied to her text. Nothing. She said something, but I was too busy concentrating on driving. I'd hit the shoulder a few times and got honked at for driving so slowly.

"What was that?"

"I said, I hope he replies soon. If we can contact someone who can tell us more about the twins, it could be very helpful."

"We can try it on our own. I watched Mother several times, and it doesn't seem all that hard. It looked like she just concentrated. As long as there's no noise, I might be able to at least sense a presence."

"I don't think that's wise. It might open something we can't handle. I'd feel much better if we had guidance first. As I said, he's quite busy and don't forget about the time difference between Canada and Britain."

I sighed. Not totally out of frustration, though. I think it was partially a sigh of relief. The thought of contacting the dead scared the bejesus out of me. Not that the info from the dark spell book made me feel all warm and fuzzy.

I glanced over at Drew while waiting for the light to change. She bit her nails. I hadn't seen her do that before. She always took such great care of them.

"Worried about the book?"

Drew nodded, still munching on her nails.

"I wish Mum or Gran could come over and help. Gran won't fly and Mum is way too busy. I think we need to sit and have a long talk with both of them before we proceed any further. I'll see if I can set it up for today."

I continued home while Drew called her mum. I could only hear one side of the conversation, but by Drew's replies, I was certain Susan was not happy about any of this. They were still talking when I pulled into the drive. She was going to have one heck of a cell bill when she got home. Drew ended the call on the way into the house.

"OK, Mum is going to cancel the rest of her appointments and go over to Gran's. She'll Skype from there. Should be ready in about a half-hour. I'll set up in the kitchen and you can get the coffee started."

I dug the notebook out of my bag and placed it on the table, along with the engraved box. Once the incense had been placed around the room, I put a K-cup in the machine and went downstairs to get more candles and a dried cedar bundle. We wanted to take the same precautions as we did at the bookstore. Unlike Drew had, I grabbed some descent sized candles that would burn for several hours.

I replaced the full coffee cup with an empty one, put a fresh K-cup in for Drew, lit the candles and incense, then darted up to the bathroom while she fired up the laptop. We were all ready when her mum called five minutes earlier than expected. Susan was in front of the computer while Great Aunt Priscilla wandered in the background, smudging the room.

"I hope you girls have cleansed the room," Susan said.

"Yes, Mum. Candles and incense too. I just hope it's enough."

As soon as Auntie P. settled, Drew caught me totally off guard.

"Before we start, I need to tell you something. Warn you actually. He's threatened *me* now, and if we don't stop him, I believe he'll come after both of you. We think his plan is to eliminate everyone in our family."

I wasn't expecting that. Drew told me she wasn't going to say anything. We'd agreed to wait.

Neither of the ladies spoke. I think they were trying to understand exactly what Drew was telling them.

"What do you mean?" her mum asked. "Why do you think he'll come after us?"

I leaned closer to the screen. "We know who he is. I've seen him. He has a very distinct port wine stain on the left side of his face."

Susan wouldn't know, but Priscilla would remember. It was almost funny watching the realization slowly sink in.

"Montgomery?" she whispered. "He's alive?"

"Apparently. Alive and well. Maybe not so much on the well side. I don't think he's playing with a full deck of tarot cards."

"Are you certain? If he's that strong, why can't I sense him?" Auntie P. asked.

"Don't know why. I looked at the old photo with a magnifying glass. The stain is identical. Yes, I'm absolutely certain it's Montgomery."

Susan finally spoke, addressing her question to her mother. "If it truly is your younger brother, why would he try to harm Marcy and Drew? He didn't even know them. How would he even know they existed?"

None of us had an answer, but I think we all wondered the same thing. Auntie P. was speechless.

"I don't know, Mum, but that's not important at the moment. We need your help with what we found in the dark spell book. Once we stop him, then maybe we'll find out why he's been knocking off our family."

"Um." I wasn't sure how to word it. "I'm certain… he indicated…."

"Stop dithering, girl." Auntie P. had little in the way of patience. "Just spit it out."

"The last time he took me, he indicated he was responsible for Mother and Granny's deaths." I sat back in my chair, waiting for a response.

Susan put her arm around Auntie P. "I'm sorry, mother."

Priscilla buried her face in her hands. "Monty, what have you become?"

We sat in silence, waiting for her to come to terms with the fact her baby brother grew up to be a killer.

After a few minutes, she sat up. Auntie was tough and set her mind to the task at hand. She'd grieve when alone.

We spent the next few hours going over the bits and pieces I gathered from the book, trying not to recite anything word for word. Auntie P. would periodically go in search of a book from her library, but in the end, we were no further ahead. Unless we delved into the dark arts ourselves, the best we could hope for was strong protection. At least we'd know exactly what we were up against.

I said nothing to them, but I'd already decided to try the physical mind invasion myself. It wasn't exactly dark magick, but it was most certainly frowned upon. Picking up on people's thoughts when they were in sight was pretty easy and perfectly acceptable, provided you didn't do it just for fun or to be nosey. Problem was, in order for it to be successful, I needed to know where good ole Monty was. My skills were underdeveloped and more than a little rusty. If Priscilla was right, and I had inherited some of our ancient ancestor's DNA, maybe I got more than just the love gene. I'd have to prepare without letting on to Drew.

It was past dinnertime when we ended the call. Drew's phone had buzzed more than once, but she'd ignored it.

"I'll get supper started while you check your messages. Maybe Randy the Magnificent got back to you."

"I told you his professional name is Loki, which is actually rather funny. Loki is the Norse trickster and god of mischief." Drew laughed as she checked her cell. "There's a text from him. He has a few hours free tomorrow. I'll send him an email so he knows exactly what we want, and include a Zoom link."

I rooted around the fridge while she spoke, but found nothing I wanted.

I closed the door and turn to face Drew. "Pizza?"

"Sounds good. Fully loaded veggie, extra-large?" She lifted an eyebrow, hoping I'd say yes.

"Sure, why not? Extra-large it is. I don't know why we're both not shaped like a cauldron. We seem to eat all the time."

"We do have an unnatural attraction to food, don't we?" Drew smiled and rubbed her belly.

When we stopped laughing, I asked, "Do you want red or white with the pizza?"

"Yes, please."

"You're such a lush, Drew," I giggled and grabbed a bottle of each and put the white in the fridge before ordering the pizza. Granny had an excellent selection of wine, but I don't recall it ever being consumed in such great quantities. We were putting quite a dent in the stash.

"While we're waiting, where are your mother's things? Particularly her crystal ball. I don't know if we'll need one, but if we're going to explore your potential, we may as well try scrying."

"I remember seeing several boxes in one of the rooms up top. Found them one time when visiting Granny. Some have Mother's name on them, but I haven't been able to get myself to go through them yet. Even though she's been gone for several years, it's still going to be difficult."

"Well, I'm here now, so you don't have to do it alone. Unless you'd rather?"

"No, it might be easier with you beside me. You're family. Maybe later we can go through some of Granny's things. There may be something Auntie P. might like to have."

Drew gave me a hug, and we headed up to the third floor. It wasn't a full floor, more like a loft, and the rooms up there weren't very big. I remembered how hot they got in the summer. The hallway was dark even though the sun shone brightly. All the windows were small, and the shutters closed. I stumbled to the end of the hall, lifted the window, and pushed everything open. An improvement, but not by much.

I opened the door to the only room at that end and switched on the light. The loft had never been updated, so the light switch was one of those old ones you had to turn. A single sconce was fastened to the wall just inside the door. It wasn't bright, but it gave enough light to see. *Note to self, call electrician.*

After crossing the room to the window, I pulled back the drapes, choking as the dust descended on me. We'd both need a shower after this. As I slid the window up, a slight breeze drifted in and sent even more dust flying. Despite all the particles floating around, the fresh air felt nice and helped clear the room of some of the musty smell.

"There they are." I pointed. "You start at that end. We don't need to examine everything right now. Just find the box with the items she would've used for her readings. I'd imagine Granny put them all together."

Box by box, we went through the contents until I found one with my name on it and lifted the lid. *My altar items.* I'd get those later. I came across

Mother's jewellery box and lifted the lid. Her ruby sparkled when the sunlight hit it. I pictured her wearing it and fought back the tears.

One evening, we had gone out to celebrate Granny's sixty-fifth birthday. I was only ten, but I remembered that night clearly. Mother had bought us both new dresses and I felt so grown up. That ruby pendant stood out against the Kelly-green satin. Hopefully Granny hadn't given the dress away. It was exquisite. I lifted the pendant out to take back down with me. I'd come back for the jewellery box later.

"Got it!" Drew yelled. "Let's get it downstairs so we can have a proper look. Pizza should be here soon, too."

I closed the window, drew the drapes, switched off the light, and followed Drew down to the living room. She placed the box of Mother's things on the coffee table. One by one, we removed the items and sat them around us.

We stopped briefly when the pizza arrived. Half a pizza and a bottle of white later, we were back in the living room. I set the crystal ball on its stand in the centre of the coffee table. It was a six-inch orb of clear quartz, not glass——heavy and expensive. The stand was pure silver and lightly engraved. Mother had kept the stand polished, and it glistened in the light. But not today. After being tucked away for years, it had lost its sheen. And the crystal needed to be charged.

There wasn't a full moon, but the sky was clear. What little moon was visible should reflect enough light to do the job. I set them on the wide sill to energize overnight.

Also, in the box were two matching silver candle sticks, a three-candle candelabrum, a brass incense burner, a Rider-Waite tarot deck, and a purple lace tablecloth, carefully wrapped in tissue paper. There wasn't really much we could do with the items, so we polished off the bottle of red while watching Bell, Book, and Candle on the Turner Classic Movies Chanel. I never tired of it. When it was over, we showered and retired for the night.

I wasn't tired, so I sat cross-legged on my bed and turned on my laptop to research scrying. I looked at several websites. They all said a dark mirror would work just as well as a crystal ball. I had an old Victorian hand-mirror as decoration on my dresser. One of those small mirrors with a handle that usually came with a matching brush and comb. It was so old black spots covered part of the reflective surface. I went over and picked it up, using my night shirt to clear off the dust. I checked the laptop and read the list of items suggested for success.

Low lighting, a white candle, and a quiet place.

I had a white candle sitting on the night table beside my bed, so I switched on the small table lamp, moved the candle away from the lampshade and lit it, then turned off the ceiling light. I made myself comfortable on the bed, cleared my mind and gazed into the mirror, concentrating on Montgomery. Unlike my dear old uncle, I had no intention of invading his mind. I just wanted to find his location.

Nothing happened, but I wasn't really expecting much. After another five minutes, the blackened glass in the mirror got foggy. I thought it was vapour from my breath, so I swiped my hand across it. Still murky. Dark shadows floated amongst the fog, but nothing was clear. I concentrated harder. Nothing more happened. The mirror cleared and it was over.

I put the mirror back on the dresser and extinguished the candle, feeling confused. Was my experience a success or a failure? I turned off the table lamp and crawled under the covers. In the morning, I'll ask Drew if she knows anything about it.

Montgomery clung to my thoughts as I drifted to sleep. Something jolted me awake only a few minutes later. He'd been in my head again, or had he?

This seemed different. I'd been in control this time. Needing to write everything down, I switched on the lamp and took my journal and pen from the bedside table.

I'd been in a building with Montgomery, but he had paid no attention to me. Closing my eyes, I tried to visualize that room. Nothing about it was familiar. A window on the opposite side was too distant to see out. I hadn't tried to invade his mind, so what happened? Could I have somehow travelled to where he was? More importantly, could I do it again? Was it really possible? Did I have that ability? There was no other explanation I could come up with. I could travel astrally.

THIRTY-THREE

I woke a little later than usual with a pounding headache. I sat up and swung my legs over the side of the bed. The sudden movement made the room spin and my stomach lurch. *Must be the wine we had last night.* When the room finally stopped spinning, I gingerly made my way to the bathroom. The shower made me feel better, but only a little. On the way back to my room, I peeked into Drew's. *Still out cold.* I let her be.

Once dressed, I went to the kitchen, avoiding the creaky step mid-way. A quick check of the cupboards and fridge showed me the food supply dwindled, so I left Drew a note and drove into town for a big shop at No-Frills.

An hour later, with the Smart car stuffed to capacity, I headed home. As I waited to turn onto Davis Drive, an ambulance whizzed by. The pterodactyls returned to my stomach, and a coldness crept through my bones. Even though it was hotter than blazes, my arms broke out in goosebumps.

As soon as traffic cleared, I pulled into the plaza at the next lights to turn around, and followed the flashing lights. I wasn't too far behind, and made it through the yellow traffic light before it turned red, and followed it into town. As I crested the hill on Main Street, I spotted the ambulance. It wasn't moving anymore. *Damn.* It stopped by Mr. Barker's store. Had whatever I accidentally released earlier come back? I asked Archangel Michael to watch over both Mr. Barker and Cooper as I pulled onto a side street. I parked by the library and ran over. The door to Antique Books stood open, a young cop guarding it.

"Sorry, Miss. Store's closed," he said. "No one allowed in."

"Is it Mr. Barker?"

"Do you know the owner?"

I nodded. "Has his grandson been contacted? I believe he's the only relative around here."

The cop looked confused. I let my mind drift and concentrated on him. Sensing he was new and uncertain what to do or say, I didn't want to get him in trouble, so I didn't push it. Someone should be coming out soon and I might be able to get some information from them.

I moved away from the door and the young cop relaxed. Pressing my face to the front window and cupping my hands, I saw Cooper and another man talking to the police. A paramedic behind the counter looked down at the floor. *Oh, God! What did I release? Please let Mr. Barker be all right.*

I focused on Cooper. He was worried, not grief stricken. Maybe Mr. Barker was only ill. Cooper twitched his shoulders as my intense stare bore into him. He turned around and spotted me outside. He waved me in, but I shook my head and pointed at the cop standing by the door. He nodded his understanding and came out to get me. The cop inside spoke with the other man and didn't notice him leave. Cooper stepped outside.

"Marcy, I'm glad you're here." He waved me to the door.

The young cop protested.

"She's family," Cooper said. "I need her inside." He dragged me through the door before the cop could respond.

"What happened?" I hugged his arm. We stood just past the counter, enabling us to see the top of Mr. Barker's head as the paramedics worked on him. The one who'd been standing now knelt, fiddling with the equipment. Mr. Barker lay motionless.

"It looks like he had a heart attack. I was upstairs in the apartment and heard the customer yelling. He was calling 9-1-1 when I came down. Gramps' doctor has been telling him to retire for a while now because of his health. That's really why I'm here. To try to talk him into moving to Halifax with my parents. We argued this morning about it."

A tidal wave of emotion rolled off Cooper, hitting me hard. He blamed himself, just as I blamed myself for releasing something in the back room.

Cooper dropped onto a nearby chair, slumped forward, and covered his face with his hands. "It's all my fault. I brought this on. If he dies, I don't know what I'll do."

"Stop it, Cooper. It's not your fault. You said his doctor warned him. This was bound to happen whether or not you were here."

I slid my arm around his shoulders and stroked his hair with my other hand. It felt like the natural thing to do.

"Ahem."

I looked up and saw the officer who'd been talking with the customer. "I'm sorry, but I need to ask you a few questions, sir."

"It's Officer Defoe, isn't it?" I unwrapped myself from Cooper.

"Do I know you, Miss?"

"No, but you knew my mother. I believe you were in high school together. She showed me some old pictures once and mentioned you were a cop. Catherine Adhamh?"

He smiled. "Katie. Yes, we were friends. Did she tell you we dated a few times? From the look on your face, I'm guessing not. Tragic what happened to her. You must be Marcy. Sorry for the loss of both your mother and grandmother. Have you moved back?"

I wasn't certain if he was happy to reminisce or was stalling so Cooper could compose himself. DeFoe glanced down at him, so I'm guessing the latter. Cooper still covered his face.

"Yes, I inherited Granny's house, so I quit my job and moved back. Haven't decided what I'm going to do about work, though."

Out of the corner of my eye, I saw Cooper sit up. Defoe saw it too. I moved away, but Cooper reached out and grabbed my arm. Defoe smiled. He must have thought I was his girlfriend. I suppose I would have made the same assumption in his place. I rather liked the idea.

Cooper told him of his grandfather's health concern and how Cooper was upstairs when it happened. There really wasn't much else he could add to what the customer said. The paramedics placed Mr. Barker on the stretcher and wheeled him out. I figured they'd take him to Southlake Hospital. It was practically around the corner.

"I need to call Dad. Maybe I should wait until I know more?" Cooper looked like a lost little boy.

"No. Call him now. If something more serious happens, he'll at least have a little time to prepare for it."

Officer Defoe let the customer leave and followed him out the door. Cooper opened the cash register and pulled the store key out from under the drawer.

"Can you flip the closed sign and lock the door for me, Marcy? I need to go upstairs and find the doctor's phone number. Will you wait?"

I thought about the groceries sitting in my car in the July heat, and Drew waiting for me to come back home. I wanted to stay, but there really wasn't anything I could do.

The groceries felt like a petty thing to be concerned about. Cooper was distraught. I could easily text Drew to let her know what happened, but practicality always won out over emotion. Besides, Cooper would be busy at the hospital answering questions and checking his grandfather in. I'd be in the way, at least initially. If I went home, by the time I got to the hospital, Cooper should be finished with the admin stuff.

"I need to get home, and you have to call your folks. You need to be with your Gramps in the ambulance. I'll look for the doctor's phone number, then I'll meet you at the hospital."

I remembered Drew's friend Randy was scheduled to call later this afternoon, and I needed to be there for that. I pictured an analogue clock and tried to work out the math. The numbers jumbled. *God! I couldn't even do simple math. Try again..* I'd be able to stay at the hospital for a couple of hours, but no more.

"I promise, Cooper. I'll see you there."

He nodded and followed behind the stretcher.

I flipped the closed sign and locked the door. I asked Archangel Raphael to watch over Mr. Barker and help heal him. He had a little book with phone numbers in a drawer under the cash register. I'd seen him refer to it a few times. With shaky hands, I flipped through it and found the doctor's phone number.

THIRTY-FOUR

Drew sat in the kitchen eating a late breakfast. "Took you long enough. Did you buy the store out?"

"Mr. Barker had a heart attack. Cooper's afraid it's his fault because they argued earlier. But I can't help but think it has something to do with me."

I put the groceries on the counter, sniffled and dropped onto the chair beside Drew.

"Because of the book?" Drew shook her head. "I doubt it. It's *our* family that's being targeted. You said he had health issues. Sometimes things like this just happen. It's called *life*, Marcy. Hopefully, it's not his time yet. It's not your fault any more than it's Cooper's. I'm sure he's going to be all right. Do you want me to go to the hospital with you?"

"Thanks, but I'm meeting Cooper there. You may as well do some more research, or watch a movie, or something. I promise I'll be back by the time Randy calls, but just in case, you need to be here.

I really hoped there wouldn't be a "just in case." I'd known Mr. Barker since I was in my tweens and considered him a dear friend. It was too soon to lose another loved one.

"Maybe once he recovers, he'll finally sell up and move to Halifax. I'll miss him, but it's better he's there than in the cemetery." I shuddered.

"Why don't you take a healing crystal to the hospital? Surely they won't object to it sitting on the little bedside table." Drew pushed away her plate of unfinished eggs.

"Great idea. I have just the one in mind. An amethyst geode."

I went up to my room and took the jewellery box off the dresser. I rooted through the small geodes I'd stashed there and picked out the best one. Then, I opened a plastic organizer that sat on the floor of my closet and cut a square from a piece of white velvet. It would show off the amethyst nicely and make it less likely to be mistaken for a rock and tossed by the hospital's cleaning staff.

Drew gave me a hug before I left. I felt bad leaving her to put the groceries away, but she understood. "I'll say a healing spell for him," she called as I raced to my car.

I cursed each traffic light as I crawled along Davis towards the hospital. My mind drifted back a couple of months to my last trip there. They couldn't help Granny. The staff wasn't equipped to deal with magick. It would be different this time. It had to be.

I reached out with my mind, searching for Cooper. *Could I sense him from a distance?* I concentrated harder. A horn blared. I swerved back into my lane, focusing on my driving.

When I arrived, Cooper paced in the Emergency waiting area. He stopped long enough for me to embrace him.

My mind remained open after my earlier attempt to reach Cooper. Wave after wave of emotion slammed into me from patients, guests, and staff. I buried my head in Cooper's shoulder and threw up my wall.

His turmoil overwhelmed me. I let go of him and stepped back. I knew exactly how he felt. Taking his hand, I guided him to an empty sofa in the waiting area.

"The doctor's still with him. I was in the way so I came out here to wait. No one's told me anything yet," he said.

"That's a good sign, isn't it? If something had happened, they would've let you know. I left a message with the receptionist at his doctor's office and she said she'd contact him right away. Did you talk to your dad?"

"Yeah. He's going to get the next flight available. Said he'd text me with the details. He really wants Gramps to sell the store and move in with us. Maybe he'll listen now."

Overwhelming loss swept through me. Even if Mr. Barker survived, he'd be taken away. All the way to Halifax. Not only was Mr. Barker my friend, he was my only resource in the area. I mentally slapped myself. Mr. Barker's health was more important. He'd have his family to take care of him. Depression settled in at the thought of Cooper also leaving. With his Gramps in 'Scotia, there'd be no reason for him to visit. Cooper's movement jarred me back to the hospital.

He'd risen and started pacing again. I got dizzy watching him, so I got up, too.

"What does your dad do?" I asked, forgetting Mr. Barker told me earlier.

"Same as Gramps. We're all helpers. Family thing, similar to yours. He has a bookstore too, but he doesn't specialize in antiques. More along the lines of Chapters, only on a much smaller scale. That's where I work, sorta like an apprentice."

A tiny ding sounded. Cooper pulled the cell from his pocket and read a text.

"Dad's at the Halifax airport now. He wants me to pick him up when he lands. He's scheduled to arrive a little before 2:00 p.m."

"I'll stay until you have to leave. I'm expecting an important call, anyway." I reached into my jeans pocket. "Here's the store key."

Cooper mumbled a thank-you and pocketed it.

"Mr. Barker?" A middle-aged, balding man in a white doctor's coat stood in the waiting room doorway, scanning everyone.

"Yes?" Cooper waved. "Do you have news on my grandfather?"

The doctor motioned to the empty sofa we'd vacated to pace. "We can talk over here."

Cooper squeezed my hand. We walked over and sat side-by side. The doctor pulled up a chair and sat in front of us. He crossed his legs and seemed quite relaxed. More like he was chatting with friends instead of talking with strangers about someone's health.

"I'm Dr. Heart, and I've heard all the jokes."

He had a friendly smile. I liked a doctor with a sense of humour.

"We've stabilized your grandfather and are moving him into Cardiac Care. He had a minor heart attack. He's very lucky, but his blood pressure is elevated. Is he on any medication?"

"Yes, I've seen him taking pills, but I never looked at the labels. His doctor should be coming in soon. He'll know what he's taking. Can we see him now?"

"A nurse will let you know when he's settled in. He needs to be kept quiet for several weeks. No strenuous activities. Does anyone live with him?"

"I'm staying with him for the summer. His wife died several years ago. Can he fly? We'd like to move him to Halifax, where we can keep an eye on him. Assuming we can talk him into retiring."

The doctor raised an eyebrow. "He's not retired?"

"No. He runs a bookstore and has an apartment above it."

"You'll have to make other living arrangements by the time he's released. Can't have him going up and down stairs. Not for some time. At his age, he's slower to recover. He really should give up working."

"Good luck with that," Cooper muttered.

I looked up when I heard Mr. Barker's name mentioned. A middle-aged man inquired at the check-in desk, so I went over.

"Excuse me. Are you Dr. Palmer?"

"Yes. You must be with Mr. Barker."

I brought him over and introduced him to Cooper and Dr. Heart.

"Maybe between the two of you, you can get Gramps to sell the store and move," Cooper said.

Dr. Palmer laughed. "Been trying for years. Stubborn man, your grandfather. Maybe he'll listen now, though. How is he?"

"We're getting him ready to be moved. He's a little groggy, but he's out of danger," Heart said. "Would you mind coming with me? I need to fill in some details on his record. Medications and such. Then you can go in and see him yourself before we move him." He turned to Cooper. "Inquire at reception in about a half hour. They should have entered the room number by then, and you can visit."

They disappeared through the door and left Cooper and me to wait a while longer. After checking twice, we were told we could go to room 4213. Dr. Palmer was already there when we arrived.

"I've heard a lot about you over the years," he said to Cooper. "He was in a for a checkup a few weeks ago and was quite excited about your visit. Is there any chance you can talk him into retiring?"

"I can hear you," Mr. Barker said. It was little more than a whisper, but loud enough.

"Do what the doctors tell you, Gramps. I want you around long enough to be a great grandfather."

Mr. Barker smiled. "At the rate you're going, I'll have to live well over a hundred to see that."

He looked over at me and winked. I wasn't certain what he was implying, but heat rose in my face. That was something I need to get control over.

"I don't want to lose you, Mr. Barker, but maybe it *is* time to sell the store. I promise to visit wherever you are. Just make sure I'm not visiting a grave site." I tried to smile, but it felt forced.

"Dad's on his way," Cooper said. "Should be here in a few hours."

Mr. Barker frowned, then his face softened. "I supposed that's to be expected. Look at me. Wires everywhere. Maybe I should think about retiring. No promises, but I'll give it some consideration." He yawned. "Kinda sleepy."

"You close your eyes, Gramps. I'll sit here until it's time to pick up Dad."

Dr. Palmer glanced at the monitor by the bed. "Everything seems fine. I'll head out now. Call me if anything changes and let me know when he's released." He shook Cooper's hand and gave me a nod before leaving.

"Where's he going to live when he's released?" I asked. "There's no way he can get up to his apartment, and he won't be able to fly for ages."

"Maybe I can fix up a bed in the back room on the main floor. I'll have enough time to get it ready. When Dad gets here we can make plans. I'm sure Gramps will agree to sell up. Did you see how scared he looked?" Cooper's voice cracked. He looked away, but I saw the tears forming.

We spent the next few hours chatting. Cooper told me about his father's store in Halifax and the city in general. It sounded like a nice place to relax, and there was so much history to explore. I'd definitely make time to visit after Mr. Barker retired.

I thought about what Auntie P. said about me and Cooper. How could I explore a relationship with him in Halifax? Was Cooper's apprenticeship far enough along for him to take over the book store? With my luck, probably not.

Eventually, time came for Cooper to head to Toronto Pearson International Airport and I went back home to wait for Randy's call. The drive home was quick as the lunch hour traffic had subsided.

I found Drew on the sunporch with a cup of tea and a Harlequin Romance. We still had some time, so I made a coffee and joined her.

"Is he going to be all right?" she asked.

I filled her in on the details.

"So Cooper will be around for a little longer than expected? That's good. Maybe now you'll consider asking him out?"

I groaned. "You're still going on about that? He'll be spending all his time taking care of his grandfather. Dating is going to be the last thing on his mind. Besides, once his Gramps is better, we can likely talk him into going to Halifax. Cooper with him. Can't get to know someone properly over the computer. No point starting something that won't have a happy ending."

"You said his dad is coming. Cooper won't need to be there all the time. I'm sure he'll be glad of a break at some point."

"Maybe. Not at the top of my to-do list. In case you've forgotten, there's a little matter of trying to prevent Montgomery from killing me. Killing us."

"No, I haven't forgotten. I've been thinking about it all day. We've got about forty-five minutes before Randy calls. Have you eaten?"

"Not since breakfast. I'm not hungry."

"Tell that to your stomach. You're making some pretty strange sounds. We still have some of that pizza left. Eat before Randy calls. I won't be able to concentrate on what he's telling us with all that racket."

"You're so funny, Drew. *Not*. Fine, I'll have some pizza."

While I was at the hospital, Drew had made herself useful by reading up on mediums. She filled me in as I ate.

"There are several types of medium. I had no idea," she said. "There's automatic writing, and sensing by touching an item belonging to the person who has passed. Some have spirit guides, others have the spirit speak through them. The medium's voice even changes, and sometimes their appearance too."

"Mother had the spirits take over her voice occasionally, but didn't have a spirit guide that I'm aware of. The deceased usually just spoke to her and she relayed their message."

"Let's hope you inherited that skill from her, and just haven't realized it yet."

"I certainly hope not. I don't relish the thought of someone taking over my vocal chords. That's just creepy. I like the sound of automatic writing. Maybe I can do that."

I settled back in my chair to give it some thought.

"Maybe automatic writing isn't for me. You've seen my hand writing. Even I can't always read what I've written. Can you imagine how much worse it would be if I did it without even knowing what I was writing?"

We burst out laughing. It felt good. We'd been under so much stress over the past week, the release was long over-due.

"OK," I said. "Time to get serious. Your friend should be calling soon. Let's get comfy in the living room. You turn on the laptop and I'll get a book to take notes. Do you think we should light some candles?"

Drew shrugged. "Why not? They won't do any harm. Besides, we aren't doing any magic, just getting some information. Do you have any scented candles?"

"Got just the thing." I dug my trusty notebook from my bag, then went over to a curio cabinet tucked in the far corner. It was made from walnut and the top three quarters had glass on the front and sides, with a mirror backing.

The shelves were filled with an assortment of nick-knacks. The bottom portion was walnut on all sides, with a door that opened to reveal more shelves. That's where Granny kept candles and incense. I was planning on rearranging, eventually. Some of my crystals would look great on those shelves. The inset lighting would make them sparkle.

I opened the front drawer and removed a glass candle holder and a vanilla scented candle. The holder was covered in a multitude of wax drippings. It was obvious Granny used it frequently. Drew had the laptop on the coffee table, Skype open, waiting for Randy. I placed the candle off to the side and lit it, then sat on the couch beside Drew, notebook and pen ready to take down whatever wisdom Randy would impart. At three-thirty, the call notification popped up.

THIRTY-FIVE

My palms grew sweaty and my stomach filled with butterflies. Correction. Pterodactyls. I felt cheated when Randy's face appeared on the screen. I expected someone dressed in a loud flowing gown, turban, maybe a beard, and older. Definitely older. Like in his sixties or something. Randy was probably in his thirties, clean shaven, cropped hair, wearing a t-shirt and probably jeans. Even though I couldn't see below his chest, jeans just seemed to go with the look. He wasn't bad looking either. *I wonder if Drew ever dated him?* I'd have to ask later. Auntie P. and Susan were both waiting for her to marry and continue the family tradition with her own daughter.

"Drew, luv. So nice to see you again. Is that lovely creature the Canadian cousin you told me about?"

I instantly liked this guy, and not because he called me lovely. He oozed charm. No wonder he was so busy. Even if he was a fraud, I'm sure people, women, would line up all day to have a reading with him. He wasn't a fraud, though. Not according to Drew.

"Creature maybe," I said. "Not so sure about lovely. I'm Marcy. Thanks for taking the time to help me. I really have no clue what to do. How do I know if I'm a medium?"

"You look more like an extra small to me," Randy said with a laugh. "Seriously, it runs in your family, so there's a good chance you can do it. You've never tried before? Your mother didn't encourage it?"

"I guess I should've filled you in on Marcy's background," Drew said, "but I thought she should be the one to tell you if she wants to."

Randy moved closer to his computer screen, propped his elbows on the table, and cupped his chin with his hands. "Oh, now you've *really* got my attention. You have to tell me everything. Come on, girl, spill."

I twisted to look at Drew. "You didn't tell me he loved gossip. He's just like one of the girls." I turned back to the screen. "OK, I'll spill. I don't mind. It's not exactly a secret. Short version, they teased me at school because I was different, so I put it all behind me, except for my crystals. Pushed it so far back that I don't really remember much, but it's slowly coming back to me. Mother wasn't one for forcing, and besides, I don't think it would have been successful if I was forced. Mother died several years ago, and Granny just last month. The time was right to get back to my heritage. I wasn't expecting to be fighting for my life, though. Now you're all caught up on the life of Marcy."

Randy stared at the computer, looking a little confused.

"What do you mean, fighting for your life? What haven't you told me?"

I waved my hand dismissively. "Oh, it's nothing really. Someone trespassed into my mind and plans on killing me."

"OK." He dragged the little word out, making it sound like it had five syllables. "So, what is it you need me for? I connect with the dead, not the living."

"I need to try to connect with an ancestor."

Drew and I took turns explaining about Montgomery and our distant ancestor and her twins.

"We need to find out more," Drew said. "Can you help guide Marcy?"

"That's a tall order, luv. I can only reach fairly recently departed, maybe as far back as fifty or so years. They've generally continued on to another realm by then. It's extremely uncommon for even the best to connect with someone who's been gone for such a long time. That relative must have passed hundreds of years ago. I can tell you what you need to do, but I won't promise success."

"Anything will help," I said.

"It's quite simple, really. You need to set the mood. It's not all for show. The low lights, candles, and incense really do help. And crystals. Clear quartz is best. You basically meditate and ask the universe for help. Either you can do it or you can't. There's no magick involved, if you'll pardon the pun. There isn't much else I can tell you, except to keep practicing. Don't expect immediate results. Try all different methods."

"Yes, I know about the different types of mediums, automatic writing, spirit guides, and such. I tried scrying last night." I turned to Drew. "I meant to tell you about it, but the day didn't go as planned."

"Tell me, us, now," Drew said.

"After you went to bed, I tried it with an antique mirror. All I could see was haze and shapes, but after I went to sleep, I believe I experienced astral travel."

I told them about the room I was in, and Montgomery. Randy seemed particularly intrigued.

"That's amazing for a first go. You may have hidden talents, Marcy. I have a feeling you'll be a good medium. Better than good. You just need to experiment more. I'd suggest you try to contact your grandmother or mother as they're close to you. I know a bit about your family, mostly Drew's immediate family. We've had some lovely chats. They've missed your visits, you know. Now I know why you stopped coming.

"I'm sorry, but I have to cut this short. I've got a client arriving soon. Let me know how you get on. I think you'll do quite well. Blessed be." Randy winked and signed off.

I closed the lid and turned to face Drew. "So, what's going on between you two? And don't tell me nothing. Your face lit up the moment he appeared on screen."

Drew lifted a shoulder in a half-shrug. "Not much to tell. We've been out a number of times. He's mentioned making it more permanent, but I'm not ready."

"You mean moving in together? Marriage? As Randy said, come on, girl, spill."

"Both. He's agreeable to either. Both Mum and Gran have been bugging me. They're more interested in a granddaughter, but they adore Randy. Might be interesting to see what sort of offspring we'd conjure up. A witch and a medium. That's never been done in our family."

"Medium. Not to change the subject, but what he said. Should I try to contact Mother or Granny? We have everything except my confidence."

Drew pulled the laptop in front of her. "Either one. Like Randy suggested, close family first. Let's see what might be the best method to start with.

We spent the rest of the afternoon and early evening researching the various ways mediums contacted the departed. I found one website that had a long list. We decided to concentrate on the most common, but I bookmarked the page for future reference. I planned on defeating Montgomery, and I could experiment with some of the other methods in the future, assuming I had a future. I wrote down the top four to attempt, trying to recall which one Mother specialized in. I think she was clairaudient. She could hear the voices. I wasn't certain I wanted to discover if I was clairvoyant. Didn't really want to see ghosts, not that they could hurt me. I put that one at the bottom of the list. My entire family was clairsentient—we picked up on feelings easily. We always listened to our gut. I was a little puzzled with claircognizance. Basically, you just knew things, as far as I could tell.

"How is that different from clairsentience?" I asked Drew. "A gut feeling is like knowing something. What's the diff?"

"You're asking the wrong person, Marcy. I guess we have a lot more research to do. Are you ready for the first experiment?"

THIRTY-SIX

We closed the drapes and turned on one lamp in the corner. Two tall tapered candles sat lit on each end of the coffee table, with the crystal ball in the middle. It should help amplify the energy, and I was going to try scrying again before we went to bed. Drew lit a stick of Frankincense incense and we both grounded.

Once ready, I settled back on the couch and concentrated on who to contact. Granny was probably too recently gone to be reached. I remembered Mother telling me once that after people passed, they went through a sort of clearing house for a debriefing or something. But I'd already felt Granny a few times. She was stubborn, so maybe she was lingering before her other-worldly debriefing.

We believed in reincarnation and that everyone kept returning to earth in another form until we got it right. We all have lessons to learn and after we pass over, we're sent back within about a month or two. Once we learn everything we were supposed to, we ascended. I decided my mother would be a better choice, as she died several years ago.

"Mother? It's Marcy. Are you here? Can you talk to me?"

Nothing at first, then the back of my neck tingled, and a gentle breeze kissed my face. The candle to my right flickered, almost extinguishing, then the curtain fluttered.

"Mother." I choked back tears. "I'm sorry for everything, but I want to learn now. Please speak to me."

The flame flared up. A fog swirled inside the crystal ball.

"She's here," I whispered to Drew. "Mother, I need your help. Can you please talk to me?"

"Concentrate, Marcy. You need to let her take some of your energy."

I closed my eyes and thought about the happy times we had when I was a child. Scene after scene ran through my mind. Something tapped into my energy.

I felt a hand on my arm. A gentle squeeze. The flames on the candles danced. Then she was gone.

"Mother, please come back." I waited. "Schist! She's gone."

"That was wonderful, Marcy. You contacted her."

"Wonderful? She didn't speak to me, merely touched my arm. She was only here for a minute. How can you call that wonderful?"

"Aunt Kathy touched you and made the flames move. I'd say that was quite successful for a first attempt. You need to take a break before trying again." Drew glanced at her phone. "It's almost eight o'clock, and we skipped dinner."

"It did take a bit out of me," I admitted. "I do want to try again, though. A quick meal, then I want to try the crystal ball again. Spaghetti?"

I blew out the candles, but let the incense burn. Drew put the pasta on and I dug some homemade sauce out of the freezer, then went out to the garden for some fresh basil. Nenka popped out from behind a shrub, startling me.

I laughed.

"You certainly get around. I need some basil. Can you guide me to the best plant?"

"Certainly, dear. I heard you talking and was just coming out for some." A worried look creased her brow. "I wasn't eavesdropping."

"That's OK, Nenka. We weren't doing anything private."

"You did quite well, you know. Contacting your mother on your first try. You're going to excel at it. I can tell. Here we are. You pick this bunch and I'll take some in to dry."

"Thank you. Nenka." When I turned, she'd already vanished.

Less than an hour later, we were back in the living room and ready for the next experiment. I was positive I'd get results, as I'd already made an attempt the night before.

"This is actually enjoyable." I looked at the items on the table. "Maybe I'll contact some of Mother's old clients. A few have already called me to see if I was going to resume her business. Granny's customers left messages, too, the day after her funeral. Between the two, I can keep busy and earn a living. How does Madam Marcy sound?"

"Please don't turn into a female version of Randy. One flamboyant person in my life is quite enough."

"Speaking of which, we never finished our conversation. Just how much in your life is Randy? He obviously wants to be in yours. Are you considering marriage? You are twenty-eight, after all. Almost past it." I giggled.

Drew gave me a shot in the arm. "Now who's not being funny? I have been thinking about it though. Randy's nice. We get along, and I would like a daughter. We'd be an interesting combination."

"That's something else I was curious about. Where do all the husbands go?"

Drew shrugged. "Not sure. As far as I know, they just up and leave. I never missed having a father. Did you?"

"No. I never really gave it much thought before. It's only recently that I realized there aren't any men in the family. I was afraid we were killing off the husbands."

"Don't worry. We're not a family of murderers. I suppose it's explained more as we marry. If I do marry Randy, I think he'll actually stick around. Now, with this threat hanging over our heads, it's made me think. If we survive this, I should have a serious chat with him."

"Whoa. What's this *if* business? We *will* survive whatever Monty has in store. It's two against one. And unlike Granny and Mother, we know what he's planning. So we don't know the details. We do know he's out there and we can prepare. If I concentrate on the crystal ball, maybe I'll be able to travel to him again and find out where he is. I don't understand why they didn't know something was wrong."

Drew grabbed my arm. "Hold on. I'm here to help you learn. That does *not* include allowing you to do something so dangerous. Promise me you won't try to contact him.

"Fine. Promise. Probably wouldn't work anyway."

Drew looked skeptical, but lit more incense, then re-lit the two candles. I sat on the floor in front of the crystal ball. As before, I only saw shapes and fog. This time, the shapes were a little more focused. I couldn't make out any details, but I was positive the human shape was male. The ball cleared after several minutes, ending my session, so we called it quits for the night. Drew picked up the book she'd been reading earlier, and I dragged myself up to bed.

As I slept, I once again found myself in that same building with my uncle. I saw more this time. I walked over to the window and looked out. I knew where this place was. The vacant hotel near the train station.

"Who's there?" Montgomery asked.

Damn. I had to get out of there. I could see him looking around. His gazed stopped at the window and he seemed to be looking at me. *Schist!* My heart thumped fast and loud. He cocked his head. Could he hear the beats?

I closed my eyes and pictured my bedroom. I was tempted to click my heels and say, "there's no place like home." Whatever I did worked, and I jolted upright in my bed. My heart raced.

He'd figured it out. I hope I hadn't pissed him off. I needed to circle my bed with sea salt. I got up and went out into the hall. The house lay in darkness. I tip-toed down, avoiding that one squeaky step, navigating my way to the kitchen for the salt.

I grabbed the container and sat the table. My heart still raced.

"Ahem."

Nenka stood in the doorway holding a tiny candle. "Are you OK? It's awfully late for you to be up."

"Bad dream. Can't seem to shake it off."

She blew out the candle and climbed onto the chair beside me. "Would you like company?"

Nenka looked like a tiny granny, with her nightcap and long nightgown. She made me feel better just being there.

"Tell me about the herbs in the garden."

Nenka talked for over a half-hour about basil, thyme, and rosemary. Just listening to her voice calmed me. I yawned.

"Feeling better, dear?" Nenka held her hands clasped in her lap.

"Yes, thank you. I'm sorry I woke you. We both should get some sleep."

When I returned to my room, I pulled the bed a few inches from the wall so I could make a complete circle. Semi-satisfied I was safe, I crawled in and fell asleep.

When I woke in the morning, cascading water sounded from down the hall. Drew was up. I dressed and headed downstairs. I heard *Season of the Witch* coming from the living room. That ringtone was Drew's mother. I raced to grab it before it went to voice mail.

"Susan. How are you?"

"Marcy, where's Drew? Is she all right?" Her tone was sharp. Something was up.

"She's in the shower. Nothing to be concerned about. Are you OK?"

"That's a relief. It's silly, really." She hesitated.

"What's silly?"

"I had a dream that both of you had been kidnapped. Must just be worry causing strange thoughts."

A headache throbbed behind my eyes. Montgomery.

"We're fine. Both of us. I have to go. Monty is trying to attack again. I need to concentrate to block him. I'll have Drew call you when she comes down. Don't worry." I ended the call.

I didn't mean to be so blunt, but blacking out while on the phone wasn't an option. I grabbed the crystal ball, cradling it in my arms for protection, then sat in the easy chair and gave in to Montgomery. Unlike the last time he invaded my mind, the room wasn't in total darkness. It was the room I had astrally travelled to.

"You've been busy, my dear. You're getting stronger. I know you visited me last night. I was quite taken aback. Have you figured out who I am yet?"

I needed to stall. Once he knew we'd discovered his identity, he was certain to kill me, then Drew and her family.

"No, not yet. Drew asked her mother, but she didn't know. She thought your description sounded familiar, though."

"Familiar? I sounded *familiar?*" He waved his hand and something out of sight smashed. He splayed his fingers towards whatever shattered. A large shard of pottery floated into view. With one quick motion, he pointed at me. The shard followed, the sharp edge hovering at my throat. He stepped closer.

"What about your grandmother's sister? Did you ask her?"

"Great Aunt Priscilla is ill. Susan thought it best not to bother her until she's better."

I swear I heard him growl. One thing was certain. He was getting impatient. His eyes narrowed. The shard touched my exposed neck. I swallowed.

"As soon as she's stronger, I'll ask her."

I already knew the answer, but I had to pretend. He squinted and glared at me. I could pick up on his feelings a little. They were heavy, dark. He tried to decide if I spoke the truth. I hoped he couldn't break through my block.

"You have three days." He snapped his fingers. The shard dropped. I jerked backwards.

The sudden change left me with a fissure-like headache opening up in my skull. My face tingled, my throat throbbed. I placed two fingers where the shard touched and came away with blood. The tingle extended down my throat. I tried to call for Drew.

"-ew."

My vision faded, like a camera aperture closing. Only a tiny speck of light remained visible. What had he done to me? I tried to stand, but crumpled into a heap.

He won't win!

In my mind I called to Archangel Michael, then repeated my protection spell over and over, lips moving soundlessly. It felt like hours before the tingling subsided. I picked up Drew's phone. It'd only been minutes.

I took several deep breaths, releasing them slowly. The headache gradually subsided to a dull thud. The absence of running water made me think of Drew. I desperately need to talk to her and went to the foot of the stairs and called up.

"Drew, I need to speak with you. Can you hurry? Drew?" There was no answer. "Drew?"

I started up, calling her again. She lay in a heap in the hallway. I raced to her side.

"Drew?" My gut twisted. "Drew?" I gave her a gentle shake. She didn't respond. Nothing else was around her. I didn't think she hit her head on anything. And there was no blood. I tried to lift her but couldn't. Had Montgomery taken his frustration out on Drew?

I stood beside her, fists clenched. I screamed.

"You bastard! It's me you want. Leave Drew alone." My throat burned. "Three days, you said. Three days!"

Laughter filled my mind. The sound sickened me. Bile rose. I swallowed. Drew whimpered but didn't move.

I got a pillow and blanket and tried to make her comfortable. Could this be what her mother had dreamt of? Had Montgomery kidnapped her mind?

THIRTY-SEVEN

I had no idea what to do. Was he just talking to her like he did with me, or was it something more? Gently, I moved her head, looking for cuts or bruises, then checked her pulse. She still had one, even it if was slower than normal. At least it was steady. I jumped when a hand touched my leg.

"Nenka, you scared the bejesus out of me."

"Is Drew unwell? I heard a thump. Did she trip?"

"No, I don't think so. I think our tormentor has some sort of control over her. When I was out of it the other day down in the workroom, do you remember how long it was?"

The tiny gnome cocked her head. "Let me think. I don't believe it was more than ten or fifteen minutes."

"And how long ago did you hear the thump?"

"Oh, only a few minutes. Didn't you hear it?"

"No, he had me earlier. I just came out of it and came looking for Drew. He must have taken her as soon as he released me."

The tiny gnome twisted her apron. "Oh, my. Oh, my. Is there something I can do?"

"Just stay with me until Drew comes around. I don't want to be alone."

Nenka nodded and sat beside me, leaning against my body.

I checked the time. "Let's wait for fifteen minutes. If he doesn't release her, I'll call her mother. She had a dream we'd been kidnapped. I guess she wasn't too far off."

I moved back and leaned against the wall.

Nenka moved with me. "We'll wait together."

Bless her tiny little heart. She was such a sweet person, uh, gnome. She only just met my cousin, but she treated Drew like part of her own family. I supposed Nenka and Tinkus were part of my family, too. Funny, though. I hadn't seen her son. Well, except his foot that first day I moved in.

"Why have I never met your son? I see you regularly, and your husband occasionally, but never him. What's his name?"

"He's a little shy. Your grandmother didn't see him often, either. His name is Nimagg."

"That was him, wasn't it? The day I moved in, I caught a glimpse of someone in the opening behind Granny's dresser."

She nodded. "I suppose you wondered why that door had been locked shut?"

"Not just locked, but blocked by the dresser, which was nailed to the wall."

"It's nothing to worry about. He's at that age where he's curious. Francine caught him watching her one night as she was undressing. The door's been sealed off ever since."

I didn't know whether to laugh or cringe. A Peeping Tom gnome.

"Is he still at that age?"

Nenka turned pink and looked down at her feet for a moment. "Yes, I'm afraid so. He's asking all sorts of questions. Tinkus is trying to get him to understand that women need privacy, and to be respectful. Nimagg is coming around, growing up. Another twenty years or thirty years and he should be adult encugh."

"Oooh." Drew moaned.

I scrambled to her side. She tried to sit up, but her pinched look told me she was hurt. Drew squeezed her eyes tight and rubbed her temples. I knew that feeling.

"Stay still for a minute and take slow, deep breaths. Lean against me."

I cradled Drew as she followed my instructions. "Was it our ever-loving great uncle Montgomery?"

She nodded. Nenka stood on the other side of Drew, wringing her hands.

"She'll be fine, Nenka. No need to worry."

Drew shifted and sat up straighter. "Is this what you go through every time? It wasn't like this the other night when he popped in to threaten me. It feels like my head's been cracked open."

"It's escalating." I touched my throat. "He's getting physical. Three days. That's all we have before—" I shuttered. "I don't want to think about that. We need to come up with a plan."

Drew grasped my arm to help her stand. "The pain is almost gone now. If he'd done this a few minutes earlier, I'd be lying here starkers. I'm glad he waited until I dried off and got my robe on." Drew giggled, wincing at the increased pain.

We both burst out laughing. The release felt good, like a huge weight lifted. We must've looked insane.

Nenka twisted her apron until it resembled a knot.

"It's OK, Nenka. We're just relieved. Thank you for sitting with me."

My grin disappeared as a thought struck. "He hasn't tried to harm any of you, has he?"

"No. We're fine. Just worried about you."

"If he makes any attempt, let me or Drew know immediately. We're OK now. You can go back to your family."

"As long as you're certain…"

"Yes, I'm certain."

Satisfied we were both all right, Nenka slipped behind a floor length wall hanging and disappeared. I'd admired the craftsmanship of it, but never gave it much thought. I should have guessed there might be a door behind it once I started finding them. The tapestry covered most of the space between the ceiling and floor, and spanned about four feet. The image woven into it extended to all four sides, without any border. The background was a forest, but one tree stood front and centre, filling about half the tapestry. A stone path led from the bottom to the trunk, ending in front of a doorway filled with a soft, glowing light. It was so realistic I could almost feel heat radiating off the glow.

"Guess I just found the fourth door. That leaves one more somewhere in the house, or maybe on the property."

I suddenly remembered the phone call. "You'd better get dressed. Your mother called about a half hour ago. I hope you don't mind that I answered your cell, but I thought it might be important."

"That's fine. What did she want?"

"She had a dream someone had kidnapped us. I suppose we were."

✻ ✻ ✻

"I'm fine, Mum." Drew paced while she spoke. "We have a deadline now. Three days. I'm putting you on speaker." She sat the phone on the coffee table. "OK, just let me get something to write on."

I raced to get my notebook and pen, then sat poised to take notes.

"Go ahead, Mum."

"A protection oil will guard you from these psychic attacks, as well as shield the house." Susan recited the recipe.

"Start with an eighth of a cup of a base oil. Your choice what type. Add four drops of patchouli, three drops of lavender, one drop mugwort, and one drop hyssop. Visualize your intent as you blend them."

"Then what?" I hoped she didn't tell us to drink it.

"Put it anywhere. It works on people and objects. Dab it, spray it. Doesn't matter. We have a meeting in an hour with the witches in the area to discuss how to banish him once and for all. I'll let you know what we come up with."

"Thanks, Mum." Drew ended the call and turned to me. "I assume you have all the ingredients in the workroom?"

"I'm certain I've seen everything listed. We should double or triple the batch. Then what? We can't just sit here and wait for someone else to figure it out."

"I'm surprised he's able to get past your angels."

"Excuse me? My angels?"

"Haven't you asked the angels to guard the four sides of the house? Your grandmother probably did, but they likely left when she died."

"You mean my guardian angel? Isn't she with me all the time? How can she guard the house?"

"No. You can call on other angels to help. You have a personal guardian, as well as other guardian angels. You really have forgotten an awful lot, Marcy." Drew sighed.

"But I'm a quick learner, and it sounds familiar. I think you're going to have to tell me everything. Pretend I'm a child just learning. That's the only way to figure out what I've forgotten, what I remember, and what holes need plugging in our defences."

"First, let's ask the angels for protection. You know the drill. White candles and incense."

Drew put on a meditation CD while I lit a candle and the sage incense. We grounded, then she asked for protection.

> "Guardian Angels, I request your help to protect this house and all in it.
>
> I ask you now to surround this house and land with a sphere of white light, from the heavens all the way to the earth.
>
> Fill the sphere of white light with protection, love, harmony and healing.
>
> Keep the sphere of white light free from all negative energy. Shine the white light and love to every corner of every room of this house, and to all edges of the surrounding land.
>
> May the appropriate helpers and angels from the Universe keep the sphere of white light shining brightly and abundantly. Always.
>
> Thank you. Blessed Be."

As soon as Drew finished speaking, I felt better. The atmosphere grew lighter, safer. We sat silently for several minutes, listening to the CD and relaxing, energizing. We needed to recharge after the attack from Montgomery. I needed to shake the feeling he was still with me.

"I don't know about you, but I'm starving. Everything happened as I was coming downstairs, so I never even got my hit of Snickerdoodles. Are you up for breakfast? This last encounter left me a little lightheaded. It'll just get worse without something in my stomach."

"Sounds good to me. How about I whip up my world-famous buttermilk pancakes?"

"World famous? Why have I never heard of them? What have I been missing out on?" I teased, trying to break some of the tension. Being on high-alert all the time dampened my ability to concentrate. With some food, a plan of attack, and my family, I *had* to believe we'd win.

"If you hadn't stopped flying over with your mother and grandmother, you'd know all about them. They're so light and fluffy, they practically levitate. I have to smother them with raspberries to keep them on the plates. You go make your coffee and my tea, sit over there, and watch a pro."

I did as instructed and watched as she mixed everything together. My gut tightened as I thought about everything I'd missed over the years. When I was younger, I played with Drew on the trips to Dorking, but the last visit had been a little strained. She was seven years older and our interests had changed. She had her own circle of friends her own age. I missed growing into adulthood with her. She could have taught me so much about the craft. At least she was here now, and it felt as though those lost years never existed.

She was right about one thing. I needed to expand my circle of friends, magickal and mundane. Drew would be going home at the beginning of August, leaving me on my own. Cooper would be gone by the end of the summer, too. *Cooper.* Could it be possible that he was meant to be my mate? *Mate.* That sounded so cold, and he made me feel anything but. I wasn't like the rest of the family. No way could I have his kid, then just let him leave.

"Anybody home?" Drew sat a plate of pancakes in front of me. "You look like you're a million miles away."

"Not a million, only about three. I was thinking about Mr. Barker and Cooper. I'm sure he'll agree to go back to Nova Scotia once he's well enough, and Cooper will go with him."

I held up my hand as Drew started to speak. "No, not ready to go into it. Not yet. I'm just thinking about what you've said. Having you here has made me realize what I've missed out on. I don't plan on getting all mushy about it, and I have slightly more pressing things on my mind."

Drew smiled and slid the maple syrup over to me, then sat down.

"I didn't see any raspberries, so we'll just have to hold them down ourselves. Load 'em up with syrup. There'll be plenty of time to sort everything out later. Then we can start planning the double wedding." Drew winked.

Once we consumed the food and dishes were done, we headed to the sunporch with fresh coffee and tea.

"So," Drew said. "Tell me about last night. Did you do any more midnight walks?"

"Yes. I visited where Montgomery is staying. I'm thinking that maybe somehow scrying is enhancing my ability to travel astrally. Maybe it's just a coincidence. It was much clearer this time, but he sensed me. He said as much when he invaded my mind this morning. I wonder if that's why he jumped from me to you? What did he say to you? Do you know where he took you?"

"No, it was dark, but I could see him. I agree that he's probably Montgomery. The mark on his face is identical. He didn't say much. He walked around me a few times. It was really creepy. He said, 'So you're Priscilla's granddaughter. I can see the resemblance.' Then he told me again that I was next, then Mum and Gran. I asked him why, but he just snapped his fingers. He's very strong Marcy." Her voice faltered. "I don't know how we're going to stop him."

"I'll do a séance tonight and see if I can contact our great grandmother. If nothing else, it'll be good practise. Maybe I can call a few of Mother's old clients and offer them a freebie. It won't be quite the same with just the two of us. Besides, if I'm going to consider carrying on with my mother's clients, I need to practise with other people around."

I had no idea where Mother's old list of clients was, or if it even still existed. I remember it'd been stuck to the fridge with a magnet. Granny may not have kept it. Occasionally, Mother would do something special and call her regulars to see if they were interested. Usually when there was a unique astral occurrence, like an eclipse, full moon, and comet, all in one night. I didn't really feel up to going through the boxes looking for a single sheet of paper. Besides, I remembered some of the names. I'd just use Granny's phone book.

Once I found the local directory, I settled on the couch, grabbed my notebook and cell, and started calling. *Shouldn't be too hard to get four people to sit with Drew and myself.* Besides, it was a small town with little to do, especially for the grey-haired set. The first four I tired were ecstatic and more than happy to come. I told them to be here by 10:00 p.m. sharp.

I'd written down about a dozen names I remembered, so I continued to look up phone numbers, just in case this panned out. Picking up Mother's old business wouldn't be so bad. I liked the idea of working from home, and I was really enjoying the new experience. Well, except the part where Great Uncle Montgomery was trying to kill me and my family.

Drew plopped down beside me, one of Auntie P.'s old books in her hand. "This is a journal of sorts, all about the witch with the twins. The old script is a little difficult to read, but I'm getting the hang of it. Someone really should transcribe all the old hand-written books and publish them. Not for the general public, but for future generations of people like us."

"Well then, why don't you do that as you're reading them? Do some research and transcribe the books at the same time. Kill two birds and all that."

"Should have kept my gob shut," Drew said. "Maybe I will do that, though." She had one finger stuck between two of the pages. "Look what I found." She handed the open book to me. "It's about the boy."

THIRTY-EIGHT

That got my interest. I hoped that whatever happened to the evil-boy-twin would help us now. I sniggered.

"What's so funny?" Drew asked.

"I was just thinking how cliché I am. I keep referring to him in my mind as 'the-evil-boy-twin'. He must have a name."

Drew pointed to the book. "Read."

I lowered my gaze and took in the characters on the page. "Whoever wrote this had beautiful handwriting, but I see what you mean about it. The words look more like hieroglyphics. I've read several ancient journals, though, so I'm sure I can get through it. Just give me a minute to adjust to it."

Slowly, I traced the lines with my fingers, imagining writing them. Little trick I learned. Bit by bit I could make out the words, and I picked it up quickly. Seems I did that a lot. Pick up stuff easily. Too bad I wasn't so quick in school. This was a snap.

"Oh. My. God." My mouth gaped.

"I know! If they could do it, why not us?"

"But wait." I looked up at her. "This is Canada. We don't have all those mysterious ancient places here. This isn't like Great Britain. What can we do here?"

"Oh, right." Drew fell back against the couch, her enthusiasm deflated.

"Let's think about it. There has to be something. True, we don't have the history that Britain and Europe do, but the land is just as old. It's only the civilization that's new." I snapped my fingers. "I've got it. The Indigenous Peoples have been here forever. They have their own stories and special places. Maybe we can find something there that will help us."

Drew sat up, her excitement back. "That could work, but I know nothing about Indigenous wisdom or heritage. Do you?"

"No, but we can find out. Maybe the local man who makes the dreamcatchers knows something. He's pretty old, so he must have heard stories. They were skilled storytellers, passing the wisdom from one generation to the next. There are also books and the internet. We're bound to find something."

"OK, let's start with the internet," Drew said. "Search indigenous oral traditions or mysterious places in Canada. Something's bound to turn up."

We set up our laptops on the sunporch and started researching. It didn't take nearly as long as I thought.

"This might be an option." I turned my computer towards Drew so she could read it. "I found a stone circle. It's nothing as elaborate as Stonehenge, but it's more than I expected to find in North America, never mind right here in Canada."

"Problem." Drew pointed at the screen. "It's in Alberta. How are we supposed to get Montgomery to go to another province?"

I waved my hand. "Minor detail. The stone circle may not even be anything other than a bunch of old rocks."

"Take a good look at those pictures. It's not just a bunch of old rocks. The circle is enormous, and there's a deliberate pattern. All the henges, standing stones, and places like that have power. The ordinary folk just don't know it yet." Drew gave ordinary folk air quotes as though I wouldn't get her meaning.

"All right, *oh, Mighty Wizard*, how do we tap into this power?"

Drew shrugged. "Usual drill. Chants, candles, concentration. That's relatively easy. You must've felt it at Stonehenge. I've been to some of the other standing stones with Mum and Gran on festival days. Evenings actually. They radiate with power. Trick is learning the purpose of the formation. It may not be what we need. Can you find anything that hints at local myths around it?"

I scrolled down the page. "You mean like this?" Part way down was the heading: *The Legend of Omahkiyaahkohtoohp*. "I'm not even going to try to pronounce that. Says here it's Blackfoot for old big arrangement. I'd say that's an appropriate name for it."

Drew pulled her chair beside me and we read the write-up together. She pointed at one of the paragraphs. "Wow, it's even older than Stonehenge and the Egyptian pyramids, and it's on the same latitude as Stonehenge. That can't be a coincidence." She tapped the computer screen. "Look, there's even a book called *Canada's Stonehenge*. I wonder if it's still available? Could be a good source of information. Maybe Mr. Barker—Oh, sorry. I almost forgot."

"I'll go visit him later today. Maybe Cooper can find it if it's not in the library or the store. Let's keep reading. Maybe something of interest will pop up." I scrolled down and found one of the old stories. Drew settled back in her chair as I read it aloud.

"For generations, local people have handed down tales of the mysterious ring. Thousands of years ago, boulders twice the size of the buffalo sat in the middle of the plains, arranged in an almost perfect circle. Several stones were set to align with the stars in the heavens. Now, little more than lichen-covered rocks remain, but the story persists. The stories vary in each telling, but the basic information repeats.

"Millennia ago, a small band of settlers set up their village a few miles from the circle. No one is certain where these people came from. They regarded the circle as sacred. A representation of a sun-god laid out before them. They left offerings to ensure good hunting. Sometimes, a small animal was tied to a stake at the centre if hunting was particularly bad. By morning the animal would be gone, the rope intact, still tied in a loop at one end and fixed to the stake at the other. No tracks were to be found, and not a drop of blood. It was as though the animal had been taken to the heavens by the sun god.

"Some of the later tales have the circle being used as punishment. A person would be tied up and left in the centre for the Gods to decide on penance. Just like the animals, the person would be gone, ropes intact, no tracks or blood.

"Eventually, civilization and progress changed their way of thinking, changed the way they handed punishment out. Laws were created and enforced, the small village disappeared, and the stone circle was left to live only in memory."

"That's interesting." I re-read the last two paragraphs. "The circle has a history of making people vanish. We could try to get Montgomery inside it. But how do we restrain him? He's not likely to just stand still and let us tie him up." I removed my glasses and chewed on the end of one arm, mulling over our new discovery.

"How do we get him to Alberta and inside the Henge?" Drew sat back, frowning.

"I think I've got that covered. Astral travel. I've done it twice with little effort, and he knows I've visited him. He has no issue with it himself, or with the mind invasion, for that matter. Maybe I can get him to agree to meet me there on the astral plane."

Drew grabbed my arm. "Are you serious? Do you realize how dangerous that can be?"

"He's planning on killing me, you, and the rest of the family. Danger isn't a consideration."

"I'm not at all comfortable with this. Maybe we should ask Mum or Gran."

I shook off her hand. "No. Maybe. I don't know. They're certain to try to dissuade me, but what other option do we have? Why don't you see if you can arrange a Skype call this afternoon or tonight, but don't tell them my plan. We'll just pick their brains. Ask for their advice. Have a major brainstorming session and see what comes of it. Maybe one of them will know how we can restrain him."

Drew bit her bottom lip and shook her head. She pushed the computer away and dragged my chair around, putting us face to face.

"Marcy, you have no idea what you're getting into. You've been away from the craft for years. You're not strong enough. Hell, you're not strong magickally at all. Maybe Mum or Gran could fight him, but not you or me. Your plan is insane."

I reached over and took her hands in mine. "I have no choice. You have no choice. I know your Gran won't fly over, but maybe your mother could. Together, all three of us can defeat him. Of that, I'm absolutely positive."

Drew crinkled her nose and gave it some thought. She puckered her mouth and wiggled it side-to-side. Her head bopped. I suspected she weighed her options and had an imaginary conversation with her mother. I watched the little Drew-show for a few minutes, waiting for her decision.

"Right. I think Mum will go for it with a little persuasion. I wish Gran would come over. We could really use her power and experience. Funny, isn't it? A witch that's afraid to fly."

"Ya, hysterical. It's almost noon. I'll make a salad for lunch and you call or text and see if they're available later today. That'll give your mother time to talk to Auntie P. and do whatever research they need to. See if they can be on Skype by what? Four our time? Maybe your mother can fly over by Monday. After lunch, I'll go see how Mr. Barker is."

THIRTY-NINE

When I walked into the kitchen, Nenka stood by the porch door, a small basket in hand. "Would you like me to gather the ingredients for you?"

"That would be a big help. Thanks. Can you get some cherry tomatoes, radishes, a cucumber, and carrots? We already have the lettuce."

As I set the table, thoughts of Cooper and Melissa popped into my mind. I'd promised Melissa we'd get together, and I hadn't been in touch since. I leaned against the counter, recalling our conversation at the museum. She studied in Cairo. Maybe she knew of some Egyptian legend that might help.

And Cooper is a helper. Maybe I could ask him to find… what? Did I even want to disturb him with his gramps in the hospital?

"Ahem." Nenka stood beside me with her basket full of veggies.

I reached down to relieve her of her load. "Sorry. Just considering a few things. Thank you for helping."

"You don't have to take this on all on your own. Make use of your family and friends. If there's anything Tinkus or I can do, please ask. We're here to help. We do more than chores, you know."

I gave her back the empty basket, and she scampered off, leaving me to wonder what else my little gnomes were capable of. Maybe Cooper could find something other than children's fairy tales about them.

I washed, chopped, and mixed everything in a large wooden salad bowl, then placed it on the table with two matching individual bowls. I was just setting a bottle of homemade dressing on the table when Drew came in.

I'd forgotten she'd called home. "That was a long conversation." I plunked on a chair and motioned for her to join me. "What did she say?"

"I told Mum everything. You can imagine she's pretty freaked out. She isn't sure how much she's going to tell Gran. Sort of a need-to-know basis. At first, she said to come back home and bring you with me. But after I told her what he did and has planned, not just for you, but for all of us, she agreed to come over. She'll get as much information as she can and be ready for us to call her by nine-thirty, four-thirty our time."

I scooped some of the salad into her bowl, then filled mine. "Eat. There's not a lot we can do right now. Why don't you come to the hospital with me? I know Mr. Barker would be pleased to see you."

"Sure. I'd like to see him. But before we go, I think we should refresh the protection around the windows and doors."

"Good idea. I hope Monty doesn't come around again. He seems to be staying away, however, I have a peculiar feeling. I wonder if Nenka or Tinkus can use the phone? Granny kept a land line and I haven't disconnected it yet. Nenka? Can you hear me?" I hadn't figured out where she kept popping out from. "Could you come back to the kitchen, please?"

Drew looked at me like I was nuts. "What? I don't know how to contact her. She just appears out of nowhere."

"Yes, dear? What can I help you with?"

Drew and I both jumped. "Geeze, Nenka. Don't sneak up on me like that."

She smiled, that familiar twinkle in her eyes. "I never sneak, dear. I'm just quiet. Do you need something?"

"Yes. Do you know how to use Granny's phone?"

"I think so. I saw Francine use it several times. Looks simple enough. Why?"

"We're going to visit Mr. Barker at the hospital. I'm sure nothing will happen, but just in case, I'll leave you my cell number."

Nenka wrung her hands. "Oh my, oh my. That awful man isn't coming back, is he?"

"I hope not. But just in case, I'll leave the number by the phone, and I'll put the phone on the floor to make it easier for you. I'd like you all to stay indoors after we leave, though."

Nenka hurried out of the kitchen, still muttering, 'oh my' over and over.

Once we finished lunch and tidied up, we drove over to the hospital. Cooper was there, along with another man, probably in his fifties. Mr. Barker lay sleeping.

"Hi, Marcy. Nice of you to come. Is this the English cousin Gramps has mentioned?" Cooper extended a hand towards Drew.

"Yes. Drew, this is Cooper, Mr. Barker's grandson. And I'm afraid I don't know the other gentleman." I extended my hand. "I'm guessing you're Cooper's dad. I'm Marcy and this is Drew."

The family resemblance was remarkable. An entire family of Johnny Depp clones. Well, almost clones. All three had the same striking eyes. It was like they could see right into your soul. But they weren't dark or foreboding. Their eyes sparkled and you couldn't help but smile. I looked at Drew and she nodded. She felt it, too. Together, they emitted a force of some sort. It wasn't the same as our kind, but it was just as strong. I hadn't noticed it with just Cooper and Mr. Barker; Cooper was too distracting.

Cooper.

Warmth radiated up my neck and onto my face.

Cooper and his dad exchanged a look and grinned. *Damn!* I was so embarrassed. I turned away and moved to the head of the bed. Mr. Barker looked quite frail.

I touched his arm. "How is he doing?"

Cooper's dad walked around to the other side of the bed. "Doctor said he's recovering faster than expected. Hopefully, we can get him out of here in a week or so."

The heat in my face cooled, but I still couldn't look at them. At Cooper. Not yet. I turned slightly and picked up the amethyst crystal from the side table. "Never underestimate the power of crystals."

I returned it to the piece of velvet and turned back to Mr. Barker. His eyes were open.

"Ladies," he whispered. "So glad you found time to visit this sick old man."

Drew came over and stood beside me.

"I'm glad you're getting better, Mr. Barker. We were so worried."

He reached up and brushed my cheek. "Don't cry, child. I'll be fine."

I hadn't realized I was crying.

"You always had a way with the ladies," Cooper's dad said. He winked at me much the same way Cooper had, but it didn't have nearly the same effect.

"I guess I'm a little emotional right now. Did Cooper mention I lost my grandmother last month? I never realized it until now, but I think I've always felt as though Mr. Barker was my adopted grandfather. I never knew my own gramps or my father. So much has been happening lately."

I dropped onto the visitor's chair and let the tears fall. I'd been holding everything in and the dam finally broke.

"I'm so sorry." I got up and ran down the hall towards to a small lounge just around the corner. I'd discovered it after Granny passed. I curled up on the easy chair and let it all out. Several minutes later, Drew came in.

"You certainly know how to leave a lasting impression with a prospective in-law."

I sniffled and ran my hand under my nose. "I do my best."

Drew pulled a small packet of tissues out of her bag. "Try this. Might work better."

I uncurled, sat up, blew my nose, then went into the adjoining bathroom. I dropped the tissue in the waste basket then splashed cold water on my face. I never realized just how rough those paper towels were until I dried my face with it. At least it was absorbent. I glanced in the mirror and groaned.

"I look absolutely horrible. My eyes are red and puffy and my face is all blotchy from the stupid paper towel." I walked back into the lounge. "I can't go back in there looking like this."

"Give it a minute or two." Drew pulled a small, unlabelled jar from her bag and applied a home-made lotion of some sort to my face. "This will help remove the puffiness."

I threw my arms around her. "I'm so glad you're here. I can't handle this alone."

Drew wrapped her arms around me. A warmth seeped into me, comforting me.

"I forgot you could do that. Thank you." Drew wasn't a healer, but she had the ability to transfer energy to people in need. I didn't really understand it, but I was glad she could do it. I pulled away.

"You're welcome. You know I'm always here for you."

"I'm better now. Let's go back to Mr. Barker's room. Maybe you can give him a little boost? Do you need much contact?"

"No. A touch will do. Most people aren't aware when it happens, unless they're magickal. They just feel comforted. I suspect Mr. Barker will know. Let's find out."

When we returned, the Barkers were chatting and laughing as though sitting at home and everything was normal. They stopped when we walked in. I went over to Cooper's father.

"I must apologize. I don't know what came over me."

"No apologies necessary. Cooper and Dad have filled me in. If there's anything at all we can do, please don't hesitate to ask."

"Thank you, sir, but this is something we have to do as a family. Drew's mother should be here in a day or two to help. Together, the three of us should be able to defeat him. Correction, we *will* defeat him."

Cooper chuckled. "Not quite Maiden, Mother, and Crone, but you should be just as effective."

"I don't think Mum would appreciate being compared to a crone," Drew said. "And I'm not sure which of us would be Mother. Probably me. I think you three match that description better. But yes, we will be stronger as three. Now there's something I need to do."

She stood beside Mr. Barker's bed and cradled his hand between both of hers. She closed her eyes and concentrated. At first, he looked puzzled, then his eyes lit up, and he smiled. He looked at me and nodded, then closed his eyes and let Drew do her thing. Gradually, the slight grey tint of his skin disappeared and a soft pink replaced it. Drew opened her eyes and gently placed his hand on his chest.

"He'll rest for a while now. I can't repair his heart, but I could transfer some strength. Unless something happens directly to his heart, he'll be fine."

"I think we should go now." I squeezed his hand. "But we'll be back in a day or two." My cell buzzed. I looked at the number on the screen. "Schist."

I knew I couldn't answer the cell in this area of the hospital, so I ran back to the lounge.

"Hello? Nenka?" She spoke too quickly for me to understand, her voice a high-pitched squeak. "Slow down." I listened as she repeated herself. "We're leaving now. Stay put and don't worry."

I rushed back to Mr. Cooper's room. "Well?" Drew asked.

"Nenka thinks he's near the house. She can feel him. It's not strong, so he's probably hanging around nearby."

"Nenka?" Cooper asked. "That wouldn't be one of your little pixies, would it?"

"They're gnomes," Drew and I said in unison.

Cooper rolled his eyes. "Whatever. Call me."

As we rushed out of the room, I heard Cooper's dad say, "She'll be an interesting addition to our family."

First Drew, now Cooper's dad. Was I the only one not seeing where this was going? Drew nudged me while waiting for the elevator.

"Don't fight it. You and Cooper are a perfect match."

"You don't even know him. *I* don't know him." The elevator doors swooshed open. "Can we talk about this later? That bad feeling I had is getting worse. I'm scared."

We stopped at the parking pre-pay just inside the hospital doors. I dropped my debit card twice before managing to pay.

We hit one red light after another along Davis Drive, and I cursed each and every one. I was just turning up Woodbine when the headache hit. Hard. I slammed on the brakes. Good thing no one was behind me. I threw it in park without pulling off the road.

"What the heck?" Drew grabbed the dashboard.

"Switch spots with me now. I don't know how long I can hold him off."

I was barely conscious when Drew pulled into my drive. I needed to get inside, behind the protected walls. Stumbling to the door, I concentrated as best I could, picturing a thick stone wall inside my head, blocking Montgomery's attempt to take control. I wasn't ready for him, and I planned on being the one in charge next time. The headache faded once we were on my property, and it continued to weaken as the front door shut behind us.

"It worked. I actually blocked him." I stumbled into the living room and fell face first onto the couch, gasping. "That really took a lot out of me." I turned my head and adjusted my glasses. "I'm ready to admit I can't fight him alone. Even the two of us won't be enough. I hope we can hold him off until your mother arrives. As you said, he's strong. But so is your mother. She's older and has more experience. I can't imagine he would've been able to figure everything out on his own, so we should have one up on him."

Drew lit the two white candles still sitting on the coffee table, along with the incense. She knelt beside me and placed a hand on my back. A small jolt of energy entered my body, revitalizing me.

"That's just it. He shouldn't have been able to figure out *anything* on his own. Someone must have been teaching and guiding him."

"He couldn't have figured it out on his own? There are lots of solitary witches. No one taught them."

"True," Drew said, "but they also don't have the same power. There's a piece somewhere that we've missed."

I breathed deeply, then sat up. "Great. And just how are we supposed to figure out that missing piece? I doubt he's going to tell us just because we ask nicely. Maybe the séance will be successful and someone will come through that'll be able to shed some light. Did you tell your mother I'm trying my hand at it tonight?"

"Completely forgot. What time did you tell them?"

"Ten. Which room do you think would be best?"

Drew shrugged. "May as well do it in the dining room. The table is round and the drapes are heavy enough to block the moonlight. Since it was your mother who did the séances, why did your gran have a round table?"

I laughed as I suddenly got a picture of Granny about eight or nine years ago.

"Some of her clients liked to watch when she made up their mixtures. They claimed it worked better if they witnessed it, but Granny said she was certain they just didn't completely trust her. Didn't stop them from coming back, though. Anyway, as she bustled around the table, she constantly hit the corners with her hip. She got sick and tired of being bruised, so she bought a round one. I think the old table is in one of the rooms on the third floor. I recall a lot of cussing when the delivery guys had to shift it."

As the last words came out of my mouth, it dawned on me. Nenka! I hadn't seen her or Tinkus since we arrived.

"Nenka? Where are you?" As soon as I stood, I fell back, still shaken by the latest attack. I waited a moment and tried again, slower this time.

Drew checked the kitchen while I looked in the dining room. "Nenka?"

"You don't think…?" Drew let the thought drift.

"Don't even go there." I raced into the hall and popped the hidden door in the wainscotting, calling for both gnomes. as I ran down the stairs. The Fae door stood open. Nenka and Tinkus peeked out.

"We're safe." Tinkus let Nenka enter the room first.

"They're here," I called up to Drew as she scrambled down the steps.

"He doesn't seem to be able to enter the house. I don't believe he's on the property, either." Nenka looked around. "But he's not far."

"I felt him too, as we neared the house. It subsided as soon as we pulled into the driveway. I agree. He's near, but not on the property. Let's keep it that way."

I wanted to hug my tiny, extended family, but was afraid I'd squish them. Instead, I knelt and placed a hand on each one's shoulder. "Please, stay alert and don't go far."

"We'll be careful, dear." They stepped back through the door, closing it behind them.

"Come on, Drew. We need to get everything ready." I detoured to the kitchen and grabbed the bottle of Advil from the cupboard. For some reason, the last dregs of the Monty-induced headache just wouldn't go away.

I checked the time. Still another hour before our call with Susan and I wanted to get a few more of Mother's items for the séance. The box we'd brought down containing the crystal ball had been tucked away under the dining room table. I went over, dragged the box out, and removed the two silver candle sticks, the candelabrum, and the carefully wrapped purple lace tablecloth. After I uncovered it from the tissue, I spread it across the table.

"Schist. It's too small. I really wanted to use it tonight. I need to get a new one before the séance. Maybe I can get a white one and place this in the centre, with the candelabrum on top."

I was putting the candlesticks on the table when I heard a faint knock. I turned to see Nenka standing in the doorway.

"Is that better? Didn't want to startle you." She smiled, trying to look innocent, but the twinkle in her eyes led me to believe she was being just a tad sarcastic. We were going to get along just fine. "Do you need anything from the garden?" She still seemed a little nervous.

"No. There are plenty of herbs drying. I don't believe we need anything else at the moment. We've pumped up the protection around the house, but

I'd prefer it if you still stayed inside for a while. The garden won't suffer from another day's neglect."

"Well…"

"Look, if he's not hovering about tomorrow, I'll help with the garden. I don't mind pulling a few weeds. I'll probably need to pick some more veggies, anyway."

Nenka fidgeted with the edge of the apron tied around her waist. "Well, I suppose that will be all right. I dread to think what that horrible man would do to us. I'm certain he knows we're here."

I wasn't surprised. If he was one of my kind, he'd be able to see the gnomes, faeries, and all the rest.

"It'll all be over soon. Drew's mother is flying here to help. In a few days, everything will be back to normal. You'll see."

She didn't look like she believed me. I didn't believe me. At least she seemed reasonably assured. Enough to sneak a half-smile before she scampered away. The twinkle had left her eyes. I couldn't worry about them right now, though. As long as they stayed inside, they'd be fine. I hoped. I checked the time. I could run to the store for a larger tablecloth and be back before Susan's call. I quickly measured the table. Seventy-eight inches in diameter. Not a standard size.

"Drew, I'm going to the store. Back in a bit."

"Hold on. You're not going anywhere without me."

"I won't be long. No need for both of us to go."

"If he tries to attack you again when you're driving…"

She was probably thinking about what just happened, but I was picturing the police photos of Mother's car with her in it.

"Yeah. Come on."

Rather than try several stores for the odd size I needed, I went to Fabricland and got a large piece of white lace. It was just after 4:30 p.m. when we returned home. Drew went straight to her laptop and booted up to Skype her mother.

"Thank the god and goddess. I thought something had happened to you two." Susan's shoulders dropped as she relaxed.

"My fault. I needed something from the store and it was a little busy."

"We're only a couple of minutes late, Mum."

"I know, Drew, but with everything that's going on over there, I was worried. It's not like you to be even one minute late."

"We're fine, Susan, and we'd like to stay that way. Have you spoken with Auntie P.? Do you have any idea what we need to do to shut him down?"

"She's extremely upset and worried, but she's checking with some of her friends. Asking what they remember about the legend of the Ancient One. There's another very old journal that was written about her. She's much older than we thought. It mentions the boy and his banishment. I don't know if the information will help. They tricked him into going to Stonehenge. It's about one hundred miles from here, but they lived around what is now Marlborough. That's only about thirty miles from the Henge. We were still working in covens back then, and they completely surrounded him once they got him there. Their combined power was enough. Many more of the stones would have been standing back then. They somehow managed to get him into the inner circle even though there was a storm was raging. A bolt of lightning hit the stone, and he was gone."

"Yes, we found that story, too, in one of the books Drew brought with her. He disappeared? Poof? Just like that?"

"The story is old, Marcy. Gone could mean he was hit directly and died. Maybe it's more mysterious, and he was sent somewhere else. You know, like those books they've made into a telly show where a woman falls through a stone and goes back to centuries old Scotland. Maybe the story isn't so far-fetched. There are many things we don't understand."

"We don't have a coven, Mum. It's just us. Were you able to get a flight over?"

"Yes. An early one tomorrow. I'll arrive just after noon your time. Your gran will be writing down everything her friends can remember, and I'll bring her notes with me. She'll keep asking and let us know if anything pertinent turns up."

"I'll see you tomorrow." Drew ended the call with her mother.

"Well, that was interesting." I rubbed my temples again, still trying to rid myself of the headache. "Maybe this stone structure in Alberta will work. You pointed out it was on the same latitude as Stonehenge, and both were roughly the same diameter. There must be a connection."

FORTY

Drew's phone dinged as we cleared up after dinner. Her gran texted us a potion to prepare for when we confronted Montgomery. I made check marks in the air as Drew read off each ingredient. *Powdered hydrangea blossoms?* I knew there were hydrangeas in the garden, but I didn't know if any of the flowers had been picked and dried. I left Drew to put the dishes away and went down to the workroom to check.

Nope.

All sorts of herbs and a few flowers, but no hydrangeas. I went back to the kitchen.

"I haven't felt him at all for ages. It should be safe to go out for a few minutes."

"I agree," Drew said. "I noticed his essence fading a while ago. I'm certain he's moved away. You're getting stronger, though. Much faster than I expected. Probably took him by surprise. Be careful. He's probably plotting something new."

Snippers in hand, I headed to the back of the garden. Granny had planted a row of hydrangeas along the south side. All different colors. Auntie P. hadn't indicated if the color mattered. I started at one end and examined every bloom. A few were almost dead, so I snipped those first. I needed them dried and the dead ones were halfway there. It surprised me just how many of the blooms were spent. Had Nenka been afraid to come out even before I asked her to say indoors? That many shouldn't have died in the short time since I asked her to stay inside. When I couldn't hold any more in one hand, I took them downstairs and hung them to finish drying.

"Nenka? Can you hear me?"

The tiny door opened with a creak and both she and Tinkus emerged.

"Yes, dear?" Despite there being no sign of Monty coming back, Nenka sounded more upset than yesterday. The worry lines across her brow were more prominent. "He's gone now, isn't he?"

"It seems so. I was curious. Have you been staying indoors more than usual recently? The reason I ask is the hydrangeas."

She looked puzzled. "The hydrangeas? What about them?"

I pointed to the blooms that now hung on the line across the room. "There were an awful lot of dead and dying flowers."

"Impossible. Why, just yesterday morning I did a full round of the garden. Any dead blooms were harvested and left in the basket over there."

I looked where she pointed. A wicker basket sat on the floor by the table. Funny, I hadn't noticed it before. There were a few flowers in it, but not many.

"I'd leave them there for Francine and she'd hang them to dry. That way, she always had pretty much any ingredient she needed. She'd pick the fresh herbs, though. I tell you, there were no dead blooms on any of those plants yesterday. Not the hydrangeas, not anything. I am absolutely positive I left nothing dead in that garden." She crossed her arms and stomped one foot. It would have been funny any other time.

"So, what caused all those flowers to die, and so suddenly? There's still more on the bushes."

Nenka shrugged.

"Both Drew and I are positive Montgomery isn't around, but would you mind staying put just a little longer? If everything still seems fine in the morning, you can go about your usual routine."

Neither responded. Now what?

"Is something wrong?"

Tinkus put a hand on Nenka's shoulder. "Nimagg's missing."

"Missing? Since when?"

"He went out yesterday morning," Nenka said. "When you asked us to stay inside, we called for him. He must have gone off the property and couldn't hear us."

"He rarely stays out so long," Tinkus added. "And he's never been out all night before. You don't think…?"

Nenka fell against Tinkus. Her shoulders rose and fell with each sob. My heart broke, but I didn't know what to do or say.

I'm sure they were thinking the same thing as me. Would Montgomery be that cruel? What was I thinking? Of course he would. He killed my mother and Granny. Why not a teenage gnome? But what would he to do him? And for what purpose? Then a thought popped into my mind.

"You said he was at *that* age. Maybe he has a girlfriend and is with her?"

Nenka looked shocked, but Tinkus grinned. Typical male.

"Is it at all possible? Maybe he has friends he's staying with?" *Did gnomes have friends?* "Or your family?" Nenka never mentioned any other gnomes except her parents. The family that disowned her for marrying a lowly house gnome. I had to force myself not to laugh at that. It wasn't funny, though. I really should learn more about them. Nimagg had been gone all day yesterday, last night, and all day today. That was a long time with no word. *Blast!*

"Drew and I will look for him. Even if he won't show himself, he'll hear us and hopefully come home." I was going to tell them to stay put again, but

I figured they wouldn't listen. If my child was missing, I wouldn't stay put either.

I headed back up and found Drew curled up on the sofa in the living room, reading. I dropped into the easy chair. "We have a problem."

She placed her bookmark and put the book on the coffee table. "Another one?"

"Nimagg's missing. Nenka's son. We need to find him."

Even though neither of us wanted to head out alone, we had no choice. We went in search of the missing gnome, fingers crossed Montgomery would stay out of my head. Drew went north, I headed south. We had our phones, and I called Drew. We needed to keep in contact. Line open, I slid the phone into my pocket. If something happened, one word would raise the alarm.

The forest to the east of the house was deep and would have to wait. We'd do that together. We walked around the property for about a half hour, calling for Nimagg. If he heard, we had no indication. I met Drew back at the house.

Nenka said he still wasn't back.

Great. We'd have to go into the forest.

After asking Áine, the Irish goddess of the fae, to protect him, we separated, but kept close enough to stay in each other's sight. I checked the time. "Drew, we're going to have to prepare for the séance soon. Another half hour, no more."

She gave me a thumbs up and kept walking.

After thirty minutes, I finally called off the search. There was no sign of him anywhere. We headed back to the house to my worried gnome.

"I'm sorry, Nenka, but we tried. It's just too dark for us to see anything. Maybe if we can find a way to illuminate the woods?" I glanced at Drew as she was an expert at creating light. "I'll call the ladies to cancel the seance.

We've asked the goddess of the fae to watch over him. Can you contact the other fae in the area and have them search, too?"

"Please don't cancel. I'm certain he's with someone, as you suggested. If this entity is as evil as you believe, he would have left his body as a warning. I'll have Tinkus spread the word. Nighttime is what the fae control. Thank you for trying," she whispered, then disappeared.

"I wonder where they live," I said. "The walls can't be that thick, can they?"

"You could try asking her. Meanwhile, it's time to set everything up. I'm certain the fae can do a better job than us in the dark." Drew gathered up the candles, incense, and other items we needed. A gnawing in my chest stopped me from helping.

"In a moment. First, I want to ask the angels to protect him."

✳ ✳ ✳

I put the white lace fabric over the large round table in the dining room and placed Mother's purple lace tablecloth over it. Once the white lace was cut and hemmed, it would look much nicer, but in the low light it wouldn't be noticeable. The contrast between the two was perfect.

Twelve-inch white candles set in the silver candelabrum stood at the centre of the purple tablecloth. Three small bowls sat on either side of it. One contained sea salt, one water, and the other a few small biscuits as offerings. The crystal ball sat in front of the chair I would occupy. Drew moved the extra chairs so they were out of the way. Earlier, I'd placed three incense sticks around the room; one sat on a small table against the wall behind my chair, one on the fireplace mantle, and the third I moved from the far end of the tables so it sat in front of the candelabrum.

Two cars pulled into the driveway as I drew the curtains tight. I hurried to the door to greet my guests. They all came together, so I wouldn't have to wait for a late arrival, and they all spoke at the same time, apparently eager to start the séance.

"I'm so happy you came back," one said.

"Does this mean you're picking up your dearly departed mother's business?" asked another.

"This way, ladies. My cousin will show you to your seats. I need a few minutes of silence so I can prepare."

Drew got them seated around the table while I took a moment to ground.

"Ladies, please, make yourself comfortable. Thank you for the warm reception. I don't know if I'll be doing this regularly. To be honest, you lovely ladies are my guinea pigs. I don't even know if I possess Mother's skill. Tonight is my first attempt, and I couldn't think of anyone better to try with than you."

I looked at each one. They sat smiling, pleased I had invited them to a private séance. I was happy I'd made them feel special.

"I haven't seen any of you for quite a while, but I remember you. This is my cousin, Drew. She'll be helping me tonight. Please don't be alarmed if nothing happens. As I said, this is my first attempt. Shall we begin?"

Without waiting for instructions, the ladies placed their hands on the table and sat with the fingertips touching. I wasn't sure if that was necessary, but what the hay? It worked on TV.

Drew lit the candles and incense, then dimmed the lights. *Why does Granny have a dimmer switch installed when she didn't do séances?* Could she have somehow known I'd end up here doing just that? I reached out and touched the fingertips of the two ladies on either side of me. I could tell they expected it. They were all so easy to read. I closed my eyes and tried to picture Mother doing one of her readings. Everyone had held hands, but this table was much too large for such a small group. Fingertips would have to do.

I cracked open one eye. The ladies had their eyes closed, and from their scrunched faces, I assumed they were concentrating.

"Before we begin, I need to close a circle around us." I had written it all out, and laid my cheat-sheet on the table in front of me. I took a deep breath.

> "I cleanse and consecrate thee, candle flame, as a Representative of the Element of Fire. May your essence bless us and bring your passion to our circle, so mote it be.
>
> I conjure the Circle of Power, by my will and by my Word,
>
> I conjure the Circle of Power, a boundary between the worlds;
>
> I conjure the Circle of Power, a sacred space for worship;
>
> I conjure the Circle of Power, to shelter us from negative energies;
>
> I conjure the Circle of Power, to contain the energies raised within;
>
> By the powers above, and the powers below, I close this circle. So mote it be."

I closed my eyes. "Are there any spirits with us tonight? Please, come forward and let us know you are here."

I glanced down at the ball. The clear crystal filled with what looked like smoke swirling around. I didn't know if that was good or bad.

"Please give us a sign to show you are here."

Drew inhaled sharply. I turned towards her. She stared at the table. I followed her gaze. The flames of the candles danced. Not just a slight flicker, but totally crazy movements.

The flames shot straight up. Drew and I both gasped, and not very quietly. All the ladies opened their eyes.

"Oh my," one of them whispered. "That's never happened before."

FORTY-ONE

How had I managed that? I took it as a sign, but of what? Then I felt it. "Don't be alarmed. Someone is trying to come through." I looked at Drew.

She nodded, indicating for me to continue.

I looked at the crystal ball. "Who would you like to give a message to?"

I sensed the presence move behind Mrs. McGillicuddy, then I heard a voice.

Tell Emma no more chair.

I looked around the table. No one gave any indication they had heard the voice.

"No more chair. Does that mean something to you, Mrs. McGillicuddy?"

"Is that my Harold?"

I was trying to remember anything about the ladies I had invited. Mr. McGillicuddy had been in a wheelchair and passed last year. It must be him. I received an image of an older gentleman standing with an Irish Setter.

"Did you have a dog? I see him with one."

"Finnegan. That's the dog. He died several years ago. Harold loved to walk him before his accident. They'd be out for hours."

"He's able to do that again. I see him standing with one hand on the dog's head, smiling."

It felt good passing along happy news. *I wonder who else is out there?*

"Is anyone else with us?" I invited any other spirits to come forward.

The flames shot up. The ladies leaned in, anticipation on their faces. They turned to look at me. No, behind me.

"Marcy." Drew didn't even try to keep her voice down. She also looked behind me. I noticed a soft glow out of the corner of my eye. I turned.

Hovering about a foot off the floor was a white glowing… something. It didn't really have a form, but it was about five feet high. I knew she was here for me.

"Who are you?" It wasn't Mother or Granny.

The glow got brighter, then exploded. The candles went out. She was gone. No one said a word for ages. At least, it felt like ages. All four ladies were smiling. I was totally freaked out and glad nothing had caught fire.

"Um, I think that's all, ladies. I don't feel anyone else." I stared at the space behind me.

"That was exciting," Mrs. Brown said. "Can you try it again?"

I turned back to the circle of ladies. It hadn't frightened them at all. I know it freaked me out, at least a little.

"I need a moment first," I told them, then whispered to Drew. "What in holy Heliodore was that? I could tell it was female and came through for *me*, but I couldn't pick up any message. It had been easy for Mrs. McGillicuddy. I actually heard Harold speak. I'm surprised you didn't hear him. He was quite loud."

"I could sense him, but only faintly. That's all. The glowing white lady, now her I could really feel. I wonder who she is, or was?"

"I wonder if she'll appear if I try again, just the two of us. I felt like I should know her."

"Yes, I got that too." Drew circled the area where the glow had appeared. "I can still pick up a bit of residual energy. Come here."

I joined her and immediately felt it. "It's quite strong. Who could it be?"

Drew cocked her head. "Strong? I can barely feel it. You're definitely showing signs of taking after your mother. Do you want to try to contact her while her presence is still here?"

Did I? Yes and no. I was afraid of who she might be. But I didn't get any feeling of danger.

"Marcy? Hello? Are you still with me?" Drew waved a hand in front of my face.

"What? Sorry. Thinking. Who do you believe she is?"

"There's nothing to fear. I don't get the impression she has any malicious intent. Do you?"

"No. If she was evil, I don't think she would have had such a softness to her. Oh, what the heck. It's not late and I'm not tired. What I am is curious. Fire up the candles and I'll give it another go."

The ladies touched fingers again, anticipation written all over their faces.

"Ready?"

"Ready."

I closed my eyes and concentrated on the essence I could still feel emanating from the space behind me.

"Are you still here? Who are you? Do you have a message for me?"

Drew tapped my arm. "She's coming back."

I turned. A soft white ball appeared, gradually getting larger and longer. I forgot about the ladies and turned my chair to face her. Drew scooted her chair up beside me.

"She feels like family," Drew whispered.

"I agree, but who? Aren't we supposed to only be able to contact people either our clients or we knew? We can't identify them otherwise. I only knew Mother and Granny. I don't know any other family who has passed over."

The spirit was now pretty much fully formed, but wasn't totally human. Not a faerie or some other spirit. It's just her features weren't completely clear. I stood and took a step towards her. I was more curious than scared.

She was a few inches shorter than my five-foot nine frame.

"Who are you?" I barely heard my voice.

"I was called Fiona."

I leaned close to Drew. "Do you recognize that name?"

"What name?"

I spun around. "You didn't hear her?"

Drew shook her head. "I noticed a faint buzz, though. What did she say?"

"Fiona. Her name is Fiona." I held my hand towards Drew. "Come stand with me."

Drew joined me, hand in mine. "I don't know of any Fiona, except from Shrek, and she wasn't one of ours."

"Funny. *Not.*"

The spirit spoke again. "You know me as The Ancient One."

Drew gasped.

"Oh, you heard her this time?" I was never one to resist any opportunity for a bit of sarcasm. Even when scared. Then it hit me.

"Wait. The Ancient One? But how is that possible? I thought we could only contact people who were fairly recently gone. Like within the last, I don't know, fifty or a hundred years. You've been gone for centuries."

"You are special, Marcy. Like I was."

"You know my name?"

"I have been watching you, waiting for you to come back."

Watching me? OK, that's creepy.

"So, if you've been watching, you know about Montgomery."

"Yes. And you are on the right path." Her color shifted somewhat, changing to a soft blue. "He's much like my son, I'm sorry to say. But you can be rid of him. I am glad you found the sundial west of this place. Your instincts are good."

She faded.

"Wait. What am I supposed to do?"

"My energy is diminishing. Tomorrow…."

She was gone.

"I heard all that," Drew said. "I think you were acting as a sort of conduit."

I turned back to face Drew and my guests. "Wonderful. I'm special and a conduit. I think you can let go now. I need to close the circle. It'll only take a moment." I looked down at my sheet.

"Lady of the Moon, of the fertile Earth and rolling seas,

Lord of the Sun, of the sky and wind,

Thank You for Your presence in our circle today.

Stay if you will, go if you must,

But know that you are ever welcome in our hearts.

We bid you hail and farewell.

Thank you for your presence in our circle today;

For sharing your wisdom and knowledge

Hail and farewell, powers of the North.

The circle is open, but never broken!"

"That was wonderful. You're stronger than your mother. I can tell," Mrs. McGillicuddy said.

"Thank you. I'm sorry it was so brief."

"Oh poo," Mrs. Brown said. "Emma got a message, and that glow was amazing. Was it a relative?"

"Yes, it was." I stood. "Thank you for coming. I'll let you know if I'll be doing this again."

I ushered them out the front door as fast as I could get them moving.

"Well, that's going to be all over town tomorrow," Drew said.

I agreed and turned on the light, then blew out the candles.

"Fiona said tomorrow. My mum will be here then. Maybe she'll have more information. This is exciting!" She gave me a hug so hard I could barely breath. I somehow managed to wiggle away.

"Exciting? I find it creepy, knowing that someone has been watching my every move my entire life. And I don't know if I want to be special. Wait. I do know. No. I don't want to be that kind of special."

"Oh poo, to quote the old lady. You're just saying that because you've been away from the craft. It'll grow on you. Besides, being 'special' in Fiona's time meant something different."

"Different how?"

"She would've been the leader. The High Priestess of the coven. She would've had to use her magick to protect everyone. We don't have covens any more. You won't need to protect anyone. Well, just us."

"Suppose. Still don't like it. I think I'm about ready to call it a night. Fingers crossed for no bad dreams or unwanted visitors."

FORTY-TWO

The next day, I flopped on the couch after spending an hour looking for Nenka's missing son. Drew joined me a few minutes later.

I shook my head. "It's no use. If Nimagg was on or near the property, he'd have heard us calling. Nenka and Tinkus must be in bits."

Drew touched my arm. "We have to be positive. There's other Fae in the area. Haven't you felt them? He could be with them."

"Other fae? Can't say I've noticed. Then again, I've been rather preoccupied." I jolted upright. "You don't suppose Montgomery would hurt one of them?"

Drew shrugged. "I don't think so. He seems to be concentrating on our family."

Just to be on the safe side, I asked the angels to watch over and protect all the Fae on my property.

After we showered and had a late breakfast, we moved out to the sunporch to enjoy the sun and the flowers blooming in the garden. "Few more hours until Susan arrives. I hope your mother has some ideas to banish Montgomery."

"She sent me a text. She's bringing a surprise. Wouldn't even give me a little bitty hint."

"Maybe she's figured out a way to deal with *him*. I know the sundial is the way to go, even if Fiona hadn't confirmed it last night. Hopefully, your mother has figured out how to harness its power."

"It's such a beautiful day. I hope that's an omen." Drew sat up straight. "What's that?" She pointed to a patch of hostas.

"What's what?" I noticed the leaves moving. "It can't be him. I don't feel his presence, do you?"

"No." She looked around, watching for something to appear. "Probably a squirrel."

I moved to the window to get a better look. "Could it be one of the other Fae you mentioned?" A thought popped into my head. "Can you tell if they're friendly? I know not all of them are nice."

Drew came over to stand beside me. "The only negative energy I've felt has been from Montgomery. Maybe Nenka and Tinkus can tell you what other folk are in the area. After everything settles down, of course."

We watched the movement of the leaves get closer and closer to the corner of the house, then it stopped.

I grabbed her wrist. "Are you certain the other Fae are friendly?"

"Well, maybe not so much friendly as not nasty."

"I hate being this jumpy." I rubbed my arms. "I know we've protected the house and property, but still…"

"He's very strong, but if he could get through, he'd have done it by now. We both need to keep watch, though."

"I won't feel comfortable until this is over."

I could hear the pattering of tiny feet running through the kitchen. Nenka burst into the sunporch.

"Nenka, I've never heard you make so much noise," I teased.

"It's Nimagg. He's back."

So that's what rustled among the hostas.

"That's a relief. Where was he?"

"At my parents."

"Where? I thought they disowned you ages ago."

"I suppose they're coming around. It seems he's been visiting them for quite some time. They knew something didn't feel right, so he stayed there until it felt safe."

"Are you going to visit them now?"

"Yes, I believe it's time to try."

"Will you at least wait until we've dealt with my great uncle?

"It's been almost a century now. Another few days won't make much difference."

I was glad to see that twinkle back in her eyes. She almost glowed as bright as Fiona had. Nenka went back to her family, quietly this time.

"That's one less thing to worry about," Drew said. "Now, do we have everything we need?"

"I'm not sure. Once your mother arrives, we can take inventory. She may have a list with her." I checked the time. "Speaking of which, I think it's time to head to the airport. She's due in about two hours and it'll take most of that time driving there and finding parking. I always manage to get lost." I smacked my forehead. "What am I thinking? My little car won't carry three people, never mind the luggage. I'll have to call a cab."

✵ ✵ ✵

Susan's flight was actually on time and she must have practically flown through customs. We found her waiting for us near one washroom with two suitcases. Once all the hugging finished, Drew asked about the surprise. Susan just smiled.

"Any moment now." She nodded towards the entrance to the washroom. Great Aunt Priscilla emerged.

If my jaw wasn't securely attached to my face, it would have hit the floor. My eyes misted. I ran over and gave her a monster-sized hug. "I'm so glad you came. What did Susan have to do to get you on a plane?"

She snorted lightly. "Susan had nothing to do with it. Just whipped up a batch of special flying juice. I have flown before, I just prefer not to. I was too upset to come over for Francine's funeral, but knowing what I do now, I had to make the trip. Little pinch of Star of Bethlehem, some Rock Rose and Cherry Plum. Add a few secret ingredients, and off to the airport. I knew you couldn't deal with this alone. It's going to take all of us."

Drew picked up her mother's suitcase. I took Auntie P.'s, and we headed to the taxi area. "Maybe with the entire family together, we can strengthen Fiona's energy and keep her with us longer this time."

"Who's Fiona?" Susan asked.

I looked over at Drew and winked. I waved over a taxi-van and nonchalantly said, "Oh, you know, The Ancient One."

The driver loaded the luggage into the trunk and Susan and Auntie P. just stood by the curb, jaws open. Drew gave them a little nudge.

"Come on. We'll tell you all about it once we're home."

Auntie P. kept glancing at me, eyes narrowed. She didn't like being kept in the dark. Susan just shifted around, trying to get comfortable. The driver must have sensed something was up. He looked in the rear-view mirror constantly, driving onto the shoulder more than once.

Auntie P. snapped at him. "Eyes on the road, young man."

He only glanced in the mirror once after that.

The drive back was strained. I was dying to tell them about the séance, and they desperately wanted to know about the Ancient One, but we couldn't talk in the cab. Drew asked about her friends back home and got caught up on the local gossip. One of her regular customers was anxious for her to return, as she needed a special order.

We finally arrived home. As soon as I paid the cabbie and he drove away, the questions flew.

"Slow down. If you'll let me get a word in, I'll tell you everything."

We piled the luggage just inside the door and went into the sunporch. Drew put herself in charge of the coffee and tea. While she took care of that, I told Susan and Auntie P. exactly what happened last night. I also outlined my plan for getting Montgomery to the sundial on the astral plane.

Auntie P. shook her head. "No, no, no. That's far too dangerous. He'll squash you like a bug. Astral travel has to be mastered before such things are attempted."

I understood why she was adamant I shouldn't try it, but what else was there? "Fiona said I was on the right path. It must be what I'm meant to do."

Auntie P. huffed. "I'd like to have a word with Fiona. Give her a piece of my mind."

"Did she tell you it was safe to connect to him that way?" Susan asked.

"Well, no, but—"

"But nothing," Auntie P. broke in. "I assume you're planning on contacting her again."

Drew came in with our tea and coffee. "Of course she is. We've got it all planned."

Part of me sided with Auntie. *Yes, we had it all planned. Did we know what we were doing? No.*

"I was hoping with all of us, we could provide enough energy to keep her here a little longer. Are either of you able to connect with the other side?"

"No. Your mother was the first in several generations," Auntie P. said. "You really could hear her?"

"Yes, loud and clear. Drew could hear a buzzing, but once we joined hands, she could hear too."

"It sounds like you've received several powers that have lain dormant for generations," Susan said.

"Oh, that's not the best part, Mum. Marcy conveniently forgot one tiny detail. Fiona said Marcy is special, like she was. Oh, I just thought of something. Maybe Marcy will have twins, too."

I punched her in the arm. "Don't even joke about something like that. Remember, that boy was evil."

"I don't think that's likely, dear," Auntie P. said. "You know, boys are extremely rare. My brother was the first since the twins. The only two born in our family. Let's hope it's the last for a very long time."

"Sorry, forgot about that," Drew mumbled.

"As much as I wish this was a vacation, it's not," Susan said. "I think we need to make plans."

"Did you find out anything more, Auntie P.?"

"Just one ancient spell, much like the other, except it calls for mullein instead of hydrangeas. I'd like to hold off on too many plans until we have a little chat with The Ancient One. How about you show me the house? I'd like to see what Francine did with it."

"That's right. You've never been here. Drink up and I'll give you the grand tour."

We finished our coffee and tea, avoiding further discussion about Montgomery, then I led them around the property.

"As you can see, Granny has a wonderful garden."

"It's much bigger than I remember," Susan said. "It's been too many years since I visited. She always came to our place." Susan looked around until she spotted the willow. She hurried over and disappeared behind the long, slender branches. Her voice drifted out. "Oh, it's just like I remember." She parted the branches and re-joined us. "Nenka is still here, I assume?"

"Right here."

We turned to see Nenka and Tinkus standing by the lavender.

"It's been a long time. Francine wished you'd come over again. A shame it isn't under happier circumstances," Nenka said.

"You've kept the garden immaculate," Auntie P. said. "I'm Priscilla, Francine's sister." She reached down to shake their hands. A finger and thumb rather than her entire hand.

"I can see the resemblance. Nice to meet you, finally. I know you have lots to discuss and we have too much work to catch up on now that it's safe. So many dead hydrangeas to clean up." They turned and disappeared into the lavender plants.

"She's very polite, isn't she?" Auntie P. said. "Not sure I'd like gnomes in my house, though. Much prefer to go into the woods and deal with the Fae there." Looking towards the lavender, she said, "Nothing personal. Now, what was that about it being safe?"

I had hoped not to mention it. "A patch of hydrangeas mysteriously withered, then Nenka's son, Nimagg, disappeared. We believe Montgomery tried getting through the protection and he took his anger out on the plants. Nimagg turned up the next day."

Auntie P. frowned. "I can't imagine why my little brother is doing this. We tried to cover up for him. We loved him."

Susan put her arm around her mother. "Unfortunately, we may never know."

We continued our walk through the garden, taking a quick inventory of the plants that might be useful for our task. When we got to the hydrangeas, Nenka was busy removing the dead blooms. Susan and Auntie P. exchanged a troubling look.

"Something evil happened here," Auntie P. said. "I can feel the residual energy. You were correct. Monty did this."

"It's still strong, but it feels like it's been here for several days," Susan added.

"A few days ago, I asked the angels for protection. Montgomery has occasionally crept around the property. He must have been here right before that."

Auntie P. gave me one of *those* looks, just like Granny and Mother used to do right before scolding me.

I shrugged. "I know. It's just that I seem to have forgotten so much. But I'm learning and remembering. I'll be up to speed in no time."

Drew stepped in before anything escalated. "Why don't you show them the work room?" She turned to Auntie P. "You'll love it."

We went back inside and down the main hall. I stopped in front of the secret panel. "Watch this." I reached out and pressed the tiny button on top of the wainscoting. The door opened with a soft pop.

"Well, look at that." Auntie P. was impressed. "I'd forgotten Francine had mentioned it."

I stepped in and turned on the light at the top of the stairs. "Welcome to my dungeon." I gestured for them to go down.

Auntie P. did exactly what I had the first time. Stood and turned in a circle, taking in everything.

"Francine told me about it, but I never imagined it looked like this."

She went over to the shelves containing the bottles of oils and dried herbs, checking each one. "We can probably use some of these." She removed five bottles and placed them on the central table. "These won't be ready in time." She gently touched the hydrangea blooms I had hung to dry.

With a click. Nenka came through the Fae door, dragging a load of the dead hydrangea flowers behind her.

"Those will have to be cleansed of the evil before you can use them in medicines and potions. However, we might be able to use his essence against him." Susan reached down to relieve Nenka of her load.

Auntie P. and Susan yawned at almost the same time.

I could take a hint. "Would you like to rest now? Or maybe have something to eat? It's after five. I can order something."

Auntie P. didn't seem happy with my plans. Understatement. I'd never seen her so snippy. She wasn't being unreasonable, though. My plan was far-fetched. Maybe if she let it resonate a while she'd come 'round. I hoped I could hit on something to please her. A nap? A full belly? Both? I suggested everything I could think of.

"Rest first, food later," Susan said. Auntie P. agreed.

Drew ordered a couple of large pizzas while I showed them to their rooms. That was one bonus of a large house. Plenty of spare room for guests. Hopefully, they'd be filled with family more often.

FORTY-THREE

Susan came down around 8:30 p.m., followed about ten minutes later by Auntie P. I warmed the leftover pizza, then set up for the séance while they ate They joined me in the dining room a half-hour later, awake and fully energized. They were eager to see if I could contact Fiona again. Drapes drawn, candles and incense lit, I opened the circle and concentrated.

"Fiona, can you hear me? I need your help. Please come forward."

It didn't take long. I opened my eyes as soon as I felt her presence. Auntie P. and Susan stared wide-eyed at the space behind me. I turned to watch as she took form.

"I see the entire family is with you. I am glad they could come."

"I heard that buzz again. She spoke, didn't she?" Drew asked.

"Yep. Susan, Auntie P., could you hear anything?"

They both said no, so I held out my arms. "I guess we need to join hands, otherwise I'll be repeating everything."

We stood in a semi-circle in front of The Ancient One. I asked the question on everyone's mind. "Can you help us?"

"I can guide you, but I cannot interfere."

"I heard that," Susan whispered.

"Me too," Auntie P. confirmed.

"Fiona, can you draw energy from us so you can stay on this plane longer?"

"Yes, I can take enough without draining you. You are all much more powerful that you realize."

I felt a touch of sorrow creep into her essence, and she changed to a soft blue again. I told her of my plan to trick him into joining me on the astral plane over the stone formation in Alberta.

"No, you must do it in person," Fiona said. "You will have to go there yourselves, all of you." She glanced at Auntie P. Did she know about her aversion to flying, or was it simply because Monty was her brother?

"Once there, you can search for his mind and let him know where you are, but you will have to break it off immediately and block your mind so he can not intrude again. Force him to come to you."

She gave us detailed instructions as she slowly faded, refusing to take any more of our strength. Fiona had taken a great deal from each of us in order to stay longer this time.

We dropped onto the chairs around the table. Auntie P. looked grey.

"Well, I've never experienced anything like that." Auntie leaned back, resting her head on the high-backed chair.

Susan reached over and patted her arm. "Why don't you go back to bed, Mother?"

"In a minute. I don't have the strength to move just yet."

I put my elbows on the table and propped my head on my hands. "I know how you feel. Fiona took more energy than expected."

I came prepared and gave everyone a piece of amethyst to help recharge our emotional energy. We each held our crystal, letting its energy do its job. A comforting silence filled the room.

Auntie was the last one to feel up to moving. Before retiring for the night, I needed to bring up my plan again.

"Auntie P., will you be able to fly to Calgary? I suppose we could rent a car, but that would take so much time. We'd lose several days. We don't have the luxury of time on our side."

"I guess I can fly out, but I would prefer if we could drive back."

"Fair enough. First thing tomorrow, we'll gather everything Fiona said we'll need and I'll see about booking a flight. I don't know whether to be scared or excited."

"Before we retire, I think we need to add more protection to ourselves. In our weakened state, there's no telling what he could do," Susan said.

Before extinguishing the candles and incense, we stood together and asked Archangel Michael to watch over and protect us. I dug into my supply of crystals and stones and gave everyone four small pieces of black tourmaline to place at the corners of their bed for extra protection against any negativity.

✳ ✳ ✳

I woke around 5:00 a.m. and went online. Luck was with me as I found four seats to Calgary on the flight, leaving shortly after ten. I also booked an SUV and a couple of rooms at the Ramada, in the little town of Brooks, as it was fairly close to both the formation and the highway. I knew from the article the area around the formation was fenced off and protected, so we'd have to sneak out after dark and break in. I made sure everyone was up and ready to leave within the hour and gathered supplies as they dressed.

The cab I hired arrived on time. No one spoke on the way to the airport. I fingered my pendant and noticed everyone else clasping theirs.

Since we were only travelling to another province, there were no issues at the airport. The plane departed on time and the flight was uneventful.

We landed early in the afternoon and grabbed a quick bite. Once we ate, phase one began. I concentrated on Montgomery. I reached out, probing for his energy, visualizing the room where I'd seen him before. He stood by a table flipping through a large book, as though searching for something. I sensed another presence, but didn't see anyone. He knew I was there and turned towards my energy.

"Hello, Uncle. It's time."

I shut him out, but not before allowing him to probe my mind just long enough to figure out where we were. It would be hours before he could get here.

As soon as I broke the connection, we started the two-hour drive to Brooks. I asked about 'Old Big' at the hotel but didn't find out anything new. We wandered around a bit and found a Walmart near the hotel. It was super-hot out, so we got cheap swim suits and headed back to the hotel pool to cool off before supper.

✳ ✳ ✳

Around 10:00 p.m., we headed out. Our destination was in the middle of nowhere, a location not easily found during daylight, never mind in the dark. The rental SUV had a GPS, so I programmed the longitude and latitude I copied from the on-line article. As we neared our destination, the computerized navigator told me to turn in eight hundred metres. I slowed. Fortunately, we were the only idiots out driving, so I could go as slow as I needed. The GPS display showed the turn, but all I saw was fencing.

"There." Drew pointed. "You just passed it."

I did a three-point turn. A narrow dirt road appeared in my headlights, complete with gate and padlock. I stopped in front of it.

"Allow me." Drew got out and approached the gate. She mumbled softly, and the lock popped. One push and the gate swung open.

She stood to the side and bowed while sweeping her arm as though beckoning royalty to enter. I drove through and waited while she closed the gate and got back in the SUV.

"Nice trick," I said.

Drew waved her hand and smiled. "It was nothing."

I turned on the high beams and drove. Up ahead was a whole lot of nothing. No buildings. No trees. No nocturnal animals, at least none we could see or hear. Dirt, rocks, and a few scatter weeds. And darkness. Miles and miles of darkness. No one spoke.

According to the GPS, we were almost there. I rounded a bend and the headlight reflected off a wire fence.

A computerized voice broke the silence. "You have reached your destination."

The entire ring of boulders sat encircled by a wire fence. Drew walked over to the gate, planning to use her magick to release the padlock.

"Wait." I rushed over and grabbed her arm. "It could be electrified. We need to check." I picked up a handful of small stones and threw them at the fence. No sparks.

"Don't think that works, Marcy. The shock isn't usually very strong anyway, and I doubt very much they'd electrify the gate. How would they get in?" Drew walked up to the fence, extended her arm.

"Wait," I cried out. "Isn't there another way to test it?"

She shook her head and touched it with one finger. "Nothing. Besides, where would they get the electricity? I don't hear a generator hum and it's too far to run a cable. It's probably up just because of some regulation. Let me take care of the lock and you concentrate on preparing yourself."

I nodded and walked back to the SUV, my heartbeat hammering in my ears. Susan handed me my backpack, and I slung it over my shoulder.

Standing between Susan and Auntie P., we linked arms and joined Drew. Before entering the enclosure, we grounded, extending our energy around the entire site, then asked Archangel Michael to keep us safe. Each of us had a specific task.

I pulled our weapons from my backpack; one jar and one white tapered candle for each of us. Drew's jar contained the bay laurel mixture, Susan's had black pepper, and Auntie P. got the cayenne pepper blend. I took the last two jars and remaining candle. One by one, I lit the candles, then stuffed the lighter in my pocket.

"OK, just as Fiona instructed. I'll start."

I followed a worn trail from the gate towards the centre of the boulders, stopping about ten feet short. I stepped away from the path and sprinkled powered mullein, circling around and back to the path, leaving roughly two feet open.

Drew cast her circle a foot from the fence, also leaving the path uncovered. Susan did the same five feet farther in, then Auntie P. mid-way between Susan and myself. Each stood guard beside the gap, waiting. It wasn't completely dark, even though it was close to midnight. The moon was in the early stages of waxing and appeared almost full, casting light in the cloudless sky. Strange how it seemed darker on the drive in. Finally, a set of headlights appeared.

I hurried towards Auntie P. and clung to her arm. "That must be him. I'm not sure I can do this. My powers are still extremely weak."

She patted my hand. "Don't fret so. You're stronger than you realize. Positive thoughts." She unfurled my fingers. "Go back to your post. It's almost time."

Walking backwards, eyes zeroed in on the headlights, I carefully made my way back to my spot. My stomach did backflips. Doubts entered my mind. *What if it doesn't work? My instincts say Montgomery has enough power to kill us with little effort. Did I just sentence my family to death?*

I wanted to bolt, get my family out of there, but it was too late. The car pulled up beside the SUV and the engine shut off.

No one got out.

"I can feel him," Auntie P. said. "He's much stronger than I expected."

Without warning, a surge of emotion filled my mind. It came from Aunt Priscilla. Typical of me, I hadn't thought about how all this would affect her. For almost a half century, she thought her baby brother was dead. *How must she feel knowing he's trying to kill us?* Her emotions flipped from joy to puzzlement, then terror.

Nausea rose and fell as her feelings washed over me. I dropped to my knees and puked. My throat burned. The surrounding ground turned black with the most foul-smelling goop imaginable. The ground under me rumbled, then absorbed the vile vomit.

"Marcy!"

I fell backwards when a hand touched my shoulder.

"Are you all right, dear?"

I took a second to assess. "Yes, I'm fine Auntie. I'm sorry. This must be difficult for you."

She smiled and went back to her place in the ring, but I could tell Auntie P. was still torn up inside.

Susan and Drew turned towards her. They felt it too. Drew rushed to Priscilla's side and touched her arm, transferring strength, much like she had with Mr. Barker.

"Don't drain yourself," I called out.

Drew stayed a moment longer, then returned to her spot. She reached her post as the car door slammed. I could feel his surprise, a shift in his energy.

Montgomery grinned and walked around the car. He opened the passenger door and reached for something. His body blocked my view, but I got a brief glimpse of a red glow.

Auntie P. turned towards me, her brow creased with worry. "He came prepared."

Whatever he tucked into his jacket pocket emitted power, but it blinked out once hidden. Monty leaned against the car, arms crossed, grinning. Was he trying to psych us out? It was working, at least on me.

How arrogant was I, thinking a newbie witch could win a battle against someone who'd obviously spent most of his life learning and harnessing the power of black magick? *Too late to think about that now.* We had to finish what I'd started. I took a deep breath and focused on Monty.

Please follow the trail. It wouldn't work if he didn't.

I released my breath when he walked through the gate and made his way up the path. He passed Drew with barely a glance. I sensed him probing her mind, but she seemed able to block him out. As soon as he passed, she closed her circle and fell in step behind him. Susan also kept him at bay. I had the feeling he wasn't really trying all that hard. Susan closed her circle and joined the procession. He stopped when he reached Auntie P. and didn't bother trying to probe her.

"Sister, it's been a long time."

"Monty, what have you become? Why are you doing this?"

He looked surprised. "Why, revenge, of course."

"But we did nothing."

"Exactly. You did nothing. My two *loving* sisters did absolutely nothing. You should have protected me. You let them take me away. I've waited so long for this moment. I've had the most powerful mentor."

He looked around. "I'm glad you're all here. Saves me some time. I would like to savour each one of your deaths, but one doesn't always get what one wants. After tonight, I will be the only Adhamh remaining. I can take my rightful place as High Priest and rule over my own coven. Rule over all our kind. I'll start with the youngest, and save you for last, *dear* sister."

Montgomery turned his back on her and continued to the centre to face me. Auntie P. quickly closed her circle, and the three of them followed him, then formed a triangle around me, inside the circle I'd cast.

He walked around, laughing.

I moved to stand in front of the gap I'd left and twisted too fast. My body turned, but my feet didn't follow. I stumbled, losing my grip on the jar of mullein. As I fell, I stretched my arms in front of me and grabbed it inches from the ground. Scrambling to my feet, I moved in front of the gap, letting some of the mullein sprinkle behind me to close the opening.

"Mother and Granny weren't prepared for you, but we are. You won't win this time."

"I'll admit you have a strength I wasn't expecting, but," he waved his arms around. "This? Nothing but child's play. Do you really think it will do any good? That I wouldn't figure out what you were up to?"

"We'll see." I motioned for my family to get ready. I'd left a small amount of mullein in the bottle and approached him, quickly sprinkling it over his feet, then dropped the bottle and stepped back.

Montgomery looked at his feet and shook his head. "Silly child. My power is much greater than yours."

We held our arms up, candles burning brightly and started the chant.

"With mullein's magick power, I ward and protect me.

I now push away all spirts, evil, and astral nasties.

With the strong influence of Saturn, this will never occur.

By the element of fire, I banish you."

I reached down and lit the mullein powder with the candle.

"This protective wild flower spell is spun from the heart.

Words for the good of all with a Green Witch's art."

The few clouds overhead moved together despite the lack of wind. The spell was working. Montgomery tried to take a step forward. He could barely lift his foot.

"Nice try, but it won't work." He managed one small step.

"Damn. The mullein powder is supposed to bind him. Repeat the chant, louder," I said.

He managed another step, but he looked annoyed.

"Foolish girl." He reached into his pocket and pulled out something bright red, the size of a goose egg. Stretching his arm towards me, egg nestled in his palm, he whispered something. It didn't sound like English. The egg glowed. It had to be some sort of crystal. I searched my mind, trying to remember the meaning of red. They often represented love, but that didn't seem to fit. Determination and empowerment. That's probably what he's using it for. He definitely was determined.

As the crystal's glow intensified, a pulse came towards me.

"Marcy, what's wrong?" Susan asked. "You look all wavy."

"What? Wavy? It's the crystal egg. It's emitting some sort of energy wave." As I stepped away from Monty, my legs trembled. My breath caught in my throat. "It's draining me."

Montgomery said nothing, but took another step closer. The binding had slowed him down, but didn't stop him. The pulsing brought me to my knees.

My family joined hands and came towards me, but whatever caused the pulsing prevented them from getting close. He placed his free hand above the egg-shaped crystal. The glow turned crimson.

I clawed at my throat, trying to release invisible hands so I could breathe. I shook my head in an attempt to clear the cobwebs, but my movement only intensified the dizziness. Spots formed in front of my eyes, blocking out my surroundings. I was losing the battle. I choked.

"Mother, Gran, look," Drew cried.

I forced myself to look up. The sky grew bright. I felt another presence. No, two.

"Francine," Auntie P. whispered.

Black clouds filled the sky, rumbling. Montgomery lowered his hands a few inches. With his concentration broken, I gasped for air. The constrictions of the pulse weakened. Monty's grin turned into a frown. Worry lines creased his forehead.

Finally able to move, I crawled to my backpack, removed the last jar, and began sprinkling the brimstone around him.

Monty turned and swatted at my hand, sending the jar flying. I crawled after it. As I reached for it, he grabbed my ankle, pulling me back.

"No." I kicked with my free leg and connected with soft tissue. Monty screamed and released me. I grabbed the jar and tried to encircle him again. This time it worked.

"We need to combine our energy," I said. "Concentrate."

The crimson glow grew so bright it almost blinded me. The black clouds shifted until they formed a giant mass directly overhead. We all joined hands, forming a circle around my not-so-loving great uncle. We repeated the chant one last time, our energy mingling with the energy from the two *angels* above us.

Monty frantically searched his pockets, then he noticed his ruby egg laying just outside the brimstone circle. He stretched his arm, palm up, and said something under his breath. The egg rocked, then slid towards him.

"Schist!" I scrambled to my feet and raced to grab it before Monty got hold of it.

"Don't touch it." Susan yelled.

I skidded to a stop. Even without Monty touching it, power radiated from it. My legs buckled. I watched in terror as the egg rose and glided to Monty.

"Marcy, we need to complete the circle." Susan came over and helped me to my feet. "Stand on the far side and join hands."

As I put a little distance between myself and the ruby egg, my strength increased enough for me to stand. I joined hands with Drew and Auntie. Susan did the same.

We repeated the chant, but to no avail. Monty spoke in Latin. A vortex formed between his fingertips and the egg. The air chilled. Time slowed. The air pressure changed, causing my ears to pop.

The glowing egg whirled closer, trapped inside the vortex, draining us of our energy as it neared. One by one, we dropped to our knees.

Auntie P. looked upward. "Francine. Please, help us." Her words were barely audible.

The bright light around the clouds softened and took shape. I recognized my mother and Granny. The forms drifted down, alighting beside our human circle. Granny floated on my left beside Auntie P. Mother settled on my right. My emotions jumbled. It'd been years since I'd seen Mother, and we hadn't been on the best of terms when she passed over. At least I'd been with Granny when her turn came. Barely visible hands enclosed around mine as

Mother and Granny joined the circle. I turned to face Mother, tears spilling down my face.

"I'm so sorry for turning my back on you and the family. Can you ever forgive me?"

"There's nothing to forgive, Marcy. You had to make up your own mind. Now, let's focus and take care this."

I turned my attention back to Monty. The ruby egg swirled inside the vortex but didn't move away from the spot. He spoke more Latin, but the egg remained stationary. Mother and Granny glowed until they reached the same illumination as the sky. Energy coursed through me. Auntie P. and Drew stood straight, strength regained. Susan was last to recover, as she had no direct contact with either of our angels.

We all glowed, only not nearly as bright. Granny finally spoke.

"Light the brimstone. Concentrate, and repeat your chant."

I let go of Mother, fished the lighter out of my jeans pocket, knelt down and set the ring alight.

"Gack. What a stench." My eyes watered from the acrid odour.

Granny said something in Gaelic and the vortex holding the egg shifted, engulfing Monty, taking the toxic fumes with it.

The ground undulated, followed by a low rumble, building into the loudest thunder I'd ever heard. A single bolt of lightened escaped from the mass overhead, heading for the centre of our human circle. The clouds vanished. So had Montgomery.

Not a trace of him remained.

The crystal egg sat on the ground where my uncle has stood only moments before. The glow from above remained, but much dimmer.

"Thank you, Mother, Granny. I miss you."

Auntie P. reached towards the glow as it faded.

"Fiona said it would take all of us," Drew said. "She wasn't kidding."

I nodded. "Maiden, Mother, Crone, squared."

"I think we should head back to the hotel," Susan said. "Someone's bound to have seen that bright light and wonder what's going on."

We gathered up the discarded jars and candles, stuffing them into my backpack. Something felt wrong. Auntie P. noticed too, judging by the look on her face.

"What is it, Auntie?" I whispered so as not to alarm anyone. "I can't put my finger on it."

"I don't know, dear. Probably just a residual from Monty. I'm sure the energy in this place will absorb it."

"You don't sound convinced. What about the crystal?" I remembered Susan's warning when I first reached for the egg. "Is it OK to touch it now?"

"Yes. Without Montgomery controlling it, you can handle it. Keep it safe, and whatever you do, don't use it."

FORTY-FOUR

Before we left the sacred circle, Auntie P. suggested we all recite a protection spell around it, just in case. Susan and Drew didn't seem to feel what Auntie P. and I did. As we turned back to the SUV, I noticed a tall shadow walking in the opposite direction on the other side of the boulders.

"Come on, Marcy," Drew called.

I peeked inside the drivers-side window. "Drew, why don't you drive Montgomery's car back? He was kind enough to leave the keys in the ignition, and I see a Budget sticker on it. I saw one in town close to our hotel. It'll be too suspicious if it's left here."

We didn't bother with the same stealth-mode on the way out. If someone spotted our headlights, we'd be far enough away from the Big Old to be charged with trespass. It didn't take long to find the car rental place.

I waited as Drew parked Montgomery's vehicle. There were security cameras everywhere, so she kept her head down and put her sunglasses on after she parked, running to join us at the curb. The ride back was quiet. We'd come prepared for a huge drain and brought along crystals to help with the healing process. We left them in the SUV to avoid possible contamination.

Since I was driving, I brought a clear quartz necklace, which I periodically rubbed. A slight pulsing hit my side where the ruby egg sat, nestled in my jacket pocket.

Auntie P. sat in the front with me, holding a quartz in one hand, and an amethyst in the other. The pretty purple stone would aid in healing the emotional turmoil. Drew held both a quartz crystal and a Herkimer diamond close to her heart, and Susan wore a quartz bracelet and held a citrine wand.

When we arrived at the hotel, we were physically exhausted, but our magickal energy was partially refilled. We all headed for the room I shared with Drew to discuss what had just happened. The only sound at that late hour was the ice machine at the end of the hall. I unlocked the door, and we filed in.

"Where do you think he went?" I asked. "Is he dead?"

Auntie P. shook her head. "I don't think so. There were no remains. And did you notice? No smell. One would think a human hit by lightning would give off the smell of burning flesh and left burnt clothing behind. It didn't feel like normal lightning to me. More like pure energy, not electricity."

"So where did he go then?" Drew asked. "His body has to be somewhere."

"There's nothing in the legend that tells what happened all those centuries ago," Susan said. "Maybe we're better off not knowing. The twin never returned, so I don't think we need to worry."

"How are *you* Auntie P.? I'm sorry I hadn't considered how this might affect you."

She shrugged. "I'm not sure how I feel. I'm glad to know he didn't die as a child and had a life, but I can't help wonder what turned him into a monster. At least I finally know the truth, unpleasant as it is. I'll say a prayer for him."

My senses told me it would take her quite a while to get over what had just happened.

After her mom and gran went to their room, Drew ordered a bottle of champagne from room service and two glasses. We wanted to celebrate our success, but it didn't seem right to include Auntie P. and Susan. We'd just killed Auntie's brother. At least, I think we did.

Drew signed for the bubbly and popped the cork. "Here's to a job well done."

We clinked glasses, but my heart wasn't in it. "Do you think we killed Monty, or just sent him somewhere else? I realize he planned on killing all of us, but it feels wrong celebrating."

Drew took a sip while she mulled it over. "I think your mother and gran took him. He's probably not dead, just in another realm. It sounds heartless to say, but it was kill or be killed. He's been banished and won't cause us any more harm."

"You're probably right. I bet that's what happened to our ancestor at Stonehenge." I held up my glass. "To a successful evening."

We sat around chatting for a while, making plans for the trip home. Then, one after the other, we started yawning. With no set time to get up, we agreed to meet for brunch.

I got up first, so I went to the front desk to check us out of both rooms, then went to the dining room to wait for the others. I just started my second coffee when Drew joined me. Auntie P. and Susan soon followed. We had a quick bite to eat and were ready to leave by 1:00 p.m.

We took our time heading back home, stopping whenever we felt like it. The trip stretched out over three days. Susan and Auntie P. decided to stay with me a few days longer and help Drew with my schooling. I was happy knowing I'd have my entire family with me for a little while, at least.

Drew mentioned Cooper on day three, and they kept grilling me about him the rest of the way home. I ignored most of the questions, which was pretty easy as they kept asking things I couldn't possibly know. I kept my answers short.

"He's about my age.

"No, I don't think he's married.

"Looks a little like Johnny Depp."

Susan liked that last one. When I told them about Mr. Barker and that I planned to visit as soon as I got back, they decided they were all coming with me.

Great.

❋ ❋ ❋

We arrived back home mid-afternoon on Friday. Nenka greeted us, anxious to know what happened.

"It's done. He won't be bothering us again." I knelt and embraced her.

"I'm so relieved. I'm certain we'll all sleep better now." Nenka scampered off, and we went up to our rooms to unpack and shower. The old house only had one bathroom, so I let my guests go first. *Mental note to self—add a guest bathroom.* Susan was putting a lasagna in the oven when I finally came down.

"We were just discussing your twenty-first birthday. It's only a few weeks away." Auntie P. said. "Susan and I have changed our minds about staying a few more days. We'd like to stay for your birthday. Can you put up with us a little longer?"

I felt like the Grinch at the end of the cartoon, only my heart grew a million times bigger. I finally had my family again. I squealed and wrapped my arms around Auntie P. "Thank you. It will mean so much more to be able to share it with you all." I hugged Susan. "Stay as long as you want. And come back any time."

I sat beside Drew at the kitchen table and gave her a shoulder bump. "Our family's the best."

"I know. And don't you ever forget it."

I sent a quick text to Cooper to let him know we were going to visit tomorrow. He replied right away.

"Great news," I said as I read the message. "Mr. Barker is out of the hospital and is resting at home."

After dinner we made detailed plans, or should I say *they* made plans—scheduling my re-education so I'd be ready to go through my coming-of-age ritual. Ever since the revelation that I was like The Ancient One, Auntie P. was adamant that I try my hand at everything.

Each of us had that one special skill, and it usually came out naturally. I seemed to excel no matter what I tried, with only minor consequences. I had a nagging feeling something had gone askew in Alberta, and I was a little hesitant to try a séance again. If Fiona came through that easily, and from so far in the past, who or what else would, or had, come through? I needed proper training before trying again.

Next morning, we piled into the rental and headed into town and down Main Street to the bookstore. The closed sign was up, so I sent Cooper a text. He came through the darkened store to let us in. The back room had transformed since Drew and I had gone through *that* book.

Most of the shelving had been removed, along with the dark appearance. The walls were now a lovely bright blue, and they'd covered the lone window with a pair of obviously store-bought curtains replacing the ones Mr. Barker had ripped down after the issue when we looked through the grimoire. A sofa and several chairs were scattered about, but the table was still there, moved off to the side, a deck of cards and a couple of tea cups sitting on it. A twin bed sat near the window, with Mr. Barker propped up on pillows.

"I guess I should make introductions. You've met cousin Drew already. This is her mother, Susan, and Susan's mother, Priscilla. Granny's sister."

"You look much like her," Mr. Barker said. "Beauty runs in your family."

Auntie P. actually blushed. I introduced them to Cooper and his dad.

"Two Mr. Barkers is quite confusing," Cooper's dad said. "Call me Steve. Much easier."

I turned towards the bed. "Mr. Barker, I just realized I don't know your first name."

"Phillip, my dear. But you can call me Gramps." He winked. *Here we go again.*

Auntie P. turned to Cooper. "So, you're Marcy's young man."

I felt like crawling under the table. The heat on my face left no doubt I had turned as red as the ruby egg. Drew snickered. Cooper just smiled.

Time for payback. "Oh, I forgot to mention. Drew might marry Randy when she gets home."

"You're so dead," she hissed between her teeth.

The Barker men seemed to enjoy the little show, but it was time to end it.

"We've come to see Mr. Barker, not discuss our family business." I sat on the edge of the bed. "How are you feeling? You look so much better."

"I feel perfectly fine, but they insist I stay in bed a while longer. After Drew helped me, I improved quickly." He pointed to a small table on the other side of the bed. "And I still have your crystal. I hold it sometimes when I feel weak or tired, and it perks me right up." His smile faded. "I hate to tell you, but I've decided it's time to retire. As soon as the doctors say it's OK, I'll be flying to Halifax to live with Steve and his family."

I swiped at a tear forming in the corner of my eye. "I understand. I'll miss you terribly, but your health is more important. I promise I'll keep in touch."

"We shouldn't tire you out too much. I think we should head back to Marcy's." Susan said. "It was very nice to meet you all."

On the drive home, Auntie P. said, "They seem like nice people. Wonderful addition to anyone's family."

"Speaking of family," Susan said. "What's this about you and Randy?"

"Well, all this got me thinking. It's time I started a family, and you know he's asked several times. I really am fond of him. We get along so well, and you and Gran like him. I think I'll call him when I get home and see if he's still willing. We should sit down and have a proper chat."

"Fabulous. Now, Marcy, what about you and Cooper?"

"Don't know." I pulled into the driveway. "I felt strangely connected to him."

"It's mutual," Auntie P. said. "I could feel the electricity between you. Imagine two of our family marrying someone magickal. I believe we're in for quite an exciting time ahead."

"First things first. I need to finish prepping for my special birthday." I excused myself and ran to my room, locking the door behind me. My mind reeled.

How am I supposed to marry Cooper when he's returning to Nova Scotia? I felt grounded here. No way was I moving anywhere. This was my home. I knew in my heart and soul I was meant to stay here, as was my future daughter. Besides, I couldn't just up and leave Nenka and her family any more than I could ignore the feelings I had for Cooper. He made me feel alive. The thought of never seeing him again was unbearable. I threw myself across the bed and cried.

Except for a few visits to Mr. Barker, and a trip to the cemetery to visit Granny and Mother, the rest of the month I spent learning everything I could before July 31 finally arrived.

FORTY-FIVE

*T*wo weeks later, I woke early, just as the sun rose. Tiny particles of dust danced in the light as it shone through the window. I threw off the covers and padded over. Not a cloud in sight. It was going to be a beautiful day.

We'd checked the time of the full moon last night—10:41 a.m. So much for the midnight ceremonies they portrayed in the movies. I would do my initiation in the sunlight. Sort of. I'd be sheltered under the umbrella of the old willow. Instead of my usual shower, I bathed in warm water infused with Lemongrass oil. Tea lights and crystals lined the edge of the tub; not necessary, but it looked pretty.

I knew from Granny's journal the ceremony could be brief. Auntie P. said the length totally depended on me. Part of the initiation was to recite a pledge we wrote ourselves.

I was ready.

Over the last couple of days, they had left me alone so I could create the pledge and finalize the ceremony I wanted. What I'd come up with was a little longer than Granny's, but not by much. I wish I'd known what Mother had done. Maybe I'd ask her if I could read her journal. Granny gave consent. I'm sure Mother would too. After everyone went back to England, maybe I'd take the time to carefully go through all the boxes stashed away upstairs, and reassemble my altar.

When I emerged from my comforting bath, the scrape of drawers opening and closing, the shuffling of feet, and snips of conversation brought a smile to my face. I made my way down the hall to my room to get dressed. I picked up Granny's letter.

"Tonight, when I'm alone," I whispered. A gentle breeze brushed a few strands of hair across my face. *Granny.* I kissed the envelope before placing it back on the dresser.

Drew came out of her room as I exited mine.

"Morning. I'm just going down to start breakfast." I gave her a smile.

"Happy Birthday, Marcy." Drew gave me a big hug. "Are you excited?"

"Excited? Why on earth would I be excited? It's only the most special day a witch can have. No biggy." I squeezed her hand. "I'm so glad you're here with me. Now go have your shower and hurry the rest of them along."

Excited? What an understatement. My feet barely touched the floor. I could scarcely contain the thrill coursing through me. A little terror weaseled in, but the thought of everything to come pushed it away. I was just about to start down when I heard my name.

"Marcy?"

I stopped and turned. Nenka stood by the tapestry, hands behind her back.

"I've got something for you." She extended her arm. Violets.

"Oh, they're beautiful." I sat on the top step and she came over. When I took them, I realized they weren't cut flowers, but the entire plant, in a tiny box.

"They're from my mother's garden."

"Oh, Nenka, you've made up with her." I leaned over and gave her a gentle hug. "Now we both have our families back. I'll find a special place for these. I think the sunporch would be perfect."

I kissed her forehead. She beamed. This really was turning out to be a truly special day. She scampered off, and I took my gift, my first birthday present, and sat it in the center of the table in the sunporch.

I had an enormous stack of pancakes ready and warming in the oven when everyone came into the kitchen.

"Drew said you were getting breakfast, so we skipped our showers for now," Susan said. "Don't want it going cold."

"Sit down. The scrambled eggs will be ready in a jiff." I scurried around, pulling plates from the cupboard, then grabbed a tea-towel and took the plate of pancakes out and sat it on a trivet on the table. The syrup was already out. I finished the eggs and scooped them onto a serving platter, then joined everyone.

"Are you ready?" Auntie P. asked.

"As ready as I'll ever be, I guess. As soon as breakfast is over, I'll go out and set everything up. I have it all together, except for the crystal wand. I'll carry that out when it's time."

When breakfast was over, Drew reached into her pocket and pulled out a box.

"Happy Birthday, cousin."

My amulet! I totally forgot she was making that. It was all I could do not to snatch it up and rip into it. Since it was hand-forged, and by family, it meant so much more. It also meant the amulet would be infused with love. Its own kind of magick. When she slid it across the table, I took a deep breath and accepted the box. I opened it and couldn't believe my eyes. I removed the amulet and clutched it to my chest. Energy seeped into my hands and arms. Reluctantly, I put it on the table to get a better look.

The silver was polished so bright I had to blink several times in order to see the design, as well as clear the tears before they formed. She had replicated the willow tree perfectly, except there was no Fae door. In its place at the base of the silver trunk was a tear shaped emerald. Round faceted emeralds sat dripping off the end of each branch, just as she'd promised.

"Oh, Drew, it's absolutely gorgeous!" I went around the table and gave her a hug and a kiss. "I'll be so proud to wear it."

She pushed me away. "Oh, don't be such a silly nilly." Her grin was almost as big as mine. "Now, you go get ready and we'll clean up here.

At 10:30 a.m. I went downstairs and removed the black velvet from over the crystal wand. Nenka, Tinkus, and Nimagg stood in a line by the Fae door.

"Good luck, Marcy," they said in unison. "We'll be watching, but out of your way."

My extended family. How lucky could one person get? I didn't think my body could withstand any more emotion. Once again, my heart almost burst through my chest. I dropped to one knee, closer to the little gnome's height.

"I'll be more than happy to have you all standing with Drew, Susan, and Auntie P. All my family together, witnessing my pledge. Hurry along. It's almost time."

A few days earlier, I'd gone back to the loft to go through the boxes with Mother's things. Her kelly green dress had been saved, and it was my size. Telling no one, I'd taken it to be cleaned. It complimented my emerald amulet perfectly.

I took a few deep breaths and grounded. Then I picked up the wand and carried it upstairs and out to the sunporch. Its power radiated throughout my entire body. My journey would start and end on the porch.

I'd already set up white tea lights leading from the door to the willow, winding through the garden, and asked Drew to light them all while I prepared. My family waited at the start of the lights. I held the wand close to my chest and began the procession. One by one, they fell in behind me and followed me to the willow.

The gnomes stood by the Fae door in the trunk. I walked through the branches and inside to a ring of tapered candles and clear quartz crystals. A small silver bowl filled with sea salt sat in the centre of the circle, along with a box of wooden matches. I put the wand down, lit the candles, then enclosed myself in a circle with the sea salt. My family stood in a circle on the other side of the candles. Doubt crept into my mind. *What if I screw up the pledge?* Normally, one would have almost two decades of training before the ritual. I had mere months. Fiona's words haunted me, as did Elspeth's reading. *Special*, they said. An amazing gift.

I looked at the faces surrounding me. They believed in me. I should too. I knelt down in front of the wand and recited my pledge.

> "Today, I pledge my dedication to the Goddess of the Earth
> and the God of Forests.
>
> I ask them to guide me on my journey.
>
> I dedicate myself as a willing initiate to the mysteries of the
> universe.
>
> I dedicate myself to strive in acquiring knowledge to help
> myself and those around me.
>
> I thank you for the blessing you have given me.

Henceforth, I will walk the path of the craft and dedicate

myself to you,

Mother Goddess and Father God

As I will, so mote it be."

I picked up the crystal wand. Strange. It didn't seem heavy. A burst of pride hit. For the first time, I actually finished something, and it was a big something. Grinning, I followed the same path back, Drew extinguishing the candles as we passed them. I sat the wand on the table beside the violets.

I didn't feel any different.

"You're officially one of us now," Drew said.

Each of them gave me a hug and a kiss on my forehead.

"Remember," Auntie P. said, "everything you do affects someone. Do as you will, but cause no harm."

✳ ✳ ✳

Standing alone at the airport, I watched the plane take off. An emptiness filled my heart. With luck, I'd soon be attending a wedding in England. Giving one last wave as the plane took off, I returned the rental and took a cab back home.

The house felt strangely empty. Having Drew with me for the last three weeks had been a joy. At least, I still had Nenka and her family for company. Wandering from room to room, I was at a loss at what to do.

Into the kitchen. Not hungry.

Down to the workroom. Didn't feel like mixing potions.

Into the living room. A novel sat on the coffee table, so I took it out to the sunporch.

I was just getting into it when someone knocked on the glass. I looked up. *Cooper!*

"Come in. What brings you here? Is your grandfather all right?"

"He's fine. I wanted to tell you Gramps sold the bookstore. We're flying home tomorrow."

My heart dropped to my feet. How could he stand there grinning?

"Oh, I guess I should mention I bought the store. More like Gramps signed it over to me as an early inheritance. As soon as I've packed everything at home, I'll be back to take over the bookstore and the backroom business. You'll be seeing a lot of me."

UPCOMING

Thank you for reading Generation Witch: Rebirth. Stay tuned for book 2 of the Generation Witch trilogy. If you wish to hear about the progress of this or any of my books, please join my newsletter at:

https://landing.mailerlite.com/webforms/landing/u0q5f2.

Purrfect Press

Reviews are Golden

I would love to hear from you! Please consider leaving a review on your favourite social media platform, Amazon, or Goodreads.

Reviews mean the world to authors. Not only do we enjoy reading how you felt about the book, but they help other readers get a feel for a book in advance, and aid authors in marketing.

Thank you for coming on this adventure with me.

AUTHOR'S NOTES

I was fortunate when doing my research to come across Omahkiyaahkohtoohp, The Old Big. There really is an arrangement of boulders in Alberta that goes by that name, and to quote Marcy, "I'm not even going to try to pronounce that." The book mentioned in the article I found online, *Canada's Stonehenge*, by Gordon Freeman, along with another he wrote, *Hidden Stonehenge*, are both available at the Toronto Reference Library. Is it a coincidence that I just happened to find exactly what I was looking for when trying to decide how to deal with Montgomery? What are the chances that out of the blue I'd find a place here, in Canada, that's on the same latitude as Stonehenge? Weird.

ABOUT THE AUTHOR

Nanci M. Pattenden is a genealogist and a fiction writer, currently working on a collection of detective stories set in Victorian Toronto and an Urban Fantasy trilogy. She also co-authors a funny paranormal series, D.E.M.ON. Tales, with author M.J. Moores.

Nanci has completed the Creative Writing program at both the University of Calgary and the University of Toronto.

She currently resides in Newmarket with her fluffy cat Snowball.

nanci@nancipattenden.com
www.purrfectpress.com
www.nancipattenden.com
@npattenden